ZOSMA

www.mascotbooks.com

ZOSMA

For more information, please contact:
Mascot Books
620 Herndon Parkway #320
Herndon, VA 20170
info@mascotbooks.com

Library of Congress Control Number: 2018907801
CPSIA Code: PRFRE0818A
ISBN-13: 978-1-64307-185-5
Printed in Canada

ZOSMA

———

Jason Michael Primrose

AUTHOR'S NOTE

If you were born before the 90s, you were born into a world without global connectivity. A world where your reach was governed by proximity to those around you. Most dreams seemed impossible and those nearest and dearest told you so. This was the world where my parents (both in their twenties) met responsibility and adversity. This was the world where I, (in my youth and my teens) met self-imposed limitation and disconnection from process.

My mother and father chose to join corporate life for medical insurance and job security and financial stability. And they stuck with it for their adult lives to support their children and their families. I don't know where or what they would be if they could, but I can say what they do is not who they are. I'm the son of a poet and a DJ.

I dreamt up this kid inside a fifth-grade classroom, literally. Allister (Or Jordan at the time), was born during my fifth-grade year inside of a spiral binder book called *Dragon Wars*. I was so obsessed with dragons and the world I'd created in those ten poorly illustrated pages, that from fifteen years old to twenty years old, I went on to write seven more books. The main characters had children and their children had children. They crossed galaxies and dimensions, discovered new solar systems. They battled corrupt kings, queens, and evil entities, and fought alongside ancient warriors, aliens, and gods.

During those same teenage years and beyond, I have waged an everlasting battle with my true self, the inner nerd who believes in magic and aliens and that what we see is not what it seems. The truth of the matter is, the universe is so meticulously constructed, can it really operate solely by chance? I believe in catalysts, and in prophecies. I believe that aliens have visited Earth and changed the course of human history. I believe that aliens could still be here, helping us progress.

It never occurred to me that if I continued to write, I'd get better. It never occurred to me that people didn't achieve their goals overnight, that they worked tirelessly and to no end for a sliver of success. Success categorized by completion, not by fame, wealth, or some other asinine measurement imposed by others. My thoughts of being an author were swept away by normalcy and tradition and of course, my perceived inadequacy. In fighting that battle, I took a long hard detour into other industries; event planning, fashion, jewelry, technology, and entertainment. And during that time, I lost these handwritten stories.

It was time to start over anyway.

"Everything after page 100 has to go," my editor said of my first 600-page reboot of the *Dragon Wars* manuscript. At 210,000 words, I thought I'd written the most epic piece of fiction ever. It was confusing. It didn't have an arc. It had too many characters and an unrealistic point of view. I took her advice with an open heart. I knew she knew more than I did. She'd read thousands of books for content and quality. I had not.

I started writing this series again four years ago when I found myself feeling caged behind other creatives, living in fear and limiting myself. Fear of my own power or fear of my own failure or fear of my own existence. Not surprisingly, my various jobs under or behind other creatives led to the acquisition of incredible knowledge that didn't relate to writing, but did relate to the business of creating. So, while creating the story and characters is hella fun, I had to look at this as a business and build a systematic process for execution in order to bring the novel to life. (Hence my belief in fate and predestined paths.)

I don't believe that I chose this subject, nor these characters, nor this storyline. I believe that it chose me, initially during some fantastical dream in my sleep. It latched on to me, and imagined pieces of this story would come to me in classrooms, during conversations, at parties, and in the solitude of my room. I consider the universe known as "The Lost Children" inescapable at this point. And I can't even promise that upon its completion it will go away. I may be compelled to write backstory and side stories and pre-stories. My motivation to finish is driven by madness, I think. Four years later, here we are!

So, to my thank yous.

Thank you to my parents and grandparents for their sacrifices. Particularly my mother's, who, as perfect as she is, I learned the most from accepting the things that weren't perfect about her. She's a living example of a superhuman with super powers. Her powers include motherhood, super strength, compassion, understanding, being a badass, and teleporting around the world. To my grandmother, who worked oh so many jobs and endured an unfulfilling marriage to raise three beautiful daughters because that's what was acceptable and right to do. To my father, who, despite our differences in our approach to life, shares my vast imagination, creativity, and unique mind. I hope reading this he is encouraged to write himself, as I know it's something he loves, almost as much as he loves me.

Thank you to my siblings. It was your transformation from rugrats to role models that inspired me to go on this journey. You have grown into incredible adults and when I began to see you for who you are, I realized we shared the urge to pave our own paths. I hope I can be an example for a reason to do so.

Thank you to the backbones of our family, my cousins, aunts and great aunts, all of whom have followed and supported my sporadic and unconventional life with curiosity but not judgment, watching and waiting like they were viewing some soap opera for a dramatic outcome.

(I'm laughing as I type this.)

Thank you to my friends who helped me bring this to life, your personalities, your decisions, your triumphs, and your mistakes are in these pages. I observed many of you with such pride, watched you change and evolve into the wonderful parents, husbands, wives, girlfriends, boyfriends, professionals, entrepreneurs, and successful people that you are today.

Thank you to my artist and his amazing team, whose talent was so magnificent he forced me to look at my writing and level up.

Thank you to my editor for your blunt honesty and your patience. For your unwillingness to let me dig myself into a literary hole. For recognizing my moods even over the phone. For your encouragement and guidance. For your bright spirit and your over the water home. For your patience through my indecision.

As you can see, I am surrounded by super humans.

———

PREFACE

Since a young age, I've been obsessed with exploring society's intricacies. We live in a world that tells us who to be, how to act, how to feel, and what milestones we need to achieve and by when. We live in a world that tells us what our purpose is, without giving us the freedom to explore those essential life choices for ourselves. How many of us know who we truly are? How many of us are even trying to figure it out? Now on the flip side—how many of us are constantly judging others by our merits, imposing our thoughts/desires/opinions on their existence? I believe it's this lack of understanding between people that is driving a wedge in our society.

The journey to self-discovery is lifelong and we are all on it. To start down this path, I had to climb out of the box society told me to build around myself. Freed from some of my mental constraints and the dream of the world, I found the story for ZOSMA, which begins the Lost Children of Andromeda series. ZOSMA is more than a story, it's a message—Zosma represents the infinite power you have as an individual—"So long as you have the consciousness and the confidence to call on it." It is the power people try to siphon from you for their own gain. They try to cut you off, and give you ONLY enough so you can function but not succeed, that 10 percent. But you can take it all back, it's yours after all. You can have 100 percent of your energy and use it to be whatever you want.

I hope that you read this novel with an open mind and an open heart. It is not my first work, but it is the first work I am sharing without fear. It is a child that I am sending out into the world to be accepted or rejected, instead of holding he or she close to my side. It will be loved or hated, befriended or be cast out, praised or shunned. This child, titled ZOSMA, can only be his or herself and nothing else. I have instilled my own confidence in this novel, so that regardless of the outcome, it will stand happy with itself for simply existing. It doesn't need my overprotection. It needs criticism, it needs failure, it needs to learn so that it may grow. And I promise to grow with it.

Twenty-four years later, a fully realized dream has come to life. The characters I created in elementary school, wrote about in high school, and hid away from the world in fear of my own potential, are born. Living on crisp, turntable pages and in vivid imagery, they feel so real to me. As real as friends. As real as family. As real as enemies. They make mistakes. They're selfish. They're scared. They're confident, impulsive, loving, vengeful. They surprise and disappoint me. They ask for forgiveness. Don't judge them too harshly for they are no different from you and me. Trying to survive on an Earth that has decided humanity's time is at its end. Trying to determine what truths to believe and what truths to question. Maybe they look like something you've seen before, but I can assure you they're not. These are the **Lost Children of Andromeda**.

CHAPTER ONE

INTRUSION

ΛLLISTER ΛDAMS

Marrakech, Morocco, 2052 A.D.

HEAVY BREATHING. RACING HEARTBEATS. The intentional pitter-patter of people moving from place to place. No, moving closer to him.

Allister Adams came to in a heap of sand, face up, every muscle throbbing, his brain included. He grunted and pushed himself onto his elbows as unfamiliar terrain and untrustworthy vision demanded his concentration. He blinked at an image of three identical buildings blending into one another and the darkness abound.

Navy gloom thwarted moonlight from reaching the rooftops. Clustered together, the far from welcoming buildings defined themselves in rectangular shapes and varied shades of grey. They towered over Allister, as if demanding an explanation from him, the outsider.

Turning toward the direction of the last step he'd heard, he squinted, suspicious of what lay beyond a stone wall's decomposing edge.

"Get up! Hands in the air!" someone shouted.

The building showed its allegiance to the city by hiding the body that carried this robust and confident voice.

"I'm getting there," he mumbled. He couldn't believe it worked. He'd completed a successful transport before, but it had never taken this long to recover from its physiological side-effects.

Six simultaneous click-clacks and a collective, fearsome whirring confirmed new military weapon prototypes charging for action.

"Hands in the air intruder!" the same voice shouted from somewhere above him.

"Yeah, okay, give me a second!"

Gun-toting soldiers slinked into view: behind opposite buildings, two waited for him to walk forward; a third stepped in front of him; a fourth emerged behind him. On the adjacent roof, a fifth and sixth aimed at him sniper-style. The double-barrel chrome weapons in sight wore prized core-reactor technology near the trigger.

Their possession of the proprietary war tech doubled his heart rate and paused his sarcasm. He was incapable of tearing his concentration from the plasma energy building in the gun's glass sphere to obey their request.

"Those aren't on full power, right?" he asked aloud. He needed the nausea to go away like now. The aches pulsed with less intensity, the fever subsided, and his body cooled. Better. He sat back on his heels, hands up, as instructed.

The plasma bonfires, though contained, gave the muddy foreground a distinguishable glow. Arriving with the orange energy's light were the details in the soldiers' uniforms, their impatient expressions, and their enlarged, exaggerated shadows. The shadows passed over Allister in an effort toward intimidation. Little did they know, he was intimidated enough by the promise of the plasma's ferocity. Still, he'd come for answers, and he'd leave with them.

Dressed in a grass green uniform and matching beret, the lead soldier motioned the gun barrel skyward. "Hands higher, where I can see them. How'd you get in here?" he asked.

"None of your business."

The soldier wouldn't understand anyway. *I transported,* he thought, imagining the conversation play out. *I transported here from the United States because I'm looking for an alien refugee named—*

"How?" the soldier demanded, voice now unsteady. His finger inched back on the trigger.

One foot situated on the ground for support, Allister launched upward and said, "I think you heard me the first time."

Click. Snap. Boom. A plasma bolt seared the upper flesh on his back. He yelled out and tumbled over, scrambling to get air back into his lungs. The weapons were on full power.

"Should've killed him," the soldier behind him said. "Charge 'em up and hit him again!"

Allister shook away the stinging. Through clenched teeth, he seethed, "You might as well put your guns down." An adrenaline rush refueled his gumption. Moving forward, he twisted sideways. *Zoom.* A bolt whistled past him. He dipped left. *Zoom.* He dodged right. *Zoom.* Triggers clicked faster. *Zoom. Zoom. Zoom.* He ducked garish streams of boiling plasma, then spun out. *Zoom. Zoom. Zoom.*

A lone, lucky shot nicked him in the bicep. He cried out. Not fast enough, not nimble enough, he was distracted by the first wound's pain. It had chased him, caught up, and kicked him behind both knees. One knee gave up and fell, pushing the sand beneath it outward. The other stayed at a ninety-degree angle, supporting his upper body's hunched weight. Nostrils flaring, he reached his dry, cracked fingers around the opposite shoulder to touch his back. Allister glanced at the blood they collected, dragged it along the thigh of his joggers and chose to keep the insults and obscenities to himself.

The lead soldier, out of arm's reach, backed away to let the gun recharge but kept it pointed at the space between Allister's eyes. Smoke, reeking of overheated metal, rose from its mouth.

"He's not slowing," the one behind him said.

"Hit. Him. Again," commanded another, coming around the corner. "Superhuman or not, these were designed—"

"To kill, I know, believe me, I know," Allister said. "Those hurt like shit, but in case you haven't noticed, they won't kill me."

The lead soldier's mouth twitched in recognition. "*Akhrus*," he said, as a fist-led arm shot into the air bent at the elbow. "You know the law, American. Our borders are closed. I suggest you leave the way you came."

"Or what? Listen, I'm not going anywhere until I speak to—"

Scattered click-clacks interrupted. Allister leapt to his feet, maneuvered in a burst of speed, wrapping an arm around the lead soldier's neck. He wrenched the gun away, took aim, and let loose its firepower. The foundation holding the snipers at an elevated advantage caved, forcing them to evacuate their posts, while burying soldiers on the ground. He spun the man locked in his grip to face him, and kicked him in the chest so hard, he flew back unconscious.

His menacing glare sent the last soldier stumbling away. "Princess Celine will make you pay," he said, dropping the weapon.

Good, at least I'm in the right place.

Allister held onto his commanding stance for appearance's sake. The orphaned gun's energy charge dwindled and its afterglow shrunk below his clenched jaw, flexed neck, and stretched shoulders. Staying attached to the man's silhouette as it waded into the grey horizon became irrelevant. Irrelevant too, was pretending to ignore the lingering sensation where the initial bolt had hit him.

His nerve faltered, and he gasped, wobbled, then took a step back to steady himself. Pain he couldn't picture compelled him to caress the area, certain flames frolicked atop already scorched skin. Yes, his shirt's fabric had been singed from existence, and his flesh remained in the same condition, tender, swollen, exposed, but there were no flames. His mother had warned him of his overactive imagination. More blood joined what had smeared and dried across his fingers the first time. Inhale through the nose, exhale through the mouth. Repeat. There was a pounding in his eardrums, while he desperately sought concentration to inspire his regenerative powers. Inhale through the nose, exhale through the mouth. Repeat.

He ran a hand through his afro. The brown ringlets, a result of mixed African-American and Caucasian heritage and infrequent grooming, deposited sand back to its home, unwilling to bring them along the next leg of the journey.

Marrakech, the Red City, had flourished as the Moroccan epicenter of merchant trade and melded cultures. Allister wandered its streets. As the wind tiptoed around him, it swept sand flecks between the abandoned civilization's haunting echoes. Overturned, paint-stripped vehicles with blown out windows. Tattered sheets hung from clotheslines. Stone temples and infamous rose-colored buildings overrun by leafy vines, cork oaks, and olive trees. The country's gem, suspended in tragedy.

"This is Marrakech now."

He dusted the tan particles sticking to his bare arms and shoulders, then untied a bandanna from his left wrist. A government-issued device known as the Cynque watch was hidden beneath. "What's Celine's location, Cynque?" he asked it, and retied the bandanna around his neck.

"Updating," it replied and repeated, "updating," and answered minutes later: "Celine Nephthys location not found."

Either the device was as useless as he'd come to believe, or Celine had evaded mandatory enrollment in the global surveillance network. Cynque, a one-stop shop for personal information: occupation, age, nationality, and citizen status (i.e. fugitive), doubled as a communication device and source of entertainment. To an average person, the watch's pros outweighed its cons. Allister was far from an average person, and his skepticism had blossomed into theories of an all-seeing government cloaked in the shiny guise of convenience. "We are all Cynqued!" the newest commercial tagline propagated. Allister liked their initial slogan better: "Cynque makes life easier."

Humidity clung to him like a needy lover, and he reached the grand La Mamounia Palace Hotel's fading memory drenched in perspiration. The prospect of confronting Celine kept him in the sweltering heat until he gathered the courage to go in.

The statuesque entrance was lined by half-broken pillars spread like downed trees along the ground. In rare cases, they leaned against sturdier companions, held up by the embrace of roots connected to the palace's upper fixtures.

Damaged chandeliers lowered his expectation for decent light. He roamed the hall's darkness. He called Celine's name over and over. Allister scowled and turned each direction in the deteriorated lobby, before he yelled, "I need to talk to you!"

A rumble, similar to a high-speed train, foretold the wind-propelled storm. Arm over his face, Allister scrunched down, using the pillar for stability and to protect his back. Sand swarmed from all sides, carving a woman's curvy hips, cinched waist, and squared shoulders—then solidified. Smooth, radiant skin sat between a chorus of twisted braids the color of midnight.

He left the pillar's support and huffed, "Celine. You look... different."

"Bow," Princess Celine Nephthys commanded, in a French-inspired North African accent.

Already crouched halfway to the ground, he replied, "I don't think that's necessary."

Fingers curved in, she yanked her arm to her body. He dropped to his knees and swayed upright. She flattened her palm, causing him to pitch forward, both hands on the floor.

She's still upset about what happened, he thought. His core muscles contracted, fighting gravity. He bowed his head. "Is this what you wanted?"

She shook her wrist, erasing the increased gravitational pull. "It will suffice," she said. "What are you doing in my country?"

"I need info on C20."

"How inconvenient for you." Celine's frown straightened. The piercing brown darkening in her eyes ignited to the purple energy of her geokinetic superpowers. Sand spilled in from the outside and sloshed like a furious ocean, flooding the room.

Ankle deep. Knee deep. Waist deep. Mouth hanging open, he edged back and debated whether to defend himself. "Don't make me fight you," he stammered. "That's not why I came here!"

"You thought I forgot what you did? When you saw me imprisoned and failed to give me a second glance? I've heard so much about this hero, Allister Adams. All I see is an impulsive, self-serving child." She raised her arms.

Okay, she's pissed about what happened. "Celine, calm down. I'm sure we can—"

More sand poured in. It swelled into a tsunami and crested, breaking against his chest. Knocked upside down, he flailed inside the earthen trap whipping en masse around his body.

"You left me to die! I beg you to find a reason... "

Her muffled words refused the tumultuous trek to his ears and kept their distance. Swallowing, a bigger mistake than paddling through the rip current, filled his mouth with flavorless particles and panic.

Stabbing sensation beneath the skin in his left arm, blood-bloated veins, and a blue glow were signs he'd tapped into Z-energy, the peculiar energy inside him. He closed his fists in an attempt to contain the power to no avail. It erupted from his forearm, dispersed the sand and blasted Celine back.

Allister rolled onto his stomach, gagged, gagged again, and threw up the grains lodged in his esophagus. Fighting the puddle of sick's smell, he turned sideways. "Crap, I didn't... mean to use that. Did... did I hurt you?"

He held his left wrist, palm exposed, demanding the Z-energy's cooperation under his breath as he waited for an answer. It behaved like lightning, crackling until its temper waned. Zig-zag shapes sank into his skin, and the energy's soft flare dulled to his natural honey complexion.

She stood over him, arms crossed.

"Look, I didn't save you, because C20 had my moth—" He coughed and wiped saliva from his chin. "I was scared. For all I knew, you were on their side." He reached for her to help him stand, to which she let out a scoff and slapped his hand aside.

"Don't be an opportunist. Just tell me why you're here."

"I told you. I need to find C20."

———

La Mamounia Palace Ruins, Marrakech, Morocco

Celine led him to an open room occupied by a mid-century wooden chaise and a sparse furniture assortment. Vines dangled from the ceiling, covered in red, orange, and pink flowers. Roots stretched like veins to decorate chipped tile. A shallow pool shimmered with clarity and freshness next to an archway leading to a balcony. Nature's luxurious accommodations.

A better-preserved chandelier spread a pure prism over a chessboard and pieces sculpted from stone. Their positions alluded to the game's tense climax, and either she or the other person was losing. Allister didn't need to ask how they moved, knowing at minimum, the princess's powers involved manipulating the Earth's crust using her mind.

The king came to Allister's chin. Fascinated, he reached for its crown.

"Don't touch anything," she said.

His head whipped toward her direction. Arched eyebrows rose. Her silky twists were pulled to the front, and the blouse portion

10

of her navy jumpsuit showed her alluring back. "And stop looking at me," she said over her shoulder. Celine had two or three years on him, which put her in her early twenties.

He froze in embarrassment, certain his ears had turned from light brown to burnt sienna. The burning spread to his face and neck, sending his focus to the sand creeping over his boots. "Sorry, I was just—" His stomach dropped. "I, um, didn't mean to offend you."

Concern for her displeasure was upstaged by a squishy sponge sound. His neck turned, and he winced, stretching his arm again to touch the layer of restored epidermal cells stitching across his back. Healing used to take a lot less time.

Allister gulped, brought his arm down, and hid it under his shadow. The cosmic-powered stone attached to the back of his hand was exposed. He fiddled with a flat piece of fabric that had loosened during his curiosity. Pulling it taut, to conceal the dull artifact, he secured its place by looping it around his palm twice and tucking the fabric ends in near his wrist and then did the same on the other hand.

With a glassy stare, she pursed her lips, then examined a fraying braid. "It's a miracle you got past the wall," she said.

"Lucky, I guess."

"And my soldiers."

"Hey, I didn't kill anyone, I wouldn't kill... anyone."

"For your sake," Celine said, deciding to invest in his eye contact, "I hope that's the truth."

He didn't know for sure but answered with confidence, "It is." His fingers intertwined behind his head and he took a few steps. "A month and a half ago, the President of the United States tells me that because I 'saved the world,' he's voiding my contract with the Andromeda Project, and by default the U.S. Government. So, I'm like super stoked they let me go free."

"Ecstatic I'm sure."

"You don't understand, that contract was hardcore. I signed my life away." He shrugged. "Whatever. Come to find out, my immunity lasts for a year. And my orders are to lay low, as in, no powers. President DeVries said when the time's up, I'll have to go back and sign a hero-for-hire deal, some crap about me helping them bring down C20. It's a joke of an offer if you ask me." He checked to make sure she'd remained engaged in the story. "C20's dangerous. Why would they wait?"

Celine stood in front of a vanity fashioned out of clay, staring at a smooth black crystal surface melded into a rectangular mirror. "What does this have to do with me?"

"I mean... you spent some time behind enemy lines. Did they tell you what they were working on?"

She flinched and cursed, preoccupied by her reflection. Almond skin, transformed to dust, escaped her shoulder and settled to the floor.

"Hey, did you hear—"

"I don't remember!"

Her rudeness mellowed, and with the smidgeon of apology in her voice, she revealed what she did remember. She remembered going to sleep one night and waking up imprisoned in a machine a year later. She remembered the psychic, Florence Belladonna, freeing her by crashing into C20's watchtower. And she remembered escaping as fast as she could.

Allister fumbled to get his words out without her noticing the cracks in his syllables. "H-How... how did you know her name?"

"I did my research. Wasn't she your associate? Why can't she help you?"

Repelled by mental walls, the question came in stifled and far off, while the woman's name, Florence, who had abandoned him in favor of her own preservation, blared between his ears.

"Why can't she help you?" Celine repeated, standing up straight.

"She's dead." He bit his lower lip. "She knew too much."

"Oh."

"Maybe you should've dug a little deeper. Can you help me or not?"

She circled him and lifted her open palm. The ground rose to his eye level, suspending a sand block over five feet in the air. She blew up at the cube. Her arid breath, as strong as the wind itself, chipped sand away and left them a 3-D sculpture of C20's former base in the Middle East and the tunnels beneath it. "I went back. Twice. The first time it was empty, although I couldn't access any of their technology. The second time, it was overrun. Your government sealed it off. Either they're protecting something or hiding something."

Allister raised an eyebrow and his neck, studying the sculpture, its layout and entry points. "Take me there," he said flatly.

"No. The Moroccan-U.S. alliance is in negotiations. It won't bode well."

If he got caught, he was screwed too. Was that the worst that could happen, being captured by the government for trespassing on classified territory? Allister buried his mouth in his palm and listened to Celine as she went on about how ludicrous the idea was.

"My friend's been kidnapped!" he blurted out.

Her eyes shifted upwards, and her chest contracted in a sigh.

"I think. I'm not sure. She's been missing for a month. Her name is Zosma. Zosma Caster."

"I have never heard such a name, and I have heard many."

"She's, uh, not from around here," he said. A wrinkle crossed his brow. "Listen, if I can find anything to point me in the right direction... "

"It's worth a few casualties," she finished. "I know your type."

Sweat beads dotted his forehead, skin glistening with sebum and saline. Allister wiped the droplets before they passed his eyebrows and pulled a computer chip the size of a mini-USB drive from his pocket. "I figure half a mil is decent for a one-way trip." He tossed it.

She caught the five hundred thousand dollars in virtual currency. Two of her sharpened nails plucked it from her palm to review it against the chandelier's light. The clear plastic techno-currency behaved like cash and could be transferred into the global Cynque banking fund without tracing its origin. It could also be circulated, if say, one wasn't part of the global Cynque banking fund. Either way, it provided assurance their association would stay anonymous.

"A bit fortuitous, too much of a coward to rescue me, yet brave enough to come here and ask me to break international law." Celine drew her neck high and tucked the chip in her ensemble's folds. "What is it you require?"

"Besides a ride?" he asked. Tight-lipped, his mind raced through worst-case possibilities. "Cover once we get there, which I remember you're good at."

"I am not amused." She stomped. Sand gathered around them, swirling at increased speed and the propulsion of a cyclone lifted them into the air.

<hr>

Abandoned C20 HQ, Former Middle East

Baking in 150 degrees of cloudless daylight, the two rode atop a chariot of sand across the Iraqi desert. Obliterated in a dust storm called the Middle Beast, dilapidated skyscrapers and houses buried under mountainous sand dunes whizzed by. Crossing three time zones at hundreds of miles per hour had put them a day ahead of his intended ambush. They stopped moving, inviting silence to surround them.

Celine's face lost its color. "I caused this," she whispered.

A mushroom-shaped watchtower held a wicked smile of broken windows and was bent near the base, as if welcoming them with a butler's bow.

If it were two months prior, the watchtower would have been patrolling the region for trespassers. If it were two months prior, Celine would be inside it, strapped to a device amplifying her sand manipulation powers beyond her control. It was that machine he'd walked by, in a rush to find C20's leader before C20's leader found him.

Her skin opened with a loud tear, as fissures split along her arm and torso. She hid them with a rapid turn of her body, and yet, in that brief moment's time, Allister saw her skin had mutated to slate rock. The simplicity of his hand pressed softly against her back calmed her heaving. "No one had a chance." She wrung her hands, eyes glued to the ground under their feet. "The U.N. blamed global warming. Any fool would know there was nothing natural about what happened."

Pressure to relieve her of her obligation elbowed its way into his conscience. He shifted his weight. He wasn't good at doing things alone. More often than not, he screwed them up. Plus, Celine was smarter and had better control over her powers.

"I thought this had passed," she muttered, shying away from his caress.

PTSD at its finest. She'd almost died there, and he, mustering all the audacity and naïveté in the world, had asked her to come back on a hunch. The tightness in his chest wouldn't leave, not until she did.

Allister pushed his hair away from his face and styled it in a bun on top of his head. "Allister Adams arrived," Cynque announced next to his ear. "30.50° N, 47.78° E. Former capital of Iraq, Al Basra." The inevitable, dreaded check-in. Decades ago, it was a choice, celebrated and rewarded on social platforms. Now, location services went right into Cynque's data-collecting brain, the same brain the authorities used to track anyone Cynqued. The hourglass had been turned over.

"The infantry is lighter the farther you get from the dome," Celine pointed out. "Do you know what you're looking for?"

"Hey, we agreed no questions."

"I doubt your government considers this laying low."

"I didn't pay for advice, I paid for cover."

Flushed cheeks joined the scowl on her face. Her reserve raised to normal, her tone's temperature lowered to cold. "I'll get to it then," she said, ahead of him, glaring at the disheveled base. She took several calming breaths, and frustrated wrinkles subsided from her forehead. "With humility, I call upon this fallen nation's ashes. Rise up and cover the route of this spirit on his search for the lost."

The tattered grey bandanna around his neck slid over his mouth and nose. Awe and envy befell him in secret. Peace, the kind Allister rarely achieved, had drowned her frustration. The door to her superhuman gifts wasn't the devil's fiery red, it was the sky's placid blue. When speaking or, rather, manifesting her will, the Earth listened, like child to mother or vice versa. Such calm must've dwelled in her heart, a calm that contrasted what unfolded on the desert horizon. Two opposing sand armies raised from the east and west, rushed at them, thundering and torrential. With her arm's thrust, the storm converged and charged forward, picking up anything and everything terrestrial in its path to aid its fury. Not wanting to miss the fun, wind joined the catastrophic distraction and kept the dust moving around after her hands returned to her sides.

"I trust you can find your way from here!" she shouted, yanking the techno-currency from her bosom and shoving it into his chest. "Stay away from my country, Allister Adams!"

It took him a minute to look down, transfixed by what she'd conjured from her overactive imagination. When he did, she'd removed her hand, and he caught the chip inches from becoming a needle in a haystack. As he came back up to thank her or apologize or explain himself, her face and body dissolved, carried away by the storm as fine, ground rock.

———

Blustery winds threatened to push the watchtower on top of a giant metallic dome. Recalling the 3-D layout Celine provided and his previous visit, he knew the dome contained the control room. The control room contained data. Hawk-sharp eyesight cut through the maelstrom and pinpointed twenty soldiers guarding it. At least she was good on her word.

Allister slid down a dune and steadied his footing on its flattest part. Moaning, he tilted his head back. Time had eluded his planning again. He had no idea how long the storm would last. A swift exhale led to straightened posture and a shoulder roll.

"Okay," he said.

Once he'd gotten in the zone, his jog graduated to an Olympic sprint, and he achieved a running speed of eighty miles per hour. Even with Celine absent, the sand's brutality escalated. Foolish and fast, he powered toward the storm, his forearms acting as shields, and when he got to its outer rim he dove in, face turned away. Losing momentum, Allister veered sideways and surrendered to gale force. His stride slowed. He sank low to listen and kept both heels up, balancing on his toes, fingertips pressed in the sand.

"We're under attack, detective!" a robust voice shouted. "Might be one of those goddamn superhumans you warned us about."

Assuming the soldier's communication had been routed through Cynque, he watched their formation restructure. Hand gestures commanded action from the cavalry, and they scampered to new posts, preparing their weapons to shoot whatever came through the cloud. Their expressions, hidden beneath helmet visors, failed to shroud their uncertain voices. "Get ready!" Allister heard a different man scream, holding back none of his frenzy. They'd gone through rigorous training in preparation for C20's retaliation, but perhaps they didn't train for him.

The elemental distraction had backfired, in that now, they'd dispatched to the middle entrance he'd planned to use.

More running. A slight pivot to the side, dodging a plasma blast, fast enough for it to miss, slow enough for him to feel the burn as it passed his ribs. An uppercut to the gut knocked the wind out of the attacking soldier and he doubled over. One down. Another soldier came at him, feet behind the first. Allister threw an elbow at his face. The soldier spun out and landed on his back. Two down. A third soldier swung a right hook. Allister blocked the punch, evaded a blast, crushed the weapon's barrel, and threw the soldier over his shoulder. Three down. He served violence cold, zipping through to the middle, taking out soldiers as they filed in to halt his infiltration. The last thing he'd wanted was a brawl, yet, after five minutes, he stood surrounded by dozens of unconscious bodies and subsiding winds.

He hopped over the U.S. soldiers, ever cautious of their recovery or the chance he'd missed one in his haste. He clambered up a dune to a somewhat submerged window. *Whoomph.* His palm hit the concrete wall. Allister's hand stung from striking it, but he needed the grip to keep from sliding backward. He heel-kicked the window's edge. It splintered. In the same fashion, he kicked it once more. Fractures wove a web on its surface, and the glass shattered.

A true gentleman, he let the sand enter first then lowered his head to peer in. Empty. Hesitation harnessed around his waist, he hovered at the edge as the hourglass in his mind ran out of sand. He had to keep moving.

His shoes crunched against the sand ridden floor. His breath shortened. His stomach tightened. It sank in. He'd volunteered to revisit the place where he'd lost the pillar of his being, Dolores Edna Adams. Two months prior, April 2052, C20 had captured his mother, Dolores. Allister led the charge to C20's doorstep to rescue her. A noble effort complicated by the organization's motives. They wanted him to come. And they wanted him to come alone.

His colleagues, Dr. Florence Belladonna and Lieutenant Leesa Delemar came after him, even when they were ordered not to. The showdown ended with the devastating energy pulse from Leesa, which neutralized the base, Florence's imprisonment and...

He pressed his hand on the nearest wall. The woozy sensation derailed his progress. If he closed his eyes, he'd see the heart-wrenching moments in high-definition, so he kept them open until they dried from the heat and blinking became reflex. An unexpected reunion with facets of his humanity that had been destroyed there—his purity (if nothing else).

Allister told himself to keep moving. And he did, one foot, then the other, and again. There was less at stake this time around, still, he found himself performing the same choreography as the last visit. Lukewarm, sheeted metal protested his heavy hand's need for support as he traversed the musty hallway, heading opposite the dome. The creaks were normal, a result of a foundation built on shifty earth. His vision adjusted to darkness revealing a canopy of wiry, metal nooses and a field of jagged steel scraps, bordered by a forest of dented paneling. Leesa's telekinetic handiwork.

The wall creaked louder, shouting at him. He swiveled to it and the wall creaked again, not shouting, he'd misjudged. It was warning him to move farther, faster. Its distress brought his attention to the rotting wounds, creases in the metal wall gaining weight and folding over themselves, spreading past him into the dark. As a result, the ceiling slid closer to his bun's curled tips, clanging in its own aggressive anger at the wall's unwillingness to try.

Hint taken, he swapped caution for speed. The floor caved and tumbled soon after. As if fueled by their own preservation, each knee lifted double time to carry him out of danger. He dove onto sturdier ground, rolled and thumped a door as the wall and the floor's final slabs crashed below.

He spent seconds on his bum; skull rested against the door, staring at dust and debris-riddled air. Catching his breath, knowing he could spare seconds at most, he felt a full minute's burdensome and unwarranted arrival. More seconds passed. He said goodbye to another wasted minute. Time continued to slip from his grasp, it fell and unraveled like yarn, while he, the kitten, pawed at it, hoping to bring it closer, to reclaim it as his own. He needed to keep moving.

Allister rebounded to his feet, faced the door, and was confronted by a name placard affixed to the office's frosted glass: Captain Jared Brandt, C20's leader.

"Lying son of a—" He punched at the glass. It didn't put up a fight and broke down the middle, leaving fragments in its corners.

Unimpressive contents. An overturned acrylic chair, wheels up. Captain Brandt's medals of honor scattered, victims of distress. "I can't believe it," he gasped, rushing over to an intact... not a desk, a miracle with a built-in hard drive. He brushed sand from the touchscreen monitor, bringing the device to life. A halo of light basked his face and the office in its hopeful glow. Tiny red dots touched the left, right, and center of his wrinkled forehead.

"No... no... no, no, no, no, no," he repeated. Additional dots connected by gridlines, outlined his lean face and square jaw in a checked pattern. They scanned his hazel eyes, and picked up texture in his arched eyebrows and patchy beard.

"Warning, facial identification invalid," an androgynous voice boomed. "Warning, facial identification invalid. Deleting files."

———

Allister kneaded the base of his neck and dipped closer to the computer. Forty percent complete. Now it was his mind's time to shine. His brain activated microscopic x-ray vision, penetrating the CPU's hardware, winding through a computer chip maze for the logic board's data storage file. His pupils, less than a foot from the device, reflected the binary code of its security grids running opposite directions. He'd found the backdoor to its hard drive, memorized the passwords, and walked in the front door instead.

A loose hair fell from behind his ear. "Open folder, Children of Andromeda," he said.

"You do not have authorization to access this folder. Deleting files," it replied.

"Access code is... D... H... E... DHEX470BCE."

"Access code accepted. Welcome back, Dr. Rabia Giro."

He covered his face, prepared for another scan, and thought, *Dr. Giro? What?*

The computer kept going: "You have two hundred thousand files remaining, what would you like to extract?"

Of course, C20 kept its content on a private server that didn't link to Cynque's public network. Extracting data to his Cynque would be too risky, would set off alarms. But he could read. He could memorize.

"Access file Mission: the Andromeda Project ruination, view only mode."

Rectangular holographic projections ballooned up from the screen and expanded in a semicircle around him. Individual bios on anyone who had ever been associated with the Andromeda Project, their names, ages, occupations, powers (if any), and status were etched in Helvetica bold next to the featured subject's flickering image. He examined them, drawing closer to the ones resonating. One employee, in particular, shared his nose, brow structure, and cleft chin.

Patrick James Adams. 33. Senior engineer. Superior intellect. Deceased. Next image. Nicolas Delemar. 58. Former General. None. Inactive.

"Inactive," he murmured. "Bullshit."

Distant shouts. Heavy duty wheels rumbling over dunes. Helicopter blades chopping through the sky. He'd flipped the imaginary hourglass over too many times. The sand had run out. The storm was over.

"Access folder, Z Protocols, view only mode."

"Folder Z Protocols requires additional clearance," the computer responded. "Please provide the access code."

"Um." He pressed into his temples and massaged them in rapid circular strokes. "It's in there somewhere."

A voice, lower than the lowest human octave spoke, "All-Allister."

Allister sprung against the wall, hands flattened on its surface. "Neight!" he exclaimed, then glowered at a creature by the entrance. "Neight, what the hell, you're alive? Where's Zosma?"

Neight Caster, the fallen alien king of a planet called Uragon, was close to seven feet tall and doused in grey armor. Creating an astral projection required incredible mental power, and it often resulted in an outlined transparent shape. But he was translucent. If one could imagine a person without their smooth, epidermal cloak, the cloak that concealed the interconnectivity by which the body is governed, they'd see, as Allister saw, that Neight's intricacies were unmasked, sketched in precise detail.

Smeared the color of muddled lavender, striated muscles in his long arms rose up like identical shield volcanoes and dipped, mimicking an unsuspecting flatland below, then rose again near the forearm, and flattened into three claws that clenched his side. Neight knelt as though he carried the burden of Atlas, boasting shoulders that could, if sentenced, hold up the heavens.

"Rabia," he began. Instead of meeting Allister's anxious gaze, his pupils traced the talons on his feet. "Rabia... wants... " Neight's image faded and returned to luminescence.

Allister resorted to shouting, as if the louder he got, the higher the probability he'd get an answer. "Come on, keep it together. Rabia wants what?"

"The Z-enerarrrrgh." The alien's head reeled back, and the astral projection vanished, a soul called back to Hades.

"Wait, how do I find—"

Boots pounding steel reverberated through the compound.

"Neight," Allister muttered and clutched his forehead.

The computer boomed, as if with anger for having to repeat itself: "Folder Z Protocols requires additional clearance."

"Right, the access code. Um, let's try... ZCW96."

"Access code accepted."

"Yes!" One at a time, the rectangles were vacuumed into the computer, and in their place, was a text file. Allister skimmed the first paragraph.

Feet shuffled down the hall. His skin tingled and he listened for their action. Windows were smashed. A door was kicked in. A young sounding woman said in a high-pitch, "Not in here, sir."

"Keep moving then," a growling voice responded alongside the whirr of charging weapons.

Allister ducked too fast, teetered and fell on his hands. Hushed but firm, he said, "Resume file deletion."

"Are you sure, Dr. Giro?"

"Resume!"

"Preparing to delete."

Light beams from their Cynques and the stench of prolonged perspiration swam over Captain Brandt's office. "Did you hear that?" the female soldier asked. Quiet as she'd thought she'd been, he deciphered the whispers in her throat.

"We suspect the intruder's in Captain Brandt's office, Detective Steele," a man said in the same gruff tone from earlier. "Some files may have been compromised. We're going in."

No chance in hell the U.S. government was taking him in. He reached for the chair and slung it by its legs. It barreled over concrete like a bowling ball. The computer met its end in a chaotic burst, littering the floor with flakes of glass. Safety mechanisms on three weapons snapped to release. Plasma beams blew holes in the walls and incinerated anything in the room with a low enough melting point. A fatal flaw in the weapon prototypes was their need to juice-up like heroin addicts in order to function. The shooting's pause answered his desperate prayer.

He didn't wait to eavesdrop on the soldiers' next moves. Allister's uneven strides thumped through the pitch-black tunnel, thanks to a piping hot new burn on his thigh. Whimpering, he grasped the area above the pain and slammed into the wall. Sand trickled from the ceiling as soldier after soldier ran across the base to catch him at the exit.

His body trembled. White energy output erupted from his left hand, dashed up his arm, and across his shoulders. He looked at the heptagon-shaped gems on the back of his hands and the dangling fabric which had concealed them. Temporal (time) energy defeated the muffling darkness and, in reverse, redrew a memorial mirage so vivid, a cave reappeared.

It was the cave. The cave Dolores died in. Amazon's Spring 2051 perfume—Preservation—attacked his nasal passages. It had been his mother's favorite—a mix of honey, ginger, and primrose. He'd inhaled it as she cradled his head for the last time, handcuffed to a bare, wired bedframe inside that cave.

"I'm sorry, Allister," her voice whispered from behind the memory's shimmering door. An apology she'd uttered after she revealed untold stories of his childhood. "I hope you can forgive me... for keeping this from you."

Reliving the memory, Allister swore he felt the heat and smelled the cinders, as the detonation of the bomb strapped to his mother's waist swallowed the sweetness of her last words on their way to his ears. The tunnels collapsed in real time, and C20's underground shimmered, returning to its present damage.

Cringing, he whispered, "Mom." The one syllable word set his escape in motion. Allister's skin lost its luster, as the energy swirled back into him. The Transporter gems dismembered him limb-by-limb, cell-by-cell, nucleus-by-nucleus.

———

DETECTIVE HUNTER STEELE
Abandoned C20 HQ, Former Middle East

"DETECTIVE STEELE, SIR, I don't know how he escaped, we went at him from both sides," the general said, standing at attention in a row of nervous soldiers.

"I can live without your excuses," Detective Hunter Steele said. "You're all fired anyway."

"Sir, you don't have the authority to—"

"You talking back to me?" he asked. Their collective head shaking ended with lowered chins. "Good, that's what I thought." He sauntered around Captain Brandt's ransacked office, thick leather boots crunching atop glass, and frowned over the gaping hole in the floor. "Clever little fuck, isn't he?"

Detective Steele was a mid-thirties, broad-shouldered figure, rocking a sleazy goatee and impeccable frame. Much of Hunter's ambiguity lay in his coal black eyes and in his imperceptible accent—he had no qualms or curiosity about his ethnic heritage and used quips to dodge invasive questions like "What are you?" and "Are you mixed?"

"A-a-as the general said s-s-sir," the female soldier stammered, "we sent a u-u-unit in from this hole here and had a second unit w-w-waiting for him at the end of the t-t-tunnel."

Hunter's eyebrow raised. "You're telling me Private Adams disappeared?" He studied the failures' faces, seeing fear, defiance, remorse, confusion, each expression dressed up in sweat and sand. They couldn't answer before he guffawed, one hand pressed against his abs, and slapped the general's back. "Man, good one." He pretended to wipe a tear from his eye, laughed deeper, and straightened up. The grin faded to a sneer. "In case I wasn't clear, you're done-zo. Pack your shit up and get your team out of here."

"You heard him, move!" The general adjusted the light on his Cynque and led the others out.

"Look on the bright side, you'll get to spend time with your kids, or pets, or whatever!"

Round and round went the loading circle of dots chasing each other on the Cynque's screen: large circle, medium circle, small circle, loop. Repeat. Their best tracking software wasn't getting a reading on Allister's device. Mid-search, his Cynque accessed its vocal programming, "Apologies for interrupting, Detective Steele, you have an incoming call from President DeVries would you like to—?"

Hunter answered the old-fashioned way and pressed the green phone button on the screen. "What's up, Prez?"

"No updates, Steele?" President DeVries asked.

"Buddy, I've been here four hours. You'll get news when I have it." He muted the Cynque, and while the president ranted about urgency, standard operating procedures, and respect, climbed out of the facility. The Cynque's rim lit up in spurts, on par with President DeVries' nagging vocals. "Stupid people and their stupid problems," he muttered, un-muted the device, then interrupted, "Hey, hey, Mr. Hysterical. Zip it for a sec. Do you know if the mines we planted here are still online?"

"They should be. Why do you ask?"

"Hold." Hunter scrubbed off unyielding specks of sand sticking to his clammy torso and neck and took a panorama of the base. "I say we bury this place. Make it look like an accident, the region was too dangerous, or you got ambushed. Get your weasel to spin a story out of it."

"You're not authorized—"

"Authorized to what? Cover your ass?"

"I hired you to bring in Allister Adams without using violence."

"Isn't that the same thing?" Hunter snorted. He fanned himself with his red leather coat. "Here's some advice Prez, you don't want anyone knowing you've got a superhuman running around the world breaking border laws." He paused to rub his slick bald head, then shook the sweat from his hand. "Plus, this kid's your best weapon against C20. The more he knows, the more dangerous he gets, and his chances of helping you go way down."

"There've been some developments stateside which need attention."

"Can I be honest? It's hot as sin here. I'm annoyed, and I can't coddle you right now," he countered, and added a smirk, "Don't worry, Allister's Cynqued. I swear on your life, I'll have him home by dinner tomorrow."

"Treat him like an asset, not a criminal," President DeVries ordered and hung up.

"One day he's a criminal, one day he's an asset, Jesus frickin' Christ!" Hunter held up the Cynque and announced, "We're clear," over their shared comm channel. "The GI Joes gone?"

His loyal crew of ruffians sat in a matte-black Boeing Osprey helicopter, "Steele" painted in giant grey letters on the side. The pilot saluted him, and the helicopter's twin engines sang with the harmony of 15,000 horses. It rose into the air, angled southwest toward the setting sun and their next destination.

Hunter jogged, arm still up to his mouth. "Cynque, activate emergency measure C20C using access code override, HS7692."

"Override approved," it said. "C20 Compromised emergency measure activated. T-minus fifteen seconds."

"Time to light it up, fellas!" he yelled, running full speed, arms pumping at 90-degree angles.

"Three," it counted, "Two."

An explosive chain reaction rippled through C20's remains. *Boom* went the watchtower foundation's bottommost layers. The mushroom head and sabotaged stalk bent, snapped, and toppled onto the dome like falling timber. Fire and smoke engulfed the ruins and stampeded toward him from above and below the surface. Hunter, tickled by exhilaration, invited death to a rousing match of tag. It licked and chomped at his heels, reached out to snag him, but missed as he executed a vertical leap, grabbed the helicopter's edge and hoisted himself up.

Not this time. He flopped into an empty seat and slapped the shaken-up soldier's leg next to him. "Need a drink after that one, eh? Where we headed?"

"Took a minute, but we got his Cynque signal sir, looks like Allister's in Morocco, 'bout a half day away."

——

ALLISTER ADAMS
La Mamounia Palace Ruins, Marrakech, Morocco

"NEIGHT!" ALLISTER YELLED, surfacing from a lucid dream. Pain drove a hasty abdominal contraction. He sat up and reached for his lumbar region.

"Bed's uncomfortable, I know," Celine muttered. "I've always been a minimalist."

By bed she meant the layer of thick leaves nesting in an obsidian bed frame.

He touched his forehead. His mind was a mucky swamp of words and images. "What... what... how'd I get back... " His Cynque displayed seven o'clock p.m. and behind its green numbers, Dolores's slender face smiled up at him. He had to have been out for at least half a day. "Last thing I remember... the storm stopped... and then... the soldiers woke up, came in... shooting."

Inspecting the chessboard, Celine tapped her lip. A four-hundred-pound stone chess piece carved as a goddess of flaming hair and exquisite robes, an obvious "queen" interpretation, lifted from the ground and moved to protect her king. It slammed into an armor-clad sculpture holding a lance upright. Allister guessed it to be "the knight." It wasn't much of anything anymore, having been reduced to a pile of rocks.

She sneered, "Check."

There was cold clay smeared on his thigh. He pressed his head down to get a better look and poked it while frowning and twisting his nose.

"You had inflammation from second-degree burns. Thought it would help, works for me."

He thought she'd cracked a joke and let one side of his face curl up to show he had some humorous sense. The clay crumbled away after a few swipes. "Nice... ha, nice try... but uh, I'll be fine. My body regen—"

"I waited a few hours," she interrupted. "Nothing was happening." Her lips pinched together and she nodded at his hands. "It wasn't luck that got you past the wall."

Cross-legged in his joggers, naked, chiseled chest on display, he peered at the Transporter gems and their fabric disguise folded next to him. Scientific research had shown that Earth's retaliation to reckless human consumption would decimate, and possibly eliminate the population over the next one to two decades. The strongest nations of the world pooled their finances together to form the Andromeda Project, expecting to accelerate breakthroughs in sustainable energy and new power sources.

He frowned. "The Andromeda Project had been hunting for these things for... like, ever. C20... C20 found them in a couple of months." Tip of his forefinger gliding over the gem's worn corners, he continued, "Makes you think... I don't know, maybe they weren't looking too hard." The swamp waters in his mind receded, and an embankment littered with harsh realizations brought fluidity to his thoughts.

How many innocent people did the Andromeda Project murder and sacrifice in their quest to find the gems' power before anyone else? Allister didn't want to know the answer, the two he'd lost, his parents, were plenty. Patrick Adams. Thirty-three, the classified file had read, the age he was when he died. Allister was eight. Superior intelligence filled in for his father's powers puzzled him. Did it mean Patrick had been a superhuman too? His mother, Dolores, told him that his father was sharp as an ax, but she never acknowledged or hinted at him being more than human. No doubt a mechanism to keep Allister from exploring his powers. She harbored fear about "them" discovering who he was and what he could do.

"Your government asked other countries for support in finding the alien artifacts," Celine said. Gazing at the queen's chess piece, she spun gold rings stacked on her finger. "Our family considered investing, then I went missing."

"But no one really knows what they do or what they're for."

"They might've figured it out. An option impossible now, thanks to you."

"It's not my fault," he whined. "They have to bond to a host to be used." Allister searched half-heartedly for his shirt and spotted it on the floor. "No superhuman would've survived what I went through. Not even you."

"We need another solution to the problem at hand."

"Can't you stop whatever natural disaster you want?"

"I do not control Earth, I communicate with it. In any case, me stopping a hurricane, an earthquake, and a drought, simultaneously?" She tied her hair into a ponytail and stood. "Not how this works, Allister. This threat is beyond what you or I are capable of."

Damn, he thought and slipped his shirt on. "Thanks for the—" he swirled his hand around the dried clay in his lap.

She flicked a stray braid away from her eye. "So, the gems?"

He dug his heels into the sand. "The thing is, well, the thing is, I don't know... how they work... except, they hurt. And they take concentration. Which I'm not great at."

What Allister left out was that for any given transport, there was a fifty-fifty chance it had been done without his intention. He got to Morocco the first time on purpose, the second time, an unhappy accident. Success rate aside, prolonged, unfiltered use, had its consequences. The most noticeable being longer recovery times. A revelation less frustrating than her accusation.

The Transporter gems' use may have been a mystery. Their origin was not. One of eight artifacts from the Andromeda Galaxy, known as the Artifacts of Evale, the gems had been concealed from those who would seek and be able to master its power. The Cavern of Transports, an extra-dimensional cave with one entrance, would disappear and appear elsewhere in random yearlong intervals. To trace its position required knowledge of detecting and tracking a temporal or time/space energy signature. Earth's technology hadn't reached that level.

"And then Neight Caster showed up," he said to himself, riding alone on his train of thought.

Faith in fantasy was required to accept bad magic luck as an excuse for why the Andromeda Project hadn't obtained the artifacts after oh so many decades of searching. Majority of the world's remaining population had misplaced their faith, especially those with money.

"I told you to stay away from my country."

"Country, Celine? There's no one here besides your minions. What are you hiding from?"

"The people of Marrakech were evacuated! I stayed to stop the dust storm before it destroyed the rest of Morocco." Celine's chin lowered. "This city was our battle ground. I'm not hiding, I'm protecting what's left."

El Jadida, Rabat, and Casablanca, the coastal cities, were what was left, safeguarded by open top domes. The domes were a dazzling construction of melded quartz crystals mined from Earth's crust, the same material as Marrakech's surrounding wall.

Arms folded, she cocked her head to the side. "If you keep up this search, you're going to start a war when what we need is peace and cooperation. Our leaders are planning a summit to discuss the planet's fate."

"From what I found in C20's digital files, peace and cooperation have nothing to do with it."

"Is that so?" Celine's posture softened, and she knelt down to scoop sand in her hands. "Is... that... so," she repeated slower.

"Yeah, looks like hiding and protecting mean the same thing all around," he said. Those jerk-offs in foreign affairs would write off their former Middle East and C20 base occupation as "protection," the same way she'd convinced herself the voluntary semi-solitude stemmed from a sense of responsibility. Falsehoods forged in fear.

Allister swished Neight's words around in his mouth, thinking how to approach the holographic encounter's absurdity with a logical retelling. He didn't give away the intel; she didn't even know who Neight was. His jaw hardened as he walked. "I don't care if you think I'm crazy, at least I'm not scared."

"You should be." She smelled the sand, sifted it through her hands, and let it fall to her feet. "It says there's an energy that doesn't belong here. If used, it will upset the balance of nature."

Shouting drew his head the other direction. Allister snuck to the entrance, no longer listening for her next sentence. He crouched beside the doorway. The crackle of plasma firing from weapons' barrels ended in blinding beams of light. One eye pinched shut; he turned his head as the stench of blistering flesh and ionized plasma plunged him backward.

Celine gasped, "My soldiers. Who would dare?"

The first and second tremors were faint, unnoticeable except the shifting sand around his soles. His other eye opened, and both darted to her. She was shaking, her emotions at their peak.

"You. You led them here," she seethed.

The tremors matured to a full-on earthquake, 9.0 on the Richter scale according to Cynque. Geokinetic energy spread the floor's length, and seismic waves continued to rock the earth beneath them.

———

Earth grumbled with the anger of a goddess. Pillars kidnapped from their foundations, ceilings and walls shredded to tile bits and chunks of marble. La Mamounia Palace Hotel, preserved for over one hundred years, reduced to debris in minutes.

Her enraged sea of braided locks lashing about, Celine's arms parted, sweeping aside the building remains. Steady waves from the epicenter guaranteed Marrakech's tumultuous collapse.

As punishment for his mistake, Allister's balance was in time-out. He lost his footing repeatedly, and alternated from falling on his hands, to his knees, to his butt. "You're bringing down your own city!" he yelled.

"This city serves no purpose if—" She cried out. Her arms and shoulders dropped. Her leg gave in. Celine said to him kneeling, "If anyone else knows I'm here." The earthquake softened to vibrations and vibrations softened to stillness as the energy retired to her skin.

Detective Hunter Steele, taller than Allister had remembered, approached wearing a casual smile, and a red coat blowing in wild excitement. A familiar, unfriendly face, their initial rendezvous was Hunter's arrival in London, where he and Leesa Delemar were hiding out following the Andromeda Project's demise. The detective had also towered behind the president, head to torso in metallic skin, when Allister was told he had one free year, and to spend it on his best behavior.

"You're in deep trouble, Allister Adams," he shouted, his skin light brown like the sand, not the moon grey color of steel. "I'm here to take you home sweet home."

Celine's short breaths came from behind, and Allister turned to see her trying to stand sans assistance. "Identify yourselves," she said, hunched over.

"Shut it, princess." Switching a triple barrel plasma gun to the left hand, Hunter aimed at her with a provoking glare fixed on Allister and feigned a pouty lip. "Don't make me hurt her."

"Screw you," Allister said.

"Screw me? Screw you! I was on vacation in what's left of Sicily, and Prez called me up for a *babysitting* gig. You could've been out partying, traveling the world, sleeping with fembots." Hunter activated the core reactor's charger. "But no. You wanted to play fugitive. What's it gonna be, kiddo?"

Armed soldiers crowded the outskirts of their conversation. Celine's power was exhausted.

Surrender?

"Identify yourselves!" she repeated.

"This isn't your fight, sweet ass, let the fellas sort it out." He pulled on the slide release, loading the energy in the gun. From rear sight to muzzle, it measured about two feet in length and had to weigh as much as a small child. Hunter shot into the air and giggled. "Taking your silence as waving the ole white flag."

Allister's silence equaled simmering. Simmering aggravation heated by Hunter's condescension. The heat spread down his upper arms, past his elbows, through his protruding knuckles. Patience boiled into vapor, and left rage in the pot, cooked, ready to serve. Foregoing a battle cry, Allister plowed, seething, quiet, at the scene starring Hunter's arrogance.

"Appreciate your cooperation, miss lady, I owe you a dance—"

Whoomph—he clotheslined Hunter. Plasma beams bombarded Allister's personal space as he watched the detective land on his stomach. One sailed past him and Celine's piercing shriek rang out louder than the battlefield. Knowing their extensive damage to him, and knowing his skin's resilience to harm, he stood in the line of fire, paralyzed by her agony. The weapons' combined efforts bore gaping, bleeding holes inches from his heart and through his stomach. One grazed his liver.

He buckled to all fours. Hunter, the soldiers, and Marrakech's leftover skyline, bounced as they spun around him.

Hunter's boot stomped on his back. Pain inhibitors firing faster and with more intensity than he'd believed possible, Allister's whole body screamed, mouth rigid and open, nails digging into his palms. Scorching hot sand invaded unprotected tissue. Hunter pushed deeper and whispered, "See, you're already getting people hurt, didn't you learn the first time?"

Allister glanced at Celine, needing her as a focal point to keep his vision from blurring further. A braided curtain did its best to hide exertion on her cheeks and a quivering chin. She inhaled. Her upper arm had been blown off and leaked sand over her fingers.

Determination coursed through his back muscles, core, and biceps, and they flexed in harmony, cooperating to push up from under the detective's oppressive heel. Hunter stumbled back, and his frustrated cry made it obvious he hadn't accounted for Allister's competitive strength.

Plonk. Plonk, Plonk. Plonk. Plonk. Plonk, Plonk. Terrestrial remnants from the La Mamounia ruins congregated as a solid rock formation, stacked stone by stone, blocking another barrage of retaliatory blasts.

"Celine, I-I'm sorry," Allister said. "I didn't know they'd—"

"I warned you. I warned you about this."

Fists swinging, Hunter broke through and barged toward them, upper body shining in his metallic mutation. Allister threw a punch, full faith and bodyweight, and missed. The detective kneed him in the chin and socked him in the jaw. An *oomph* left his lips as he spun in the air, then slid along the ground, ending up next to her bare feet. Blood oozing from his wound sank into the sand under him.

"Whatever you need Adams, we can help," Hunter teased.

"You're violating international law!" Celine boomed.

"Yeah, and I'm sure you're violating the king's curfew. You thought I wouldn't put two and two together when you kicked up all that dust in Iraq? Come on, baby, you know better."

"Were you or were you not commissioned by the U.S. government?"

"I can't answer questions right now."

"Then Allister is under my protection until you can."

The orange evening sky disappeared in Allister's periphery, and his cheek hit the sand. Hunter had halted, his backup otherwise occupied, sinking in quicksand. Celine, lifted above the battlefield on a piece of oval-shaped slate, had her good arm stretched out.

"Don't," he moaned.

She raised her hand flattened to the sky and, starting with the pawns, her chess cavalry joined her in the air, sprinting to the place where the detective stood. Hunter jumped from side to side into, not away from, danger, smashing through rock like they were playing a game. The unused queen came from the side like a left hook, and knocked him to the ground with such aggression it sent him sliding through a building's foundation in reverse. Check. He repositioned his hands to catch the brunt of the interior's collapsing boulders, surged his arms upward, and threw off the sagging structure. Shoulders drooping, a visible loss in his signature pride, Hunter's focus shifted from Allister to Celine and back. He wiped his mouth, spat and yelled, "This isn't over!"

Her slate rock slab displaced the sand as it settled.

"Are-are you okay?" he asked, hair matted to his forehead, torn shirt covered in blood.

"I've overextended myself." She scowled at the injured arm, whole again, though made of compacted sand. "And you've overextended your welcome."

Allister wrenched as a healed stomach brought back the knot in its pit. Fat and connective tissue marched across the wounds like an army, coating them with a hypodermic layer. He expected that in forty-eight to seventy-two hours, when the epidermis repaired, the haunting burn would dissipate. Time would tell.

He felt her staring at him, he assumed in both curiosity and disgust. He'd chosen to remain on his back, pretending to be busy fiddling with shirt scraps. When their tired gazes met, he mumbled, "You saved me."

"I did it out of respect for your existence," Celine said. "I wish you'd done the same for me."

His mouth sewn shut, he contemplated basic ideology of respect for others that had diminished in human cultures over the last twenty or so years. Allister never wanted to be a culprit to such a crime. He adjusted his body to lay on its side, fixated on the fiery horizon beyond the quartz wall and the tail light of Hunter's helicopter. A dot polluting the picture-perfect sunset.

Celine's modelesque figure had transformed to sand. The loose, granular substance spilled out, cascading over her shoulders and hips like they were cliffs. He reached for her in an attempt to rescue her from disassembly, as she allowed the soil-sand mixture to claim her legs. Nowhere near as concerned as he, she opened what remained of her mouth.

"I'll have a plane waiting in El Jadida," she gurgled, her sandy, dripping torso and face melting into the planet's crust. "Take it wherever you want, as long as it's out of my country."

—-—

ZOSMA CASTER
The Subconscious

"LEESA DELEMAR, ARE YOU HERE?" Zosma Caster asked in a melodic voice.

Traced in vague white energy lines, physical echoes of humans she'd encountered drifted close to her astral form. Her three-fingered hand extended to touch one. Confusion drew it back. Nicolas Delemar, Florence Belladonna, Bridget Sparks, Jared Brandt, Dorian Xander, Russell Ashur, and Rabia Giro, the former Andromeda Project's core members, were present in her foggy subconscious. Where was—? Allister. A smile crossed her face, which gleamed a lilac complexion. The clarity of his presence rivaled the other figures. Propelled by her palpitating heart, she floated to him.

"I'm here." A hand, likely belonging to the airy voice, touched her armored shoulder.

The fog dispersed. Cape, double-breasted tunic, two letters "A" and "P," conjoined at the same line representing the Andromeda Project logo; Lieutenant Leesa Delemar had returned dressed in death's bleakness. The fading shapes were redrawn, and her cold touch brought life to their interactions with Zosma.

"I felt my memories slipping," Zosma said. "I was not sure if it was a dream or—where am I?"

The question begged context. Did she mean the physical plane or the astral plane? A subzero chill pushed on the environment from outside her mind. Shivers rattled her subconscious. Her body must be somewhere cold. She'd landed somewhere cold. Three memories flashed in order: Z-energy erupting from her enflamed skin, she and Allister transported to the thermosphere, waking up surrounded by—

"Your physical body? I can't be sure. This is your subconscious," Leesa answered, peering into the void. "There's a place I need to take you." Light pulsed from her fingertips, gifting dimension to infinite dark. It took a sharp upward turn, creating a wall of energy blue as an ocean. The Lieutenant strutted the wall's direction and said, "Your father's spell left your psyche vulnerable, hurry."

Zosma followed. *Z-energy lives on,* she thought, grateful and worried.

Thick fog crept back in with purpose. Leesa, steadfast and unaffected by diminished visibility, didn't notice it sifting between memories and the people who represented them. Distracted, Zosma fell behind and exclaimed, "My memories, they are fading again!"

"One of these isn't a memory, it's here to take them away," Leesa said, then shouted, "Show yourself, creature!"

Zosma held Leesa as their eyes darted from one wispy Andromeda Project member to the next. "Where is Rabia?" she asked.

"Run," Leesa said so only she could hear.

Their frantic feet tapped the fabricated floor. The fog, so dense now it was like liquid nitrogen, assumed a serpent's shape and doubled. Two cobras. Two pairs of soul thirsty, vile red eyes, whipped ahead and reared to strike, separating her from Leesa.

Terror morphed the energy wall's serenity to the chaos of an impending supernova. Bolts licked outward in a shuddering crackle; one snake hissed, disintegrating, struck from behind by their might. The beast grew with its companion's destruction and swore vengeance in snake's tongue, coiled in itself.

Zosma didn't need to see to know that the energy wall parted near the bottom. Leesa had kept going and shouted from the opening, "Leave it! The wall will stop him!"

Cackling reminiscent of Dr. Giro's pomposity pierced the emptiness. Zosma presumed it laughed in defiance, at the protection promised by what she believed was a figment to pacify her loneliness. No choice but to obey, she traded her offensive attack for a swift exit.

Leesa commanded the energy through her black-gloved hands and built a ten-foot warrior outfitted in grey reflective armor and a bull-horned battle helmet. The phantom guardian's spiked shoulders swaggered, and its rusty knees squeaked as it stepped to confront the onslaught, equipped with a sharpened spear. "You will guard this sanctum blessed with the strength of an entire people. Nothing gets past you," Leesa told it. "Nothing."

At the first opportunity, Zosma jumped forward, tucked, and rolled across the open threshold. From the other side came a bright flash of Z-energy and the howling concession of vanquished fog. The knight had done its work.

Silk straight hair blew in Leesa's contorted face, as streaming light from her palms connected to the turbulent wall. Energy waves crashed together, closing the passage to Zosma's reimagined conscious. A triangular red door formed.

"The spell you spoke of," Zosma began. "The one my father cast?"

"Neight Caster kept our minds separated to hide you and Z-energy from the Universe. Your body was turned human, molded to resemble me, a form acceptable for Earth's narrow perspective. For a long time, you didn't know about me, and I didn't know about you. But he came."

"Allister." She smiled again in spite of herself and the stress she'd experienced in his charge, draping her arms over her body wishing they were his. "The magic of Uragon... " Her face sank "... is not foolproof. I woke up, and lost control."

"I expected it. There's no way you could've controlled this."

"What was that thing? What does it want?"

"Dr. Rabia Giro, he's been waiting for me." Leesa walked back and forth, hugging herself. "Erasing your mind lured me out." Mid-stride, she froze. "His influence is... he can't be here. I can hide. If I hide, can you summon me?"

Because they occupied the same mental space, Zosma was privy to her thoughts. Leesa had a level of emotional intelligence, but if she were a software program, it'd be antiquated code. Compassion felt inconsistent to her current linear, logical thought processes. Digging to its root, the concern wasn't so much for Zosma's welfare as it was for the Z-energy's.

Leesa ceased musing. Zosma gazed at the under-construction refuge encircling them, a replica of her planet, Uragon's countryside. To the right, orange hills bled into sky-scraping mountains and ended like an unfinished painting. Set in the center, a stone tower straddled what was to come and what already was. To the left, a blank canvas.

"It is magnificent."

"The rest is yours to build," Leesa said. Her astral form glitched, losing what little color it had. Yanked back by invisible force, Leesa flew head over heels until she struck and was sealed inside the energy wall.

"Leesa!" Zosma screamed. "Let her go, I cannot do this without her!" She rushed toward the vertical energy barrier. Calm, intact, but their connection to each other blocked. Knowing a terrifying influence on the other side itched to invade her haven, Zosma waited, powerless.

—‑—

C20 Lab, Somewhere Cold

Zosma's sun yellow eyes opened to humans gawking at her like an experiment. Those stares were not unlike ones she'd seen from her own people. Horror and fascination culminating in the same collective action: discrimination, putting her in captivity, labeling her an outcast. Panicked breaths condensed as they escaped her plum lips. She swallowed. Multiple voices spoke in hushed tones, though one dominated over the others, unfeeling and loud, next to her pointed ear. Rough rubber bombarded her personal space.

"The alien's awake, Doctor," a male human said. "I need to put it under again."

She was an experiment.

"Wait, I want say hi," a voice squealed, quieting the room. Horridly pale and plump, Dr. Rabia Giro loomed, a fluffy mustache plastered beneath his nose. "Good morning, Princess Zosma," he greeted with an elder's smile and strange accent. Using a fat finger, he double-checked the burly straps restricting her to a padded operating table. "Sorry for trouble, have to make sure you don't escape."

Does he think these can hold me?

"You were there, inside my head," she said. "What did you do to Leesa?"

"Lieutenant Leesa Delemar is dead. You killed her during your... awakening," he said.

Her wrists rotated under the straps to relieve chaffing and encourage circulation. Zosma tensed and whispered, "That is not possible. I saw her. She helped me."

The Lieutenant's wispy voice replayed from their conversation in her psyche.

"For a long time, I didn't know about you, and you didn't know about me," Leesa had said.

You didn't know about me, the sentence fragment repeated. Allister's arrival to the Andromeda Project shifted the tectonic plates representing Zosma's consciousness and, in a month's time, coupled with feelings of betrayal, Z-energy's power rose like magma through the cracks.

I woke up, and lost control, Zosma thought, knowing it was an understatement when she'd admitted it.

The sensation of pins and needles tap dancing on her cold skin was a painful reminder of the searing, catastrophic energy pulses that erupted from her and threatened the planet's northern hemisphere.

"I expected it. There's no way you could've controlled this." Leesa had given her the response as some sort of consolation.

This. The Z-energy, it was uncontrollable, yes, but it was hers.

"I saw her," Zosma repeated, less convinced.

"Your imagination, child. Be right back, don't move."

Compared to science facilities on her planet, the laboratory and its technology were inferior. Simple robotic assistants mimicked basic functions. Acting as extra hands, they worked alongside humans smothered by long puffy garments. Few left their bodies exposed, they'd designed warm fabrics to fit over their misshapen five-fingered hands, wrapped their dull white, brown, and black faces in thick, knitted textiles and shielded their ocular organs behind clear plastic protection. Cold was a human weakness. One of many.

The chill in her bones made sense.

To date, the majority of her experiences on Earth had been limited to similar scientific labs, except when she traveled Europe with Allister inside Leesa's body. Zosma's mind was aware and had taken ownership, perceiving the adventures as her own. It was the first time she'd been able to experience Earth's natural beauty and eclectic culture.

Then, she woke up and lost control.

Freedom to explore taken from her, she was back to a centralized computer brain. Electron microscopes. Machines speaking in beeps, hums, and clicks, passing secrets of their endeavors to keep her restrained. Primitive, easy-to-understand language, deciphered in seconds. Her synapses fired, and she opened her hands to expel power. Nothing. "These devices stop me from using my energy. Where is it?"

Next to the computer, Rabia nodded sideways at a massive glass bowl sandwiched by two flat white disks. "Your power is there."

Zosma's eyes narrowed. He'd told the truth. Her power source, Z-energy, flowed inside of Neight Caster's energy prison, the famed containment center. *There's no way I could've controlled this.*

At birth, she was called the star's goddess. Her beauty and abilities foretold to surpass any other being in the galaxy. Uragon's Princess, destined to hold the highest honor on their planet, Neight's crown. It had been less than fifty Earth years since Uragon fell to invaders and Neight and Zosma began their 2.5-million-light-year trek as refugees from the Andromeda Galaxy. For her years on Earth, the containment center had served two purposes: to make sure she didn't eradicate the planet on accident and their intergalactic enemies wouldn't find them.

Her mind went blank. Vacancies in her thoughts and feelings, attributed to the suppressed connection between her and the Z-energy's power. Tingling sensation flew up her spine. Memories bubbled to the surface. The time she manipulated matter to form an army against Uragon's conquerors.

"I remember," Zosma muttered. Straining her entirety, she summoned the Z-energy.

The man called Rabia Giro stroked her arm. She recoiled. "Give back my power and fight me like a true warrior."

"I am not warrior, I am scientist." His hand burst. A collection of grey mist encircled the operating chair and prowled, as it had done in her mind, toward her crown-less forehead. Thin blue energy formed a film around her and a loud *zap* blocked the attempted infiltration. "Why is not working!"

The human male from earlier scrambled to his computer screen. "It's achieved 1 percent access to Z-energy, Dr. Giro."

Enough access to stop him from entering her mind again. Knowledge of Rabia, his motives and actions, ached for recognition, tugged at her attention, yet, they were shrouded, connected to Leesa's psyche in the distance and not hers.

For a long time, I didn't know about her, and she didn't know about me.

"I have controlled wielder of great energy before. She was like you, strong, lost, confused." Rabia cupped her chin like she was a child. "We can work together to save humanity and many more."

"No one will control me," she said, taking back her chin. Returning strength loosened the straps, sending blood to her six fingertips. "I am not her."

"Two percent access, Dr. Giro," the man called out. "We have to cut off n—"

"Do it then," Rabia said. His parasitic mist wriggled toward her. "Will be painless."

The containment center's override system activated, taking Zosma back to 0 percent access to the Z-energy.

CHAPTER TWO

CYNQUED

DR. RABIA GIRO

C20 Lab

C20 OPTED TO FOREGO non-disclosure agreements and anonymity to ensure privacy. Instead, Rabia suggested their operations exist off the grid, a few thousand miles from civilization. On the continent's surface there were no identifiers, but isolation underground had kept their survival secret for months.

Born in Bulgaria, Rabia spent twenty years working the industry, publishing research on the acceleration of human genetics and applications in clean stored energy. The manuscripts circulated prominent science communities and fell upon the Andromeda Project directors' laps; they were beyond intrigued. In 2040, they recruited him to study Neight and Zosma's alien genetics and energy.

Rabia fished a disinfecting wet nap from his lab coat pocket and wiped his hands clean. "Hard to keep you at 0 percent access," he said. Over many years, his heavy Eastern European accent had lightened to fragmented English.

The lab's robot assistants were dormant, and he'd dismissed his staff to their solitude. The room and its appliances were given dimension by the containment center's feeble glow. In recent days, he preferred minimal artificial light when he worked, he found it less distracting.

He massaged his forehead. "Your power, it always finds you." Two chubby fingers dragged across the containment center's monitor, rotating the diagrams and measurements. Its computing style and language belonged to an alien civilization, the Uragonians. They communicated using one million plus identical circular symbol variations. He'd found black a mainstay around their circumference. The symbols' interior coloring, whether solid or in gradients, were mixed and matched with triangles, squares, octagons, etc., dictating their deeper meaning.

Forming sentences in the language had become second nature. Deciphering the functions and formulas governing Uragon's advanced knowledge of physics and energy hadn't become anything aside from confusing. He was a geneticist after all, not an engineer. Hands clasped behind his back, Rabia swiveled to look at Zosma and gather his thoughts. She slept in stillness, hair draping her armored shoulder pads, brow furrowed in hostility. He nodded and resumed tackling the complicated science. "Impossible to keep you... " his voice trailed. Any access to the Z-energy would awaken her, and the machine's numerical measurement tools revealed her closeness to gaining 1 percent.

The containment center's alarm rang. Complaints about the inefficiency of the algorithms the machine used to block her power leaked from Rabia's mouth.

"You cannot read it, can you?" Zosma asked. Her statement held no inflection, no boast.

"Quiet," he snapped, tapping his knuckles against his lips. "I will remember how to read this forsaken language... in matter of time."

"Where is Alli—" his name caught in her throat. She cleared it. "Allister," Zosma finished.

"I owe explanation for actions. I know this." He reached her bedside unprotected, no gloves, no heavy coat or scarf. "They will tell you I am evil, but I am in business of self-preservation."

Following her vacant irises, he inspected the ridges separating the metal ceiling.

"I do not believe preservation means to them, what it means to you," she said.

Another obnoxious fit of the alarm's ringing. He resisted the inclination to override the containment center as she rose from 1 percent to 2 percent access to the energy. "It does not," Rabia answered. "However, poor imagination come from missing perspective. Humans have not seen, so cannot fathom what would mean to evolve."

Her limp arms dangled off the metal cot's edge, and her chin fell to one side, touching her shoulder. "They are not ready for evolution," she said.

"I will ready them," he assured her. "Or you prefer they perish, like your race?" Greyish particles flitted from his figure and settled on her like seedlings in ripe soil. It was the last chance he had to influence her or risk losing the most valuable player in his game. As if a gunshot sounded, the race for control began. They spoke formalities on the surface, while a wrathful battle occurred for her subconscious. Mounting energy access made her a formidable mental warrior, but Rabia had more practice. Round one ended.

"You are fortunate for my disadvantage."

Rabia smirked. "I need you to be, as they say, blank slate."

Silhouettes of the Andromeda Project's former team members skulked about her subconscious, evading absorption into his cloudy mist. Nicolas Delemar, the man who'd raised her as his human daughter, was the first to go, destroying her connection to a parental figure, the position Rabia wanted for himself. "I promise humanity's continued survival, why you resist?"

"If the death of this world means you fail," Zosma said, "then I am obligated to allow it for the good of the universe." Four percent Z-energy access. Her lips pressed together. Her back arched.

Telekinesis kicked in and the cot rattled. When it was over, her torso flattened. She whispered, "I am alone now. Leesa is gone."

"Yes, give up, Zosma," Rabia soothed. "These creatures can't accept you for glorious being you are. I will make them understand. Together we show them what you can do." Dormant for decades, Zosma had an infant's impressionable mind. Seeds of influence germinated in her mental terrain sprouted a dense forest, tangling her thoughts in darkness and doubt. Pressing on her arms, he penetrated her intentions with inky grey eyes, hunting for Allister Patrick Adams's lingering astral presence. He must be the last domino to fall. Her purity was what Rabia needed.

"I will not let you take him." Zosma's chin shook, and her forearms flexed beneath his oversized palms. "You are more than evil, but you are less than me," she said in a steady low pitch.

"What you think you know of me?" he asked, face-to-face, wearing a grandfather's smile. His mist permeated throughout her mind, delivering new thoughts, desires, beliefs.

"Nothing. I see... nothing," her voice cracked. "I know now why I feel this way."

The game at its peak, he outlined her noble cheekbone without touching it. Her irises cleared and adopted the same color as his.

"Zosma?"

"Yes, Dr. Giro. What shall be my first task?"

He clasped his hands to his chest. Her energy access levels stabilized at 10 percent, the standard level for keeping her subdued and effective. A level assigned and regulated via the containment center. "Time to make introduc—" Rabia's smile faded. He cupped an elbow in one hand and stroked his chin. Out of all that was lost—the childhood she'd lived as Leesa Delemar, the familial relationship to Nicolas Delemar, the obligation to and the activities from the Andromeda Project—one thing didn't change: her longing for Allister Adams.

CAPTAIN JARED BRANDT
C20 Prison

CAPTAIN JARED BRANDT'S BEARD had grown to his cheekbones' highest point. Gone from a clean-cut, polished official to dirty hands, picked-at fingernails, and clusters of hair trying to survive an ever-expanding bald spot. The smell of decaying fish seeped from his pores. He bent his head to his armpit, taking a whiff. His face shriveled. Breathing fresh air or eating a decent meal were activities too far from recent to be remembered.

"This's how veterans end up," Jared said. His southern drawl was one you'd find in Southeast Kentucky. Military tours and worldwide travel for twenty or so odd years hadn't softened it the slightest.

His elbows rested on an ice tablecloth draping a table bolted to the floor. Midsection, wrists, and ankles, shackled. He should've frozen to death. The ice touching his shirt sleeve was an inch thick and thickening, but the knot in his throat had been there for days, the pounding migraine, weeks.

"When I get where I'm goin' on the far side of the sky," he hummed the lyrics he forgot, then sang louder, "I'm gonna land beside a lion, run my fingers through his mane, or I might find out what it's like to ride a drop of rain!" Beneath dried blood, his palms held warmth. He wasn't going anywhere, anytime soon.

Mist puffed under what Jared had convinced himself was an airtight door. A shape, sculpted in black smoke, materialized as the stout geneticist.

"You don't get off so easy." Dr. Giro knocked on the door. A guard opened a peephole. "Get me prisoner's dinner." The door cranked open. Dr. Giro retrieved a covered tray. The door cranked closed. "Eat before gets cold," he suggested, removing the lid to reveal a fatty ribeye, garlic-mashed potatoes, glazed brussel sprouts, and a biscuit.

The meal reminded Jared of Sundays after evening Bible study. "No broth today," he murmured, shaking his head. Wrist shackles grated the ice as he leaned away. "This a trick?"

"You stopped yelling like madman, so I decide to reward you. Remind you what freedom feels like," Dr. Giro replied.

Jared slumped lower in the chair. His stomach spilled over the camouflage pants he'd been captured in. "Shit. Since I joined the military, I've never been free."

Dr. Giro cut the steak in slow strokes. Tantalizing juices from its rare interior dripped onto the plate. The fork punctured the tender beef, scooped a teasing of mashed potatoes, and the doctor held it to his mouth. Unable to control themselves, Jared's teeth ripped the helping off. The doctor continued feeding him like a toddler until the meal finished.

"Drink," Dr. Giro insisted.

Water hurried to catch up to the party in his stomach. An unraveled mind nourished, the why and the how became clear again. He nodded. "So, you're the *savior*," he said in air quotes, "break out genius of the twenty-first century, Dr. Rabia Giro. And here I am," he boasted, "Captain Jared Brandt. The pioneer in humanity's advancement! C20's leader! We'd make a pair, that's fer certain. But I suppose ya got what ya needed from me, cheers to success." Jared lifted an imaginary beer mug and shoved it forward. "Why didn't ya just kill me?" He looked at the empty plate, then at the man who'd spoon-fed him. "You want somethin'."

"Not about what I want," Dr. Giro said. "You see how rewarding can be when you cooperate."

Jared took in the stone slabs, low ceiling, and frost-enveloped walls. "Where are we? No wait, lemme guess. The North Pole?" The chains jangled as his fist beat the layer of ice on the table. "I knew it! The North fuckin' Pole."

"You are member of C20, Captain Brandt. Are you ready to resume our work?"

"See, that ain't freedom." He rolled his eyes. "Go on ahead and kill me. I ain't helpin' you." He scrunched the Henley's sleeve away from his wrist and touched the skin. Regular body temperature.

Sometimes superhumanity was more curse than blessing. A transparent force field, typically invisible to the naked eye, had intensified during Jared's time in captivity and turned as opaque as Rabia's motives.

"If killing you were easy, would be done," Dr. Giro said, herding ice beneath his round fingertip. "This was test. You pass."

"Still playin' yer fuggin' games!" He swept the tray and its contents from between them. The tin plate, the silverware, its rectangular top, clattered to the floor.

"You will join. Or you will suffer," Dr. Giro said and picked up the empty glass.

Jared's sunken, insubordinate eyes peered closer to read Dr. Giro's body language. Relaxed hands, even stance. Passive. "You want Allister." His laugh bounced off the prison walls, amplified by its hollowness. "Well, I suggest ya do the cooperate thing. I got nothin' to lose."

"I expect your arrogance."

"Good, cuz if ya want me to do somethin' for ya, I gotta be alive for. Better ask nice." He shrugged and sat up straight. "Cause you. Can't. Make. Me."

Rabia faced the door and pulled his shoulders up to his ears.

"Had a feelin' gettin' hold of the Z-energy was a small part of yer plan but the Transporter gems must be pretty important too. Outta curiosity, how long were ya looking for 'em?" He paused after his question, watching the doctor with as much pleasure as was possible for his condition. His need to understand surpassed the need to survive.

"Longer than you can comprehend." Rabia whipped around. "Transporter gems are means to later end."

Mentioning Z-energy and the Transporter gems brought the Andromeda Project's memories. The Andromeda Project's memories brought memories of the closest thing he'd had to a brother. Drumming up his past mistakes reminded him that being a pawn cost him freedom.

Patty Cakes was the nickname he'd given Patrick Adams, his childhood friend. He blamed their falling out on PTSD, after his second tour in Afghanistan, when it was jealousy: Patrick's beautiful marriage, Patrick's brilliant kid, when Jared had the same shit and didn't appreciate it. Their last words to each other, the night Zosma landed on Earth, were rock-hard surface anger, and if they'd dug a little and broke soil, forgiveness would've sprung like a well. Hearing how they took Patrick out... messed up, sick... he wouldn't wish it on his worst enemy.

A goddamn bullet to the skull, he thought. *What kinda monster would kill a man in front of his kid? Have I killed a man in front of his kids?* At least once. War was a helluva drug, a hallucinogen with a terrible decade or longer come down. He rubbed his chest and took a deep breath.

He couldn't believe it all happened in a six-hour time span, the events fuzzy, not in order. Zosma's ship spiraling to its end, so bright in the country sky the stars weren't visible. The dazzling blue energy expanding from the crash, which sent Cumberland and his family up in flames. Bewildered, he spent a couple hours looking for Allister and Dolores, then hightailed it. The military troops left knowing everybody was dead or dying.

Fixated on the glass twirling in Dr. Giro's hand, Brandt went from staring at it to through it. "Where were you during Cumberland?"

"Had to wait for opportunity." The door opened at Dr. Giro's command, and he stepped into the hall's darkness. "Remember why you join C20, because of death and destruction caused by Andromeda Project."

Revenge and its hypnotic spiral had convinced Jared that infiltrating the Andromeda Project, ransacking their facilities, and bringing down the organization, would be proper retribution. Payback for his losses. A successful mission executed two months ago. Somehow, he'd lost as much as he'd intended to take from his enemies. Being a pawn had cost him, well, it had cost, *him*.

"I offer you place in our mission to discover key to human salvation or, you feed your guilt and defy me, until you starve and die."

Small victory. Small smile. "Hear that?" Jared rattled the chains holding him to the table. "It's freedom, Dr. Giro. I got nothing to lose."

FLORENCE BELLADONNA
Belladonna Castle, Province of Como, Italy

FLORENCE COULD'VE SQUANDERED her irrefutable privilege with world travel and expensive objects. She pursued a covert political career as a giant screw you to her entrepreneurial family, finding passion in making change and not amassing wealth. A self-made woman with a family-funded Ivy League education. Some would call it an oxymoron.

Her well-managed reality in the public eye suffered two back-to-back blows: her father's death announcement and an airplane attack intended to end her life.

A month to the day, she thought. She'd spent weeks in seclusion, caring for her family's castle on Lake Como, whilst getting as close to normal life as a "dead" socialite could expect to achieve.

Cynque local news had released a developing story on her.

"I'm listening Giovanni," she said in a British-American accent. Opening a door, preparing a meal, or reading the morning news were accessible and managed via artificial intelligence imbued in the castle's functions.

"Florence Belladonna," the computer, Giovanni, read, "eldest of two siblings, sole heir to the Belladonna fortune, dies at age thirty-seven in airplane bombing."

Cynque watch destroyed, the particulars buried with a fake body. She touched her forehead and pushed her lips to the side. A big favor she'd have to repay, and she was annoyed as to how, since joining the Andromeda Project had been a favor, and now she was in hiding because of her affiliation.

"I doubt anyone's gonna believe that garbage," a gritty, rugged voice joked from the foyer.

"How can I help you, Detective Steele?" she asked. Egg whites scrambled hard and gluten-free toast sat untouched next to her. She was emotionally committed to the round cedar breakfast table, bending over it and stirring her espresso. *Tap, tap*, went the miniature teaspoon. She turned. "Well?"

Hunter grinned as if he had some triumph to celebrate. "Was in the neighborhood, thought I'd say hi."

She scoffed. "I sensed you sniffing around out there like a novice. Giovanni, return security measures to maximum." Manicured fingernails clicked the stained wood. "Not sure I want to know how you found me," she said, "but since I know you like to brag, by all means." Florence waited, one arm up on the back of the chair, appreciating an array of citrus and magnolia trees and the region's famous camellias.

"Ready to come out of retirement?" Hunter teased, snatching a sword off the wall and prancing her direction. "No choice to be honest, your country needs you."

"Which country? I have dual citizenship and zero patience."

"The one that paid me to save your life. Twice." He held the sword in the light. "This yours?"

Four calculated steps later, a firm grasp on the sheathed weapon, she answered, "Yes. One of many."

He let her take it. Florence put it in its decorative place and sauntered to the table.

"I know you have a soft spot in your 24k gold heart for Allister Adams. Has he contacted you?"

Allister. Saliva built up beneath her tongue. Her heels' clicking slowed to a stop. Hunter's stomps didn't. His breath stroked her neck, egging her fingers toward her favorite sword, the dragon-handled weapon she kept on her hip. He snarled. She spun around. Restrictive, yet void of pressure, his metallic hand caught her wrist.

"I never understood bounty hunters. Hard to be loyal when you serve the highest bidder," she said, leaving her fuchsia-painted lips the least bit parted.

"Isn't it though?" His lustful eyes traveled from her mile-high cheekbones to the pointed toe on her lace boots. "I prefer the term detective. Can't believe you wear those things to breakfast. I hope you wear them to bed too." He positioned his hand around her waist. "I risked my life to fly halfway across the world and pull your limp body outta the Atlantic." Hunter yanked her closer. "The least you could do is answer a simple question."

"I doubt he knows I'm alive." She resisted the impulse to body slam him and faked a smile, going so far as to touch the stubble on his hard-edged chin. Little tactics helped open his mind to her telepathy. "Thank you, by the way. Although your bank account must be even more thankful than I."

"Your ex, I mean, President DeVries owes me some techno-currency. Tell him to pay up, will ya?"

"We haven't spoken since... " Her words took a detour and wound up back in her private thoughts. Her chin dropped.

"Yeah, yeah. Anyway, Prez wants you to come back to the states and help sort this C20 mess, get Allister on our team." Hunter pressed against her and licked his lower lip. "I figure if I offer you a night of fun you'd agree to his terms. I promise, I'll be gentle."

"I won't." Florence kneed him in the groin. While keeling over, his face hung in perfect position for a flying back kick, and her stiletto's sole connected with his temple. He staggered.

"We'll have a night of fun when my leg grows back," she sneered, distancing herself.

He growled. "That wasn't very nice."

Telepathic power surged through her forehead. "To answer your question: I'm not ready to go back to work." She released the globules of crimson energy on him.

Hunter's head, doused in psychic power, rolled back, his knees buckled, and his body hit the floor.

"Shame, you won't remember this lesson in respect. Let's see what you've been up to."

Allister Adams

Moroccan Desert

ALLISTER... ALLISTER... ALLISTER, a woman's voice called in his head. *Allister!*

"Go away," he moaned, dallying in a dream state. "Go away... "

The woman's haunting call turned harsh, a prickly version of the last syllable in his name.

"Sir. Sir, 'ey, sir!"

He woke to a lady in a ragged dress and torn shawl, hovering beside the two-seater row.

"Move!" She shook with impatience, burlap bags stuffed in her wiry arms with vegetables, bread, and clothing spilling forth.

"Sorry," he mumbled and thrust himself against the window.

She sat down in the aisle seat, turned up her nose, and spat, "'Bout time."

The railcar sped to its next stop along electric tracks at 375 mph. Commuters dolled up in suits, their upright posture and hands folded neat in their laps, were traders, bankers or politicians. By contrast, he wore tattered remnants of a shirt and gauze stained the dull maroon of dried blood. Eco-conscious laws and native Moroccans' adaptation to heat required the train's air conditioning unit to pump on low, amplifying the smell of charred flesh and oxidation. Noses were shielded. Eyes darted his direction. Throats cleared, and whispers started.

A six-foot-four, two-hundred-pound mixed-American man (plainly African-American as far as any onlookers were concerned) was a hard thing to hide in a country like Morocco. Allister slouched and his knees pushed against the person's seat in front of him.

The past poked him in the side as if he weren't in enough pain. Snot drizzled onto his upper lip despite the air's dryness. He wiped his face using an entire arm, careful not to undo the opaque fabric around his hands. That would be grand, unveiling the Transporter gems to a train full of strangers. Inhaling deeply through his nostrils, he sucked in stray emotions to make sense of the last three days.

Captain Brandt wasn't the one pulling the strings. No, Dr. Giro had created C20's files, and Dr. Giro could destroy them. Those access codes had been embedded in the computer's security module; it would've taken weeks for a hacker to find them. About eight weeks if he took a stab at it. He sucked his teeth. The U.S. soldiers knew what was going on because as soon as the general called in an attack, they moved center. He imagined the CIA had their top computer scientists breaking down C20's security system to extract the files while the region was being "protected." The Ops team hadn't gotten far, as the entire encryption had been intact when he penetrated it, and even then, some code threw him for a loop. If they were the last ones in there, the president might've captured Captain Brandt. Captain Brandt would know where C20 had moved.

Learning what the U.S. government knew and combining efforts wasn't the worst plan; he had a ten-thousand-piece puzzle on the table and no one to help him put it together. The idea of seeing Brandt's smug face made his blood boil, and he was hot enough as it was.

Allister recalled his first encounter with the captain, working as a barista at a small cafe in D.C. The gig was supposed to be temporary while he decided on a college or a career, and helped pay bills. After two years, it had become a bad habit. Day-to-day tardiness and lack of focus were roadblocks to productivity. The fat check Captain Brandt wrote the cafe's owner weeks later explained his premature termination. Payment for setting Allister loose.

In that section of D.C., people couldn't loiter, or the soldiers took you in. He was close to getting picked up when Captain Brandt came to save the day and sell the dream. Any hard-up super human would be intrigued by a bundle of cash, a few choice words about saving humanity and once-in-a-lifetime opportunities. The Andromeda Project was convinced Allister's gifts (the ones his mother had told him to suppress and thus, were useless) would lead them to the Transporter gems. He passed two assessment tests and a field test with record-breaking scores. Next thing Allister knew, like a sucker, he was enrolled in the Andromeda Project. Their prized recruit. It turned out, Brandt, commissioned by Dr. Rabia Giro, wanted to use Allister's gifts to lead C20 to the Transporter gems.

Joke's on them. His thumb rubbed the bump on the back of his hand. Irony. Taking a train, though he held the cosmic power to move through time and space. Depending on the perspective, he'd either been cheated out of his destiny or squished headfirst into it, on a path determined to tear his heart and soul to nothing. Power gained. Love lost. He bent his neck and let his head touch the window, gazing doe-eyed through translucent glass.

"Next stop, El Jadida Station," a male computer voice announced.

El Jadida's proximity to water had been a blessing and a curse. Being spared from drastic climate change across the North African region didn't stop rising sea levels. Celine's semiprecious stone walls were impressive, regardless of her distance from the city. He wondered if she'd be there to make sure he left and didn't cause trouble. Or if he'd caused too much trouble and she never wanted to see him again. She would've made a good ally.

She hates me for sure, he thought and crossed his arms. It was his own fault, behaving that way, knowing his powers weren't holding up to their usual standards.

The train had gone underground and rose up from the depths like the engine that could, riding parallel to the horizon. Evening arrived during the journey, filling the sky with a moody purple. He turned his wrist to reread the most recent Cynque message.

Per their agreement, his service to the U.S. government was on pause, yet, like any other Cynqued individual, the device logged his movements. The message informed him he'd been downgraded from hero status to fugitive. Allister shuddered, the plasma burns on his body had made that clear. Fugitive was written in capital red letters next to his name. He bit his lower lip. It'd be impossible for him to travel in the United States, and if Morocco had implemented the Cynque scanning system, the moment he left the station, they'd attempt to restrain him and send him to the nearest deportation facility.

"Cynqued ya, huh?" the toothless woman next to him squawked. "Heard dey bringin' it here next. Won't Cynque me. No, no, no. Don' wanna be tracked."

Her words brought unwanted attention and he slouched lower in the seat.

"Look at you." She pointed. "You already shook!" A French roll fell to the train floor. She scooped it up, chortling, and cleaned it with her shawl.

Passengers' stiff bodies jerked as the train pulled to an abrupt stop at El Jadida railway station. Domestic travel guaranteed his smooth exit, and Allister stepped onto the main boulevard, realizing he had no idea where to go.

———

El Jadida, Morocco

In need of a shirt to replace the cloth fragments clinging to his biceps and waist, Allister meandered awning to awning through rain-soaked streets. In the outdoor market's freshingly trendy selection he found a sleeveless light green top with white embroidery detail and a pope's neckline.

He backpedaled and asked, "How much?"

The bearded young man cast a glassy look and observed Allister head to toe to head. Grunting in disapproval when he reached the frizzy, brown curls, he ripped the shirt and its hanger off the wire. "Closed," he said.

"Sir, I'd like to buy the shirt. How much?" Allister asked in Arabic. Shared complexion and adopting the native tongue worked opposite his favor.

The merchant, who was not Cynqued, snatched the decorative cloth off the table and broke into irate mumbling under his breath. "American" flared up after a string of curse words disguised as harmless adjectives. Allister opened his mouth to protest the insults.

"I trust this is sufficient," a woman's buttery voice offered. An open satchel of gold coins jingled as it plopped.

"Hmph," the merchant grumbled, fishing the balled-up linen from a packed bag and hurling it at him.

Allister jumped back as he caught it, said, "Thanks," then mumbled, "jerk."

Defense tankers polluted the pedestrian river flowing crowded intersection to crowded intersection. And their big wheels dwarfed the Moroccan soldiers next to them. The regime wore ill fitted uniforms, helmets, and reflective visors. Their semi-automatic rifles embodied the old-fashioned way of thwarting civilian and terrorist resistance.

"Get moving, two minutes to be inside!" the soldiers commanded, leaking from their posts and into the streets.

The stars showed up, refusing to wait for the merchants to dismantle their pop-up stores or the consumers to finish their shopping. Night stretched its hand and blanketed haggard stragglers scurrying to their Riad-style homes. Doors slammed. Shutters closed. Lockdown had begun.

"Follow me," the hooded woman said and took his wrist, hauling him to an alleyway. El Jadida's patrol squad strutted along the cobblestone street, looking for curfew violators to punish. The two dipped farther into the shadows.

"Is your tracking on?" she asked. Her rigid grip squeezed his carpal bones closer together than was comfortable.

A nod toward superhuman strength. "Celine!" Allister's heart did backflips. He threw his free arm around her. "You're okay!"

Neither prepared for the outburst, she stepped out of his grasp and he stuffed a hand in his jogger pockets. "Sorry," he said and smoothed his hair. "It's just, I'm alone here and I didn't know where to go and... how'd you find me?"

She removed the hood, then crouched to pluck a twig jammed in his bootlaces. "I have eyes everywhere."

Hours had passed. Allister lay awake in a rundown hostel, thinking about the voice he'd heard on the tram. The voice mimicked the phenomena he'd experienced while communicating through telepathy. He didn't know any living telepaths, and Neight Caster, the highest probable candidate for performing a similar feat, had the deepest voice he'd ever heard.

Celine examined her braids' ends in a mounted oval mirror. They whittled to sand and blew to the other side of the room.

"Still learning, huh?" he asked, peeking under his gauze. He found new skin and exhaled relief. "Me too."

"I am responsible for maintaining the walls around the other cities lest they flood," she said. "It's why I've dwelled in Marrakech alone."

"With great power comes great sacrifice," a quote from the wise, purple alien, Neight Caster. She needed to concentrate. She needed peace. Another set of scales he'd tipped during his impromptu vacation.

She wrenched herself from the dusty mirror, crossed her arms and saddled up by the bathroom door, rather than taking the spot next to his shirtless upper body. "Did you find anything?" she asked.

"Yeah, some files. Pretty sure C20 survived. They're not in the Middle East." Allister sat up. "But I know they're somewhere."... *tending to unfinished business*, he thought. "I don't think Detective Steele followed me."

If the paycheck was worth it, Hunter Steele was entitled to track his bounty to any country's jurisdiction. That said, Celine had been pretty prescriptive about her territory and even if she hadn't, her power spoke for itself.

Allister's jaw stretched. Consecutive yawn number five. An hour nap sandwiched between two seats on a train didn't replenish enough stamina to go at his current pace. He dozed off at the height of their conversation.

The Cynque's hardware unfolded in his mind's darkness. Navigating its software components, pinpointing essential features and functions, he found the logic board which held security override measures. He ought to use the brain stocked with his father's superior intelligence in tough situations—but fighting gave him such an addictive rush.

"What of your friend?" Celine asked.

Her indignant face came into focus.

"Nothing concrete," he replied, alert, awake. Allister thought about what Dr. Giro wanted with the Z-energy. Zosma was the only living being in the universe with unlimited access to it, the doctor would need her to conduct research and/or experiments. "Wait a minute, Dr. Giro's done testing before. On General Delemar."

"Who? What?"

"General Nicholas Delemar. He founded the Andromeda Project. With my father."

Sleep wasn't happening. Allister stormed to the bathroom, crumpled shirt in hand, and shoved open the door. If he was a fugitive, he was going to act like one. He wrestled the garment over his head. "Cynque, disable tracking system, access code: W3$L&YDV4!3$." As the Cynque authorized the encryption, he squinted at a violet hair sprouting from the hairline.

"Confirmed," the device said. "Location services are disabled."

"You can't leave. It's the middle of the night," she said and blocked him as he tried to exit.

"I have to. Tell me where this plane is, I'll fly it myself."

"Why do you need a plane? Why not use the cosmic power you've stolen?"

He shouldered her as he passed. Two steps from the door handle, his voice raised, "I told you I don't know how. And I didn't steal them. I—never mind." Allister sank to a squat. "I have to find General Delemar. He's alive. Are you going to tell me where the plane is?"

"Think about what you're doing," she said. Violet energy accumulated in her stern glare. The rickety building swayed under moving earth, and the mirror lost its grip on the nail, fell and crashed onto the desk.

He exhaled, coercing anger's flush to subside from his cheeks, then searched her face for cooperation. Celine flopped on the bed, hands pressed to her scalp. Broken shards weren't the sole casualty in the miniature earthquake. Cries from other rooms made it known her emotional lapse hadn't been contained. An air horn sounded. Footsteps climbed the clay stairs. The hostel's manager yelled for tenants to flee in case of an aftershock.

Arms spread out, she quivered. "Meet me where the dome touches the sea. There's a private airstrip."

The manager unlocked the door and rammed it open. "What're you doing, you stupid American?" he asked in Arabic. "Go, go!"

Wind whistled behind him. Tiny bits of sand, spinning in circles where Celine had been, vanished through an open window.

DETECTIVE HUNTER STEELE
Cincinnati, Ohio

"GOOD MORNING," HUNTER SANG to a homeless couple sprawled on an apartment building porch. His leather trench fell right below the knees, which he gave thanks for in light of the conditions. He climbed over them and kicked the man on purpose.

Sewage and urine plagued his senses up four flights of dank stairs. "Gross!" he exclaimed, stopping short. A football-sized rat shuffled past his feet. He punted it. It squealed.

He entered the condemned building's top floor and scoured the hall for an apartment number: 5-2, 5-3, 5-4...

"Honey, I'm home!" he whooped as he pounded the flimsy door labeled 5-5. "Dorian Xander! Open up!" No noise drifted from the apartment, no Cynque broadcast, no streamed music, no AI communication, no sound.

A door swung on its hinges and banged a wall. "Hey, shut the fuck up, asshole. My wife's tryin' to get my kid back to sleep," said a male tenant as cadaverous as the building itself.

"Get back in your shitty box, loser!" Hunter yelled. He brushed his jacket aside to flash the foot-long gun in its holster.

The pale-skinned addict ran into the door frame on the way backward. "I don't want no trouble. I just need quiet. I'm about to freak, man."

"Dorian, three seconds and I kick in this door. Three. Two. One and a half."

"He ain't been here in days," the neighbor said, and retired to the apartment and his child's incessant bawling. "Shut that thing up or I'll beat the piss outta both of ya!"

Hunter heard a crash, a woman's yelp, and a door slam. Poverty's song. Domestic violence and crying children. Sounded like his house growing up. "Idiots. I should burn this place down," he said, checking his pockets for a miniature explosive.

The door's warped wood mingled with the lock's tarnished and rusted metal. Hunter lifted his foot and kicked it open. Four fingers ran along the entryway table in a standard occupation assessment. Dust levels hinted at an extended period of absence. He wiped the filth onto his pants and returned his hands to the trigger, spotting—

Yellow bananas on the countertop, a hint of green stem. Their ripeness, evidence the squatter had been there within the day. "Who'd he rob to score these bad boys?" He separated one from the bunch and leaned on the kitchen island ledge to admire the grim sky. "God, this place sucks."

Los Angeles ravaged by fires, droughts, and earthquakes. New York's population decimated in a flash freeze. Miami eradicated by tsunamis and super hurricanes. The government spent butt-loads to revive those markets and achieved no success. Meanwhile, Cincinnati and other cities like it were wastelands. Abandoned houses and cars, high-priced commodities, inescapable problems and socioeconomic statuses far below the poverty line. Cynque technology wasn't integrated or enforced there. "Middle America," neglected and officially left behind. If Dorian wanted a place to live in seclusion, he'd made the perfect choice.

Hunter peeled the banana and took a bite. "The man, the myth, the legend," he said, mouth full.

Dorian Xander's thin frame reflected in the window. He clung to his position adjacent the door, amber eyes bright and damp, elbows pressed inwards, fingers white from clenching the unused keys. Rain had given a shine to the nineteen-year-old's jet-black locks and canvas backpack.

Still chewing, Hunter said, "Don't give me that look. You don't live in a goddamn fortress." He dropped the banana's leftover peel and made his way to the foyer. Dorian jumped, fists up, wheezing through a mask resembling a dog's muzzle.

"Cool it. You answer my questions, you keep this shack. If you don't." He pulled out the square bomb, placed it on the counter, and patted it like an obedient dog. "The last time you heard from Allister Adams, go."

Dorian fumbled his keys onto the hook next to him, thumbed the activated Cynque he'd been issued, looked into the room's corners. Nerves. Anxiety. Lying preparation technique Hunter called it. Do as much as possible, then spout a false answer. The observer, absorbed in distracting behaviors, was more inclined to believe you.

"That a yes or no?" Hunter put his hands on his hip. "I read up on you, champ. What was it thirty-seven people you killed? Got my record beat. My goodness, a whole damn neighborhood, and on Christmas Eve. Those screams must be haunting." Middle finger tapping the bomb's activation button, he smiled. "You know

I counted about twenty units on the way up. Nine occupied. Ah hell, what's a few more notches on the belt anyway?"

Dorian shook his head and waved his arms.

"Oh, you really don't talk? I thought Prez was screwing with me." He paced the kitchen. "Makes sense, sound powers and all." The refrigerator swung open. He grabbed an aluminum water bottle, raised it as a toast and took a long swig. "Fine. I'll give you the long and short of it. U.S. Gov is looking for our old friend C20. I know what you're thinking, and no, Allister, the hero of heroes, didn't beat them. They need him to though, or this world's going to shit."

"How did you find me?" a computerized voice asked.

"Smarty pants here uses the watch to communicate. Your parents would be so proud if you hadn't... ahem." Hunter finished the water, winked at him, and crumpled the container against the counter. "The gag is, you're government property. You know that, right? We let you live in this dumpster because you don't serve a purpose. Cynque records everything you say and do, every message you send and receive, every place you visit outside this disgusting hole." He checked the bomb's time and turned it, so Dorian could see. Five minutes. "See how that works, you ask a question, I answer. Now your turn. Go."

"Have not heard from him," the device answered on Dorian's behalf.

Averted eyes equaled lies. Communication between close colleagues wouldn't go radio silent. Most people kept in touch those days, it was harder not to. Hunter took steps to corner Dorian. "You sure he hasn't come to you for friendly advice?"

"Yes."

Denied a third time.

Hunter dug into Dorian's clavicle and lifted him up. "Best thing about my job is I can rip your head off and call it research."

The gothic-inspired teen squirmed, restraining his cries. "Let's boogie playlist activated," the speech assisting Cynque announced. Alternative music blared through a surround sound system.

"What the—" Hunter let go.

Tears gushed down Dorian's emaciated cheeks. Five twists unhinged the muzzle covering his Peruvian skin, and it dangled at his jawline.

"Xander, be nice," Hunter said. Metal crept over his stretched neck. His chest, having turned metal also, contracted at the pain of skin being ripped off the bone. At the pain of his transformative superpower in action. "Not so fast!" Hunter's massive metal hands clamped Dorian's throat shut before it produced a peep. The kid sputtered, blunt nails digging at Hunter's grip. Pulsing concussive energy dwindled as Dorian went unconscious.

"Allister's gonna be real tore up when he hears about this."

The bomb had thirty seconds on the clock. He dropped the dead weight, dashed out the door, and thumped down the stairs, exiting at the exact time as a calamitous boom. Fire and smoke spewed from the fifth floor. Witnesses protested neither his presence nor his actions.

"Incoming call, President Wesley DeVries. Would you like to answer?" Cynque asked.

"Ignore." Hunter adjusted his artillery and asked the Cynque, "Who's next on the list?"

"Former Andromeda Project recruit: Bridget Taylor Sparks. Location: Fort Miami. Incoming call, President Wesley—"

"Ugh! Answer."

———

Chicago, Illinois

Hunter's foster parents referred to him as a living birth defect. He spent years of his childhood locked in an unfurnished room.

He learned meditation to manage his superhuman powers, and on his sixteenth birthday, he finagled an escape route by absorbing his cotton blanket's physical properties and tossing himself out the window. Neighbors frightened by the three-story fall and his skin's threaded texture called the police. Men and women in white suits wrote a five-hundred-thousand-dollar check, and his parents sold him up the river.

The laboratory's experimentation on his ability's limits caused him to permanently absorb and assume the properties of the three strongest metals: chromium, tungsten, and titanium. Later, he discovered transformation was detrimental to his health, straining his heart to the brink of cardiac arrest. Advised not to attempt becoming metal from head-to-toe and to choose bringing forth the armor with care, he resumed meditation to battle three main triggers for its unsolicited activation: stress, anger, and fear. He recalled the metals, in parts and pieces throughout his body, a limb here, a torso there. His weight training regimen made his strength superior. Adding his metal exterior made his strength herculean.

UV rays beat through Chicago's mid-morning haze and humidity held moisture hostage on Hunter's skin as he trekked across the White House courtyard.

"Don't touch my car. I won't be long," he said to the security guard at the entrance. Irked he had to wear a shirt in the first place, a button-down no less, he left his electric sports car, hazards on, parked in the cul-de-sac. He breezed through a metal detector and chuckled, holding his arms out while they searched him. "I think I know the rules by now. I left my besties in the trunk."

"Clear." The investigating soldier ushered him in and scanned his Cynque.

"Hunter Steele. Detective. Approved," the computer said.

He saluted the help and descended a steep marble staircase.

The White House had a new building's scent: fresh laid floors, painted walls. Just under two-years-old, it was constructed in 2050 after a successful North Korean terrorist bombing in Washington, D.C. An aboveground museum paid respects to the original, while an underground compound was used for conducting government affairs. A receptionist directed Hunter to bland hallways and squiggly, energy-saving bulbs, a.k.a. the classified section. He stopped for a second frisking and a body scan. "Two-factor authentication, I like it."

Escorted to an elevator hidden inside a wall, Hunter scanned his Cynque and pressed a camouflaged button the same black marble as the interior. It didn't light up.

"Welcome, Mr. Steele," the press secretary said when the doors opened. "We appreciate you coming on such short notice."

Gotta pay the bills, he thought. They strolled in tense silence to a sliding door leading to the Oval Office. The press secretary scanned her Cynque and gestured for him to enter.

Wesley DeVries, the nation's current president, swiveled in the chair, arms crossed. His chin nudged Hunter to a brown leather love-seat. "Please, sit," he said.

True to its name, Hunter found the Oval Office more impressive than he'd envisioned. From architectural preservation to the U.S. Seal's placement. Their forefathers would be proud.

"What's up, Prez! Nice digs," he said, then asked, "Who's this?"

The press secretary sat opposite him, legs crossed, clutching her forearm near the Cynque. "I'm Press Secretary—"

"I'm kidding, Weasel, I remember."

President DeVries snickered.

"It's W-h-y-zelle," she corrected and shot the president a glare. Clara Whyzelle had wrinkles showing her age and sagging jowls to match. The fair-skinned woman patted her conventional up-do and adjusted her pinstripe jacket.

77

"How do you keep getting them to appoint you, aren't you the reason we're in this mess?"

"Detective, enough." The president cleared his throat and smoothed the spotless desk. "Before we move on, can I offer you a shot of immunojuice or a probiotic water?"

"If you don't got scotch, I'm good." He crossed his legs. "I was on my way to sunny Florida, worst state in U.S. history. Wanted to get some sun, ask some questions. What's so urgent?"

"Your behavior," Clara said.

Hunter pointed at the withered politician sitting across from him. "Prez, between you, me, and the wall, you've got major media problems." He turned and rested his feet on the bald eagle's giant wing. "Plus, your instructions were pretty clear," he said, then mocked the president's voice. "Do whatever it takes.'"

"I know what I said. We can't operate by those rules anymore." Wesley wrung his hands "I don't have that kind of power."

"Mr. President, do you have any power at all?" he asked in a faux professional tone.

"Detective Steele," the press secretary interrupted, "What you did in Cincinnati was unacceptable."

"You think you can do better? Be my guest."

Nine square panels sprang to life, playing the apartment complex explosion. Volume muted, captions ran the screen's width. A recorded clip from a bystander's low-definition V1 Cynque camera revealed a man in a red trench watching flames climb to the clouds.

Casualties, casualties, casualties. People worried too much about death. His tactics were unorthodox, but people didn't hire him because he was gentle. They hired him because he got the job done. Gritting his teeth, Hunter uncrossed his legs. "Whatever, they were all meth heads anyway."

"What about Marrakech?" Wesley replied, tilting his head. "King Nephthys is threatening retaliation. He wants to pull out of the summit and take Africa with him. We can't afford to lose anymore allies. Do you understand what we're facing?"

"A bratty, arrogant kid. You keep playing nice guy, Allister's gonna undo everything this administration banked on your re-election." He rose from the leather cushions and pointed at President DeVries. "Don't act like I didn't warn you about this blowing up in your face. You look like a fool, Prez, and blaming it on whoever's closest is not a good move." The press secretary alternated her leg positioning and rearranged her pant legs. The president chose to focus on the door instead of Hunter's words. No one cared about the muscle or the muscle's time or the muscle's opinion. "Forget it," Hunter mumbled, "as long as I'm paid, I'll abide by your stupid politics."

The president's finger tapped the glass desk. "Clara, I need a minute."

"Of course, Mr. President." She dipped her squirming chin and hurried out.

"This is a matter of life and death," Wesley began.

Plopping down, Hunter blew air through his lips. He'd heard the speech a thousand times and made a habit of tuning it out after he'd listened to its entirety in U.N. meetings and campaign briefings. America walked around, chest puffed out, claimed it would steer the human experience in a positive direction. Lofty goals from an outside perspective, considering the U.S.-led Andromeda Project failed to accomplish any major missions, and the country hadn't recovered financially or economically from recent natural disasters. Skepticism from other nations' leaders aside, he mouthed alongside the president.

"C20 is a terrorist organization. They need to be terminated, and we need Allister to do it," Wesley finished.

"Yeah, yeah." Hunter clapped. "You nail it every time. Starting to think you believe that garbage."

Whoosh. The door opened. In a flurry, wind glided across Hunter's nape, as heels, one loud thump, one soft click, one loud thump, one soft click, walked behind him. "Somebody needs another lesson in manners."

Hunter recognized the woman's voice. He worshipped her like a queen and loathed her like an ex-wife. "Another veteran working on this?" Scrunching his fingers like a hungry baby, he cooed, "Dr. Belladonna, I missed you."

Florence sported a bushy ponytail, her hip cocked, her hand positioned above the curve of her thigh. "Give it a rest, Steele."

"There are quieter ways to investigate," President DeVries said, "and I expect a professional of your talent and experience to know that."

"Alright, alright. So you want the twit brought home unharmed." He shot to his feet and rubbed his brow. "What now?"

Frozen mid-step, his legs and arms tingled, urging him to move. He told himself to break free, but an unseen force repressed the commands. Florence, infected with a smoky red glow, touched the sword's handle on her hip and circled him.

"Now, you answer to me."

Released. A baby's crying rang in his ears, shuffling his thoughts. "Ha-have you been ca-caught up to speed?" A wide smirk disguised him stumbling over his feet and words. "If not, I'd b-be happy to debrief you."

Wesley's head jerked sideways. "You're dismissed, Detective Steele. We'll be in touch."

"Cool." He flipped them off while walking backward and tripped over his heels as he continued out the open door. "If you need me, I'll be at the beach."

FLORENCE BELLADONNA
White House, Chicago, Illinois

CHICAGO HAD BLOOMED during the economic collapse. Major industries, technology, finance, entertainment, media, and apparel, salvaged their companies and migrated to the less volatile climate and terrain. Growing to the most populated metropolis in America, the new nation's capital was built on sustainability and global warming propaganda and boasted the strictest environmental laws in the country.

"Becoming a workaholic again?" Florence asked, seated on the president's bed. Her toned human leg was crossed over her bionic one. Two fingers pinched the sheets. The black silk set hadn't changed since she'd chosen it a year ago. She smoothed the crease her tampering created. "I told you, you need balance."

Three floors deeper, inside Wesley's private living quarters, her heart beat as if it had grown fingers, intent on scratching its way out of her chest.

"Cynque, open top drawer, access code: DRFLB." A loud hiss released, absorbed by the room's artless walls, and his shoulders relaxed above an acrylic dresser powered by artificial intelligence. Telepathy let her see what he saw. His mind open, unfocused stare fixed on forgotten moments. Their photo at his inauguration: Florence hugging him in a floor-length jade gown. The fierce temper of her matching eyes. Six years. Hard to believe.

Her breathing slowed, and regret's syrupy taste soured in her mouth. "You should've let me go," she said and swallowed, reliving the memory inside his mind telepathically. "Would've been safer for us both."

Wesley hiked up his trousers to scoot onto the bed. "I wasn't concerned about safe. I was concerned about you."

"I know Wes, and I—"

"Let me finish." Their fingers intertwined. "When I thought I'd lost you, my biggest regret was not telling you I loved you before you got on the plane."

His cologne's woody scent bestowed nostalgia. Florence caressed his five o'clock shadow, lifted his chin. Her lips parted, drawn to his by magnetic attraction and suppressed desire. Logic threw itself between them, and at the last possible second, she turned. Her metal appendage, a fusion of alien technology, energy-enhancing psi crystals, and synthetic skin, looked back at her, blending in, but not well enough, similar to their relationship with mainstream society. Florence had decided not to be a president's wife long ago. Telepathic prowess dissolved his emotions, and hers.

"How are you... after the accident?" he asked and wiped his eyelid.

Florence stiffened, pulled her hands to her chest, and slid off the bed. "Better." Three-inch-heeled Christian Louboutins had them forehead to forehead.

"I know you're disappointed I had to do it this way."

"Contact me by sending some low budget bounty hunter to my private estate? Yeah, was a bloody shame. You could've called."

"I've called the properties I knew about."

Twirling her ponytail, she muttered, "Lake Como's new." Florence threw it behind her and asked, "Did you ever think I might need to process the fact that my associates believe me dead?"

"One. I gave you a month. Two. You've pretended to die before. And three, I wouldn't have done it if it wasn't urgent."

"The world leaders are pissed. They say we dropped the ball, and to be frank, we did. Besides letting a lunatic run the Andromeda Project into the ground, Dr. Giro's betrayal? How'd that slip by?"

Wesley shrugged. "We got anxious. He did too."

"He? Wait, wait, pause. I thought China, Russia, and Korea orchestrated this and Dr. Giro was the minion."

"No. Not even close." The president let the floor keep his attention and kept his shoulders flexed. "Dr. Giro's plans to bring the program down were in motion for months, maybe years. When he resigned he said, 'The Andromeda Project no longer suits my needs.' He recruited those nations, not the other way around."

Her mouth fell open. "What? You and the other directors knew Dr. Giro was a traitor, and you didn't stop him?"

"It doesn't matter what we didn't do then. We need to act now."

Spurts of perspiration drove her to the bathroom. A washcloth hit the sink bowl. The faucet's sensor, triggered by her hand, plunged cold water over it. She wrung the cloth and pressed it to her face.

Brazil, the United States, the UK, Russia, China, and Korea, had formed and funded a partnership destined to end in greed and first-to-market opportunities, The Andromeda Project. President Wesley DeVries had served on the board, accompanied by six others—collectively known as "the directors."

Though the directors accused DeVries of "nepotism," a heavy background in strategic management and execution, and the United States' anxiety brought Florence to the Andromeda Project. Hired on disguised as a psychiatrist, she spent two years tracking their primary mission's status (locating the Transporter gems)—and dug up staggering back story in the process. Twists like murder, turns like deception, and a laundry list of reasons why they'd continued to fail. Incompetence and sabotage were potent when mixed.

Florence's last memories from the final battle at the Andromeda Project splashed in; clearing everyone's mind of her existence, gaining a telepathic window into Rabia's psyche, leaving Allister to fend for himself.

"By the way, CIA says Adams disabled the Cynque's tracking. Don't know how you're going to find him!" he yelled through the bathroom door.

"I'm a telepath for God's sake!"

Florence emerged minutes later fresh, straight-faced. He straddled the archway, waiting for her return.

"Either you have no intel on where C20 is and what they're doing, or, you have some intel and you're just not sharing it," she said.

"I swear, I have no intel on where C20 is."

She sighed, leaned to him and whispered, "*Entre nous.*" Her lone pinky finger lifted. He lifted his too, and they interlocked in secrecy. "Allister's found."

"And they wonder why I keep hiring you."

"Let's say I decide to trust you and bring him back. What happens next?"

"America saves humanity."

———

ALLISTER ADAMS
Old Manhattan, New York, New York

DRUGGED, DRUNK, HOMELESS, and frisky, forceful escorts coexisted in Central Park. An off-limits zone, as were many neighborhoods to its north, such as Harlem, Washington Heights... the Bronx. Extreme temperatures had condemned more properties than were worth saving, and they referred to the areas which had suffered mass exodus as Old Manhattan.

Lower Manhattan, a place called New SoHo, became a microcosm of New York's elite. The metro systems implemented a Cynque verification filter. Employment in New SoHo meant second-class citizenship and entry and exit at programmed times according to an algorithmic scheduling system. Dwelling in New SoHo meant unfathomable wealth and coming and going as one pleased.

"We kill Earth! Earth kills us! We kill Earth! Earth kills us!" sign-wielding teens repeated in unison, protesting capitalism and the continuous exploitation of dirty fuels and wasteful energy. They crowded Allister, then marched into Old Manhattan's busy crosswalk, not caring to make it to the other side before the light changed. Unleaded gas was ten dollars a gallon. They had a point.

He strolled to the street corner and balanced his soles on the curb as cars whipped by. He'd traded in his cultural shirt for a navy tee and a black longline hoodie.

A college-aged man and woman slogged to a stop in his peripheral, their curved spines burdened by unknown tasks. He peeled back the hood's fabric to see the closest student's Cynque screen. Quantum physics review notes, dictated. The twenty-something-year-old woman cursed, rewound the transmission, and listened again. The man dipped his head to catch her frantic eyes, rubbed her back and said, "Courtney, we studied all night. We'll do fine."

Allister studied quantum physics at eight years old. A never-ending encyclopedia in his head contained information and occurrences unconfirmed by human scientists. For instance, he knew who built the great pyramids and it wasn't the Egyptians. He knew Stonehenge was a gateway, not giant stones arranged in a circle. He thought college was about learning useless facts, but the two students' interactions showed it was about growth and support, bonding with peers.

Throw in high stakes, volatile personalities, superhuman powers, and voila, you had the Andromeda Project. The program where he'd anticipated character building exercises and a curriculum in line with his accelerated learning curve. His peers there had been Dorian Xander, Bridget Sparks, and her.

Spit poured into his mouth faster than he could swallow. Leesa Delemar. Twenty-four. Lieutenant. Telekinetic. Deceased. The glowing picture from C20's files captured the glitter in her cerulean eyes and the bounce in her chocolate tresses. At the beginning, she'd behaved as a trained death machine, her combat style calculated and murderous.

He savored the thought of their first touch, how he'd melted her lifeless demeanor and stormed her emotional vault armed with charm. From those depths rose a spirited, compassionate, loving woman. More than a peer, and a friend, he missed what she represented: a traditional life, a potential family, an escape from his destiny. Mourning her death was awkward. Knowing she'd existed as a fabrication, the impossible-to-maintain dream of Nicolas Delemar, a man unwilling to let his dying daughter go. Leesa was Zosma in disguise.

He should've known when his powers reacted to hers. Then duh, the Z-energy pulses. How had he not seen it?

"Watch it, you piece of trash," a jittery, suited man scolded. His downcast eyes rejected Allister's dirty joggers and untied, battle-worn boots.

If I'd cleaned up, Allister thought. Or paid better attention to his surroundings as he'd practically shouldered the man off the sidewalk.

Glass and chrome structures joined the waking sun on the eastern horizon. New SoHo's privilege shined with intricate architecture and blaring Cynque advertisements. "Life's better when we're Cynqued," one read. Patrol posts took shape, and plump guards working their booths monitored incoming cars and pedestrians. Mount Sinai Hospital was positioned at the outermost edge, right across the first checkpoint.

"Cynque?" the guard asked.

Allister hid his wrist by his thigh, wondering whether to scan in and undo his elusion or—

"Sir, Cynque please?"

"Um, I... " The line grew behind him. He scratched his chest, eyeing the crowded entrance, and pulled the hood to conceal himself more. He floundered to find an explanation for why he shouldn't scan. "I-I need treatment, at the hospital. It's an emergency."

"You don't look like there's anything wrong," the guard replied. His light-headedness begged to differ.

"There's a hospital in Harlem for your kind."

"Is there a way to keep those lowlifes from coming down here?" a woman asked. Allister identified the African-American woman, dressed in diamonds and an orange charmeuse jumpsuit. Frustrated people of different shapes, sizes, and ethnicities shared her view, commiserating as a collective, shouting and shoving him aside. Allister staggered to the nearest bench.

White light oozed from the hoodie's pockets and he removed his hands. The two cosmic artifacts were booting up beneath knuckle length sleeves. At eye level, the transporter gems shined a vibrant green color, and active temporal energy broke down his atoms, creeping from his feet, to his knees, to his waist, to his neck.

The merry-go-round: Old Manhattan, New SoHo, angry New Yorkers, whirled faster. Mouth clenched shut, he smothered vocalized agony and transported against his will.

Mount Sinai Hospital, Border of New SoHo, New York

"Ugh." Allister twisted his neck on cold linoleum and sat up to massage a hammering headache. At the realization he'd transported to Nicolas Delemar's hospital room, he sprang to his feet at breakneck speed. The Transporter gems were known for precision.

C20's classified files had pegged General Nicolas Delemar, the former head of the Andromeda Project, as "the vault" due to his invaluable knowledge.

The general carried the burden of failure on his way to the grave. Responsible for the Andromeda Project's inadequacy.

Responsible for Zosma's awakening. Responsible for Allister's possession of the gems. Due to the acquisition of rich and powerful enemies, whoever set up Nicolas Delemar at Mt. Sinai knew he needed protection. No matter how hard the wheel of fortune spun, the prize would be death.

He observed the sleeping man's machine-assisted breathing in tempted silence, gauging whether U.S. government tucked him under those cotton sheets, or C20. The lowbrow grimace Nicolas had chosen when he shot Patrick Adams in the skull was tattooed in Allister's memory forever. Blood rushed to his head. Face hot, neck veins swelled to the point of rupture, his skin stretched across his knuckles as he made a fist.

"I've run through this moment in my head over and over, thinking about how I wanted to kill... " He steadied his quaking voice. "I know my mom wouldn't want me to, but you, you, don't deserve mercy." Allister released his fingertips from his palms' captivity. "When I told Leesa what you did I promised her I'd let you live. I knew hurting you would... hurt her." Nostrils flaring, he gripped the tubes pumping oxygen to the man's lungs, liquids into his bloodstream and yelled in a whisper, "Are you listening to me? Wake up!"

Rapid beeping indicated oxygen loss to Nicolas's brain. The general gasped. Allister let go and clutched his heated chest. "I wouldn't kill anyone," he'd said to Celine in Morocco. Now he speculated whether his declaration had been made in faith or fear.

Nicolas's coughs poked holes in the silence. "Private Adams?" he sputtered, "What are you—? How long have I—?"

Allister's blood simmered, and he inched closer, straining to picture the distorted, smock-wearing demon as a human being. "Why'd you do it?"

The general, a risen corpse sentenced to suffer, glared at Allister. "Because your father was a fool. He betrayed his country to help that stupid alien."

"You say one more thing about my dad and I swear—" Allister tore Nicolas from the white cocoon's protection by the collar. "I'll rip out whatever's keeping you alive."

"Go on. Go on and do it. I'll die knowing you destroyed Patrick Adams's legacy."

Allister snarled. The fist returned, and raised to punish Nicolas's mouth for its words.

"Do. It."

He pulled the general close, glimpsing sagging skin and wrinkles in a mummified face. "I lost Zosma. If you can help, I'll look for some self-control. Do you know where C20 is?"

"What a fearless leader, just like Patty Cakes." Violent coughs punished his sarcasm. "If he were half as loyal, he'd still be here."

"You do want to die," Allister hissed through closed teeth and pushed him back.

Nicolas settled onto the bed. "You don't have it in you. Deep down you're a self-centered coward, just like him. You grabbed the gems instead of saving your own mother."

"You're a son of—"

"Shut up, Adams," the general barked, raising his hand. A round device equipped with a large red button dangled between his fingers. "I activate this, the feds come running. You'll be blown to dust before you can inhale." He set it on his lap. "I have a question. You were the last person to see my daughter alive. Did she die in peace?"

The mention of Leesa lowered his shoulders and un-flexed his muscles. "Why do you care?" he asked. "You treated her like a caged monster."

"Like a caged monster!" Nicolas coughed up blood, wiped his hands on the comforter. "You naive shit. You have no idea what I sacrificed to keep Leesa alive."

"You're right. I don't know what you sacrificed, but I damn sure know who. Neight. My father. My mother. The innocent people

89

of Cumberland falls. And for what? Zosma woke up. The energy overloaded Leesa's mind. She was killed or erased or... "

"Leesa was erased the day Neight merged her and that creature. I had to cage the monster inside her." His cheeks shook as he delivered a plot-thickening line, "The directors agreed testing Z-energy was too dangerous after the pulse flattened Cumberland. They voted to lock it inside the Containment Center and Zosma's mind in Leesa's body. Keeping the energy separate kept Zosma dormant."

Allister swept hair from his brow and placed both hands on his hips. "You didn't listen. You kept experimenting on yourself."

"Dr. Giro convinced me it was for the best." He leaned back, running his fingers over heroin needle holes in his shriveled forearm. "The Z-energy did this to me. We tested human compatibility using gene therapy to grant access to its power. At 8 percent, it supercharged my cells. Made me strong. Resilient." He made a loose fist. His tone wavered. "Then I got weak. Found out, supercharging... killed them faster. I was cycling through new cells at a rate I couldn't sustain. My body gave up."

Nicolas's aging accelerated. Not the answer he'd come for but worth the trip.

The Z-energy was proprietary to the Uragonians, granting them power in various percentages depending on heritage. Decidedly, Z-energy was not for humanity, not for their cells or their bones or their limited mental imaginations. A source of magic that would, if given the chance, corrupt, corrode, and confuse the body's basic processes.

By some stroke of luck or subjection to the same gene therapy he wasn't aware of, Allister had 25 percent access to the Z-energy of his own to use. His brutish ways and poor training produced the Z-energy's un-aimed bursts, off-center beams, and the occasional tantrum over his skin with no significant result.

"What about Zosma?" Allister asked.

"Keep up, Adams. Shit, for someone so smart, you can be a dumbass. Dr. Giro wanted to experiment with Z-energy, so, he reset the Containment Center. Leesa's energy access levels hit 100 percent. Their bond or the spell, whatever you want to call it, broke."

"He triggered Zosma's awakening on purpose."

Nicolas gave him a sarcastic, double-thumbs up. "Near the end, Giro's stupid rants stopped making sense. He said we couldn't grasp Z-energy's importance, went on some tangent about how this planet and its people need guidance. I was too sick for it to make sense, but here." The general reached under the pillow, then held his Cynque in the air. "The password is Leesa. There's a folder you'll want to read through, a program called Hex Fourth."

Allister snatched the watch and studied Nicolas's stiff upper lip and hateful eyes.

"You think knowledge brings you closer to happiness. The more you know, the more miserable you become. That little boy who frolicked into my office fifteen years ago has been ravaged by betrayal and death, and it's the most beautiful thing I've ever seen." The general's snickering turned to heaving.

"I don't care what you say about me. If you know where Dr. Giro is, tell me now so I can stop him."

"You don't even know what you're stopping." Nicolas shrugged and took a turn for the delirious, activating the hospital bed's panic button. "If you visit Belladonna's grave, thank her for saving me. I suggest digging up the body. Make sure she's actually there."

There was a buzzing outside the door. A Cynque scanning.

"You were stalling," Allister said, backing away from the bedside.

"If I was stalling, they would've come a lot sooner."

A muffled voice carried betrayal through the door. "We know you're in there, Allister. Hands up or we shoot on sight."

No delay for a plea or response, the door burst open and plasma weapon-armed CIA agents shuffled through the doorway. The leading agent blasted his rib.

Allister toppled, screaming. An inferno spread through his side and over his body. Unable to complete a thought, move a muscle, or fathom recovery, he curled into something primeval. A bullet to the skull would have been mercy.

Betwixt his anguished cries, he heard boots and a man's deep voice utter a callous comment, "This is the second time you've ruined my vacation." Hunter Steele lifted him high enough to land a steel-fisted punch to his face.

CHAPTER THREE

ULTERIOR MOTIVES

Allister Adams

CIA Satellite Facility, New SoHo, New York

"Please state your name for the record," a woman's computer voice instructed.

He blew air through his lips to take the edge off then stated, "Allister Patrick Adams."

Drenched in eerie green light, CIA's interrogation room had Cynque surveillance in the fibers of its walls, while a two-way mirror hinted at important officials watching what transpired. Heavily armored American soldiers had arranged themselves in a staggered line around the three-hundred-square-foot room.

He opted not to sneak a glimpse at his swollen face, nor did he dare touch the bandaged wound on his stomach.

President Wesley DeVries stood across from him, arms folded tight and high. He'd fired off a list of ridiculous questions and his face scrunched in impatience for their answers. "We won't get anything done like this, Mr. Adams."

Targeted red beams formed constellations on his body. Every gun trigger in sight was being stroked or pulled by an antsy finger or two. Allister cleared his phlegm-coated throat and said, "I'm not telling you anything as long as I'm a bullseye."

The president swiveled left, then right. "You heard him, stand down."

"Over my dead body," Hunter said, his flexed biceps and twisted smirk pleading for action or impulse. "This kid's a time bomb."

"I can hear you," Allister replied.

"That's an order, Detective Steele."

The detective's reluctant gesture sent the soldiers' gun barrels from 90 to 45-degree angles.

Memory took the reins and drove the horse and carriage back to a month ago. "Last time I saw her, we-we were in London." Allister tugged at hair by the fistfuls. His voice wavered, a jumble of confidence and despair, "We were okay, then, and I swear, it was out of nowhere. The Z-energy took over her. A telekinetic storm ripped the Montage apart, and I knew a pulse was coming because she was... so hot... nuclear hot, like the sun." He got up at a glacial pace. "You're fishing."

President DeVries confronted Allister's intimidating frame. "This is tough for you, I know."

"You know what's tough? Believing you don't already know what I'm about to tell you." His foot tapped once, twice, three times. "We were in the thermosphere. The Transporter gems took us to the... yeah, she released the energy, and I got blown back to Earth." He glared at the president. "You know the rest."

"The locals said they found you alone, incoherent," President DeVries said and dropped his arms. "They also said you died on the way to the hospital."

"If I died, even for a split second, I wouldn't have these." He flashed the Transporter gems "My turn. Where're my friends? Dorian? Bridget? Are you hunting them too?"

"Your friends are safe."

"Wrong," he replied, and tilted his head at Hunter. "Dorian said this asshole tried to kill him for no reason."

"Miscommunication in proper protocol for bringing you in, right, Detective Steele?"

Hunter growled and waved, dismissing the accusation.

Wesley continued, "I apologize on his behalf, moving on. You infiltrated a territory occupied by our soldiers and destroyed Captain Brandt's computer. We were close to discovering crucial files to help us locate C20."

"Fake news. You weren't close at all. I didn't see anything in the database about C20's new location, and I read the whooole thing."

"Impossible. There were at least a million files, and you were there for thirty minutes."

"I read every single one!" Allister shouted. Multiple hands shuffled President DeVries behind the soldiers in formation. "I read them," he said, softer. "That's how I found General Delemar."

"Get out of my way." President DeVries pushed through the group, drew in a deep breath, and took a step closer. "What else did you read?"

"Stuff."

"Look, whether you accept it or not, we're on the same team."

"Let me stop you there," Allister said. "I agreed to come because you told me you wanted to help."

"I thought it was 'cause you were crying on the floor like a bitch," Hunter retorted, whacking a fellow soldier's arm. "Right?"

"We want to help," President DeVries said. "Help you stop C20 before they take over the world."

"Wrong again. I need help stopping Dr. Giro before he experiments with Zosma's power." He turned to the windowless door and said, "Hear the difference? Yours is political, mine isn't."

"You don't have a choice. You violated the terms. Not to mention you're a walking weapon of mass destruction, especially with the cosmic artifacts."

"Two months ago, the Andromeda Project fished me out of a coffee shop." Allister jerked his head around and pointed at the president as he limped toward him. His adrenaline levels hit the ceiling, dousing his side's throbbing pain in numbness. "My biggest problem was showing up on time and remembering to put the muffins out before the line got too long. You did this to me!"

In rage and sorrow, he'd seized the president's collar, holding him inches from the ground at eye level. Red, eye-socket-sized circles burned holes in his skull. Others followed, aimed at his lungs and spine.

"Don't shoot him. He's not going to hurt me." The president cupped his shaking hands and said in a soothing voice, "Allister, put me down."

"I lost everything I loved trying to be your hero. I'm not doing it again." He let President DeVries's feet touch the floor and lowered himself into the seat.

I thought you'd say that, said a distinct voice inside Allister's head. It was the same one from the train.

His skin washed out, mouth wide open in distrust and, although gazing at her reflection in the two-way mirror, he didn't notice her at all. Unable to speak, he found himself having to remember to breathe, stunned as her name bounced inside his skull. "I-I don't believe it," he muttered and spun around.

From her skin's vibrancy and the infamous red lip color she often chose, Dr. Florence Belladonna and her ageless silhouette were intact. "I'm alive, Allister. I've been alive."

"I've been alone this whole time, and." The sentence cracked and broke in the middle. His heart contracted. "You're not... you're not real."

"I am, and it's time to take this hunt underground." Florence walked to him and bowed. Taking his cheek, she pulled his head into her embrace and whispered, "I'm here to help you, not them. I came back for you, understand?"

In a trance, he nodded, and relaxed against her.

—•—

CAPTAIN JARED BRANDT
C20 Prison

CAPTAIN JARED BRANDT wore a thin, transparent energy field as a jumpsuit. Keen to Dr. Giro's scrutinizing stare, he slouched in the chair and tapped his knuckles to the rhythm of melting water's monotone dripping.

Tufts of white hair clung to Dr. Giro's otherwise barren scalp like the last few trees in the Amazon rainforest. His once cinnamon brown skin had become tawny in sunlight's absence.

"You work hard, sacrifice so much. But, here at C20, we don't accept failure," Dr. Giro said. "I need your first mission complete."

"Answer's no," Jared responded.

"You bring me Allister, or I'll make you do it."

Drumming up other distractions by plucking the icy surface, or whistling his favorite songs, still led him back to the geneticist's coal black irises. The longer they fixated on him, the opaquer the disruptive energy field became.

"Good luck gettin' through this field," he said, leaned forward, then whispered, "Don't forget, I been a POW."

Dr. Giro blinked, his concentration disrupted. "I remember your past, Captain, and realize physical torture would be waste of precious resources." The doctor lifted a Cynque tablet (nicknamed CynqueT) from his lap and gave it to the captain to hold. "I thought we chat over movie. Watch," he said, pressing play.

A cinematic story faded from black into a major natural disaster montage from the 2030s, 2040s, and early 2050s. The Middle East spiked to infernal temperatures in 2047, leading to mass evacuations. And afterwards, the "Middle Beast" storm in 2051 eradicated anyone or anything toughing out the heat. Category 6 hurricane "quintuplets" drowned Florida and the Caribbean in 2045. The final, arguably most disturbing, footage featured the Pacific Southwest's devastating 9.5 earthquake in 2032, which halted domestic technological development, and pushed progress back twenty years. Screaming children soaked in blood. Families clinging to wreckage for dear life.

Jared twisted his mouth, feigning an unchanged mood. "This ain't war. Shit happens. At least they're dying from somethin' we can't control."

A time lapse began. Jared's mouth opened as wide as it could stretch. Year by year, a simulation showed Earth's immune system at its strongest, determined to cleanse the unstoppable parasite, humanity. Oceans forced humans to move farther from the surface. Seismic activity tore the crust apart. Weather anomalies plunged civilization into a pre-technology age. In the last prediction, Old Faithful erupted with a *kaboom*, spraying ash and lava over the entire United States and reigniting a volcanic chain reaction through the ring of fire. The screen faded to black.

"That ain't possible, not in our lifetime," he stammered with nervous laughter.

"Hard to believe you have ten years left. Such delicate species, such delicate infrastructure."

The captain's wobbling hands held the tablet like a child he was afraid to drop. "There's no fixin' it? If it did happen, I mean? Just boom, ten years an' bye-bye people?"

Dr. Giro tugged upwards, prying the tablet from his grasp. "Why you think Neight Caster want to leave your planet so fast? He foresaw this."

Humanity had two choices. "Extinction or evolution," he mumbled. "How's Allister fit in?"

"If Mr. Adams is not allied with C20, future you saw is certain."

"So, what if he is?" he asked, losing his composure to another agitated laugh. "Ya got another future layin' around here somewhere? I'd love to see it."

"I need him."

"Listen here. I been on the wrong side, an' I'm done. Patrick made me Allister's godfather to protect him, an' I went an' sold him to the Andromeda Project, an' tried to sell him to you." The disruption field flashed to transparency. "The kid's brilliant, strong like his daddy. If he's gonna stop this from happenin', he don't need you an' this to get it done." His arms opened to reference the underground base.

"Ah, ah, ah." Mist separated from Dr. Giro's body and slithered toward Jared's unprotected nose. The disruption field didn't return to protect him.

"Syria, 2036. ISIS had taken the whole country. Our unit was locked in a tunnel under the main city for a week. No lights, a buncha dead, tortured civilians rottin' next to us. Air raid took out the caves, the tunnels. There was soldiers down there, no one knew. An' I survived thanks to my trusty gift. What I'm saying is, it ain't checkmate yet. I been through worse."

The geneticist folded his hands. "We shall see."

Particles siphoned in Jared's ears and up his nostrils then barreled down his throat. He convulsed, gagging and groping for the blunt edge of the table he was chained to.

"Welcome back, Captain," was the last thing he heard as Dr. Giro's influence infected his thoughts.

———

DR. RABIA GIRO
C20 Basement

AN ENGINEERING FACILITY had been constructed in the C20 compound's lower level. Like the living dead, the organization's hired scientists and soldiers filed in from all sides each morning to complete their day-to-days. At its close, the workers filed out to subpar meals in communal kitchens, and restless sleeps in single-occupancy cabin quarters.

Rabia's enthusiasm hid behind a tightened grimace. He sported a polyester lab coat, as if the room wasn't fluctuating around 40 degrees Fahrenheit. Beneath the coat he wore his staple ensemble: a patterned orange chest plate and wool pants tapered at the ankle. As he walked, he asked, "Mr. Ashur, what's status?"

Russell Ashur, his lead engineer. Faithful. Brilliant. Starving for recognition. "Almost there, Doctor." He hurried to a computer screen. "Confirming access levels and the energy's location."

Better funding than the Andromeda Project, gave them better technology. State-of-the-art CPUs, two to three monitors each, surrounded engineers and physicists working in frigid silence. Behind clear, titanium, floor-to-ceiling energy absorption barriers sat Russell Ashur's greatest achievement: the U-generator prototype. The containment center and the U-generator (named after its adaptation of Uragonian tech) were fraternal twins. Whereas the containment center held the Z-energy safe from the world, the U-generator would use the Z-energy as a power source for the world.

Rabia, Russell, and their team accepted the challenge to study and recreate the substance or combination of substances strong enough to withstand the Z-energy's radiation, an exercise essential for the generator's success.

Though fueled and empowered by scientific principles, Z-energy was magic. If it could be dreamt, it could be done, and if it could be understood, it could be mastered. Neight Caster boasted the Containment Center's simplicity and promised it didn't call for an additional enchantment or incantation to contain the energy, "It is mastering the relationship between metals, matter, and energies," Neight had said when questioned. "A skill you do not possess."

The statement, seasoned with the savory taste of a challenge, fed Rabia's rabid stubbornness. He knew the magnitude of their struggle, and refused to acknowledge that he'd underestimated the energy's complexity.

"Z-energy system found," the computer announced.

Russell, skin dipped in a lush pecan and a touch below middle-aged, rubbed his neck and stretched to look at the generator again. Condensation puffed in front of his face, while he watched hypothetical outcomes populate in real time. "That's not right," he said and removed his fur hood and gloves. "Sheesh, you're not cold?"

"Would be warm if you got generator working. I have meeting with C20 board in forty-eight hours. Test now."

"I'm not confident in the system's stability," he replied, reviewing the energy levels. He smoothed his wavy, unkempt hair. "It's wanting to transfer more than the generator can handle."

"Move." Rabia edged Russell over to reread the algorithm's predictions and frowned.

"See."

"Protective measures in place, yes?"

"Ish."

"Test it."

Russell cocked his head to the side and pushed his glasses onto his face. "Start the transfer." Another engineer initiated the process. "Here we go," he muttered, lowering himself into the nearest seat with a fist over his mouth.

"Transferring Z-energy," the computer said.

Blue energy snaked through the U-generator's power rods. As a collective, the dozens of hollow tubes salvaged from Neight's spaceship wrapped the core like Saturn's rings and kept the energy contained during distribution. The spherical core, filling with Z-energy, creaked in steady rotation on its axis. A deafening buzz consumed the room as its speed increased, and consecutive beeps and dings signified empowered energy cells. For added security around the core, they'd built a durable but thick titanium alloy semicircle and a neutralizing ion field equal parts cation and anion. Held in place by foot-wide poles, the generator took up

700 square feet, supported a disruptive bulky design, and cost a billion dollars to construct.

"Five percent access achieved," the computer told them.

A rotting smile stretched over Rabia's face. Unparalleled luminosity engulfed the room. Goggles shielded every eye but his. He tilted his head back and squeezed Russell's shoulder. "Full of promise. Now, use weapon."

Russell stood upright, pupils shrouded in white mist, and nodded. The protective barrier had an entrance where he scanned his Cynque. It opened with profound obedience. He waded through the unnatural tension between expectation and reality, unfazed by the machine's ominous presence. He picked up the gun and looked to the audience for reaction. Marionettes on strings, in an uproar, they performed, offering encouraging claps and piercing whistles.

The energy, coaxed from the whirring generator, powered the weapon with blue life. Aiming at the energy-canceling barriers, Russell fired. Dr. Giro mouthed victory when the wall absorbed the blast.

Russell flipped the gun, then faced the generator, as if seeing the monster for the first time. It delivered more energy, replacing what had been used. He tossed the object away. He waved his arms. He mouthed, *turn it off.*

Rabia's smile flattened. Russell was not mouthing those words, he was yelling them. Yet, a barrier designed to cancel energy, cancelled all energy, even sound.

"Ten percent access achieved," the computer said.

The room's celebration quieted to murmurs. "Is he okay?" a newer physicist asked, lifting her goggles. The pulsating weapon, burdened by the energy's access, exploded. Shrapnel banged against the protective wall, then deflected back into the center, clanging on the metal floor.

"Hmmm," Rabia said, bowing to the computer's screen. "Generator's pulling in 5 percent increments. Is not set to stop at 5 percent."

The physicist gasped. "The generator isn't programmed to stop? If there's nowhere to send the additional 5 percent, Mr. Ashur's created an unstable energy system."

"Turn it off?" an assistant asked them.

Rabia waited, the energy's glow reflecting in his unbothered eyes. A pulse fanned from the core. The barrier splintered while absorbing the blasts entirely, suffering hairline fractures on its surface. Remaining energy retracted. The U-Generator powered down. A graveyard hush settled over the lab.

"I severed the connection," the physicist said. "A second one might have... "

"Check on Mr. Ashur," Rabia ordered.

Engineers' heads emerged from under their forearms. Action returned to the room. Multiple scientists shrieked as Russell hoisted himself up, then collapsed.

"Everyone out!" He pointed a finger at the physicist and said, "Except you, Ms. Eberle." He left the computer and knelt to check Russell's wrist for a heartbeat.

Blood formed blotchy stains on the engineer's puffy coat near cuts from the weapon's metal. Huddled, too shocked to inhale, Russell asked, "You-you knew this would happen, didn't you?"

Rabia's thumb located the injury on Russell's triceps and applied pressure. Russell howled. Wet thin liquid seeped up to his hairy knuckle as he drilled deeper, summoning more anguished cries. He wiped the gore on his coat and resumed standing. "You are here to make sure this works, not to question my commands."

"Medics are on the way," Ms. Eberle said and shrank back.

"Good. Repair barrier for next demonstration."

Five ski-suited men in masks entered. Rabia, rooted to the floor like a great oak tree in a storm, let the commotion swirl around him in a long-faced hush. They collected Russell's body onto a stretcher and wheeled him to the infirmary for treatment.

———

ZOSMA CASTER
C20 Infirmary

ZOSMA HAD HEARD RABIA refer to the room, located on C20 HQ's middle floor, as the base's infirmary. Machines measured human vitals. Massive heaters guaranteed bearable temperatures. Accessible through a tunnel connected to the lab, he asked her to meet him there expressing utmost urgency.

She floated, her razor sharp facial features, and needle-straight hair visible to anyone in decent proximity. The hooded cloak draping her skintight Uragonian battle armor scuffed the dingy floor as she landed for a closer look.

Paper sheets and a naked, unconscious human body covered a long, padded table. She neared the limp figure, which she identified as a man via his anatomy. Under false light, he glistened with the sheen of a broken fever, clearly on the verge of his last shallow breath. Such delicate creatures. She recognized him, though certain she shouldn't have, as the engineer from the Andromeda Project. His name eluded recollection.

A clear bag labeled "adrenaline" pumped liquid into the engineer's veins. His cheek twitched.

"Hmm, should be awake now," Rabia said.

She brought the cloak's hood up, freeing her from light's truth, and shook her head while shrouded in the privacy of the garment's shadow. Shackles rested against the table's side. She wanted to believe it was a dream. She'd never been bound by them and, yes, of course she'd chosen to be there helping Rabia preserve the Earth. C20 was her home on this strange planet.

Air escaped faster than she could take it in. Uragonian tears released hydrogen ions when combined with elements in Earth's atmosphere, causing them to become acidic. One oncoming drop would reveal her awareness.

"Zosma?" Rabia asked, at a whisper's distance.

"Yes." She faced him, head down. "Do you require my assistance?"

"Perhaps."

He returned to his duties and she, distracted by medical machines, robotic assistants, the genetic scanner, drew closer to the latter. Caressing it brought back... Russell. Russell Ashur was the patient's name. He'd built the Andromeda Project's gadgets.

"What did you say happened to the human again?"

A woman and man entered the room. "We came as soon as we... " the woman cut herself off as they ran into each other side-stepping Zosma, "could."

"Keep him from going into coma," Rabia instructed and nodded Zosma's direction. "Activate G.A.M."

She initiated the Genetic Analysis Mechanism, which from her assessment was just a glorified body scanner. The machine isolated Russell's epidermal, nerve and muscle cells and showed them a microscopic view of its work on the screen.

"Analysis complete," the machine announced. "Cellular biology diagnosis: Radiation damage. Human tissue is not equipped to handle direct exposure to pure Z-energy." On the zoomed in screen, skin and muscle cells disintegrated one after the other.

"Exposed to pure Z-energy, how?" she asked, approaching the master computer.

"We are building important device for directors," Rabia replied. "No more questions."

Zosma flinched at the word "device" and took a sharp breath. "The energy is degenerative. It will continue to break down his cells until he is no more than dust. I can stop it, if it is your wish."

"What is worst case?"

"The human perishes."

"Proceed."

She let the cloak fall behind her elbows. Her fingers drew circles, and curled into fists.

Z-energy poured from Russell's orifices, smelling of a scorched forest. His body convulsed as the magic of her people was sucked out of him. The energy wrapped around itself in the air and traveled to her waiting palms.

The absorption's force blew the cape and Zosma back. Knocked over chairs banged into machinery. The shrieking human helpers thudded against the wall. Rabia stood, hands clasped, uninjured, and unmoved.

Reconnecting to the energy swept a brief, vivid memory over her: discovering the containment center at the Andromeda Project. Looking at the infinite Z-energy inside it shaped like her. Realizing her psyche was bound behind a magic wall inside Leesa's mind.

What am I doing? Zosma thought.

"That will be all," Rabia said. His forefinger took her chin. A grey swarm dispelled the memories, reeling in her concern and putting her at peace. "Return to your duties," a deep voice, deeper than Rabia's echoed in the condensed mist, then repeated in Rabia's accent, "Return to your duties."

"With gratitude, Dr. Giro." She increased the space between them, eyes on his paunchy face, and pivoted, marching away in steady rhythm.

—-—

NEIGHT CASTER
C20 Basement

NEIGHT CASTER ROLLED OVER, unsure how long he'd been unconscious. In his six centuries alive, he'd fallen from the majesty of being Uragon's finest warrior and respected king to the current, humbling position as Earth's prisoner.

Like all beings from the planet Uragon, he was blessed with Z-energy manipulation. Neight used the energy via spell casting to bend reality to his will and manifest desires from thin air. The Z-spells demanded reasonable, focused outcomes, otherwise chaotic explosions and his own self-destruction would ensue. In theory, his freedom could be conjured, and he'd chosen to spend his twenty-five plus Earth years in captivity observing the complex organisms known throughout the universe as humans. To pass time. To bide time.

The engineer, Russell Ashur, had devised a method to restrict the alien's magic potential by using his superior technology against him. Approved and implemented by the Andromeda Project circa 2040, power suppressors emitted electromagnetic waves, quelling the brain's ability to call upon supernatural powers. So, no, the transparent, hollow cube of reinforced titanium holding him was not entirely his choice.

Dr. Rabia Giro, an expressionless enemy, ceased his slow, repetitive knocking and dusted frost from his crisp collar. "Time to wake up, Neight Caster."

Neight pressed his clawed hand against the alloy to rise from the seated position.

"I heard you using Z-energy," Rabia said.

True. In a state of duress, he drew on the source and used Z-energy to project his astral form. Searching across oceans, mountains, and deserts for Allister Adams's radiating soul to pass on a message. The power suppressors activated, cutting the energy off before he'd gathered enough to finish a sentence. Desperate and relieved, Allister had begged for any sort of clue, and in Neight's miscalculation, he was unable to deliver it. He must find another opportunity.

"Dr. Giro, want to have a look at this?" an engineer piped up.

Neight slumped back to the floor and growled, "Tend to your fruitless efforts."

Rabia shrugged his husky shoulders and returned to the intricate basement layout.

And what a layout. An unfamiliar machine prototype nestled amongst fiberglass walkways. Scientists dwarfed and dazzled by computer monitors, double-checking calculations. Miniature lifts carrying engineers to pumped up, life-threatening heights. Constant and (for the moment) unsupervised movement, egos and decision-making.

Rabia's hatred for him was entrenched in the prison's design. Invasive walls sat close to Neight's shoulders, denying his arms their full wingspan, as if there wasn't ample space to spread out in the basement. Right angles stared at him from the low ceiling's upper corners, nearly parallel to his six-foot-nine peripheral vision. And though sitting front row to C20's operation, with light and sound stimulation bombarding him, the isolation felt total.

A woman wearing multiple oversized sweaters powered through the entrance. She glanced at the capsule, lured by Neight's gaze, but didn't slow down.

"Good, you're here," she said, rushing up to Rabia. She blew a jet-black strand from her face and peeled the sweater sleeve back to tap her Cynque. "We have a solid theory why the experiment went south."

"Wait for Russell."

Shivering, she closed the topmost wool sweater. "Is Mr. Ashur awake yet?" she asked. "It's 9:00 p.m."

The doctor touched her shoulder, locking them in a staring contest.

She straightened her posture and said, "Understood. When Mr. Ashur recovers, we can review." The strand fell into her face again. Unconcerned, she left it hanging and joined her fraught coworkers.

Rabia strolled, laced fingers on his belly, and touched his nose to the prison.

"They cannot see me," Neight said.

"Would be unproductive," he replied. Warm breath's condensation on cold material took hold and became mist, spreading and enveloping the exterior.

"What is C20's purpose?"

"Like your Andromeda Project, C20 is me pooling this world's resources to find way back home. But less selfish. My plan helps humanity. C20 investors knew sacrifices were coming, even their own in some cases." Somber mist trailed behind the doctor as he explored the capsule's perimeter. "More progressive nations know is time to evolve. I promise to prepare them."

"There appears to be more to it than that."

"Yes. A good king is always observant," Rabia said smiling, and clicked his heels together. His palm teased a round green button on a dashboard attached to the prison. "I call this prison Atomic Separator. Centrifuge mechanism made special for you. You get one answer to question. Answer wrong, I press button now. Answer right, I press button later. Ready?"

Neight's claws expanded and contracted. He gave Rabia his full attention, chest high and proud. "As I will ever be."

The mystical mist reminiscent of Rabia caught up. It didn't settle back on his skin. It lingered like cigarette smoke at a dive bar. "Artifacts of Evale, harness power of great eight civilizations." His mouth turned up into a double-sided smirk. "One belonged to your people, Uragon's Z bands of unlimited energy. You know where they are?"

I never told the Andromeda Project about any other artifacts, he thought and answered in a booming voice, "Those bands are lost somewhere in the universe with the other six artifacts."

"Not all artifacts protected same way. No, this one, if I remember right... " He shook his forefinger. "This one your people kept veerry close."

"I have heard the story has many versions. According to our ancient transcripts, they were scattered to prevent activation." Neight kept his wide, grey jaw from moving and moonlit eyes from widening. Broadened shoulders, an honest face, and his towering stature reinforced his contrived confusion.

"You claim not to know missing artifact locations, yet, you knew two were on this planet before you arrived, is right? Or we pretend is not true?"

"I came to Earth to get farther from Andromeda's Sanctuary... to protect Z-energy and Zosma from tyrants, such as you."

Rabia's eyes flashed grey. Neight's vision lapsed.

"I suspect you were looking for Transporter gems," Rabia accused.

He avoided direct eye contact with Rabia in order to keep his concentration and lifted a glowing hand to block further attempts. "You are as entitled to your theories as you are your treachery," he said, cringing. "You will not find anything in my head useful to you."

"You know more than you say. I have search Zosma's psyche for clues, unlocking door after door." Rabia burst into blackness and his voice echoed through the 100-foot ceiling bunker as the cloud thinned and evaporated. "I seek answers. Faster I find, better for you, her, us. Don't you want to be free, Neight Caster?"

———

DR. RABIA GIRO
C20 Lair

CYNQUE VERIFICATION, voice activations, and ocular or face recognition were flawed procedures for accessing the sacred control room. Rabia Giro relied on atomic deconstruction to enter and leave, ensuring no one would infect the nucleus of his communication like he'd infected so many others. Fifteen-foot-thick walls encased the dome, swimming under a concealed ice shelf inside the base.

Fog spilled from holes in the wall, crept along the floor, piling on itself, and carved Rabia's body from the dense cloud. The Korean director, the Chinese director, and the Russian director waited for him. Discretion regarding their identities had become moot and instead of blacked out visuals and distorted vocals, hardened expressions and privileged lives played on six-foot screens.

From left to right: Chung Tae-Won, a plump Chinese software genius known best for perfecting Cynque technology, buying up Samsung, Apple, and Google, and taking the entire consumer electronics and AI market share. Jane Wenyin, a thin Korean businesswoman, who grew her family's manufacturing by supplying materials and machines to produce energy weapons used by C20, the Andromeda Project, and major military powers. Last, Aleksander Karjavine, a handsome ex-party boy, who'd mastered global finance by devising the new digital-based techno-currency. Together, they controlled the intangibles by which the world measured its interconnectivity. Communication. War. Finance. For them, C20's mission served as the next natural step in their individual legacies: innovation in energy. A field confused by solar and wind power, derailed by hydrogen-generated (electric) power and stifled by oil moguls and utility monopolies.

"We have six generators in development," Rabia said, opening the meeting.

"I won't go to market with an untested product," Jane warned, speaking near perfect English.

"Testing is good, making progress."

Chung snorted. "Have you figured out how to make sure energy remains stable?"

"No, Mr. Ashur and his team are working on energy movement between generator and containment center." Rabia checked his nails. "When finished, we update current models."

Jane popped the cork on a champagne bottle. "Has Zosma been cooperative?" she asked.

"Very good, very helpful."

"Good. Because disasters are brewing right now. A blizzard over Moscow, a monsoon in the South Pacific." She poured the Ace of Spades, set the bottle next to an empty identical companion and gripped her champagne flute. "And, this is a rumor: scientists are saying Mt. Vesuvius is about ready to blow. They're predicting a catastrophic event that will turn Naples into the twenty-first-century Pompeii. We don't have long, Dr. Giro."

She spoke of the catastrophes like they wouldn't affect her, sitting on a chair fashioned to resemble a throne, legs crossed under a diamond-studded gown. Rabia grinned as his fingertips formed a steeple... the things people did to attain immortality's sweet taste. "We working fast as we can."

"You sure you can pull this off?" Chung's fat chin fell into a frown. "Starting to sound a lot like General Delemar."

"Patience, patience," he urged his three supporters. "Summit is where we make our debut."

"You heard Wenyin, creep, we're past patience, this is twenty-five-year fiasco thanks to U.S. My country is starving, freezing, we need resources." Aleksander reviewed the blueprints, which included the energy-to-distribution ratio, and the machinery work flow. "We have one shot deal, it better work."

"Yes." Jane picked up the glass and took a sip. "Our buyers won't be so eager now that they know how volatile the energy is."

"Thanks to Bazzo Sparks slandering C20's name to potential investors. I want him dead," Aleksander said. "Every time he opens his mouth, he costs me money."

Rabia bowed, both arms out. "Done."

"Our demonstration has to prove effective and safe for key leaders and target partners," Jane continued. "We're proposing a singular solution for the world's energy consumption problem. Going to be a hard pill to swallow for those who have significant stake in fossil fuels, electricity, and nuclear power. We will reconvene tomorrow."

Windows into the directors' lavish lifestyles blanked to opaque slabs. The room dimmed.

"Meeting adjourned."

CAPTAIN JARED BRANDT
C20 Basement

JARED TAPPED A METAL GRATE in every effort not to engage in conversation. Standing guard like a good soldier, he thought about why he felt gratitude for the refreshing shower's coconut scent, about the therapeutic nature of a good, clean shave, about how else to ignore the alien's words floating at him from the capsule.

"Your power has come a long way since I first analyzed it," Neight said, hovering Indian-style in the cylindrical prison's center.

Back in 2037, Jared had squealed at the alien's physical appearance. Piss scared right out of him, he jumped into Patrick's arms, whose strength gave from laughing so hard. Patrick had encouraged him to trust Neight as an ally and an equal, citing the 90 percent similarities in their genetics. A difficult mentality to embrace for a man who'd been trained that the enemy's incompatible ideals, either religious or cultural, were as incompatible as their looks, skin color, or nationality.

"What does it mean when you can disrupt any process you put your mind to?" The alien's three toes morphed into sharp claws, and they clicked as they hit the floor. "Jamming a weapon. Stopping an engine. Blocking energy. I hope I am making sense."

Perfect sense, Jared thought.

"Do you miss Patrick Adams?" Neight asked. "I miss him. So kind. Generous. Loyal."

He surveyed the room and sidestepped farther from the capsule. "Yeah, well, he's dead," he whispered harsh-like, swinging a hand in the air, the other glued to his ribs. "And it's your own damn fault. I got no sympathy. God, do you even know what you did?"

"I know what I did, and I am not sorry for sacrificing my life, so you, Allister, and countless others could be here to see your destinies through. Florence Belladonna's family aircraft flew within five hundred miles of Cumberland during the landing. She would have died. What if Florence had died?"

Jared knew. His head lowered. Tides of converging sadness and misguided resentment formed a whirlpool in his mind.

"Yes." The alien nodded. "Now you see, I see everything. Not just what is visible."

Jared retreated to the communal workspace to distract himself and found a fresh basket of irritations. He picked at his thermal, giving the lanky medium height engineer beside him dirty looks and said, "Can you stop grindin' yer teeth, Ashur? It's annoyin' as shit."

"Sorry, nervous habit," he mumbled. Russell Ashur, bandaged from wrist to shoulder on his left arm, wore a sling.

Shit, what happened to him?

Kitten heels clicked against cold concrete. "Dr. Giro's requesting another test. We aren't ready," an attractive young Asian woman said to Russell, breathless. Red warmth consumed her pale cheeks.

"I get it, Myra. We can't limit the energy transfer," Russell said.

Myra, beautiful name, Jared thought. *How'd a nice lady like her get recruited—*

"Mr. Ashur, please listen," she insisted, "the two machines aren't calibrated to work together, talk to each other about how, when, and why to use the energy. To create a functioning system, we need to make adjustments to the containment center."

"I know, I know." Exasperated, Russell's uninjured hand towered above his head and fell to his side with a dramatic slapping noise. "I know. I wanted to circumvent the issue. Please explain how you'd go about changing a machine's function, built on physics principles we don't understand."

"Need some help?" Jared offered, clearing his throat and nuzzling Myra by accident. "Oh, 'scuse me. I—"

"—have an idea," Russell interrupted and sprinted to the nearest computer. "Bring up the calculations for locating the Z-energy system."

Jared stepped back to watch Myra's thin, tapping fingers fulfill the request.

"There they are," she said, and rocked her hip to one side, a sweater sleeve over her mouth.

"Hope this works." Russell's chin moved up and down in rapid succession, keyboard to screen, while, one-handed, he pounded new formulas into the computer's database. His index finger pushed his glasses up.

"What you work—"

"Make sure it finishes uploading!" Russell screeched to Myra, hurrying away, then yelled, "I'll be back!"

Myra pointed with a chewed off nail. "We're working on this," she said.

The first U-generator prototype sparkled like a shiny new fighter jet. Six generators were scheduled to get their titanium barriers installed, and thirteen generators in development had their base framework. Jared wasn't known for brains and tried to follow the machine's properties and purpose as the explanations flowed from her glossy lips. He asked her personal questions, watching the flickers of light catch her freckles instead of listening to her responses. He'd picked up enough to send flutters throughout his chest cavity. As modest as she was mind-blowing, Myra Eberle was extracted from Stanford's doctorate program at twenty-two to be C20's lead physicist.

Swooping air sent a chill across Jared's shoulder blades. He covered his mouth on instinct, afraid to inhale the mist.

"Are we ready?" Dr. Giro inquired. "We better be ready." He sat posture perfect, one booted foot on a stool and the other fastened to the floor.

Myra shrank. "I'll prepare the team," she said and rushed off.

Jared turned to watch her go and choked on his spit mid-swallow. "Zosma...?"

"Dr. Giro, the final materials have been received and assembled," the alien woman said, "I am eager to learn the next phase."

He gaped at her, glanced at Dr. Giro, who hummed, oblivious, reviewing Russell's work on multiple computer screens, and gaped at her again.

"I don't believe you have met." The doctor turned, gesturing an introduction. "This is Captain Jared Brandt. He helped pioneer C20 operation in infancy."

His jaw had unhinged expecting him to produce words, and hung there waiting for a coherent acknowledgement or greeting. It had been twelve years since Jared saw her alive, post-landing at a top secret holding facility and never in her current radiance. Her hair, a field of magenta desert roses, surrounded her face. The princess wore a tempered smile and hovered just above the ground. As she did, he glimpsed her royal beauty under the flying cape: violet skin, incomparable bone structure, and muscle density concealed by golden armor.

"Whew, hey," he said. "Hey, Zosma."

She floated in his personal space, touched his thin, chapped lips, and sloped shoulders. "As seen through each other's perspective, Captain Jared Brandt," Zosma greeted. She drifted back, her arm bent at the elbow, vertical in the air.

He scratched his neck, unsure what to do next.

"In Zosma's culture they touch forearms to form bonds in trust and friendship," Dr. Giro said.

Zosma pursed her lips as Jared edged toward her.

"Yeah, uh nice to meet you," he said, tapping his forearm to hers.

"You are supposed to say, 'I accept the truth of you as you are, here and now'," she scolded.

"Sure, that too." Having staggered back and no longer in earshot, he nudged the doctor and mumbled, "What's she doing here?"

"Dr. Giro is giving me an opportunity to use my power to help humanity," she answered. "In return, I can stay on Earth and make this my new home."

"Right," he said, stretching the single syllable word by the tail.

To him, Zosma being accepted by humanity was about as likely as her making it back to the Andromeda Galaxy. Emerging awareness came as a single conscious stream, penetrating the cloud in his mind. One unrestricted thought lead to another, then another. A threat to Dr. Giro's influence.

The longing in her voice sparked confusion about her true motivation, and like cancer, suspicion spread in him, making him confused about his own true motivation. Jared stroked his face. He'd been tricked, and a placebo attack had left his mind mist-free.

"Zosma prepare for exit, I meet you on bridge to finalize strategy."

"As you wish." She placed a hand over her stomach, dipped her head, and returned to the air.

"I admit, C20 would not be this far if not for your dedication," Dr. Giro said to him. "Do not make it worthless. Come."

Exercising tenuous independence, he followed Rabia, listening to each word explaining C20's mission for inconsistencies. Whether through meticulous rehearsal or blatant honesty, nothing rang alarms. He moseyed away only to be dwarfed by the energy-canceling wall and the U-generator prototype itself.

"Ahh, she's gotta power this puppy!" He knocked hard on the protective barrier. "And she ain't got a clue, does she?"

"It promises to save billions."

C20, conceived to help humanity, an abstract painting with a complex background and blurry foreground, none of which fit together comfortably.

"There is always catch," the doctor said. "Prepare for worst, hope for best. I have gift for you, special plasma weapon."

"Aww, you shouldn't have." Jared's brow relaxed. He shrugged off his qualms and asked, "When do I get to see my godson?"

"That's spirit," Dr. Giro said, looping a hefty arm around his shoulder. They walked back toward the giant steel doors they'd entered through. "Will be glorious reunion."

FLORENCE BELLADONNA
Belladonna Mansion, New SoHo, New York

FLORENCE SENSED THE SORROW for her death and relief for her survival dissolving into contempt for her deceit. Allister had refused her assistance getting up the mansion's stairs, and by the time they reached the foyer, his tears had dried, replaced by cold, bloodshot eyes and a hardened jaw. Their heartfelt reunion froze to ice in the climate of reality.

"I live in a dumpster compared to this." Allister glared at the oil painting collection lining the hallway of Belladonna family members from the past ten centuries. Italian or African descent or both; dukes, duchesses, lords, counts, queens, knights, and an emperor legitimized her often challenged pedigree. "Hmph, no wonder you're so rich," he noted.

"Let's see," she began, "in a month's time you've pissed off the U.S. government, infiltrated a top-secret facility, and leveled an entire city. Am I leaving anything out?"

"Think you nailed it. By the way General Delemar says thanks for saving him," he spat and threw his hands out, "except he thought you were dead, like I did!"

"Don't take it personal. He knew the Andromeda Project inside and out. It had to be done." Florence dismissed his tantrum and guided their voyage deeper into the house. They entered the sun-lit sitting room, though neither were keen to sit.

"It had to be done, I had no choice," Allister mocked. "You need a new script."

She kept a flat tone, combating his frustration with apathy, and delivered her next line, "I assume you obtained some useful information."

Chasing her down on an off-balance gait, then wrenching her upper arm, he screamed, "Why'd you save him after what he did!"

He was nothing like the Allister she remembered. Instincts kicked in. She took back the limb and executed an elbow jab to his bandaged side. He looked up at her, doubled over, breathing like the room was robbed of oxygen.

"Don't make me do this." Florence's hand spread out, a psionic energy orb whipping round it. More aggressive measures weren't necessary.

Allister's chilling yelp didn't end in retaliation. It ended with his cheeks soaked in tears. It ended with him crumpled on the floor, begging.

"It hurts, everything hurts."

She kneeled. Crimson energy separated into each palm, and she held them next to his head. "What's happened to you?"

Florence entered Allister's mind by boarding an imaginary rollercoaster traveling at light speed. A captivating, yet dizzying laser light show flew by in broad darkness, and she was ejected into the astral plane, destined to fall the inevitable distance to the subconscious surface she chose. Over years of training, deep-probing telepathy, though effective, hadn't become less daunting.

She hit the ground, sending a clear telepathic ripple through Allister's psyche.

His heart beat as if no blood would ever be enough. It thundered in her ears and in the air. Every fiber in her being linked to his. She felt vehement fear, anger, devastation, smothering life in the heat of emotion. "This can't be the same place, the houses, his parents, the..." She bent to pick the withered brown grass. It whittled to dust between her translucent fingertips. Dead patches spanned for eternity beneath a blackened sky.

Florence recalled a different world: Z-energy blue grass growing in abundance, houses holding his mother and father's fond memories, and their astral images keeping hope alive. What had happened to the luminous sky? The stars, planets, and galaxies representing his magnificent intelligence and understanding? What had happened to his guide, Neight Caster?

A silver glow pulsed where lifeless vegetation met the atmosphere. Two distorted shapes, aiming to be round, resembled binary stars positioned on the horizon's opposite sides. *Transporter gems,* she guessed. They fought to penetrate the clouds and pushed through in spurts, bringing temporal energy's light to the darkened setting. Thickening air restricted free motion, and she crawled toward a little boy's silhouette. "It doesn't make any sense," she struggled to say.

"You shouldn't have come down here," he said. The cross-legged child tended to and dwelled over three looming tombstones. Patrick Adams. Dolores Adams. Leesa Delemar.

Mismatched explanations about Leesa's disappearance and forming no true friendship while working together gave Florence liberty to throw any attachment to her in the river carrying away distractions. But she fished for sentiments and reeled them close. She witnessed dying without death, her colleague's capable body deteriorating in Allister's arms as Zosma reclaimed her stolen life.

"Oh, my goodness."

"What's the point of having these powers if I can't save the people I love?" eight-year-old Allister asked.

Any answer sounded insensitive, scripted or lacked perspective. She had only ever loved one person, and she suspected neither her love nor her power would save him from the inevitable.

"You're holding onto emotional pain," she said. "And it's holding the physical pain with you as well. You can't punish yourself for what's happened." Gazing at Allister's perceived failures etched in stone, Florence touched his shoulder to make him face her, to see the trauma's mental scarring. He refused her request. Her bodily functions stopped. She felt suspended, stuck, bogged down by his rejection. An excruciating, unbearable pain stabbed through to the crux of her soul. She jerked her hand back. "There's nothing I can do," she whispered. "You hold absolute power here. You must find a way to restore your psyche."

A loud vroom began Florence's journey in reverse. She launched skyward, traveled backward through the same nausea-inducing ride, and woke up to Allister cradling his side and using the wall to stand. Guilt squatted on her chest like a tenant refusing to pay rent. "Have a seat," she said, moving a plush patterned chair to him.

He dropped into it and turned away from her. "How's Dorian?"

"Dorian's safe, recovering."

"What about Bridget?"

"She's where you left her, in Florida. No one's going after her."

"It's my fault Detective Steele went after Dorian." He sniffled. "I... wanted to make sure."

Florence took refuge in the chair's matching love seat. She rearranged her floor-length skirt to conceal its slit and the unwanted souvenir from the Andromeda Project. After a booby trap bomb went off during C20's attack on their base, too much tissue damage left her few options short of amputation. Rabia's motives for installing the alien-infused tech remained unclear. The psiborg leg responded to her thoughts and was twice as strong as its human counterpart. Sometimes it felt too light and she forgot that beneath pigment matching fibers; hard wires, metal alloys, and crystals commingled. If uneven steps didn't remind her, the psionic energy it channeled would.

Allister's lip twisted to the side.

Propping her elbow on the couch arm and her cheek on her fist, she massaged the area where numb upper thigh met the foreign enhancement. "It doesn't hurt," she said.

"Why do you do that?" he asked.

"I'm telepathic. It's involuntary."

"It's rude. I don't blast you with blue energy and say, oh sorry, I have energy projection." He let his head rest on the chair. "Are we doing this? Or are you babysitting me?"

"Why do you think you're here and not in a prison?"

His shoulders relaxed. Allister's tree of angst had deep, thick roots. "Save yourself, it's what you're best at," he'd said to her as the Andromeda Project crumbled around them. The last words in her head, as she drowned in the Atlantic Ocean, and the first when she woke in the ICU in Milan.

"I had to make a difficult decision, I wouldn't have left you behind otherwise." Florence uncrossed her legs and stood. "To your point, how do you expect to save others, when you can't save yourself?" Slowing her stride, she turned her chin to her shoulder. "Look at you."

"Hmph, that's your apology?" Allister inhaled and struggled to stand. "It's fine. You did what you had to do."

"It's evolution, the strong survive."

"And the rich, the cunning, the selfish," he added.

She eyed a purple streak in his hair. "When you're ready, I'll be in the computer room. I encourage you to leave your attitude here."

———

ALLISTER ADAMS

Belladonna Mansion, New SoHo, New York

"THIS IS MY father, GIOVANNI," Florence announced, arms wide, palms up. "What's left of him at least. It's an artificial intelligence program."

Skirt swishing left to right, right to left, drawn out steps carried her into the buzzing room. She turned in jewel-embellished heels. The older sister he never had, waiting for him, the much younger brother to catch up during a tiresome outdoor adventure's end. He limped in, aided by the door frame's narrow width. He watched her watch him, her expression aimed at sympathy but reading as impatience.

The CPU's motherboard was installed on the farthest side and floor-to-ceiling monitors were installed on the one nearest him. Public news and private transmissions sang a tragic song. One told the world's truths. One showed how those same truths were spun into the tallest tales. Hard to recognize which was which.

"How much did President DeVries pay you to find me?"

"Technically, Detective Steele found you." She flipped her hair. "Which means I don't get paid."

His cynical grunt held an inkling of scorn and appreciation. He slumped against the entrance. "How'll you keep the lights on?" The trust tightrope connecting them was stretched to a frayed center, contingent on the motives (if any) concealed under her navy silk getup.

"New look?" she asked.

The man bun on his head loosened, then liberated, he tousled his overgrown mane and pulled the stark minority growing at the hairline over his eye. Violet strands had multiplied to a violet clump. "I think it's a side effect. Could be from using the Transporter gems? Color's kinda random." He let the follicles curl to their natural shape. "The gems are stressing me out. And I haven't slept. And I'm not healing. I don't know what the hell is up." He pushed the hair back and hunched forward, defeated by his own admission.

"I told you why. It's your problem to fix," Florence said. Nicolas Delemar's Cynque dangled from her forefinger. "I take it you haven't accessed it?"

"When would I have?" *Forget it,* he thought, it wasn't worth the sarcasm. "No. Password is Leesa."

"Giovanni, do me a favor and manifest the keyboard for me. I'll also need you to open your software backend."

"I'd be happy to, Dr. Belladonna."

The Cynque clinked on a waist-high glass table's surface. She bent, typing on the table's embedded keyboard, taking breaks to recall memories and stroked the watch as if it held them. Her typing resumed, then stopped. She shook her head, highlighted and deleted what she'd written and clicked her nails. Grinning, she muttered, "Wrong interactor." Her chin and gaze, parallel to a monitor, dared not falter as her fingers attempted the unknown feat at their fastest pace. For the third time, language spread the wall's length.

It was a legacy coding language called Viper. Allister leaned close. Although outdated compared to Cynque's programming, its fundamental theories echoed in all encrypted software, providing compatibility between two incompatible systems.

Astonished by Florence's proficiency, he ogled at cyber security layers peeling away to let her enter the password, establish a private link, and initiate the download.

The computer dinged and said in a smooth androgynous voice, "Download complete. Which folder should I access first Dr. Belladonna?"

Letters, numbers, characters, and symbols on a dimensionless black setting, language rendered immaterial, dissolved, leaving a warm tan screen inhabited by files and folders totaling in the millions. She gave Allister a skeptical glance.

"Delemar mentioned a program called, Hex... Fourth?"

"Doesn't ring a bell," Florence replied. "Giovanni, open folder Hex Fourth."

"Accessing folder Hexforth."

Ah Hexforth, not Hex space numeral four. He scratched his head, the familiar syllables he'd reunited hoping to find clarity felt incomplete.

Three blueprint sketches enveloped the room. He cupped his neck, inspecting the CAD file labeled "U-Generator Energy Distribution Prototypes." From the notes he gathered two models weren't feasible. The available input/output ratio tested insufficient for the joules needed to maintain continuous distribution.

"Dr. Rabia Giro endeavors to construct, what?" he said, reading a short description beneath the last approved model. "Construct twenty U-generators?" He glanced at Florence and read on, "... for the purpose of harnessing Z-energy. U-generators will use formula listed in Exhibit E, to draw the energy from its source." Allister's head got closer to the flickering image, he swallowed. "Which has been hypothesized to reside in the Containment

Center. Said energy will operate as clean energy and be distributed throughout said medium, for public and private use, subject to premiums as set forth by the... " his voice pitched in shock as he finished, "controlling entity known as C20! What the hell is this?"

In a word, vague, and Zosma's name wasn't mentioned a single time.

"This is pure madness," she said.

It went on to state that the U-Generators would be available for private sale to major cities and utility partners worldwide at C20's discretion.

Date commissioned: March 2052, a month ahead of the Andromeda Project's downward spiral.

"Look," she said, pointing. Giovanni played the next round of evidence.

In the video stream dated November 20, 2044, the camera focused on a bland boardroom of stuffed old geezers. One in particular, well past his sixties, tilted a mic and began, "Neight Caster, you tried to leave the planet without adhering to your promise. A promise to help us mitigate a catastrophe *you* predicted. Please explain to the board why we should trust your council and continue the search for these gems you spoke of. It would seem to us, they don't want to be located, and you don't want to help us locate them. Dr. Giro has presented a reasonable, if not better alternative to your original proposal."

Silly for Allister to see Neight Caster using his claws to anchor himself to a metal podium. An alien testifying in front of congress for God's sake. "Senator Phillip DeVries, allow me to put it in terms you can comprehend. Should this world you cherish as your home become uninhabitable, the Transporter gems can open gateways to new worlds for you to explore. They hold the key to limitless manipulation and movement through time-space. I know it has taken over a decade to detect their power, but I assure you, they are far more valuable than the Z—"

"Your honor," another member of the senate scoffed, "this is the same thing we've heard year after year. Doesn't he have any new material?"

Senator DeVries gulped and spoke up, "Neight, understand that we're facing trillions of dollars in losses and damages from these natural disasters. We've had to take loans and aid from our enemies. The American people don't care about mystical space travel. They need water. They need food. They need heat and power."

The other senator joined in. "Our way of life is crumbling and what the hell do you care? You can just hop on the next space ship out of here and leave us to die."

Her outburst provoked the crowd's ensuing uproar. Neight's lips straightened. The podium squealed as he tore it from the foundation. Their angerless screams prevailed over its clanging along the floor.

"I wonder," the alien said, grinding his claws, "has Dr. Giro explained to you what Z-energy will do if, say, there are not proper protective measures in place?" His hand opened, and Z-energy burst into sapphire blue flames in his palm.

Desperate murmurs mingled with frightened prayers, they scrambled over and around each other to attain maximum distance. "Has he made it clear human biology is not equipped to sustain prolonged exposure to its pure form?" Raising his arm above his head, letting the blaze grow and soak the room in its burning shadow, Neight continued, "Or informed you it causes cellular deconstruction at an atomic level?" Human clusters huddled in corners. "I thought not," he said as the fire poofed to smoke.

Allister connected these details to what Celine had said in her sanctuary. The train towards humanity's preservation had chugged along a track whose destination was the Transporter gems. Him derailing that dream had sent the train toward what many believed was a dead end.

Nicolas was wrong. A second Cumberland incident wasn't the reason the directors didn't accept Rabia's proposal. It was fear of Neight. The same Neight who had always been gracious, patient, and wise. Allister wanted to blame a lapse in judgement, for that, that arrogance, that abuse, that violence. It had to be asked, what kind and loving king let his entire planet die to protect living energy anyway?

Human logic told him Neight had made a cruel and unfair mistake. Yet Allister's instinct drove him to provide the same protection to the living energy, who had a face, and a personality, and a name. Zosma.

"I-I read a research document from the Z-protocols folder at the base. There's a clean energy initiative the world nations are scrambling to figure out."

"I'm aware of the initiative. I just wasn't aware of this initiative. Wesley must know." Florence crinkled her brow and tapped the responsive walls.

Allister wandered wall to table to wall. "They were a decoy... the gems... if he'd escaped in 2040 like he'd planned, we'd never know about the Z-energy."

"Or would we?" she asked quietly, engulfed in blueprints, dated 1973. Diagrams isolated Arecibo observatory's massive upgrades in communication capabilities. Communication, which allowed Earth to receive Neight's transmission four decades later. Written in the bottom corner: Commissioned by Rabia Giro. "Can't be right."

Heart pulsing in his ears, Allister swiped to find the project's before and after photographs: Dr. Giro scowling amongst smiling astronomers, Dr. Giro shaking President Nixon's hand. Black and white souls trapped in grainy film. He wasn't the same plump man, though obesity often came with age. Noticeable black dots bled across his torso, as if the pictures had been developed in an unsupervised dark room.

Allister looked north. "Dr. Giro wasn't alive in 1973, so how..."

Florence had kept swiping and landed herself in the 1900s, losing twenty years after each leftward hand motion. Scanned typewriter messages, telegrams, ink and pen handwriting on paper, on scrolls. They weren't the Andromeda project's files or C20's files. These were personal records, and the content carousel ended on a withered book titled *The Book of Ancestry.*

Their mouths hung open in disbelief, and she sank onto the table. "I need to get in touch with Wesley to—"

"Incoming message, Captain Jared Brandt," his Cynque announced. "I can read it aloud for you, Mr. Adams?"

Among the insanity he'd witnessed, the name hit him like a tidal wave. "N-no."

"There is a location request in the message, but your location services are turned off. I can re-engage your location services to give you an estimated arrival time and book transportation to Cumberland Falls, Kentucky."

"No. No, no, no."

"Cumberland Falls? Captain Brandt?" Florence asked, "Allister, what did he say? What's he want?"

He backed into the doorway and managed to stay on two feet, puffing, straining as the Transporter gems' white glow out-shined her luxury fixtures. A tightening energy cocoon outlined his physical shape. Telling himself to breathe and go with it, he prepared for what came after the tingling sensation—conflicting gravitational force and transported molecules.

———

Cumberland Falls, Kentucky
Allister rallied several nausea-reducing breaths as the gems returned to their signature dulled green. The Transporter gem's "transportation" ability was baked so deep in myth, who on Earth could fathom, let alone survive its reality? In action, every bone

was pulverized, every living tissue shredded, skin, clothes, organs, taken apart by temporal energy like broken things needing repair and stripped to basic atomic, even subatomic forms. As if being crushed milliseconds later in infinite fusion and compressed through a singularity weren't jarring enough, he lost memory and coherence with the brain's discombobulation.

On the upside, he stayed awake post-transport.

The front door's red paint chipped down to the wood. The roofed awning's missing shingles. The lumpy brick driveway leading to two-story glory. A striking setting for a suppressed childhood memory, the home he grew up in.

World frozen in the seconds between what had happened and what was to happen next, the scenery reminded him where he'd transported and why. He buckled. Air thrust against his face as he landed in the street, scraping his knees on its jagged stones. He stared at two fistfuls of pebbles grinding in his palms, waiting for the world to move again, for his heart to find its beat. Glassy eyes summoned the courage to rise, and, once again, face preserved devastation.

Cumberland Falls' flaming end murdered half a dozen apple trees in the front yard and the garden his mother had tended to in her spare time. Not to mention the abrupt end to treasured family moments, he and his father fixing up the old Mustang, even when it wasn't broken. His mother's home-made cornbread.

On the heels of catastrophe his physical superpowers came into full bloom: speed, strength, and accelerated healing. His body's cellular tissue regeneration in particular added complications to his already hard to manage intellectual superhuman powers.

Allister's childhood serenaded him, and the coniferous taiga's sweet aroma brought back the extreme Russian summer in 2041. Dolores carried two recycled grocery bags, packed to the brim with cured meats and farm-grown fruit. His favorite things to eat. She led them the long way home, through Zaryadye park, ignoring the slipping bags to maintain a firm grasp on Allister. He insisted he could carry one, that he was big enough to help. She refused and instructed him to keep up.

Their brisk stride halted at Saint Basil's Cathedral steps. He didn't realize what it meant that they were surrounded by gawking tourists in perfect poses, unusual couples pushing empty strollers, and random men sporting bad socks and trendy hats. Allister remembered his mother whispering to a stranger about Nicolas Delemar and the Andromeda Project, stretching his collar to keep him next to her. She repositioned the bags, so they sat on her hip, and snapped, "Sit still," then asked her confidant, "How close are they?"

A covert meeting veiled as casual conversation in a hectic square.

"They are here," the person replied.

Dolores snatched Allister by the hand, dashed across the cobblestone and into an empty street. Nine-year-old Allister stole a second glance at the man, nearly twice his mother's height, and gasped. The stranger flickered like an old television. It had been a hologram.

Curiosity left him at an oncoming truck's mercy. Its brakes screeched. Allister flew, hit the ground on his side, and rolled over himself until he lost velocity and came to rest on his back. The driver cursed his mother's carelessness while Allister wailed, high-pitched and raw, blood seeping from bruised flesh and a shattered humerus. Feigned emotional reactions swept Red Square, bystanders left their fake conversations to offer their services. One even yelled they were a doctor.

Dolores huddled next to him, casting her matronly shadow, cradling his arm. Moscow's police unit swarmed the scene and, by coincidence, foiled the spies. Not a minute later, she'd hoisted him up and fled the accident. He begged her to slow down, her tears and her pace. She waited for the crowd's insistent recommendations for medical attention to melt behind them, then she obliged, lugging him into an alley.

"I'm fine, Mom," he said. Holding his wrist, he pinched his eyes shut and let the blood trickle away from the reconnected skin. "See! Nothing to worry about."

In April 2052, that moment and its relevance to his future became clear. The Andromeda Project had captured the accident on tape. Captain Brandt played it for him at the second interview's conclusion. Was it the part where Dolores interrogated the odd seven-foot man? Or when the truck rammed his stringy boyish frame? No, it was their hideaway shrouded in perceived safety, in the alley, where his body's autoimmune system stitched him up like a rag doll. Brandt's voice repeated in his head. "Ya can't fly under the radar anymore, son."

"Like hell I can't," he said aloud. Cold enveloped him. He shuddered, imagining Cumberland's lost souls clawing at his vibrant, warm flesh. His presence was a perversion to their peace, the last surviving reminder of their unfair demise. Well, one of the last.

Footsteps. Sandalwood and citrus-scented aftershave. Rubber-soled boots crunched gravel as they approached him from the rear.

"I know, son, whole thing's pretty messed up," the voice said in a Southern drawl too close to his father's for comfort. Captain Jared Brandt strolled into the garden and gazed at its barren acres. The house seemed to mean as much to Brandt as it did to him.

"Ya let Delemar live." The captain smacked his lips. "Yer father would be proud."

A rising temper blasted whatever cold Allister had felt to steam. "You have five seconds to tell me what you know about the U-generators."

"You don' even know what happened or what's happenin'." Brandt bounced on his toes and hugged himself. "We can work together ya know, Patty Cakes watchin' us save the world."

Pure anger roared from Allister's throat. His mouth opened so wide he could only see Captain Brandt's sturdy build bouncing in his tunneled vision. "How dare you" and "murderer" and "bastard," he screamed in no particular order as his fists pummeled the captain's disruptive energy field. Blow after blow, boom after boom, the punches' kinetic force dispersed through the strengthening field. Built-up energy backfired and Allister's body smashed the damaged asphalt. He blinked at the starless evening sky.

Hands planted, his abs contracted, and his legs kicked into the air, bringing him to his feet. He wiped his cut-up knuckles on his shirt and put fingertips to palm for round two. His uppercut began the skirmish. Brandt dodged. Allister took a left hook to the mouth, a right hook to the chin.

Brandt pressed a button under his palm. Tiny metal panels clinked, encasing the captain's arm to the elbow, while wires snaked out, writhing parallel to his veins, and connected to circular twin gun barrels. "I don' wanna hurt ya, son," he said.

Allister dragged his tongue along the inside of his lip. "Too late."

And in the sinister stillness of the sprawling abyss, the captain shouted across the cul-de-sac, "I think Zosma's in trouble."

Wind and gravel overtook them in a profound *whoosh*. Her name had given godspeed to his movement, but hearing the word trouble, stopped his attack. Heels pressed together, legs straight, facial expression furious, Allister bent down and asked, "What did you say?"

CHAPTER FOUR

ON THE BRINK

ALLISTER ADAMS
Cumberland Falls, Kentucky

ALLISTER PREPARED for tormented, vengeful Neptune blues, but Captain Brandt's eyes were pools of shame and remorse. Their genuine worry thawed his grimace. "You have five more seconds," he muttered.

"I know you and Lieutenant were close," Brandt said, powering down the gun, "and when I saw Zosma, I figured she'd have her memories, on account of they spent so much time together."

Two fingers slid across Allister's chin. "You saw her?"

"Did more than see her, I talked to her. Dr. Giro introduced us like we were strangers." He pressed the button on his wrist and the device retracted. "She looked right at me. Ain't say a word. I'm willing to bet there's some wires crossed up there. He rebooted her or somethin'."

"I read about the Z-energy... and the generators."

"Intel ain't easy to come by these days." The captain explained how he'd left the computer at C20 intact and how certain he'd been the government wouldn't destroy it because they were in his words, too damn nosey. "I made sure those files were there when you came huntin', And I knew ya'd come huntin' even though they told ya not to." He shrugged. "You're stubborn, just like yer daddy."

Unable to stomach the captain's tone, Allister hocked, spat the resulting loogie over his shoulder, and headed to the driveway. "Stop doing that," he said.

"Doin' what?"

He touched the porch railing and answered with grit, "Pretending you knew him."

"Patty Cakes and I, man, Friday night football games durin' season, the diner for milkshakes and wings. He always had his eye on yer momma, sweet Dee—"

His reminiscing touch escalated to a tensed grip. The wooden railing snapped.

"Allister, I—"

"Don't you dare apologize!"

"I swear I didn't kill her."

"You brought her there! Put her in that cave! You-you, buckled the straps, and you set the bomb's timer. You might as well have."

Brandt recoiled. "I'll never," he started, running his hand along his cheek, "I'll never be able to forgive myself for what I did."

"Good. I'll never forgive you either." His fury burned the captain's regret into an ash pile to be taken by the wind. He didn't care. He refused to care.

"Stakes are high. Those machines don't just harness Z-energy, Zosma's gonna have to power 'em."

Simple as the mention of her name, Zosma's whereabouts and wellbeing took priority. She was in present danger. With her, Allister could right the wrongs. He could make up for past mistakes. Saving Zosma was almost like saving his mother. At least he'd know he was capable of saving others, and by default, capable of the virtue he ached for.

The idea of losing someone else he loved sent shooting pain through his head. So much was to blame for what happened to Dolores, and so much of the blame fell to him. He released his grip on the past, ignored the pain in his head, and thumbed for compromise on the emotional bookshelf. Arms unfolded, he about-faced.

"Brandt?"

The captain held his stomach. Raised veins, engorged and blackened with corruption, crept over his neck and head. "Get outta here. Dr. Giro... tricked... me," he wheezed, crumbling and falling unconscious.

In peculiar awareness, Allister checked the starless sky and stumbled back without speed or guile. Despite the southern night's thorough darkness, his favorite constellations were missing... Perseus, Taurus, Cassiopeia. Haze twisted as it poured out of Brandt's mouth and hit the ground. Absence explained.

"Good evening, Mr. Adams. Captain Brandt has, as you say, left the building."

Mist at his waistline and suspended in the lower atmosphere had collected and molded.

"I knew first day at Andromeda Project, you were answer I'd been looking for." Dr. Rabia Giro—yellowed nails, greyed teeth, splotchy skin—glided his direction and into arm's reach.

No matter how hard he gritted his teeth, thought violent thoughts, fanned his hatred for Rabia and bolstered his concern for Zosma, motor functions didn't show up. He couldn't speak, let alone raise a fist to punch, a leg to run. Gasoline's pungent smell soared up his nostrils. He gagged, or rather, his brain sent an urgent request to engage the reflex, though his throat could not obey. Cloudy grey pupils drilled an iron glare through him and slimy tentacles born from the doctor's mist wriggled across his cheeks and tugged at his mouth's corners.

"Neight's little hybrid," Dr. Giro sneered, cupping his jaw. "Broken."

———

FLORENCE BELLADONNA
Cumberland Falls, Kentucky

THE BELLADONNA CORP Gulfstream jet's engines roared, speeding up to its Mach 1 maximum.

Florence balanced on the passenger seat's edge. "Giovanni, keep us in the air for as long as you can. I'll make this quick."

"Happy to assist, Dr. Belladonna. Turning on holding pattern navigation sequence," Giovanni informed her. "Distance to Cumberland Falls, fifteen minutes."

She scooted back and activated her telepathy, imploring Allister to concentrate on her voice. The plane's lights and interior faded in a pink energy ripple.

Her mind catapulted into the ever-expanding collective of consciousness known as the astral plane. Any savvy telepath, any worthy telepath, accessed the realm as she'd done, with a squint and forefingers fastened to their temple or forehead. The Astral Plane lived between myth and theory, in a home built of grandiose claims and abstract descriptions. Wholly a mystery to those not plagued by or, (depending on your perspective), privileged to psionic energy manipulation.

The Astral Plane's eternal highway stretched around and through the universe, and on its pulsing energy tarmac, thoughts going faster than the suggested speed limit of light, zipped to destinations in the waiting minds of the cosmos.

And this is where Florence came, sensing a disturbance that transcended the physical realm. To wage war against a perverse disruption to the purity of free thought, a fog settling onto lanes, causing traffic, accidents, havoc.

Allister's subconscious beckoned. She reached her hand into negative Space, wrapped her fingers around the fabric of the macrocosm, and pulled it to her. Her astral form gained weight, depth and dimension, conjured as an energy representation of her physical attributes, and with it, she navigated to the heavy glob

146

surrounding his mind. The atmospheric disturbance bearing down on its terrain blocked her ability to read it, to assess its viability.

Concentrate on my voice, she insisted.

Toes pointed, she plunged, racing a blackened sky to the parched grass spanning Allister's psyche. Arms back. Elbows locked. Chin out. Her shimmering form torpedoed ahead, falling so fast the ground came to meet her. Speed had given her marginal advantage, positioned to touch down a fraction of a second before the murky mist threatening to swallow her whole. She performed a graceful airborne tumble and landed on one knee.

Mist plowed the surface, lightning struck, and wind screeched, as if a dense cumulonimbus had descended and unleashed its power.

"Dr. Belladonna," Rabia said. His voice, deep and raspy, his body, a swarm of black bees fashioned to a man's shape. "What an unpleasant surprise."

"I could say the same," she said, hands up. "Get. Out." Psionic energy lines retraced her astral body, fortifying its presence.

"I wonder, can you fight on two planes at once?"

The cloudy, swirling mass erupted. She ducked her head; arms crossed in front of her and conjured a psychic force field. Visibility a complete stranger, she shouted for Allister inside its protection, and like a beacon, blue light penetrated the murkiness. She sprinted in its direction, hoping it meant he was somehow okay.

Stifling air's immense pressure crushed her mental stamina. The force field, its sole purpose to deflect the mist's brutality, flickered and cracked, striving to hold up its end of the bargain. The cloud's thickness thinned as she battled through, and she burst free, panting and stumbling. Little Allister, valiant and irreproachable, held the madness at bay with his tiny arms pushed forward and Z-energy streaming forth.

She'd planned on taking shelter behind the gravestones of Leesa, Dolores, and Patrick, and scoured the horizon. Gone. She did a second sweep, searching for another psionic landmark.

Flat, dead terrain met her at each turn, until she found a blip bathed in the Transporter gem's tapered light. A candidate for the safe-haven where his deepest thoughts could live.

Energy sparked on her heels, flowed up her body and set alight her fingertip. She pointed to the spot below them and by rotating her wrist, drew a circular platform.

"I... can't fight," he said, going from two raised hands to one. "The influence... too strong." His legs gave way as blue light shorted out.

She caught Allister on his way to slumping face first in the grass. "Rest for now. You'll need it."

Rabia's essence reared, billowing on itself like volcanic ash clouds. Her crafted transportation took off, whizzing them toward shelter faster than her own feet were allowed, even in the extended reality-warping of the subconscious.

Florence wasn't given the leeway to perfect the platform's levitation and balance. The sustained roar in surround sound drove her free arm's wild swings, as she repelled tentacle attacks from all angles with energy bursts.

She checked on the eight-year-old lying unconscious at her feet, then she turned, violating the cardinal rule: don't look back. A rule for good reason, as the abyss galloping after them had compounded. Darkness expanded to the left and right, above and below. And in her diversion from steering, it converged in the foreground to enclose them.

She held her breath and a strained squint, crouching breast to knee. Psychic energy gripped and stretched a small opening's edges, letting them squeeze through. Lifespan exhausted, the platform dissolved. Two astral bodies tossed onto the grass, rolled and stopped outside the house Allister had grown up in. A sanctuary reborn: two stories, brick, and a shining door sporting a new coat of red paint.

The more unique the structure to his experiences, the better it'd protect his inner psyche. Good for him.

A soft mold of Rabia's chubby face formed inside the cloud and birthed a prideful and triumphant smile.

"You came," Allister whispered, awakened.

"I did."

The boy's voice spawned sensibility and checked her ego. Waging against the obscure influential presence required imagination and strategy, endurance as well, no question but, it was not a limit test of her telepathy's brawn. Her priority was to keep Rabia from consuming Allister's fragile mind, not to win. She gathered him, whisked them through the door and slammed it shut.

The door disappeared, shutting them in. Tears brimmed wide eyes looking up at her.

"Will he get in?" Allister asked.

A funnel cloud's enraged winds rattled the foundation and walls in response.

"Not if you don't let him." Her rose-colored psychic power sidled up the structure, sealing rifts formed by the storm's savagery. In their undeniable vulnerability, she stroked his cheek and hugged him like the child she'd never have. Nevertheless, she felt distracted. Energy lines giving her figure proportion dimmed.

"You have to focus. If-if Dr. Giro gets hold of you, none of us stand a chance." Arms wrapping her torso, she stepped away. Pieces of her astral form detached and burned up, like embers flitting from a fire. An occurrence too real to be explained by a weakened telepathic connection. In the absence of atmosphere and of elements, it'd be impossible for fire to burn inside the sacred place she'd gone, for heat to rise into the thousands of degrees. Inconceivable incidents, even in the extended reality-warping of the subconscious.

Physical trauma slammed Florence into reality head first. The plane's pitching and rocking, loud sirens and brisk beeping,

Giovanni's uniform voice warning about their low altitude. She dashed to the cockpit and heard plasma bolts zooming by outside the window.

"Giovanni, why didn't you wake me up!"

"Apologies, Dr. Belladonna, I had to engage shield systems and extinguish fires in the main cabin," it answered, "and I found it difficult to manage multiple tasks."

Strapping herself in the pilot's seat, she pulled up on the controls, but it was too late.

ALLISTER ADAMS

SCATHING HOT PLASMA shot through the air. Captain Brandt, a jittery puppet, succeeded in blowing the jet to scraps. The tingle in his mind was gone. Florence's psychic presence was gone. Allister's chest tightened.

"Do not fight me," Dr. Giro coaxed, "You seek Zosma? I take you to her."

Mist power claimed Allister's hair and seeped down his creased forehead. *Not if you don't let him.* The statement repeated in his ears, louder and louder, eventually absorbed in the kaboom that destroyed the house. A tsunami of flames rushed outward. Dr. Giro's neck rotated the advancing fire's direction.

There came weakness in the doctor's mental blockage. No longer afflicted by the sinking in quicksand sensation, Allister explored commands for motion. He found the response positive, arched his back, flexed his hands. Radiant blue energy corkscrewed around his balled fist, breaking up the tentacles swimming on his skin. They unwound, slinking down his body, retreating over dirt and pebbles, and assimilated into the doctor's lurking shadow.

"Tell me where you're hiding her!" Allister yelled.

151

Kicking. Banging. Choking noises. Even with a glance, his vision pinpointed Florence's location, confined in a burning cockpit, her psiborg leg snared by the crushed dashboard.

Dr. Giro had reached Brandt, whose hands were clasped at his neck's nape, nose touching his knees. "If you let her die, saves me trouble."

Allister hesitated.

"You always do right thing, Mr. Adams," the doctor taunted and grabbed the captain by the collar, "is why you lose."

Allister knew better than to make the same mistake he did with his mother. Blood pumping through his veins, he ran to the house. The fire had closed in, but neither singed fingertips and forearms, nor air polluted by carbon monoxide and particle matter, dissuaded him from tearing brick slabs and metal sheets away. He found Florence, unconscious by that point, and used her bodysuit's puffy sleeve to drag her closer.

He hoisted her over his shoulder to return to the blazing street. The stars had arrived to offer their condolences, while flames hunted for more brush to burn but experienced no luck. Anything susceptible to combustion had done so on impact. Beyond the heat and hazard of incineration, he laid her down and she awakened.

"You alright?" he asked, staying stooped.

"My sword," she said first, gasping. In a hoarse whisper she finished, "I need to get my sword."

He settled a hand on her back. "Hey, hey, take it easy."

A crescent moon suffused Florence in resurrection's godly glow. She managed to stand, still coughing, and snapped, "I'm fine." She limped to comb the wreckage for her kindred weapon, not slowed down by first-degree burns on her arms or smeared soot and bleeding micro-cuts on her face.

"I can't tell if Brandt was lying or not," Allister mumbled. His face relaxed in a vacuous expression. "It was like we were both ambushed. I don't know. He sounded sincere."

Florence threw her arms up. "Are you not disturbed by what's happened inside your head?" Her chest rose and fell, rose and fell, lungs catching whatever oxygen the inferno had left behind. "I haven't felt mental power like that."

"It's okay. You did what you had to do."

"And you as well. Thank you for saving me."

Efforts worth their weight in gold. His warmed gut was a comforting exception to the tension.

Foot tapping, she wiped her running nose, then a dripping cut on her cheek. "I don't have much luck with planes, do I?"

His mouth curled. "Seriously though, you're pretty banged up. Don't you think you should chill for a second?"

"Chill for a second? Allister, we need to find Dr. Giro." She shoved her hand into her jumpsuit's pocket and presented a tarnished Cynque in her upright palm. "This is our lead, it belonged to my father. I was reluctant to read through and relive the horrible things he did."

"But?"

"I forced myself to. It's been, eye-opening." Florence massaged her head, testing each kinky lock of hair to make sure none had been burned off and finished her trek to the smoking wreckage. "Bazzo Sparks sent it via private messenger. He's a young finance guy who has been managing Belladonna Corp for the last four months."

"Oh God." Allister pivoted each direction she went as she searched. "Sparks? As in..."

"There you are," she said, flipping the sword around and holding it out. The dragon handle gleamed gold, out-shining the steel, aluminum, and brick pile she'd retrieved it from. "Yes, as in closely related to Bridget Sparks."

"Do you think he knows something?" he asked.

She slid the coat's lapel aside to reveal a leather embossed sheath around her waist and tucked the weapon away. "I think he knows a lot more than we do."

———

BRIDGET SPARKS
Campbell Recovery Center, Ft. Miami, Florida

THE OCEAN'S SALTY SMELL breezed through the 102-degree air temperature, to the balcony where Bridget Sparks observed the testy Atlantic waters. She stared out at what used to be sand, and was now stacked boulders to combat any incoming storm's surge.

Florida's bottom half had been submerged by consecutive Category 6 hurricanes, which drowned majority of the state population in an unforgiving barrage of hundred-foot tsunamis and flash floods. Beachfront properties were a thing of the past. Buildings on steel risers and elevated highways prepped for the predicted rise in sea level, unless something worse happened first.

The state's southernmost tip was dubbed Fort Miami for its heavy occupation by the U.S. Coast Guard, and was established in what had been Orlando.

Campbell Recovery Center was the kind of rehabilitation facility you'd find by a body of water. It encouraged indoor meditation in the mornings. The rooms and halls were decorated in tropical pinks, teals, and whites. Dried Conch shells lined toilet tops and were affixed to walls. Moody nurses changed embroidered towels daily. The center served as a government-assisted hospital extension for patients who didn't have any place to go, and Bridget Sparks didn't have any place to go.

She'd been in the hospital for six weeks, recovering from multiple facial lacerations, brain damage, and internal bleeding. Her waking hours had progressed to four to five per day, and contrary to her nature, she'd weened herself off pain medication.

Bridget's nose wrinkled at her frost white hair. She supposed that's what undergoing stressful cosmetic and medical surgeries would do. Shaving the right side bald in drunken rejection of traditional female beauty had resulted in uneven growth, however, the color was an ash blonde pre-surgeries. She picked at a scar next to her ear, found another on her forehead, and sucked her teeth.

"How do you feel, Ms. Sparks?"

Numb. Besides, the surroundings were too sterile for her to feel anything. Bored of scenery, Bridget diverted her attention to the handsome middle-aged doctor straddling the balcony doorway, pouted and pointed out her discovery. "Be peachy if it weren't for this bloody scar."

"It'll heal." Dr. Gerald Campbell yawned, and wiped away the tears. "Give it a few months."

"I don't got a few months," she scoffed, elbowing him aside to stomp into the room. "You never told me who dropped me?"

"Some young kid. Wasn't in much better shape than you, truth be told. He vanished before I could take a look at him." He tapped his Cynque, sending her hospital admission report onto the animated screen spanning the room. "He didn't know much about you."

Allister Adams, the undercover troublemaker. She spruced her angled bob to give it more volume, wondering what ingenious cover story he'd dreamt up to get them to take her. The grin faded. Her Cynque displayed the time, location, temperature, and the message she'd received from Dorian Xander telling her to "be careful" because "they were coming." They, she assumed, meant the U.S. Government. Because, they, the Andromeda Project recruits, were under contract. The agreements were lopsided for all of the superhumans, even Allister, but Bridget in particular had lost her Australian citizenship and become property of the United States. They'd be along to collect her soon enough.

"I gotta check out early, Doc." She dragged her fingertips across the itchy polyester blanket. No sparks. She turned her trembling hands to inspect her palms. No electric currents ran through her veins.

"What'd ya do to me?" she asked. "Sabotage? Experiments?" She thrashed the hard mattress, kicking her legs. "Show me my diagnosis!"

The doctor's chin wrenched back. "Ms. Sparks calm down or I'll have you sedated."

"Show me!" she shrieked, grabbing his Cynqued wrist to scroll for details. In the diagnosis they theorized by the plaster in her lungs, concrete dust on her skin and glass in her face, she'd been buried in a building demolition. "Bugger," she moaned and plopped on the bed like a punished teenager. She may or may not have overdone it with her powers and caused one. Unnecessary roughness on her part.

"We started having unusual blackouts hours after you were admitted. I went digging for info." He paused, gawking at her short shorts and mid-riff shirt, then shot his eyes to the ceiling. Fifty-two pages into Cynque's search engine, he'd found backlinks to the dark web. URLs swept away in the internet cleanse of 2048 talking about the Andromeda Project, their alien studies, their shady dealings, and their superhuman recruits. Based on what he found, he brought in power suppressors.

She delivered an icy scowl. "The fuck were you thinking bringing dampeners?"

"You were tampering with electromagnetic fields. I weighed serious options, including turning you in. My center lost three patients when the, when the life support machines went off." He rubbed his chest. "But, you weren't recuperating as I expected, so... so I blamed the thunderstorms."

Clever scapegoat. There'd been a severe storm daily for two months. In any case, his power suppressor idea hadn't worked. The blackouts stopped on their own.

"How bloody kind." She pulled her hair outward and twirled it. "Sorry mate, I'm not interested in some bored ER doc's sympathy."

He opened the door to exit the room. "I'm a neurologist," he said back. "I'll be happy to get you reassigned."

She crawled to the bed's corner and tucked her legs under her thighs, bosom pushed toward him. "Wait, wait, wait. I didn't mean... It's, it's loads to process. You could've gotten in trouble and you still didn't turn me in. What gives?"

"I knew it wouldn't end well," he replied, back to her, one foot out the door. "They gave you a tough time over there, sorry for your hardship."

"Spare me. Did you find out why it stopped?"

"There's a slightly plausible explanation."

Bridget bounced her bottom on the bed to bring her curvy frame upright. "Go on, don't be shy. Won't hurt my feelings."

Dr. Campbell's eyebrows damn near touched his hairline when he turned around. "We have more appropriate clothing options, Ms. Sparks."

"Oh, I'm golden." Standing on her tippy toes, she pressed against him. "Spill."

"You've been turned off."

"I've never been turned off before."

Inhaling, the doctor shifted focus to and from the framed Chicago and San Francisco skyline pictures on opposite walls. Bait on the hook, fishing line out and he didn't bite.

Bridget fell on her heels. "You mean, like a light switch?"

"Sort of. I detected a distinct change in the neural pathway you used to exercise your power."

In layman's terms: the road to electricity had been blocked and thus curved elsewhere. A reroute begged a new destination and therein lied the inexplicable. Her hands went numb on their way to clamp over her mouth. Blood left her cheeks colorless, rushing from her head to generate feeling in her arms.

"I need to phone a relative," Bridget said.

He hid another yawn with his sleeve and pointed to the CynqueT next to her. "All yours," he offered and closed the door.

A neurological diagnosis felt shallow. If the setback linked to her superhuman genetics, which she believed it did, there were two people she knew who had long history and expertise in the field: her ex-boyfriend Russell Ashur and Dr. Rabia Giro.

Four rings buzzed in her ear. "The number you have dialed is unavailable at this time," a machine announced.

"Don't ignore me," she said and redialed.

"Hello, this is Bazzo Sparks."

More excited to hear his rural Queensland, Australia twang than expected, she exclaimed, "You tried ignoring me, you little wanker!"

"Oi, if it isn't my favorite sis. How the hell do you keep getting my number?"

"Baz..."

Muffling his voice, Bazzo asked, "You're in trouble again, aren't you?"

"When am I not in trouble?"

He exhaled. "Ah fuck. You really got the best timing, I ever told you that? Hold up."

Formal greetings, introductions, and small talk plagued the background: meet Mr. and Mrs. so and so, President this, Prime Minister that.

Bazzo joined at the end, "Thanks for coming, Professor Burgoyne. Dr. Baker, looking good. King Nephthys, how's your daughter? Just kidding, pleasure to see you, be right in." He pretended to laugh at a bad joke then said, "Can't chat Bridg, business in Swedish country. How much coin ya need?"

"Geez, I don't need dosh, Baz." Turning to one side, Bridget stroked her scarred forehead again. "I think the gov's on my tail. Can ya come get me?" AC's chill sent shivers down her arms. She climbed onto the bed and pulled her legs in to rest her head on them. The sunset had painted a brilliant orange and magenta layer across a cumulus cloud cluster's underbelly. "It's a long story," she finally said and let loose the secret weapon. A baby voice, the one that had often worked to get her what she wanted. "C'mon, I haven't asked you for a thing in five years."

"We haven't talked in five years, ya arsehole," Bazzo retorted in a higher pitch, then went down to a whisper, "I'll see what I can do."

BAZZO SPARKS
Campbell Recovery Center, Ft. Miami, Florida

"WHADDYA MEAN she's not allowed visitors!" Bazzo Sparks shouted. "She rang me, and I moved my whole week around to get here!"

"I'm sorry, sir," the young male nurse said. "Dr. Campbell says she's not well enough to have company. Come back next week." He left the L-shaped desk to commiserate with a slender woman in floral print scrubs.

"Where's this doc?" he asked.

"I don't know how I'm going to feed my family," the coworker cried, slumping her shoulders for a much-needed hug from her colleague. "We've never had an outage for this long."

The male nurse squeezed her. "I didn't know it spread all the way to Norlando. Cynque news said it was contained."

Lightning's negative charge soaked south Florida's atmosphere. Bazzo smelled it. He thrived on it. Shame to hear another electrical grid had gone down. Bigger shame to hear no one had done a thing about it. The rumor was that the state's engineers weren't paid a reasonable wage to keep up and the Coast Guard's engineers were for major disaster relief, not day to day labor. He glowered. When lightning struck there, it struck hard, and the people paid for it.

He looked around. No patients in the waiting room. No security guards. His eyebrow raised. Bingo. Tall guy in a white coat. The nurses still preoccupied, he moseyed toward the stately individual engrossed in a CynqueT.

The nurse sprang from behind the desk. "Sir, you aren't allowed to—"

"It's okay, Nurse Graves," the man interrupted and spun to face Bazzo. Creases filled his tight smile's corners, eyelids stretched taut above his twitching cheek. "I'd be happy to help, Mr....?"

"Sparks. Mr. Sparks." Bazzo squinted, chin nodding upward, and asked, "You good, mate?"

The doctor smiled wider and replied, "Yes, Mr. Sparks. Thank you for asking."

On the tablet were Bridget's full name and blood work results. The man, labeled Dr. Campbell via electronic name tag, tucked his propriety work behind him. "Who were you asking for?"

Bazzo invoked his expensive etiquette training. "I'm here to see Bridget Sparks. Please."

"Oh, I apologize. Ms. Sparks can't have visitors."

"Look, yank, don't be a dickhead. I'm bloody knackered," Bazzo blurted out, "I just need to get the bill sorted and we'll be on our way."

Dr. Campbell's enthusiastic inflections sank into a calm, even depth. "No need to rush, Bazzo, we have plenty of time."

"How'd you know my—"

Snake's hissing or insect's buzzing, either sound described molecular mist treading through air.

"C'mon, Giro, using my fam to get to me? You could've sent me a meeting request like the old days." His hand opened and electric bolts darted across the ceiling, brightening the overhead lights. Dr. Campbell crouched, arms shielding his body.

Hot grease sizzling in a fryer described the mist's elimination. "What are you talking about?!" Dr. Campbell exclaimed, still crouched. "Who is Giro?!"

The light trick worked.

Nurse Graves and two female workers ran to help the doctor stand. Dr. Campbell appeared normal again, flustered, but his features had relaxed. "Don't worry about me," he said to his employees. "Make sure the generator wasn't damaged. If we lose power again... "

"If ya lose power again you'd have to call it quits on this dump." Bazzo grabbed Dr. Campbell's lapel. "I can either charge the hospital generator, or drain it. Where's Bridget Sparks?"

Dr. Campbell declined the onlooking staff's suggestion to phone the authorities, reiterated the importance of keeping the power on, and dismissed them to their tasks.

"It's plenty of trouble keeping this place running as it is." He gave Bazzo a stern look, said, "Take her, I'll delete the records," then exited in a flurry.

His baby sister stumbled into the lobby's flickering fluorescent light. "You made it!"

"What in the bloody hell are you wearing!"

Her open mouth twisted to a grin. "Still over protective, ay?"

"Piss off. Get some clothes on and meet me out front. You're coming with."

———

A tuxedoed driver carted them to the airport in Bentley's fifth anniversary hydrogen-core-powered model. Spaceship, grey exterior, black leather interior. Bazzo and Bridget weren't born or raised in luxury, so his silver spoon had taken getting used to. Thoroughly acquainted, he opened a sparkling alkaline water.

The curious girl he'd taught to fish drew her knees onto the cushion to face him. "Hmm, an even bigger bastard than before, by about twenty centimeters," Bridget said, sizing him up. "Ya went out and made a man of yourself."

Twenty-eight years old. Tailored, Tom Ford suit in navy. Sun baked blonde hair gelled and combed over. Solid gold Cynque. He sank in the seat. "Yeah, yeah. It's just stuff."

Yelling matches with their mother and mental instability stemming from her electric powers drove Bridget to abandon the family at eighteen. From the night their powers arrived, him nineteen, her seventeen, to the moment she slammed the screen door proclaiming she'd "never be back as long as she lived," his sister had gone from a scrawny, awkward girl to the shape and self-assurance of an older brother's worst nightmare. Somehow wanting to be a biologist became living the fast life in Sydney, bouts of prolonged drug and alcohol abuse, plus weekend shifts at a strip club.

"You seem better, stable," he said.

She stared at her ice blue heels. "Takin' it day by day."

Chipped nail polish, semi-permanent scars on her face, a criminal record. They'd gone in opposite directions. He tried to swallow the lump in his throat. "Been a wicked few months for you?"

"Years." Bridget's chin dipped to her crop top's high collar. "Wicked few years. I done some terrible thi—"

"Bridg," he interrupted, "I been looking for ya, 'bout a year now. Mum got real sick, wanted to heal things up between you two. Ya know, before..."

"She alright?"

"Takin' it day by day," he mocked. An electric spark darted over his lashes.

Sniffling, she said, "Five years is heaps of time to not talk."

"You were hard to reach, and I don't mean that as a dig."

Over that five years he'd launched a comprehensive private investigation on his dime, adamant about her whereabouts. The Feds shut it down months later, assuring him his sister wasn't missing, she was taken care of. Disliking the answer, he contacted the last people who'd seen her: old party friends in New York and Los Angeles, the owner of the strip club where she'd worked. Dead ends. Literally. Overdoses, suicides, homicides. So tragic and so easy to cover up.

Bazzo gazed at well-watered palm trees through tinted windows. "I knew about the Andromeda Project, didn't know you were in the mix. My boss clued me in. Also said he'd kill mum himself if I did anything to jeopardize the deal."

"Mum or me? No brainer really."

"Had to pick my battles for sure, but, I made Mr. B promise they'd treat you right."

"Alert: Florence Belladonna has used Cynque device 5684," his Cynque announced.

He sat up. "Show me where."

"Here you go, Mr. Sparks," it replied, opening the map to her last tracked coordinates location.

Close. She must've collected his gift.

"Urgent update: the Swedish president counter-signed the agreement," the device said, then asked, "Is the wire approved for four million euros?"

"Yes, send to the Swedish National Bank from account ending in 2261."

"Right away, Mr. Sparks." It buzzed. "Transaction complete."

"No U-generator for Sweden."

He unbuttoned a third button on the white dress shirt and wiped his sopping forehead using the jacket sleeve. In the car's cool 70-degree temperature, his posh demeanor overheated and unraveled.

"What's on with you?" She side-eyed his Cynque and said, "You're acting, weird."

Damn right. He'd penetrated the elite 0.1 percent, a society gated by wealth, status, and association, governing the world and its complicated operations. Socioeconomically, it was the least safe place to be, on the radar. Car bomb attempts to sniper attacks at five-star accommodations to poison in expensive champagne to beautiful armed women. Day in and day out he fluctuated somewhere between invigorated and terrified. Wealth, like magic, had come with a price. And shame on his Bond complex for the willingness to take on its dangers and its perks.

His enemies' failure, he chalked up to laziness. The organizations and individuals threatened by his rhetoric hadn't done their research. Catching the champagne was dumb luck. The other attempts were futile when his power detected anything in a five-mile radius using or producing electricity. Imagine the rhythmic time bomb's ticking or the heart's electrical system. A sniper or assassin's heartbeat had a distinguished crescendo as the time to pull the trigger, or make the kill approached. He knew every note like Mozart's *Symphony No. 40 in G Minor*.

Goosebumps raised the hair on his arms. "Get down!" he exclaimed.

A bullet ripped through the front windshield and the driver's skull, killing him, and exited the rear windshield. The Bentley lost minimal speed and veered onto a semi-crowded sidewalk. Its digital control dashboard blinked red warnings, noting the car's proximity to moving subjects and inanimate objects. The vehicle computer searched for a source of reliable information to correct its driving pattern.

"Navigation disengaged. Please re-engage Cynque for navigation capabilities," it warned. Verification for the steering mechanism popped up. Five illuminated green circles in the shape of a hand for fingerprint scanning and one illuminated square underneath for the Cynque.

Bazzo stretched his left arm around the slumped driver to align his wrist against the square. Each time the car went over a bump, he grimaced and Bridget covered her ears, neither of them knowing whether it was a civilian or something less gruesome. Such obstacles forced the car to give up more speed as he struggled to gain its trust.

"Please pair Cynque for auto-navigation," the computer squawked.

"Hurry!" Bridget shouted, tapping him, "Those idiot folks in line aren't moving!"

"Please pair Cynque for auto-navigation," it repeated, with similar, heightened urgency.

The Bentley continued to move at damage-inducing speeds. Approaching drivers honked. Car tires screeched. Frightened people yelled. Unfolding havoc muffled by sound suppressing windows.

Bazzo peeked above the dashboard and scoured the sidewalk ahead. Dozens of desperate citizens stood in their path, waiting in a line at Fort Miami's primary shelter. For food. For supplies. He prepared his conscience for human bodies' impact and blood splatter in the event he failed to connect to the system in time.

"You've got to be fucking kidding." He turned sideways, giving his arm the ability to extend, and wiggled his wrist. "C'mon Cynque."

A red beam zipped left to right scanning his device. "Pairing, Bazzo Sparks," it said, then confirmed, "Welcome, Bazzo Sparks. Please scan finger—" He flipped his hand and held it out in front of the glowing finger shaped circles. "Fingerprint scan confirmed. Engaging navigation."

"Baz!"

"Oi!" Bazzo jerked his hand to the right.

The wheels obeyed his instruction. Their car swerved, jumped the curb and missed colliding with stalled traffic and the block-long hoard of poverty-stricken Floridians. Bazzo reached over the dead driver and opened the door. "Sorry, mate," he said. Clicking the seatbelt off, he shouldered the body out onto the pavement and scrambled into the driver's seat.

"Engage self-driving measures, Mr. Sparks?" Cynque asked after he slammed the door.

"It's a bit late for that, ya reckon!" He ruffled his hair, then steadied his ten fingertips and leveled them to operate the digital steering wheel.

"I knew they'd come after me," Bridget said. "I shouldn't've dragged you into this."

"Ha, they're not coming for you. They're here for me."

———

Bridget Sparks

Bazzo turned off the rearview monitor, ignoring the blameless lives the self-driving car had taken and the unprovoked damage it had done, both of which called for their acknowledgement, and their apologies. He shunned Bridget's occasional muttering and anxious swaying and unanswerable questions.

"The self-driving measure should've auto-engaged," Bazzo said quietly. "Blasted trigger is hardwired."

The Bentley's interior distortion was but a glimpse into what must've been the alarming remnants of its frame. Irate onlookers bombarded the sidewalk, Cynque's to their mouths, undoubtedly giving testimonies and their car's description to law enforcement. For the second time Bridget was a moving suspect, expecting sirens as she tallied up casualties.

"Are you good?" he asked her, coming out of shock and easing into denial.

Bridget nodded.

"Good. It's no one's fault, got it? Don't let that rubbish in ya head."

She picked at her nail polish and nodded again. "Ok."

"It's no one's fault," he repeated.

The ambiguous "they" trying to kill her brother nagged at her. "Are you a fugitive?" she asked.

Bazzo smirked. "Cynque tells me I'm a CEO, but yeah, me and the yank gov been on delicate terms as of late. I'm not sure that's what we're dealin' with."

As if to answer, four blacked-out Suburban SUVs zigzagged lane to lane, cutting off vehicles to intercept them.

"And we are takin' the freeway." Bazzo slammed on the brakes and rotated his right hand clockwise. Virtually connected, the digital wheel turned underneath it, spinning them one hundred and eighty degrees.

Her body hurtled across the backseat. Her spine hit the deformed passenger door.

"I'd strap in if I were you," he said.

She blew her hair out of her face. "No shit."

Their perilous drive needed her brother's full and undivided attention. They drove on the right side of traffic, and the wrong side of traffic, steering clear of head on collisions with quick acceleration and sharp turns. She hauled herself onto the chair as two SUVs snuck from the rear on either side. Agents leaned out their windows, toting energy guns she'd seen at the Andromeda Project.

Hands by her ears, she ducked, screaming Bazzo's name as plasma blasted the window, showering her and the backseat with hot glass and molten car chassis. The agents sped up.

Their gun barrels obtained a clear shot at Bazzo's skull. With an erratic wheel twist to the left, the Bentley rammed the adjacent

Suburban. It swerved, drove up the central divider, and flipped on its roof.

"Just like in the movies," Bazzo said, flexing his fingers and pushing them forward. The car accelerated and he repeated the same twisting action to the other side. The second SUV carrying armed agents was crushed in a concrete divider and Bentley sandwich and left in a spinning frenzy.

The Bentley's exterior held. Bridget's sanity, did not. Shrieking carried her clambering over the arm rest and into the passenger seat.

"Hey, hey, it's gonna be alright, trust me," he soothed. His mouth tightened, jaw muscles bulged above the bone. Currents danced across his knuckles.

The third SUV's engine shut off mid-intersection, and a bus tore through it. Bridget exhaled, curled toward the arm rest, and peered through the rear window. Big, expensive mess to clean up for a city with a lot of other big messes to clean up.

Fort Miami's silver blurred in open highway. She assumed they'd run into a river of never-ending brake lights, but there weren't cars crammed in bumper-to-bumper traffic on a weekday afternoon. Unusual for a substantial metropolitan.

"I lost my powers," she said.

"Sis," he started, gripping her ankle and shaking, "y'ave gotta learn to let go of the self-hate and embrace who ya are. Stop fighting it, it's part of ya."

Easier said. Her throat dried up.

"Ya been out here on your own long enough." He returned his hand to the wheel. "We gotta to stick together."

"Mr. Sparks," his Cynque said through the car's speaker, "Dr. Belladonna's flight path has new destin—"

"Pull it up," he interrupted.

"Fort Miami executive airport is the final destination," it said. "Shall I update the navigation?"

"Don't ask dumb shit, Cynque. Take us to Dr. B."

"Navigation updated."

"I had three tasks given to me by my boss on his deathbed." He lowered his voice. "Number one: rewrite the Belladonna will to include his oldest daughter; number two: find her."

"In two miles," it interjected, "take exit 8A for Better Boulevard, then keep right."

"And three?" Bridget asked.

Bazzo switched lanes and turned to her. "Make sure Rabia Giro doesn't—"

Forty tons of falling metal crashed onto the street.

Succeed, Bazzo had said. Muted by her sharp cry as she reached over and whipped his arm to dodge the fiery aftermath of an exploded Mack truck. They careened toward the vacant highway's shoulder. Loud and harsh, the Bentley's tires squealed to a stop.

"Christ," she said and let go. "Pay attention."

"I asked ya to strap in."

She buckled the seatbelt and covered her mouth. No matter how unnatural the occurrence, neither was keen to ask the other where the eighteen-wheeler had come from. Bazzo straightened the wheels to drive forward. Bizarre quiet inside and outside, magnified the sound of them kicking up gravel as he picked up speed along the shoulder. He tapped his knee, looking up every so often.

"Somethin' ain't right," he said. "Keep 'em open."

They merged onto the main road and resumed their getaway. The stone overpass ahead appeared innocent. Its rusted steel railings protected a row of dirty cars parked parallel and single file. She raised an eyebrow at the sporty Honda civic from the early 2020's. Guessed the make and model of the previous years' BMW i15. Their family had purchased a caravan model Prius, which came next, but never got around to affording the third generation flying Tesla, the last car in the row. Her gaze drifted higher.

Frantically, she beat her hand on the glove box. "Oh my gawd, oh my gawd, Baz, what is that!"

Backlit by Florida sun, a cloaked figure hovered above them in the sky. Cracks traveled through the bridge's crumbling foundation and the railing snapped, as if squeezed by the hand of God. Laws of Gravity no longer applied to the unoccupied cars lifting into the air.

"Look out!" Bridget screamed and crouched in the seat, expecting any of the abandoned vehicles hurtling toward them to wreck their reunion. Holding herself tighter at each street splitting crash, she mumbled promises to heaven of all the good things she'd do if her powers returned to save them. *Boom!* The Bentley skidded left. *Boom!* The Bentley swerved right.

She opened her eyes to the red Honda's hood crunching against the road in front of them. *Kaboom!* It blew up. The Bentley jerked left. Flames bum rushed the passenger side. Bridget twisted away and their car's equilibrium failed.

Bazzo leaned his full weight to the center, shouted, "Sit still, will ya!" and pushed her, so as to lend the extra weight to his effort. Abrasive maneuvers to keep the Bentley, which rocked back into place, on four wheels. Bridget gripped the door handle in one hand and her brother's arm in the other.

The creature landed on the interstate, surrounded itself with energy, and spread its arms to each side. Unavoidable in every sense of the word, the unleashed energy wave barreling toward them covered eight lanes of highway.

Bazzo took his hand off the accelerator. "Hold tight," he insisted and pulled them lower.

The blue inferno's deafening rumble warned of scattered automobiles and uprooted asphalt, of its nigh fatal impact. She cringed, bracing herself for—

Her involuntary screams. Her weightless body. Her lungs contracting with such speed the air had no chance for escape.

They tumbled backward mid-air, until the roof touched her head too hard, smashed in on brief but violent contact with the road. Gravity returned, using her body's one hundred and thirty pounds as justification to throw her around the interior.

Bridget strained to keep her grip on the door, on her life, and on Bazzo's sleeve, as the Bentley rolled over itself, propelled by the reversed force of the speed it'd been driving.

———

Bazzo Sparks

Demolished metal car frames had further demolished their metal car frame. Sweltering air from the engine's recent combustion rushed through the windowless rectangle.

Throbbing above Bazzo's chest, beside his neck stalled any immediate movement. Shooting pain arched shoulder blade to clavicle. The nerves screamed at the slightest pressure, even when intended to assist their escape.

If the neurons would stop bloody firing, he thought.

Placing his right hand near his left shoulder, his lips formed an "O" as he exhaled. The bone pushed back from light coercion and he counted down in silence from 10, and got to 4, 3, 2—in a gut-wrenching snap, the bone returned to its socket. His murderous scream dwindled to, "Ahhhh, mother fu—" as he clenched his jaw, squeezed his eyes shut, and rocked. "Stop bloody firing," he pleaded. His brain listened to him, as anything run on electricity would, and his pain's intensity level subsided to moderate.

Bridget's head dangled upside down, parallel to his. The roof so close that her tangled, short hair spread across the felt fabric ceiling. His capable arm unbuckled his seatbelt. His spine scraped millions of tiny glass fragments as he slid onto his back. He unbuckled Bridget, straining the less battered half of his body to cradle her on the shallow drop down. Bazzo grasped her torso and hoisted her through the driver's window. They spilled next to the car.

He situated her on the pavement to search for physical injuries. Above her now fattened, black eye, the sewn-up wound had been busted open. "Wake up," he urged, "c'mon, wake up." He moved her bangs from the bleeding mess.

Whoom. The car flipped over them and squashed to obsolescence against concrete. He cowered, pressed to his sister's motionless body. It missed his head by an inch. Rotating his neck, he analyzed the assailant. Whoever or whatever the creature was had feminine curves and an irregular heartbeat, scratch that, heartbeats, plural.

If scared or startled, the woman might've slowed her pace and spoken, to diffuse the hostility churning between them. She advanced, patient and predatory, face concealed. An emblem flickered in the sunlight.

The reflective patch on the cloak's collar read C, and a smaller patch next to it read, 20. Together they spelled C20.

"I always end up working on the weekends," Bazzo said. He concentrated on the powerlines, and they answered his invocation, as anything run on electricity would. Crackling with immense voltage, his palm outstretched. Jagged electric lines surrounded his legs, trotted up his torso, and morphed him into hissing white currents.

Concentrated bolts slammed into the woman, flashing up and out like lightning forking through clouds. She slid away from them.

Bazzo grunted. "Need more juice."

Planting her feet on the asphalt, she pushed her hands out and, halting backward motion, walked against his electric force.

His weakened veins constricted, parched of their power. The electricity sizzled to steam. He frowned and squatted next to Bridget, who stirred.

"Baz, what's happening?"

"Remember how I said they're here for me?"

She nodded, wearily accepting his hand and rising with him to her feet.

"Good, now get outta here."

"I can't leave you, we just—"

"Bridget... Sparks?" the woman asked, disregarding their skirmish to approach her. "The electric goddess. I am not supposed to remember you. How is this possible?"

"Hold on a tick. Now whatever problems are between us stay between us." He moved his sister behind him and glimpsed the purple complexion under the hood. "Zosma?"

Helicopter blades beat the air. Again, the woman exercised indifference towards him, swiveled, and zoomed to challenge the newfound interference.

"Go home, Bridg," he said, turning to her. "It's time."

Bridget wrapped him in a hug, whispered, "I'll see you there," and took off running on a slight hobble.

An earful of monstrous, earth shattering booms divided his attention. Boeing AH-72 helicopter's 30mm revolver cannons unloaded their rounds. Airborne, Zosma somersaulted over herself, alien armor glistening like a blessing from Apollo, C20 cloak blown to rags. She slowed her rearward flight, and when the cannon fired again, a telekinetic bubble thwarted its intention.

C20 had outdone themselves. White uniformed agents descended concrete sound barriers in pairs. They configured themselves as a defensive line and scurried across the freeway, shooting forearm-affixed plasma weapons skyward. The AH-72's disbanded and circled out of firing range.

"Baz!" Bridget yelled.

A trio of agents carried her, heels kicking, to a hovering stealth grey aircraft whose four underside thrusters gushed heat and fire. He thought she'd made it to the brush. He thought she'd made it to safety.

"Your nomen knowledge yields no mercy. I have been ordered to end your life," Zosma said. Her voice was flat and heartless to a degree he felt certain she had no personal feelings about him whatsoever.

"That's a kicker, 'cause I was ordered to save yours," he said.

Projectile shrapnel sped at him. One-handed, he flipped. It missed.

Zosma's attack remained incessant, resolute. Employing molecular manipulation, she sculpted sharpened swords, knives, and spears out of dislodged bumpers and stray engine parts within eyesight, and telekinetically hurled them at Bazzo. Flipping the same direction to avoid becoming impaled, Bazzo's legs touched the air, and a concerned peek toward Bridget made his twist too shallow. A jagged metal hubcap sliced him at the ribs as he rounded the turn. He landed on his feet, sagged to his knees, then spat on the pavement.

He scanned the battlefield. They loaded his sister up the aircraft ramp. The hatch closed. Thrusters ignited.

And he wasn't out of the woods, yet. Warm blood stained his white shirt. His fingers slipped through the clean rip in the cotton and checked the wound for tenderness. Skin-deep, thanks to electromagnetic reflex. He flinched when skin touched skin and abandoned the activity to watch the triangular shape shrink into high altitude. Mum would never forgive him if his sister died in his custody.

Electricity sparked around his trembling fist. "Bring her back," he said angrily, teetering upright. "Make them bring her back."

"I do not know her fate," Zosma said. "I do, however, know yours."

He didn't think his throat could get any tighter, already constricted by his lack of responsibility, but her rough, three-fingered hands compressed, denying circulation in a telekinetic chokehold.

His hand went limp. His power fizzled out. He moved on to option two.

Blessed by their proximity, knowing his voice wouldn't carry, he sputtered, "Rabia's using you." Asphyxiation won, and the returning helicopter fleet disappeared behind his falling eyelids.

ALLISTER ADAMS
Ft. Miami, Florida

FLORENCE MULLED OVER Allister's question before she'd said, "I don't dig too deep into my father's motivations."

Because why would Giovanni Belladonna need a bullet-proof jet furnished with military-grade weapons? Allister shrugged. It was apparent the knack for acquiring fancy, dangerous toys ran in her family, and wasn't on her mother's side. The closest listed aircraft on the old, inactive Cynque, had collected dust in a Washington, D.C. Air Force hangar. One of ten planes at her beck and call, waiting for action. Wish granted.

Hands flattened on the ceiling, he darted window to window in the cramped cabin. Skyscrapers waded in the dark grey smoke dashing past them.

"Hear that?" he asked.

"P.Hydra 80s, the military's new pride and joy," she said.

P for plasma. Spot on. He'd forgotten that her Harvard University PhD in psychiatry, her blush warmed cheeks, and soft tones were ploys to mask her true love, combat. Martial arts, weapon mastery, and warfare strategy were courses she'd aced through life experiences to earn a PhD in survival.

Where's the fight? he thought.

"They're close," Florence answered, then added, "Sorry. Habit."

"Cut it out, Florence!" The conflict ringing in his ears was replaced by one nerve-racking, bone-rattling *zoom*, then another. Two fighter jets approached on either side. He made his way to the cockpit and sandwiched himself in the archway.

"Incoming transmission from unknown aircraft. Retrieving," Giovanni announced, and read the message aloud: "This is Second Lieutenant Edward Brooks, U.S. Army. You're flying in restricted airspace. Raise altitude now."

"Military clearance level: Top secret, Dr. Florence Belladonna!" she shouted at the CPU. "Send."

A *swoosh* confirmed its transit, and a response came an instant later.

"It seems your clearance level is, in the Lieutenant's words, not valid for this rodeo," Giovanni said. "He has offered you one minute to comply."

"This rodeo? Giovanni, scan for logos, power signatures, and facial recognition." Panels on the wings squeaked, waking from slumber and stood at a slant, increasing the drag. The plane's acceleration slowed. "Hold on," she said to him. "I've never done this before."

Nothing to hold on to, he gulped, fastened his hand to the wall, and rooted his feet in a wide stance.

Panels creaked back to flatten the wings and the aircraft pitched down. The engines roared as she banked left, dove lower, then straightened out to accelerate between a set of high rises. She banked right, looped around the buildings they'd passed, and fired off a string of obscenities. The plane rolled on its axis as she whipped them into an evasive turn to dodge rapid fire. They flew at a vertical angle through two buildings married by a mezzanine floor. A space narrower than he'd estimated. The jet's reinforced titanium armor tore at the buildings' concrete exteriors and shattered their glass windows as it soared to the crux of battle.

If Second Lieutenant what's his face had followed them, their thunderous journey would've masked the pursuing aircraft's demise.

Stomach turned inside out, Allister rested on the first plush seat he came into contact with.

"Scanning. Logo identified: C20. Logo identified: U.S. Army," Giovanni said. "Power signature identified: Bazzo Stephen Sparks. Power signature identified: Zosma Caster."

"Zosma..." He staggered to the plane's rear exit. Heeled boots thumped after him.

Florence touched his shoulder. "Allister, opening the escape hatch will destabilize the cabin pressure."

"Then close it the second I'm out," he snapped and bent over to look for her. His mind one place, his feelings a separate place than that, neither vying for reason nor patience. "I-I have to get to her. It's my only chance."

Not too high above an eight-lane freeway, Zosma levitated, engaged in aerial confrontation with five circling helicopters. The U.S. army emptied their M265 launchers. Plasma-core-infused warheads whistled through the air. Queasiness in his stomach bubbled to fury as they detonated. An energy ring backlashed, demolishing the surrounding surface with concussive force and a rising ash cloud swelled where Zosma had been floating.

Their altitude fell. The jet rattled. He snagged Florence by the arm to avert her fall, gave her a firm look and said, "You remember the Middle East? If they keep this up, she's gonna go nuclear."

"Fine." Florence turned and said to the computer, "Giovanni, find somewhere to put us down."

His fist pounded the hatch release. It cranked down. Wind stormed the cabin amongst earsplitting sirens and Giovanni's nagging alerts. On his back, he slid to the platform's end, steadied his feet on the sharp edge and catapulted into the atmosphere like a skydiver.

Burned vegetation and petroleum engulfed him in a *whoosh*, and the helicopter's rotating blades sliced louder and louder and louder as they got closer and closer and closer.

The two pilots inside evacuated the instant his body crushed the snout. Thin air in the troposphere and the impact left him winded. The helicopter spun out and nosedived. He dug his fingers into cast iron and aluminum to keep from slipping, and rode the spiraling contraption downward. It'd looked so much easier when superheroes did it.

Less than a minute from impact, he leaped off, curled into himself, and hit the street sideways. Nervous about his equilibrium, Allister situated his feet on the highway, staying crouched to yell, "Zosma!" Tumbling induced nausea called for a breather. When it passed, he finished, "I've been looking for you."

Three elements able to withstand the exorbitant heat of nuclear fusion; iron, nickel, and silicon had been mined from a blue giant star's core, forged into Zosma's Uragonian battle armor, and doused in a 24k gold coat.

She glided to him wearing a hardened scowl, cast in the muted Z-energy's blue. "Why have you been looking for me?"

"I... because..." His heart squeezed life from his vocal chords. "I was worried."

"Did you have some idol fantasy imagined about our union?" The sweetness in her voice and its melodious inflections were treasures lost in manufactured words spewing from a robot. "I am saving this planet. I am saving your people. Dr. Giro has told me my power can stop what promises to be the end of the human race."

"He's lying to you, he has to be." Allister trekked to her, rapt in her amethyst skin's smoothness. He took her hand, traced her fingers. "Please," he pleaded, "listen to me. Stay here. We can help you. I can help you break free."

Her slanted eyes straightened. The mean grey color in them, the cloudy grey belonging to Dr. Giro's power, dissolved. She blinked at their mingling anatomy and guided his coarse, soiled palm to her face. "I fear I am not myself."

Though poisoned by Dr. Giro's influence on the inside, her intoxicating scent had endured. The chemicals in Earth's atmosphere interacted with Zosma's epidermal cells to produce a blend similar to warmed honey, lemon, and ginger.

Thumping boots on the pavement broke their embrace. Zosma pushed him out of harm's way and a thin field reflected plasma blasts back at the charging U.S. soldiers. Darkness and frustration returned to her brow. "I come to kill the heathen who seeks to sabotage their survival and they attack me?" she bellowed, hovering higher. "I suppose even the ungrateful must be saved." At sonic speed, she ditched lowered altitude and vanished beyond the afternoon's blue.

"Look what you did!" he snarled at the soldiers. "She was telling me about C20!" He squatted on his toes, hands together in faux prayer and pressed to his lips. Deep breaths cooled his body and returned him to center. "I was so close."

"Were you?" A deep, sarcastic voice asked.

Veiled in none other than Hunter Steele's burly shadow. "Yeah, I was," Allister snapped. "Surprised you're here. Last I heard they fired you."

"Last I heard they put you in time-out." Hunter's glare dissolved into a painful grimace. Metal crept across his knuckles, twisting up to his biceps. Fully equipped, his arm peeled back.

Allister thrust his chest out and pulled his arms back, preparing for the detective's swing.

"Hey, mate, leave 'im alone," a man said in an Australian accent.

"If it isn't my favorite CEO, Bazzo Sparks. How you been ole' buddy?" Hunter asked, never taking his eyes off of Allister.

"I'll be better when Dr. B tears you a new one," he spat.

The Belladonna's defense jet purred as it descended to the street, where it was welcomed by a sea of upended vehicles and military personnel. Down the hatch Florence marched, sword hitched to her waist, doing her best to hide irregular strides in a leather one-piece. Allister and Hunter sidelined their brewing physical altercation.

"Detective Steele, what's going on here?" she asked. "I have orders from the president—"

"I have orders too, sweetheart," Hunter jeered, "from the director of National Intelligence, the Secretary of Defense, the Secretary of Foreign Affairs." He motioned to the soldiers and their weapons aimed to injure. "You coming the easy way or the hard way?"

"I make one call and you'll be on Cynqued jobs by morning." Inches from his face Florence poked his metal chest. "This can't be your jurisdiction."

"Really?" His hands spread to the destruction around them. "Superhuman sightings? Alien refugee gone rogue? C20 on state soil? I think it is. Let's face it; you three already look like shit. So how about just surrender."

Armed air tanks aimed at them. A good hundred troops, decorated in varied ranks, ached to prove themselves. A two-mile-wide perimeter barricaded by the Coast Guard hadn't allowed civilians, media, firefighters, or law enforcement to breach it.

"We'll go!" Allister said. "We'll go with you. As long as I get a private meeting with President DeVries."

Florence twirled around and whispered to him, "What do you think you're doing?"

"And you can escort us," he continued, cracking his neck, then his knuckles. "But we take the jet."

"Are you loony?" the man named Bazzo protested too loud.

"He's smart." Hunter smiled. "Smarter than both of you, at least. You heard him ladies and gents, we're heading to Chicago." He pointed two fingers at his eyes and at them. "I'm keeping an eye on the hardware." The detective retreated to a squad transport utility helicopter and hollered, "You'll get your meeting, kid. Don't you worry!"

"I hope you know what you're doing Allister," Florence mumbled.

"I have no idea. I'm just taking a page outta your book and playing by their rules."

———

U.S. Airspace

Padded yellow leather cushions made the ride a tad more comfortable than the cabin's stuffy atmosphere. Allister slouched in a rear-facing seat, adamant about existing in silence. Bazzo's back was to him. Florence rode in the cockpit, unwilling to discuss the fallout.

Zosma's initial reaction to his arrival stung something vicious. A black hole opened in his heart, and upon its collapse, he crumpled the chair's arm. "Sorry," he muttered to no one. He loosened his grip, attempted to reshape it, and gave up in the absence of Florence's outrage. The aluminum had been crinkled beyond repair.

The nerve, asking why he'd looked for her when the reasons were clear as day. Because they'd spent two weeks traveling across Europe living in sexual bliss and emotional freedom. Because they'd learned about the Earth and its beauty in unison. Because during their last encounter she underwent a traumatizing transformation from human (Leesa) to Uragonian. Because he'd transported them to space, to save her and the Earth. Because he'd lost her and felt responsible. Because her eye color haunted him.

Brandt didn't lie to him during their skirmish in Cumberland Falls. Zosma was alive. Not just alive, she was living, breathing, speaking, flying. To inhale the smell of hot tea on a winter morning, to perceive the cosmos through round shivering windows, to feel ten thousand degrees of desire, and to hear words spoken with otherworldly inflection. Proof Brandt didn't lie. When her white cape became undistinguishable among Florida's puffy cumulus clouds, he knew he'd given up too soon. He could've done more to make her stay, or at least done more to help her remember Dr. Giro's treachery. But what better way to make Earth her new home than to help power the generators and save the planet? Dr. Giro had given her purpose, and it occurred to Allister that she craved purpose more than pleasure.

Cheeks tickled by the brief instant where her touch was all that mattered, his Adam's apple bobbed in his throat and tinkering fingers agitated the disfigured metal. His hand yanked to his lap.

"You must be Allister, heard a lot about ya," the Australian man said. "Name's Bazzo."

Turning his head at snail's speed, Allister replied, "Yeah. I know who you are." His elbow fastened to the window sill, and he wedged his chin between his thumb and forefinger, peering down at deteriorating Midwestern states.

Bazzo hastily switched chairs to sit beside him. Though his right eye had been decorated in purples and blacks, he seemed intent on staring a hole through Allister's temple.

"What?" Allister asked.

"She was sent here to off me, ya know." Bazzo unveiled an ice pack and pressed it to his eye. "Doctor's orders."

"Why would Dr. Giro want you dead?"

"I know heaps about C20. And I'm telling my business mates not to invest in his technology." He wiped scum off his brown dress shoes and squashed his tousled hair against the window. "They took Bridg. Guess we both got skin in the game."

Allister rotated the hoodie strings in his dry fingertips. "Guess so," he said.

"You knew her well?"

"Well enough."

Florence swept past them and took the chair opposite Bazzo. "Bridget's one of the strongest superhumans I've ever treated, she'll hold up alright."

"Whatever ya say, Dr. B."

She kneaded her hands, pulled at the armpits of the skintight jumpsuit, and tapped the psiborg metal; Allister hadn't seen her nervous before.

"Ya can ask me anything," Bazzo said.

"Don't know where to start," she mumbled.

The Aussie did. Two years into a gig at an investment firm, he'd been pitched an acquisition by well-known business vulture Giovanni Belladonna. Some artificial intel startup he had been trying to offload. Bazzo, whiz that he was, ran the numbers and voted "strong pass."

"So, he did the psychic thing, and, long story short, I don't like blokes in my head." He chuckled, then moaned. "Must've liked the fight in me, 'cause he gave me an offer a week later."

"Adorable story, however..." She bent her head and let hair fall over her eye. "I was referring to our recent investments and your position at Belladonna Corp."

"Ah... the Andromeda Project and C20. That's a tale if I ever told one."

Bazzo's tale was as informative and action-packed as promised.

The Andromeda Project's operating output had surpassed available cash flow and Giovanni's silent partnership in 2047 plugged holes in a capsized ship. An embarrassing detail, considering the organization pooled its initial funding round from six founding countries and began their quest somewhere around 2030.

"Yeah, Mr. B was late to the game, but after fifteen years they had a lead on the Transporter gems. And the payout on those... whew. I never seen so many zeros."

"Pfft. Why're they worth so much?" Allister asked, plucking one. "They don't do anything."

A defensive lie. He didn't know how to do anything with them. There were endless applications of drawing on such power: deconstructing matter and sending it elsewhere, voyaging to other worlds and galaxies, eliminating human waste off world. Varied use cases for the same eventual outcome: humanity's exodus from their dying planet.

All promising notions had been thought through and discussed in real time. According to Bazzo, the Transporter gems became a pipe dream. C20's directors, Aleksander Karjavine of Russia, Jane Wenyin of Korea, and Chung Tae-Won of China, were working both sides of the coin, and approached Giovanni to head off the Andromeda Project's impending failures. They believed Rabia Giro would be the one to save humanity, and he'd do it using the Z-energy. Bazzo advised his boss not to put all the eggs in one basket, when said basket (the Andromeda Project) was sinking.

Allister reversed his posture. He leaned over the aisle, buried his other elbow in the knee farthest from the window, kept his arm upright, and wedged his chin between his forefinger and thumb. "Hmmm, what else?"

Bazzo tossed a hand in the air, waving it to and fro. "It was a free-for-all, no rules, no commitment. I sent the first wire, I reckon twenty million? Pennies in the grand scheme. A month passes, these dipsticks are going on 'bout wanting to build another base, wouldn't tell us where. Asked for more zeros, exclusivity, non-disclosure, non-compete. We said no." He sat up and lowered the ice pack. "They pushed and pushed. Me being me, I set up a where-the-fuck-is-my-money-going meeting. Mr. B wanted to know the end game."

"My father and Dr. Giro met in person?" Florence asked.

"Right-o. Twelve weeks ago? Irony, I tell ya. A scammer getting scammed." Bazzo scratched his head. "Point is, Mr. B wasn't keen on the plans to quote, 'rescue humanity,' and he... " He tapped his temple. "... Dr. Giro's mind."

"I don't think anyone knew he was a telepath."

"They still don't. He took that one to the grave." Bazzo shook his head solemn-like, and added, "Ya dad came back shook up, swore on your life about a deeper meaning to the Z-energy."

She leaped to the seat's edge. "Where'd it leave the company? And the contract? And you?"

"The old man's noggin' never recovered. The contract, handshake deal, wasn't solid. I took over as CEO, found you and told as many peeps as I could the U-generators are a fraud."

"You don't know that," she muttered.

"I know he wouldn't've lied to me."

"You're one of few." Florence flipped her hair and hurried to the cockpit.

Allister stood, chained to the airline seat by his own hand and hesitation, wondering whether to comfort her or let the tantrum run its course.

"Think you know who to trust?" Bazzo called at her back, "Ask DeVries about the meeting in Milan with ya dad."

———

BRIDGET SPARKS
C20 Prison

WARMTH ESCAPED BRIDGET'S BONES like secrets she couldn't keep. Her knees curled to her forehead. She wanted to be whisked to the safe place under her bed, a beloved hiding spot whenever her parents argued over whose turn it was to make dinner, or whose fault it was they'd had superhuman children. Her esophagus twisted in knots, and she evoked her more pleasant childhood memories.

Running through fields on their parents' farm. When Bazzo had taught her how to swim. When he'd taught her how to surf.

Their first family road trip. Dry and stinging, her eyes popped open for the fifth time.

"Baz..." she whispered.

Snippets from their short reunion redrew the purple-skinned woman's vivid silhouette and replayed her unwavering aggression towards Bazzo. She wondered if he was powerful enough to hurt her, or if she'd laid waste to him and the U.S. military in one fell telekinetic swoop. *She called me the electric goddess.*

Once upon a time.

She dabbed her palm on the splitting headache's obvious culprit, the gash in her skull. The absent Cynque meant she didn't exist and couldn't be located, and as each hour passed, the cell felt more and more like a coffin bolted shut.

Confronting lower body numbness and upper body shivers, she trekked toward light penetrating a peephole. If she yelled someone might hear her. If someone heard her it was probably an enemy. Wheezing, she collapsed. Ice-cold chains writhing beneath her pants' fabric compelled her to scoot away.

The door unlatched and opened. Russell Ashur entered, his arms entangled in a thick blanket, his snow pants tucked in his boots. Attempts to grow a beard had resulted in random patches on his round cheeks and the C20 logo on his parka divulged his allegiance. Too cold to shout, powerless to punish him, she stared, waiting for him to speak.

He pointed to her forehead. "Dr. Giro says he's going to fix it."

"Te-tell 'im I-I'm not a f-fan of m-mad sci-sci-science." Her stomach flipped, and rising body temperature paused hypothermia's advance. The thought of the doctor's stubby, hairy fingers coming within a centimeter of her face. Detestable.

She traced the unguarded injury, stewing over what she'd done to Russell and what Russell had done to her. They'd spent months together entwined in a casual sexual relationship. Russell, infatuated by her beauty and electromagnetic awareness, fueled a case for her importance as an Andromeda Project member, not a time bomb to be detonated in battle. Right before the relationship caved in they were on the same page, working toward the same goal. Getting each other's rocks off.

She, snarling like an injured lioness, watched him with a skeptical glare as he dropped, edging closer on his knees. Pinching the blanket's corners, he tossed it on her, then clambered to get up as if she might pounce. Twenty degrees warmer and electrically charged, Russell would've been a crisp carcass.

Eighty degrees of an authentic Outback summer beamed under the blanket, and though wrapped in a cocoon inescapable for her or the heat, not an ounce touched her chilled skeleton.

"I wouldn't stick around to see me warmed up." Her jaw hardened. "I'm planning to slit your throat for what you did."

"You don't mean that," Russell said.

"I meant every bloody word, you bastard." Her brow fell, the shivering returned. "Do you feel important now? Is Rabia bowing at your feet for your genius?"

Russell's remorseful brown eyes flinched behind circular lenses. He rubbed his gloves together and looked every direction except at her.

"What gives? Bringing me here anyhow, my powers shorted out." Her tongue ran across her numbed lips. "I'm sure ya knew that much." She sucked her teeth and kicked the blanket away, hollering, "This thing is shit!"

"I was scared." He bent to meet her at eye level, fought to say his own words, and not someone else's. "You opened up to me, and I got scared."

"G-get out."

"I came because..." he choked. Syllables fluctuated as the words sputtered out. "Because I haven't been myself for a long time."

"Get out!"

"Your powers aren't gone, they've evolved," he muttered, distant, foggy. "He'll be here soon. Fight the influence, if you can. It's everywhere. He's everywhere." Russell scanned open the door. "Thing is, I thought you'd help me get back to who I was. But it's who I was."

Dimness returned. Boots crushed ice between his long strides. An elevator dinged. He'd be back. And she'd repay him for the cold, sharpened statement he'd drilled through her two months prior, "You're nothing to me."

Her heart beat so slow she swore it had stopped. Her body temperature, not a tick above water's freezing point. Halfway to standing, palm flattened against the metal interior, she wailed and fell against the door, seizing and foaming at the mouth like an epileptic. A winter morning's frost spread over her limp arms and legs, and the convulsions lessened to shudders. The elemental outburst distributed ice along the walls, decelerating the air's molecules to a perpetual cloud of condensed moisture.

Breathing returned to normal. Movement belonged to her again. She put her hands up in disbelief. Crystals embedded in pinkish-blue skin refracted even the faintest light.

Her iced soul welcomed patience as she snuggled to one of the prison's corners. The transformation wasn't a secret or a surprise. Russell knew. Dr. Giro knew. A destination for her neural pathway had formed.

———

ZOSMA CASTER
C20 Base
SOARING THE HEAVENS to and from her mission, Zosma witnessed the perilous truth of human existence. Children born into poverty; starving nations; mass migration to lands less susceptible to a

dying world's wrath; and, yet, didn't carry an ounce of sympathy. Appalled by their inherent brutality, she reconsidered saving a people who refused to welcome her. They weren't capable of welcoming each other.

Humans craved Z-energy's purity and, per Rabia's explanation, needed it to survive. *Did they deserve to survive?* she pondered. Plasma canons melted human flesh in a single blast and bombs carried more joules than her incinerating pulses. Z-energy wasn't a gateway to survival. If humans were doomed to destroy themselves, her power would be a catalyst to speeding it up, not slowing it down.

She removed the glimmering tribute to royal heritage on her head and placed it on the crystalline vanity. The reflective oval attached to it reminded her of the "soul speakers" on Uragon, although on her planet they told her things, showed her things. This showed herself. (Self-reflection taught plenty, find anyone who'd tell you different.)

Singed strands in her violet mane, her chin's sharp angles, and the plum of her silken cheeks, delicate beauty oppressed by a hooded cloak. She found perversion in her body's perfection. The upper arm's creamy skin marred by slashes from shrapnel. *Impressive*, she thought. Her skin prickled.

"Allister," she whispered.

Fanged teeth bit her finger as the prickling worsened to burning, and magical Z-energy flames manifested on her skin. The distance between her and her reflection grew. As if the floor had caved, her body zoomed downward into a chasm. She'd expected a painful landing, but woke up in a warm, comforting place.

Joy galloped through her heart at the fresh rain smell, at Uragon's geraniums and irises in bloom. Springing into flight, she rushed to the tower's edge to look at countryside reminiscent of her home planet's elegance.

To the north, rainbow archways, luminous roads, shooting stars, and obscure planetary bodies represented her cosmic knowledge.

And the little red door protected the sacred space from Rabia's influence.

"Welcome," a tender voice said. It was in her skin, on her clothes, in the sky, in the grass. "I brought you here to show you."

Leesa's buoyant words triggered the memory that started it all. Zosma was locked in the castle's tallest tower after declarations of war reached Neight's ears.

Monster. Ender of worlds. Harbinger of apocalypse. The living bomb. An infinite number of names with the same meaning. She remembered the rioters, claiming she would bring about Uragon's ruin. Funny, how when things are put into the universe, they happen. More than a century shrouded in exploitation, violence, and hatred, and, for approximately forty of those years, Zosma had no access to sensory input or output. For all those deaths, and a 2.5-million-light-year expedition, she'd fled far enough to get trapped in her own mind.

"Don't let him separate us," Leesa whispered, "If he does, he'll get in and he'll find them."

"What does Rabia Giro want?"

"Directions. He's looking for the power you have."

The flames sank to her lavender skin, void of sensation. She blinked at her reflection, emotionally unchanged, allowing the dream to be what it was. Shivering followed, not at the cold, it meant nothing to her. Gliding the four-hundred-square-foot living area, she said, "I know you are here, observing me."

Like a genie summoned, pumping steam chopped through her quiet breathing and shot down in a single burst. It spiraled, outlining Rabia Giro on a bed that had never been slept in. "I am here, Princess Zosma," he said.

"Bri—" She detained the name in her throat, a name she wasn't supposed to remember. "The prisoner is in the basement as you requested. I was not able to kill the superhuman you refer to as Bazzo Sparks. I met interference from flying war machines and..." her voice trailed off.

"And?" He rose, like a priest to give a homily, and his forehead wrinkled as he leaned away from the overhead light.

"You dislike light."

"I think light dislikes me."

Rabia's true motives rested on the horizon but would not rise above the mountains and become the mid-morning sun. The hood fell and gathered at her neck as she reached upwards. Long, flat hanging luminaires flickered in response to her attention. "Why is my energy being tested?"

Although shorter than her by inches, his extremities drifted, projecting a shadowy aura. His looming presence stretched to over eight feet. The light fizzled. "You aren't to ask questions, we discuss this. You are here to answer." Rabia turned, standing in direct opposition, and asked, "Why you let Bazzo escape?"

She drew the cloak's extravagance to conceal her face. "I was overpowered. I apologize."

"What is done is done," Rabia scolded. "You will accompany myself and C20 team to Summit demonstration. Is your chance to show world's leaders you are key to saving Earth."

CHAPTER FIVE

Allies & Enemies

WESLEY DEVRIES

The White House, Chicago, Illinois

PRESIDENT WESLEY DEVRIES brooded in the Oval Office. His unflinching eyes were glued to the wall panels feeding him heart-wrenching accounts of imminent doom. Fifteen feet of snow had been dumped on Moscow, a record high. Their news reported thousands without food, water, or power, and hundreds dead. The South Pacific's monsoon had eroded and washed away cement risers along with the villages they were constructed to safeguard. A 7.4 earthquake had struck Naples. The city was unprepared. The body count was astronomical. Hours after, geologists recorded an increase in ground temperature and released images of an ash cloud forming above Mt. Vesuvius's gaping crater.

He muted the surveillance, rested his elbows on his desk and let his head sink into his hands. The duty to protect billions, domestic and abroad, had pulled the last few days' decisions in multiple directions. Pressure from major security agencies, investigative bureaus, and the other government branches—reminded him his personal feelings weren't acceptable.

They'd crossed uncharted territory, dealing with concepts and creatures no one could predict or make logical sense of. No precedents existed. No political prowess could've prepared him. Intuition lugged him from behind the desk.

The entrance to the Oval Office slid sideways. His executive assistant popped her head in. "Mr. President, are you ready to see—"

Florence burst in the room followed by the absolute last person he wanted to see, Bazzo Sparks.

"Wesley Phillip DeVries!" Florence shouted, arms bent at the elbow and swinging with every stride. Her hair bounced behind her.

He gave up trying to swallow and hid his hands in his pockets. The woman he loved pumped toward him, distraught, inconsolable, gorgeous. Give credit to preparation for the casual response, though he didn't have words to back up his body language. She searched for his attention. He knew better, such a connection would demand he speak the truth or deny an accusation. Reveling in silence, he counted the contusions on her body and scabs on her face.

"Don't look at me like that," Florence said, her tone raised and exacting. "I- I can't believe you'd go behind my back and..." Her posture deflated, as if the realization landed on her shoulders. "I keep giving you the benefit of the doubt. I keep making excuses for you."

He succumbed to her request for eye contact. "You're hurt, and I'm not sure where this is coming from. I think you should sit."

"You met my father on his deathbed and you kept it from me."

"Shit."

"That's your answer? You have some nerve."

Wesley told Florence as much of the story as he felt comfortable revealing. He'd known of Giovanni Belladonna as a business mogul and her father. Up until his death the IRS, CIA, and FBI had been after him for fraud, money laundering, offshore accounting, even terrorism.

"I met your father because I had to sideline the investigations. What he knew about C20 and Dr. Giro was more important."

A tricky game that got Wesley impeached. He remembered the twenty-hour interrogation. "You're proposing we halt all pending warrants, subpoenas? Are you protecting America's for-profit business sector or Giovanni Belladonna?" the Speaker of the House had asked.

"The world," he muttered aloud, present day. Such a presidential answer. No wonder the charges were dropped. He looked up and into Florence's eyes. "Florence, please rest, have some water."

"I don't need rest. I need answers." She crossed the room. "What're you going to do now? Belladonna Corp is yours and the charges—"

"Oh, we'll get the estate sorted, DeVries," Bazzo interjected and chuckled. "I been clearin' the books for a couple months, and we paid off outstanding taxes according to the agreement."

Florence tucked a stray curl into her ponytail's smooth sides and asked, "Which was?"

Wesley's hands moved around the trouser pockets. His head went skyward.

"Which. Was," she repeated.

He gritted his teeth and glared at Bazzo.

"Tell her, mate."

"Sure," he conceded, hovered next to the entrance. "Preferably, in private."

He swiped his Cynque. The door opened. Bazzo threw up the peace sign and walked out. It slid closed and clicked to lock.

"You might want to sit down," Wesley offered.

"You might want to start talking," Florence retorted.

Lips curled in, he paced, brushed the desk's edge at each passing, then stopped and faced her, in a trance.

"Florence, don't do this." He resisted her psychic intrusion, burying thoughts, repelling her mental advances. "Once you do, there's no going back."

Deep pink burned around her pupil's edge and consumed her corneas, eyelids, and lashes. They stood forehead to forehead, nose to nose, heart to heart. Her glimmering hand rose, and pressed against his cheek as she whispered, "I thought we practiced upfront honesty. I know now you tell me what you want me to know."

The probe intensified, combed his mind, compelled the truth from his sealed lips.

"A few months ago, your father and I met up in Italy to discuss going against Rabia and C20, and he proposed a deal."

"A deal with you?"

Giovanni gave Wesley an ultimatum. Either take Florence out of the Andromeda Project and associated missions, and keep her out, or continue to use her for the government's pursuit of the gems and C20's downfall. If he chose the latter, the tax debt and any charges against Belladonna Corp had to be wiped. It was the sole trade Giovanni would accept for putting his daughter in constant peril.

Florence fumbled for the bookshelf, and it proved sturdier than her wobbling frame. She sighed, stroked her shaking wrist across her forehead, and released him from the telepathic hold.

"What was I supposed to do?" he asked. "Your father didn't want you to absorb his mistakes, neither did I."

"Wesley, I don't believe you." Florence sniffled. "After the accident, I spent night after night telling myself I made a mistake. You were willing to give me a fairytale on a platter. What kind of person refuses such an offer?" The salted drops of water ran along her eyelids. Wiping one tear would extend an invitation for others to join. Her voice softened. "Tell me the truth. It had nothing to do with me, did it? You wanted to make sure you had your superhuman sidekick."

"You're being ridiculous. This has nothing to do with how I feel about you, or what I wanted for us. I mean for Christ's sake, you volunteered for those missions yourself!"

"Beside the point! When I volunteer, it's on my terms." She grabbed her chest, short of breath. "And the Andromeda Project was a bloody favor I owed you that you cashed in on at my expense. If you loved me, you'd have vowed not to involve me."

"I needed you. America needed—"

"Exactly, America does need something doesn't it? What do you know about the Z-energy?"

Evasive maneuvers had brought the situation under his control, and he rushed to catch her as she blacked out.

"I'll always love you." Wesley planted a kiss on her forehead. "But this is bigger than us." Twisting his wrist up, he said into his Cynque, "Turn down the dampeners, Detective Steele."

———

ALLISTER ADAMS
The White House, Chicago, Illinois

"I CAN'T HEAR ANYTHING," Allister said. He was stretched over four lounge chairs lining the wall beside the oval office. He swung his legs around, jumped up, and pressed his ear to the door.

Two lamps on either side of Bazzo flashed as he adjusted their voltage. "Paranoid much?" he mocked and joined him. "Dr. B and DeVries are old colleagues." Electricity zapped the door's keypad, powered down its lock mechanism. It opened. "I doubt he'd—"

Florence was out cold, head propped on the couch's arm.

"DeVries, what have ya done this time?"

"Shhh," Allister whispered. Lights on. Nine panel televisions inactive. No Secret Service. Tuned in to in-progress banter, he circled the room and landed on the United States seal in its center. President DeVries and a woman conversed.

"Mr. President," the muffled voice said, "the World Energy Summit is our best chance to convince fellow nations that what

C20's doing needs an ethical hand. If we leave it to military governments like Russia, China, and Korea to control the world's energy, they'll control... the world."

"They'll get rid of us," Wesley said.

"The second they have the chance." The woman spoke poli-talk without missing a beat. "We need to take the operation, finish what they started. And Allister needs to be the frontrunner."

"Do we know what happens to Zosma in this scenario?" the president asked her.

"Do we care?"

Hydraulics at work reverse-spiraled the United States seal open. Allister looked down and wrenched away, chest heaving, as a pant-suited elderly woman and Wesley ascended on a platform.

"You're a liar!" he snarled.

The woman screamed and flattened herself on the bookshelf to let him charge by.

"Slow it down, partner," Hunter said, easing from behind the bookshelf. He had not one, but two large plasma weapons aimed at Allister's head. "That's right. Now back it up."

He obeyed, stepped back on the leading foot, and continued reverse-trekking an acceptable distance from the Commander in Chief and ended parallel to Bazzo. Wesley stood bewildered.

Two overhead lights went out. "What's the play here, mate?" Bazzo asked. "Shoot to kill, a scuffle?"

"Nice suit, *mate*." The detective stroked the trigger with his finger. "I'm sure you don't want blood on it, so quit the tricks."

Another light fixture died. "Doesn't answer my question."

Hunter aimed down. "Speaking of questions, which leg do you want Allister to lose first?"

"I'll keep my legs, thank you," Allister said, elbowing Bazzo.

"Fair enough, no more tricks."

Electricity sparked in Bazzo's palm. Hunter went to fire, but Bazzo snapped and blew up the gun, rocketing him backward.

Allister tackled the stumbling detective in a bear hug, and they smashed into the wall. Its concrete reinforcement kept them in the room, so he crushed Hunter's cheek against it. That was for the plasma blast to the ribs. He lifted him by the neck and plowed his skull in there again. That was for the punch to the face.

"Let's go, Allister, leave 'im!" Bazzo shouted.

"Fat chance. Daddy got a big payout to make sure this goes as planned." The detective expanded his arms, throwing Allister off and socked in the stomach.

Oomph. Allister careened backward, and split the president's glass desk in half. It crashed into a million jagged pieces.

Rotating his wrist around, Hunter said in a high-pitched voice, "Aww, did you think you were going to save Zosma and frolic into the sunset?"

The woman had hightailed it. The president tiptoed next to Bazzo, who held Florence in his arms. Allister's lips sealed into a thin horizontal line.

"You're working for somebody else," he said.

The wrist rotation stopped as Hunter's smile faded. "Yeah, I'm working for the real power players, not figureheads. Have to make sure you stay put." He used his foot to flip his gun from the ground to his hand and pointed at Wesley and Bazzo. "Don't move a muscle."

Hunter's mouth dropped and so did the gun. His skull spurted red psychic energy. Allister checked over his shoulder and nodded at Florence. Some unresolved moment or traumatizing detail Detective Steele had locked away, was redisclosed by telepathy at its deadliest. The six-foot-four powerhouse screamed for the "crying and yelling to stop", covered his ears and curled in a ball.

FLORENCE BELLADONNA
Belladonna Mansion, New SoHo, New York

RETURNING TO CONSCIOUSNESS, Florence groaned and shifted positions to sit up on the heirloom couch. The warm body next to her fidgeted and an anxiety-stricken inhale shot tea tree, eucalyptus, and peppermint up her nose. Oil ingredients in an organic body wash. Good guess but, no, it was Wesley, mouth buried in his hands. Her awakening and sudden movement catapulted him to his feet, and he fired off frenetic questions asking how she felt, what she needed, could she hear him, could she stand.

Her palm flattened on textured suede. She rustled a handful of hair.

"Ugh," she said, expanding her eyelids. "I feel like I've been hit by a train."

Bazzo tilted his head. "Psychic hangover for sure. You did a number on Steele."

"Florence," Wesley said.

Their last discussion and his warm deceitful smile made her stomach churn. She slapped him in the face, and it felt so good, she did it again.

"I deserve that."

"You're a traitor and a liar," she said, and shoved him. "You deserve worse."

"You two weren't supposed to leave this house, remember?" He placed a hand on the cheek she'd attacked and looked at her. "Reports came in about Morocco, Cincinnati, Cumberland... and Ft. Miami was a goddamn disaster. National Security and Foreign Affairs were all over it." His imitation featured a booming authoritative voice, "Use force, round everyone up, even Zosma." He double tapped the Cynque.

Unfolding his arms, Allister entered the room. "Even Zosma? You think your shitty artillery is enough to bring her down? She didn't even blink."

"I can admit Detective Steele wasn't the best candidate. He's a violent showoff, and we weren't prepared for a full-scale assault."

"Are you listening to me?" He strutted up to the president. "She's under Dr. Giro's control, which means if you want to stop C20, you go through her."

"We'll do whatever we need to do to take down their operation and get this situation under our control," Wesley said.

"I'm not hearing anything about saving her."

"I don't know what to tell you. It's not a priority, it never was."

"So, first you... you trapped Zosma's mind in a human body and kept her locked in a machine. Now you want her to be an energy source. Why does she have to be for destruction or for power or for advancement or for anything but herself?"

"I mean, we don't have any other options, Mr. Adams. We're depending on the U-generators to work."

"There's no other way?" He rolled his eyes, shook his head. "There has to be."

A ten-thousand-piece puzzle on the dining room table, and Wesley hid the missing pieces.

"He's right," Florence said, irritated. "Do we trust Dr. Giro? No. And somehow, you and a handful of moguls trusted him to come up with a solution that's in humanity's best interest? And there's no backup plan. C'mon, Wes."

"Florence, you and I both know that's a gross oversimplification."

It was split. Many financiers had listened to Bazzo and were fearful. They believed the Z-energy was dangerous and wanted alternative solutions to preserving the human condition. Others, eager to solve their problems, believed Z-energy was God's way of shifting power from Western nations.

"I'll handle this." Bazzo snapped his fingers. "Gio, wake up."

"Welcome home, Bazzo," Giovanni said. "It's a pleasure to see you again."

"How ya going? Initiate I-mode."

"Splendid! Thank you for asking. I've initiated I-mode."
Metal sheets cranked down over the windows, cancelling the day's warmth and light. They sealed in the floor and the "sun" room became the interrogation room. Harshness settled in her bones. She closed her eyes. Now they had to do it the hard way.

"Do me a solid and pull the president's emails for the past 365 days, key words Andromeda Project, C20, Allister Adams, Zosma Caster."

"Right away," it said, and set to work. They flicked onto the screen one after the other. "I've retrieved the information requested. What would you like me to do next?"

Bazzo faced the compilation, arms crossed. "Highlight and extract all sentences with those subjects in them. Statements, no questions. Assemble into one document, please."

"Absolutely."

"You've made your point," the president said.

"Good. I'll stop him, when you start." Bazzo smiled at her. "See, no telepathy needed."

No wonder her father liked him. She strode to the illuminated wall and read an email snippet.

"Hacking is a federal crime, you know," Wesley replied and took a deep breath. "We're wasting time. The World Energy Summit's in two days. If Allister doesn't help us... you know, never mind. You need to see for yourself. Show them the video, Sparks."

"Your crappy propaganda? Piss off. The film is shit."

"Show us," Allister said, sulking in the corner.

"Ya heard 'im, Gio."

The computer ticked, clicked, hummed, and pulled up a clip titled "Catastrophe 20" from the president's inbox.

"You want to know why you're so important, Mr. Adams?" Wesley thrusted his hand at it. "It's all in here."

Old faithful obliterated their beloved Midwest farmland, and eight consecutive year-long winters cursed the nation. Canada and Russia's northernmost cities froze overnight. Fires spread in countries straddling the equator. Super hurricanes dumped water on already battered coastal regions.

Bazzo sucked his teeth.

"Using depressing footage to promote personal interest?" Florence asked. "This isn't an election campaign, Wes."

Wesley stared at his polished black shoes. "I didn't say it was. Moscow's buried in snow, the Philippines are under water."

Allister pointed his direction and said, "Explains why you'd be parading me around as some big American hero at the World Energy Summit."

"You signed on the dotted line." Wesley leapt from his seat. "Those gems are U.S. government property, and so are you."

"I'm no one's property," Allister growled, their noses centimeters from touching.

"You help us, or you leave Zosma to her fate in Dr. Giro's hands. It's as simple as that."

"God, my mother was right about you and this phony operation."

Bazzo side-eyed her like, are you going to handle this or not? Reading an expression could be as effective as reading a mind, and she'd sat on the sidelines long enough.

"There's more. I know there's more." Florence confronted the text from his compromised government inbox. The topmost sentence gave her the shovel she needed. Psi energy channeled through her palm, digging into the type of deception only Wesley could've gotten away with. Secrets tumbled down her psyche like an avalanche. Whatever she thought she believed was destroyed by rock-hard truth. "You knew where Zosma landed after the explosion," she paused, "and you let them develop the generators on purpose."

"Siberia." Wesley let out a heavy sigh. "She landed in Siberia. C20's team picked her up before we got to her."

"It's your fault Dr. Giro took her," Allister said, "It's your fault she's possessed by him."

She waited for his impulsive violence to have to execute telepathic suppression. He radiated a vengeful peace.

"You got what you wanted. C20 did your homework for you." Allister marched past the door and yelled back, "Good luck getting it!"

"Stop him!" Wesley grabbed her. "He's a billion-dollar liability."

"Me?" Allister asked, turning, his forefinger against his own chest. "I went to Cumberland Falls, have you seen it? It's a cemetery. Your handiwork." Blue energy circled his left knuckles, and he opened his fist to let it dive into his palm. "And screw your energy summit. Electric Wonder here can play your savior." He stormed out.

"I'm gonna not take offense to that," Bazzo said.

Florence dragged her human leg alongside her psiborg one to her great-grandmother's couch. The wall's cranking began, and she watched afternoon light dump shadows onto the marble floors.

"I need to process this." Her words crowded the runway, unwilling to take flight. She cast her eyes upward. Wesley's silhouette was tormented by a photon mob, giving a halo illusion he hardly deserved.

Faint. What she felt and feared would come after the hot flashes. Her mentor. Her lover. She'd trusted him. Giovanni's accusation was sound: Wesley had confused his exploitation as being in love with her, and Florence had confused it with trust in her. Boil away the fluff: lavish vacations, poetic words, and gaudy diamond rings, what he loved about her was what she could do for him. It was impure. It was revolting.

Wesley's internal battle tempted telepathic intrusion. His desire to take her clammy hands in his and provide reassurance meant he'd make a heart-fueled effort to smooth her anger with a phrase like, "I was protecting you." A bullshit excuse when he'd thrown her in the arms of danger by omission.

Bazzo's brow scrunched, looking at the president's face, then her face, then back to his face. "Something going on with you two?"

"Florence," Wesley said, "I didn't tell you about Zosma because—"

"Save it." She sat upright and tightened her ponytail from opposite ends. "Bazzo, we leave for the summit tonight."

ALLISTER ADAMS
Old Manhattan, New York, New York

AN IMPATIENT SUN raced to its next destination around the globe and brought the first evening flush. Old Manhattan partiers roamed trash-ridden avenues, whooping and hollering, breaking glass and offering cheers to a better tomorrow. Allister swiveled, evading a gay, intoxicated couple, then descended concrete stairs to a musty duplex and kicked the door open.

A single mother's desperate need for income afforded him the temporary dwelling. He'd paid in techno-currency, and no questions were asked. He sulked by the kitchen's core features: Maplewood cabinets, an old-school linoleum sink, a griddle, and a dorm-sized refrigerator. Like a surly wife, a hard mattress outfitted in thin sheets waited for him to reach the bedroom.

Lying flat, Allister stared at a corroded ceiling; cracks and warped plaster foretold its collapse—a similar situation to his own mental stability.

Blue energy scurried through veins in his left arm, the equivalent of countless stinging needles trying to break free from beneath his skin. Stinging pain easy to ignore in an adrenaline-fueled battle but not alone in a basement on a metal bed frame. He wondered why it always conducted through his left arm, never his right and shuddered, spreading his fingers to release his apprehension.

Z-energy sold as a commodity had two paths: either a program where limited and controlled access established high premiums based on demand, or a program that provided public access, subsidized by government taxation, where conscious consumption was law. Was the goal humans living together and basking in its infinite power? Whose preservation was at stake: an individual, a nation, or a civilization? Unless personal agendas surrendered to a greater good, owning the energy and its distribution rights dialed down to who could do it first. Regardless, the U-generators' asking price begged hefty investment capital and adoption would be based on a region's wealth.

Zosma wasn't a utility or a resource to be owned. She was a living creature. Whether C20 or the U.S. Government won, she lost—her freedom and her future. A familiar story, the princess's life or an entire world's fate.

Repetitive knocking flushed his thoughts down the drain. He sat up. "Who the f—" Boots striking uneven concrete cut him off. He scolded himself for the loud noise and tiptoed to the bedroom door frame. The knocking persisted.

He wanted to ask who was there, because there wasn't a soul he'd told he was here. An enemy would already be inside shooting holes in him, but an ally... an ally might take this more cautious route.

"Allister, they told me you're here. Open the door or I'll open it myself."

Celine again.

"Coming, I'm coming!" he exclaimed, sprinting to the door. He flung it open. "Who is they?"

"Not the wind, nor the trees keep secrets from me," she said. Mud and clay solidified into her legs. "I've some news."

He rushed her inside when her body was whole and asked harshly, "Did anyone see you? What are you doing here? You can't just show up." His restless eyes landed on her.

She stood shoulder to shoulder with him, lips pursed, nose shoved in the air. "America's filthy," she said. The hand clutching a lily-white shawl opened to let blood flow. Her finger sailed across the window sill. "I'm attending the World Energy Summit."

"Good for you. I'm not."

Celine drifted away like a forgotten song lyric. Dancing dust tumbled from the apartment's corners, spinning above her writhing hand. It coated her skin and hardened her exterior.

"I lie awake at night, hearing Earth whisper in fear of its own destruction. The roots, the leaves, the animals, they tell me there is an unnatural thing here."

Allister opened the fridge and stuck his head in. A lone pickle jar rested on the door. He unscrewed the lid to inhale its contents. "You mean Zosma?" he asked, sliding one out.

"No."

Crunching and chewing, he cocked his head. "Z-energy?"

"I'm uncertain. Whatever it is, it can't stay or—"

"That doesn't tell me anything." He slammed the jar on the counter and wiped pickle juice on his pants. "Did the president put you up to this? You know what? I don't care, I'm not going to the summit. It's what he wants."

"Allister!"

"I don't want to talk about it anymore!"

"Then be quiet and listen." She forced him to face her. "The World Energy Summit is hosted in Vancouver." Her voice lowered. Her beating heart bombarded his ears. "King Nephthys has been promised a miraculous demonstration by an unknown entity. Technology set to change the world. I know one organization who'd issue such a promise."

He did too.

Disheartenment tore him from her grasp and took him to the door-less bathroom. The mirror had an infection of speckles and blotches. His lips turned up as he found clearness in its corners and examined the increasing number of light violet hairs in his beard. Longer, curly versions had invaded his scalp. Their sudden mutation presented no correlation he could trace (i.e. abusing his powers), as Z-energy came and went as it pleased.

She didn't give him the privacy he needed, and their eyes aligned parallel and met in the mirror. "Can you use them yet?" Celine asked.

No glint or gleam, the Transporter gems denied the bathroom's bad light and held to their pale mint color. He shook his head. "It's hard to go anywhere when you don't have direction."

Celine's midnight locks swung to and fro as she glided to the door. "Listen to them rather than telling them what to do. I'll get us to Vancouver." Her tone turned to solid rock. "Dr. Giro will be there."

Allister paced in a circle, fists clenched in the air. He ended up at square one, facing his obscured reflection, palms fastened to the sink bowl. He turned its knob. The faucet sprouted cold unfiltered water. He buried his head in soaked hands, rinsing revenge's noxious craving from his pores and came up for air. All his superhuman strength couldn't break the chains that constricted his options. He squeezed the porcelain so tight it snapped under his weight and shattered on the dingy floor. "I know," Allister admitted, "and if I want to save Zosma, I have to kill him."

RABIA GIRO

C20 BASEMENT

DEDICATED ENGINEERS AND SCIENTISTS, bundled in scarves, hats, and quilted coats, hunched close to their computers. Rabia waited in the lowest light possible. His gaze jumped from snaking veins in his hand to the steel wall and back. The yellow skin splotches that afflicted his wrist and hairy forearms trudged to his elbow. It wouldn't stop there. His thumb, disfigured by a yellowed and cracked nail, thumped in slow rhythmic increments.

The steel wall rippled like a lake disrupted by a skipped rock, became double doors, and cranked apart to let Zosma fly through. She landed and marched to him. "You requested my presence, Dr. Giro?"

"There are people who think your power is dangerous," he started. "They want to see you destroyed." The computer behind him exposed three digital images. "So, we destroy them first." Target #1: Bazzo Sparks. Target #2: Florence Belladonna. Target #3: Wesley DeVries.

"They are mobilizing faster than you predicted," she said.

"Faster than we predicted."

"If I am to be included in the collective we, that is incorrect, as I had no expectations."

"We, as organization, Zosma Caster. The one you are part of. Are you clear on—" His hand shot out and coaxed a figure from the shadows. "Mr. Ashur, come join us."

Russell Ashur, cowering and layered in warm clothing, crept into the faint light.

"How long you been there, spying?"

"You want her to kill the president?" Russell asked.

Black mist emanated above and around Rabia. He rose and bellowed, "I ask how long?" The room shook. What little light shined, fluttered in fear. For seconds, the basement lived in darkness.

Russell plunged to his knees. "A few minutes, please," he choked, "I'm sorry." His glasses fell and cracked on the stone floor. "Yes. Kill. Wesley DeVries is distraction. I know what America wants: control." Rabia cut his sparked, reddened eyes at the intrusive minion. "We do what's necessary to preserve entire human race. No politics." The attack vanished as if it never was. "Go, Mr. Ashur. My patience wears."

"The-the-the simulation's tested positive," the engineer said and reached for the frames. Splintered lenses broke as he tried to remove the smudges with his shirt.

Zosma floated beyond Rabia and commanded Russell's glasses and their fragments to rise. Blue energy traced each edge and corner and fused the pieces together. She lowered them onto his astonished face. "The cold, it does not bother you?" she asked the doctor.

"Our enemies threaten success and salvation. Do not fail this time," he sneered. "You are dismissed Zosma."

"Of course, Dr. Giro." With a slowness that begged sarcasm, she bowed and left the area.

"I simulated the absorption cycle Neight used on Zosma's ship to get her here. What is used, it powers what's needed, the rest goes to the generator," Russell stammered.

"You are saying you found solution to stabilize energy system?"

The engineer didn't blink or look up, and nodded his answer with his lips smashed together and eyes on the dirt under his nails.

Well done, Rabia thought, then glowered at him. "I promise great strides to directors and world leaders. Make certain we deliver."

Russell clambered to C20's U-generator testing area. He was a man who craved recognition. Insecure, overzealous, and rejected by the scientific community for his wild ideas and lack of published research; the perfect specimen to infect, and influence. Steering Russell's movements had served Rabia's mission and, in some ways, fulfilled the engineer's own purpose. If nothing else, tenacity proved he'd be a worthy asset in the doctor's new world.

Only Rabia heard the clapping echo through the basement. He swiveled at the sound and ambled to the basement's deepest crevice.

Neight continued tapping his palms together. "I am impressed."

"What you babbling about, Caster?" he asked. A chunk of skin fell off his chin and squished on the metal. Annoying, yet painless.

"Ironic you chose to conclude your research on this continent. Fitting. I can do nothing but appreciate your flare for sentiment."

"I spend my life studying human genome, how it works, limitations, adaptations, compatibility." Rabia's chin reached for the half-mile-high ceiling. He kicked his legs up, and paraded around the prison. "My results would fascinate you."

"I do not doubt this. They are an intriguing species. Though, I believe you mean you spent his life studying the human genome." Neight pointed at his plump body.

Done playing the mighty steed in the merry-go-round, he stopped in front of Neight and twirled a finger around the capsule's scramble button. "If centrifuge rips you apart, how long to put yourself together?"

"At my current power levels, long enough for you to fail." His head bowed in faux respect. "About two Earth weeks."

"Good to note." Rabia walked away with pep in his step. Louder, he continued, "Is stunning, you built machine to house your planet's 'core' reactions, reactions a body can't endure."

"Mastering Z-energy is a lifelong journey, and you are incorrect to infer a physical body cannot be capable. It demands time, training, and mental strength. As for the containment center, it was created to delay the inevitable, which is all you need to know."

Rabia assumed the "inevitable" meant its detection and misuse.

Illuminated grids, graphs, diagrams, and equations linked the containment center as the location for the energy source. Z-energy manifested inside the off-white fishbowl, swirling like Jupiter's giant red spot, only blue. Stored three floors above them, the invention replicated the properties of Uragon's core and contained the energy's constant chemical reactions by repelling them into itself.

"Since we are on the subject, I have update for you regarding our progress." He vaporized and melted into the walls, taunted Neight with god-like omnipresence. "The hypothesis was incorrect. Containment center is holding cell. Zosma, your darling Zosma, is true Z-energy source."

———

FLORENCE BELLADONNA
North Vancouver, British Columbia, Canada

FLORENCE, BAZZO, WESLEY, and Dorian arrived in British Columbia's new capital by town car. Among rows upon rows of verdant hills, Douglas firs, and Sitka spruces, nature's hooting, cawing, and chirping carried on endless conversations. Fishing boats and small yachts rocked steadily, bumping against North Vancouver's docks. Its inner harbor was alive with seafarers, who complained and swigged beer outdoors. Her telepathy on overload picked up their rebellious thoughts. Blaring sirens and the city's sundown curfew would eliminate them.

"Thanks for pulling this off Baz," Florence said.

"Glad my dual-citizenship was finally worth a damn." Bazzo pushed up the butterfly door, got out of the driver's seat and stretched. "Can't say it was tough this time around. This bloody summit is open doors for any nation who's stayed afloat and has some Techno-cash to blow."

"You make it sound so frivolous. Many of them are attending out of genuine concern," Wesley countered.

"For themselves," Bazzo said.

Florence pointed at Wesley and Dorian. "As non-citizens, you two are allowed twenty-four hours here. Let's make them count."

"Remind me how you got them to agree to host this summit in the first place?" Bazzo asked the president.

"They owed us a favor," Wesley snapped.

Florence rolled her eyes and said to Bazzo, "Yes, because I caught the assassin responsible for the Canadian Prime Minister's death."

An assassination that caused the Great White North to flip from a peaceful democracy to a militaristic dictatorship. Strict visa laws had kept Canada's borders gridlocked. No fugitives, no immigrants, no foreign businesses, no exceptions.

And enter Mother Nature, since being the world's most changed social and political infrastructure wasn't enough. Each summer, the Pacific stole an increasing amount of Alaska's permafrost. An entire state literally melting off the map promised to put Vancouver Island, Burnaby, Delta, and Richmond's main areas underwater in five years. Hence moving the economic epicenter further north.

Florence stood, dwarfed by another estate belonging to her. A sprawling log cabin, hand hewn from timber, and built on a fire-forged stone foundation.

"Thanks for coming." She twisted her body to Dorian Xander, whose shoulders had shrunk from the forest's noise. "Keep in mind what I told you, listen to the silence." She handed him one hundred and fifty thousand dollars of Techno-currency packed in a single chip. "As promised."

Focused on his untied bootlaces, Dorian gave a short nod, and closed his hand around it.

"I thought it'd be cooler," she mumbled, and bunched her sleeves up.

"West Coast weather," Bazzo replied. He greeted the two house staff, who came to collect his travel bag. "Get Dr. B's first, mate," he said and pointed at a Gucci weekender.

"Welcome back, Mr. Sparks," a woman said. "Hear you're in trouble again."

"No one's been 'round here, right, Margy?" he asked.

The plain young woman paused mid-scuttle and stared down the steps at him intently. "No, sir."

"Good, let's keep it that way."

Wesley slung his hand luggage over his shoulder and grumbled aloud, "Didn't know this existed."

"You weren't supposed to," Bazzo retorted. He picked up his bag and gestured to Florence. "After you."

Margy took the initiative to settle the guests' belongings in their assigned rooms. Meanwhile, Bazzo led them through an open entryway, past leather couches dressed in exotic Afghans, and stopped under a ceiling of intertwining logs next to a barren fireplace.

"Hello, Bazzo, Dr. Belladonna, welcome home," Giovanni said.

A comical juxtaposition embedded artificial intelligence in the vintage property. Despite her distaste for technology, having a globally connected system provided irrefutable convenience.

"Gio, control room access, please," Bazzo said.

"Voice recognition confirmed. My pleasure."

The fireplace compressed and disappeared into the wall, revealing the computer's mainframe. More operations base than relaxing fjord view getaway. Enthralled by satellite surveillance and inundated with blue light, Florence tripped and barked, "Don't touch me," as Wesley went to catch her.

She avoided his pleading stare. It required confidence in her courage to look in his intense grey irises and not be swept off her feet by the river of betrayal and lies running between them. Arms crossed, jaw sliding across the hinges, she threw her hair in a messy bun and mustered an even tone, "Giovanni, I need you to run a biographical on Dr. Rabia Giro."

"Would you like to run it on the Cynque global database?"

"No. Go stealth. Hack into Google's private search engine. They'll have archived data from before the cleanse."

"Whoa, Google. That's a throwback," Bazzo said. He found an office chair in the corner to park himself in. "C'mon Gio. Hurry it up. You're still plugged in, right?"

"Confirmed. I have access and I've found five matches. Would you like to choose one?"

Five men were pictured in glitchy squares. No mouth went uncovered, and an astonished gasp escaped anytime a member of the small audience read the next biography. Generations of born and bred scientists, Rabia Giro the third, fourth, fifth, and so on. However, their unique lifespans, birthplaces, and physical attributes didn't align in her head.

"Copernicus... Galileo... Isaac Newton... Darwin... Einstein... he assisted them all," she said.

"Dios mío!" the Cynque in Dorian's pocket shouted, missing his typical melancholy context.

"Mmm, it looks like a lineage to me," Wesley said.

"Except they don't look to be related," Bazzo offered.

"You sound as crazy as General Delemar," the president scoffed. "Sorry, but I've been through this exercise. When we developed the power suppression system, Dr. Giro and Captain Brandt were the two resident superhumans."

"Let me guess, you guys made 'em guinea pigs?"

"They volunteered. At any rate, the system worked by linking, for example, transmutation to a gene sequence. Russell tested the prototype using Giro's DNA and found out he was human."

"First of all, there is no way Dr. Giro's human. Second, I think now's a good time to discuss the folder from General Delemar's Cynque," she said. "Open folder Hexforth." Dating back to the 1900s; photographs, signed research documents, blueprints, and handwritten letters piled evidence onto an unsettling mystery. "I've had the images in it cross-referenced. Our friend Dr. Giro's been studying the Z-energy long before the world's problems started."

———

Fifteen minutes later they filed into the living room. Wesley loitered near her, shifting his weight, clearing his throat. "Florence." He stepped toward her. "Please. Say something—"

"I can show you to your rooms," a woman proposed.

Florence turned her back to Wesley and faced the head of property affairs, who had arrived with helpers to escort them to their lodging. "Wonderful, thank you, Margy."

Bazzo waited for them to leave then said, "It's not totally his fault. He's the president. Politics takes hold. Protecting what's left of the free world... blah blah blah."

"Yeah, he's the president. He's a lot of other things too." She toyed with an imaginary ring on her finger, adding, "We were engaged, for about a month." Florence's mouth twitched. She wanted to smile at the potential for happiness and a family.

"Um, come again?"

"You asked if there was anything going on."

A blank look took over his face.

"With Wesley and me." She tapped her boot on the wooden floor, inhaled, and strolled toward the kitchen. "Forget it. Espresso?"

"I'm good."

The old-fashioned hum of grinding coffee beans dropped a double shot into a porcelain cup rumored to have originated in the sixteenth century. Her father had used the handcrafted three-cup set for his daily morning, mid-afternoon, and evening brew.

Lord Giovanni Belladonna, dead at eighty.

"You're growing up so fast," her father had said to her at thirteen. If anyone were to ask what happened to the girl who used to enjoy ballet lessons and recitals at the Broadway Dance Center.

To the girl who liked pretty dresses. To Lord Giovanni's little lady. She'd say the truth happened and demolished the facade of her fairytale upbringing. At sixteen, she found out the man who'd given her everything was worth nothing. Yes, Giovanni had more money than God, but he was bankrupt in morals. She took up fencing instead.

Florence peered at the dark, steaming liquid. In two months she'd adopted her father's same habit: one double shot, three times a day. Drinking it paid homage to him, though she hadn't shed a tear for his death. She took a sip. Strong and bitter, like him.

"He hired me at twenty years old. Granted, I'm a genius," Bazzo said and winked. "Still, he took a chance, showed me how the business worked behind the scenes."

"I haven't spoken to him in twenty years." Her lips pressed together, then parted as she finished. "But, I'm glad. I'm glad he had you."

According to Bazzo, her father didn't believe in love. He'd admired his eldest daughter for being headstrong and determined, favored her because of their shared psychic potential. Even if she'd tricked herself into thinking she didn't need validation, it felt damn good to hear.

"Reminds me, I need to show you the library," he said.

Florence's mouth fell open. Adjacent to the entranceway was a reading room wrapped in a mesmerizing library. Thousands of books, real bound and printed paper books, lined its spotless shelves. As she stepped past the room's manual sliding doors, she stepped thirty plus years into the past. A time before digital had taken over. Cleaned in preparation for their arrival, she inhaled fresh pine and musky oils. Her heart fluttered at round oak tables, leather armchairs, a diamond one-hundred-and-twenty-eight-light chandelier.

"This is a dream. I can't believe my father owned anything this... magnificent."

"Your dad owned some kick-ass literature," Bazzo said. "Now, you do." He wandered ahead and searched the library's inventory at eye level, then got on his toes to check the higher shelves. "Ah, there it is." With both hands, he yanked a bulky, withered book sandwiched among two others of greater size. "His fave. Raved about this one, said it held the universe's secrets."

Florence deserted her idol gazing to join him at the largest oak table, which was built to a height that encouraged reading on one's feet. "*The Book of Ancestry*," she mumbled and traced the woven binding. "I've seen the name."

He curtsied. "I'll leave you to it."

Inside the book, she saw her name etched in Giovanni's distinct calligraphy on a folded note. She flattened it on the table, and then she read:

Florence,

If you're reading this, it means you've come home. I'll never be able to explain why I did the things I did, but I can imagine you've seen how corrupt a world can be. I learned how to navigate it a long time ago. The future here is grim. On these pages, you'll find our past, which you must understand to forge our continued existence. The language in this manuscript has been lost to mankind as it was not theirs to begin with. Use your telepathy to read it. My eighteenth birthday gift, the sword of Psion, is tethered to you. Do not underestimate its strength or yours.

Regards,
Lord G. Belladonna

Florence laid a hand on the paper as if it were the shiny lapel of her father's favorite tuxedo. She exhaled contempt, inhaled understanding, exhaled apathy, and then halted, not ready to inhale forgiveness.

She unhinged the serrated sword from her hip, curled her fingers around the handle, and liberated it from the sheath. The silver gleam dancing in diamond's light matched her psiborg leg. Upon further inspection, she found infused in its blade were the same tiny purple crystals infused in her artificial limb. Psychic energy rose off of her shoulders without her conscious command, startling her. The sword slipped and clattered on the table. She slammed the book shut, which stopped a chorus of whispers from singing in her ears.

World Energy Summit, Deep Cove, Vancouver

"Your father told me you can't protect a woman stronger than you," Wesley said, as he tied his bowtie. "Now I know what he meant."

Florence crossed her legs in the limousine's backseat. Her arms, soaked in black evening gloves, draped her thigh, while Deep Cove and its homogenous forest borrowed her attention. Better that than lending it to his words.

"Fifteen years and I've loved you more each one," he said.

Her pupils shifted to her eye's corners. Her neck turned above a bare shoulder sturdy as a wall his confessions could not break.

Short, wavy hair moved beneath Wesley's hands, as he held her gaze with the same determination as the words spilled from his soul. "Do you understand how empty I feel? I didn't know how to cope with - with losing you. And if I'm being real, I don't want to. I've done everything I can to keep you close. To keep an eye on you. You're all I have."

"Wesley, stop it."

"Florence, Florence. Don't drag this out, I made a mistake. I've made mistakes." He folded his lips in, reached across the seat, and offered a light touch on her gown's frill. "If we can enjoy one evening together, it'll be worth all the ones we've missed. What're you so afraid of?"

Florence flashed back to what she'd believed were her last moments on Earth. The plane shredded to bits by the time it plunged into the Atlantic. Ocean rushed through her lungs and bundled her in death's blanket. Her certainty that she'd die there, unloved and forgotten. In a single memory, a thirty-minute make-up application became a Matisse of cosmetics and tears.

Wesley wiped them, captured her makeup-smeared face in his hands and kissed her on the lips. She softened to his embrace and turned her body to indulge. He caressed her psiborg leg.

"Don't." She pushed his hand off but squeezed it for support.

He took her chin, touched her leg again, and said, "This is part of you. Accept it. I have."

She smoothed her hand over Wesley's hairline and said, "I'll try," then deserted the love scene.

Reapplying blush, eyeshadow, and eyeliner was a ruse to reconstruct a telepathic barrier to contain her emotions. Being a stranger to affection and best friends with solitude pushed Wesley, the closest thing to family she'd get in her lifetime, to the outskirts of her mental walls.

Wesley rolled down the window. A gentle wind rescued his scrunched forehead from sweat's gloss. His handsome, youthful face brooded above a patterned, fuchsia bowtie. It matched her striking ensemble, though, it wasn't the occasion's principal accessory. The sword slept at their feet.

"How do you plan on getting that inside?"

"You know how," she said, as she stroked her lashes with the mascara's wand. Florence screwed the cap on and dabbed her lower lid.

Burdened by god knows what, his heel bounced while the left thumb tapped the right thumb's knuckle. She snuck a selfish peek at her ex-fiancé's thoughts and found him conflicted by his love for her and his fear of losing her. Being afraid to lose people was a dangerous way to live life. Especially people like her, who were already lost.

Lightning forked in silence to an unsuspecting ground, and thunderous booms gave delayed warning. Rain's sour smell hinted at an on-time arrival, but remained fashionably late, waiting for conflict. The World Energy Summit's remote venue was a restored mansion inspired by the British Columbian parliament building. An exquisite granite, marble, and andesite sculpture set against the indigo backdrop of a summer evening. Soldiers patrolled the perimeter of a forty-foot spiked gate.

Wesley dug for her hand, holding it tight while they passed shrubbery on their climb up the driveway.

"You look beautiful," he said.

She wrapped her arm around his neck and kissed him for the last time. "Thank you, Mr. President."

Event staff assisted her vehicle exit. Teeth clenched in a contrived smile, Florence entered the public eye and executed polite waves to people she'd heard of or met as a child.

"Welcome, President DeVries. There were some last-minute invitees added we need to review," a young woman said, her words rushed. "They're waiting for you in the study."

———

A narrow, linear-columned runway spilled from the foyer into the main hall, where intricate celestial stories, posed as murals, were painted on its stone ceilings. Angelic warriors, elemental gods, armored men and women, and a red-eyed demon illustrated in eternal conflict.

Wesley returned from his briefing, sidling next to her as staff members directed them to a door.

"Hi, Mr. President, welcome, right this way," they said and watched them pass. "Dinner is served."

Did you find out? She projected.

Glad you brought the sword, Wesley thought and glanced at his Cynque. *Stay alert.*

Tyrian purple wallpaper stretched behind elongated mirrors, whose intricately molded frames atoned for being crafted in cheap metal. A modest chandelier twinkled.

Champagne glasses reached the attendee's hands. Sweet desserts and savory dishes decorated a sanded and glazed cedar table in the dining room's center, while aged, oaky Italian reds and buttery French whites were poured in faux camaraderie. The tension slipped down like a satin nightgown.

"King Nephthys," Wesley greeted the Moroccan diplomat with a bow, "glad you made it. Will we be seeing Princess Celine this evening?"

"She's not feeling well." His curt reply was missing its reciprocal bow. He scooted by to take his seat. "I trust there'll be no superhuman incidents."

"No, your highness. It's been handled."

Major nations from the five U.N. groups promised to represent by sending the who's who of their elite. High-net-worth individuals or respective elected or appointed officials showed up and showed out from countries like Morocco, Germany, India, Nigeria, Mexico, Canada, Turkey, Egypt, Argentina, Norway, Austria, Poland, the UK, and Brazil. They enjoyed lobster tails, filet mignon, roast, asparagus topped with poached eggs, and caviar.

"I don't remember seeing her on the list of invitees," a dignitary from Austria gossiped.

"She's the late Lord Belladonna's daughter," the Norwegian Queen answered, "representing Italy and his filthy company, I suppose."

The German prime minister snickered. "I heard she was dead."

"Isn't this the second time?" his consort quipped. Glasses clinked. Laughter ensued.

People loved to weave their personal truth into the world for consumption. Florence tossed her hair. Her forearms flexed as she picked up her steak knife by the acrylic handle and held it upright.

"Let them talk, sweetheart, let them talk," Wesley said, lips parted, not moving.

"Would you like a glass of our 2028 Marchesi Cabernet Sauvignon?" a waiter asked.

Grinning, Wesley answered, "Yes, she would."

Too distracted to appreciate the meal's tantalizing flavors, Florence took calculated sips of her dry, full-bodied drink in fifteen-minute intervals. She never swallowed and spit it into the glass. If all went as planned she'd discard it on a circulating collection tray before anyone was the wiser.

Amidst casual conversation, Jane Wenyin, the former Korean director for the Andromeda Project, passed her a fake smile and the dessert tray. The woman sat opposite Chung Tae-Won, the former Chinese director, and on the table's far end, a menacing Aleksander Karjavine, the former Russian director, shoveled roast into his mouth. Three traitorous tyrants responsible for funding C20's research and development efforts.

Aleksander squinted at Wesley after a few glasses of cabernet and pointed. "You better have plan, DeVries. I love good meal, but I would not fly five thousand miles for one."

Wesley's posture straightened to the insult. "Too late."

She coughed, knocked off guard, and brought the cloth napkin to her lip.

By contrast, the table joined in nonchalant laughter at the unexpected joke. "No, seriously, thank you, Mr. Karjavine. You bring up a good point. This is the perfect time to address the reason we're here." Wesley left the table and moseyed behind the guests, performed his speech. "If you take a look around the room tonight, you'll see a plethora of different faces, nationalities, religions. At the end of the day, we're people, we're human, and we're fighting to survive. It's easy to forget that in your own home, surrounded by your country's traditions, laws, and military protection. It's not enough anymore." He looked down. "What we're facing is elimination. Unless we work together to preserve our way of life. We've found the Transporter gems, the most powerful thing known to man besides Z-energy, and thanks to Allister Adams's cooperation, we've had time to study them and figure out how they work."

Light clapping disrupted the president's sentiment, or as Florence would call it, the president's gigantic lie.

"We're talking about opening new doors, in the figurative and literal sense. Let's do it together," he concluded. "I propose a toast to evolution and advancement."

They quieted to eerie silence, no doubt reflecting on what it meant to them individually, and for their countries.

"To humanity," Jane said.

"To humanity," the room repeated, raised their glasses, and drank to their own desires.

"Where's the superhuman?" one of the gossipers asked.

"We'll be moving to the next room," a waiter announced. "The summit commences in ten minutes."

Wesley returned to sneak a kiss, and her head jerked back.

"What a riveting speech," Florence said and shoved past him. She collided with a woman on her way out the door. "I'm sorry, I wasn't paying..." Her voice went cold. "Attention."

Jane Wenyin. The petite socialite smirked, picked up the solitary champagne glass on the table, and pursed her glossed lips.

"You look well," she said, "cheers to your swift recovery."

The drink tumbled into the basin Jane called her mouth in three classless gulps. Florence imagined peristalsis working the bubbling liquid down the woman's should-be cigarette-rotted esophagus and depositing it in an acidic, oily pool of the event's cuisine. An eighty-five-year-old body with brand new organs and shiny, plastic skin. She'd lived in her country through four generations of political unrest and stood as living proof that, in their world, immorality equaled immortality.

"You staying for our surprise demonstration?" Jane asked, "It is revolutionary."

"I'm on the edge of my seat," Florence replied and clenched her dress fabric by the nails.

"The Andromeda Project was worthless. My business damn near collapsed because of its failure and so did the global economy. I was forced to invest the leftover scraps of my portfolio in C20's solution."

"It's not the solution I'm concerned about," she blurted, "It's the person leading it."

"And the United States is a more agreeable option? Tsk, tsk, Doctor, I thought Lord Giovanni taught you better than that." Jane's finger rimmed the glass. "You have seen what happens when you get in the way. This time, I'll make sure the job's done." She let the glass go and watched it shatter at their feet and feigned shock. Cruel reminders to her attempt at orchestrated murder. "Come along, little lady, you don't want to be late," she said and strode out the doorway.

Florence jumped after her, fists charged with psionic energy. "Hey, hey." Wesley tugged her by the elbow. "You have to relax."

Deep breaths melted the energy and she turned. "This is me relaxed. That woman is a b—"

He raised his eyebrow and a finger to her lips.

"Witch. She tried to have me killed."

"I have to go in there, take a minute to cool off."

"Wesley."

"Yes."

"He's here," she mouthed.

"I know," he mouthed in response. "Stay alert."

She traveled the corridor on her toes and groped the depths of an oversized, sapphire-studded clutch, gauging the appropriate time to slip behind a column and check her father's Cynque for Bazzo's overdue status updates.

"Can I help you find the conference auditorium, beautiful?"

Florence turned enough to catch Hunter Steele's cheesy smile, and touched the telepathically invisible handle of her sword. "Detective Steele, what are you doing here?"

"My, my, my. Hello to you too," he retorted. "Who else would the U.S. hire to run security but the best?"

ZOSMA CASTER
World Energy Summit, Deep Cove, Vancouver

HAIR COILED AND PINNED in a magnificent up-do, Zosma's chiffon dress and sewn on cape plunged over her alien curves. The intricate, ever-present crown and its lustrous stone were conspicuous contradictions to her most convincing human costume, and cast an eerie glow on the leaves, twigs and dirt that plagued the mansion's untended roof.

The man Zosma had met, Captain Jared Brandt, leaned on the ledge next to her. She exhaled as they witnessed the third lightning flash in under a minute.

"Storm's comin'," he said.

She remembered the captain. His decorated red uniform and his reluctant obedience. They'd worked together during the years she paraded around as Lieutenant Leesa Delemar. He changed from the soldier to the traitor. Slighted by corrupt policies and nonchalance toward human life, he embarked on a revenge quest against Nicolas Delemar and the Andromeda Project. Actions which were trivial in the universe's grand scheme, had wrenched through reality, altering more timelines than she cared to imagine, including hers.

"Humans are puzzling creatures." She watched him scrape at the ledge. "Admirable fascination with the unknown. I wonder, must they endeavor to control it?"

He broke eye contact and pressed a button below his palm. The weapon jutted out and reformed atop his forearms and locked in place. "We're scared of anythin' better or bigger than us."

"Is not every being in this universe?"

One of two wrist canons' gears cranked. She stepped away from the ledge. Light drizzling threatened her beauty, yet never touched her.

"If my power helps heal this world, I can be a symbol for preservation rather than destruction. The longing for belonging grips the minds of the strongest and weakest alike."

He activated the second canon. "I'm nothin' but a lost soul."

"You can change your truth if you change your perspective." Her dress spread around her as she levitated off of the ground.

Nodding, he stared up at her. "You an' Neight are somethin' else, I tell ya."

Dry to her hollow bones, she floated to the winding staircase, and gave him a final smile, before she disappeared into misty submission.

ALLISTER ADAMS
World Energy Summit, Deep Cove, Vancouver

A STREAK OF HOT SILVER split the sky, followed by the requisite thunder crackle. Black clouds billowed from the east, drenching the Canadian wilderness in the rain's heady scent and pattering drops.

Allister stared through fogged windows, waiting for instructions that wouldn't come. He huffed and rearranged himself in the BMW's roomy backseat.

"Is there a signal or?" he asked.

Celine sat behind the driver's chair, left leg folded over right. "What is in there is unnatural."

"I'm still confused, who're you talking about?"

She went to speak, and no words came out.

"Uh, Celine?"

"The rain," she mumbled. Sand speckles fell from her cheek and landed in her lap. "I won't be able to hold myself together."

He jabbed a thumb at the downpour. "You didn't do this?"

"I don't play with the weather."

"I mean, okay, but rain's not what's scaring you. So, why're we out here?"

"Antarctica is covered in 15-million-year-old ice," she spoke slowly and fixed her shawl in a trance. "If you want to know a planet's secrets, that's where you go. The ice told the ocean, the ocean told the rain, the rain told the soil, and the soil told me: Dr. Giro is—"

"I'm going in. You're freaking me out."

She didn't protest.

He threw his hands up, opened the door and ducked out onto the sidewalk. Crouching beside the car, he estimated the distance to the vegetation encompassing the venue. Aggressive ivy and hostile vines snaked around the gate's titanium bars the full forty feet up. Unruly shrubbery planted in equidistant rows offered him solace between their leaves, if he could get to them. A soldier patrolled past him.

He bolted.

"Hey," the soldier sneered, spotting Allister beside the decorative hedges. He threw an elbow across the man's jaw and knocked him unconscious. *Click.* Seconds before a blast released, he spun outward and wrestled another armed soldier into a headlock.

"Let go of it and I won't hurt you," Allister said.

The soldier kept a firm grip on the trigger. He cursed and tightened the choke hold. His assailant's neck arteries and veins compressed. The gun hit wet tarmac. Allister's head swiveled in the soaked darkness to confirm no one had seen. "If anyone'd told me five months ago, when I was baking croissants and restocking sugar packets, that I'd be..." Runoff water carried the sentence away. Anything that had happened in the last five months sounded too ridiculous or too sad. He took a breath and dragged the limp body across the concrete.

Gears grinding inwards moved the hydraulic system of a hidden entrance. He thought he was heading for a sly, quiet infiltration prior to the stressful undertaking of heroics, but the stark white spotlight shining in his eye had to belong to a Cynque or military artillery.

Allister stood at the opening, hands in the air, knowing it best he give up to get in. The light vanished, and the colossal property with its eyebrow style windows, and cavernous mouth of french doors, scolded his carelessness. Rapid, multiple white flashes weren't paparazzi welcoming his arrival, they were a lightning storm on its worst behavior.

"Good morning, Sir Adams," Detective Hunter Steele said, his strapping frame unveiled. "Welcome to the party."

"You mind letting President DeVries know his guest of honor's here?" Allister yelled over nature as he entered.

———

BAZZO SPARKS
World Energy Summit, Deep Cove, Vancouver

"I BLOODY HATE RAIN," Bazzo said. The uncomfortable masked uniforms had questionable ventilation systems, but he gave silent thanks rain didn't touch his bare skin. He tended to have adverse reactions to it, as any electrically charged superhuman would. The person next to him stood silent and still, obedient to a fault. He tilted his neck and whispered, "Mate, you in there?"

They didn't break character.

Hunter Steele marched toward him, bearing a hostage. "Bringing in Allister Adams!" he shouted at his wrist and shoved the staggering body.

Bazzo and the soldier both straightened up, although their camouflage made them nigh invisible.

Oh god, he thought when they entered the double doors. *I gotta get inside.* He nudged the person he believed was his partner in crime. "Wiggle your fingers, I can't tell if it's you."

Dorian nodded. Thunder, lightning, heavy rain—loud noises, especially blended, had triggered a sonic energy buildup. He clutched his now glowing hand, then shook it up and down, left and right. The energy dissipated.

He and Dorian were stationed at the majestic entrance. Concealed by lowlight and cloudburst, they scampered around the side of the house and flattened against the wall. Chest moving in temporary exhaustion, he said, "If I use my powers, I'll fry the whole guest list. This is fucked."

A loud boom sent Dorian to one knee. The side door swung open. Two soldiers walked out as Bazzo ducked below eye level and froze.

"Steele promised me fireworks tonight. I'm disappointed," the first said.

"Night is young, man, night is young," the second replied. They congregated out of earshot, too enthralled to look their direction.

"Hey, mate, pull it together."

Dorian patted Bazzo on the chest in gratitude. "Good on ya, let's go in."

FLORENCE BELLADONNA

"THANK YOU FOR YOUR PATIENCE," Wesley said to a chattering audience. "Please, quiet down. We're ready to begin."

The auditorium doors banged open. A disoriented Allister, drooling blood and spit, was escorted inside by the armpits, his feet dragging behind him. The murmurs circulating the room hushed.

"Detective Steele, what did I say about violence?" Wesley left the podium to help Allister onto the ground-level stage and into an armed chair.

The conference hall's wooden panels absorbed collective gasps. Dim, mood lighting fell, wrapping the room in secrets. None shined on Dr. Rabia Giro, as he hobbled from stage right.

"Welcome, all," he rasped and leaned forward to each of the five U.N. groups.

Haggard. Pale. His ears and nose had morphed from rounded organs to sharpened ones. To which he blamed malnourishment and isolation. "It was kind of U.S. to let me join. We complete our first devices and are eager to show you, the lucky few. Thank you, Jane, Chung, Aleksander, for invitations, it is honor to be present for this pivotal gathering in human history. Believe me, I know. Mr. President, allow me."

Wesley stiffened, huddled beside Hunter, who'd transformed, then folded his metal arms over his metal chest.

"Dr. Belladonna. Is no wonder we've gathered to rub elbows with socialite of such poise and skill at manipulation." Dr. Giro neared the stadium seating's bottom row. Taller than she remembered. Bolder than she remembered.

Confusion at his word choice commenced among the attendees. *Allister? Allister can you hear me?* she asked, jaw clenched so tight she felt her teeth would shatter from pressure.

"Many know her as political activist, renowned psychiatrist, and daughter of infamous Lord Giovanni Belladonna." He gave a short, sarcastic clap. "However, what I know, which you do not know is that Dr. Belladonna is superhuman." His shifting eyes stopped on her.

A moment she'd spent six years avoiding, from calling off the engagement to quitting politics to playing dead.

"*E' vero*, Doctor?"

Led by Jane's head turn and porcelain veneer grin, her peers examined her like a zoo animal.

Florence protested. "I'm not sure what you mean?"

"I think you know what I mean." Dr. Giro entered the audience like a prosecutor engaging a jury. "Ladies and gentlemen, not only is she superhuman, Giovanni, rest his soul, was also one." Parallel to her in the aisle, he continued his character assassination. "Their power rests in telepathy, and for those who do not know, that is ability to read thoughts, control thoughts."

A crack of thunder trumped her heartbeat's loudness. Her temperature touched the vaulted ceiling. Forget the last six years, she'd spent her life avoiding this moment. The elite's inescapable stares dissected her sweaty face as she clutched her chest in utter silence.

"President DeVries has been lying to you all." Dr. Giro descended the stairs. "Dr. Belladonna is not psychiatrist, she is weapon. He used her telepathy to shut down Korea missile efforts. Hired her undercover to retrieve Transporter gems for U.S. government. And now, he's employed her and Bazzo Sparks to dissuade this world's leaders from paving path to your future. Why do these things? Are you not one people as he so eloquently preached?"

"She should be allowed to explain herself," an Indian diplomat said.

"I don't want to hear it, lock her up," a financier from the UK argued.

"An absolute disgrace to our society," said a third. It was the Norwegian Queen, of course.

"50 years successful in business," Aleksander sneered, "Because I always knew better than to trust Giovanni."

She sensed Allister's concentration lapse again.

"United States wants to seize my hard work by force, say I am terrorist. No, I am scientist. And they twisted this poor child into thinking he is their hero when he is their pawn."

The guilt in her was a steel ball, heavy enough to keep her weighed down, not quiet.

"It's... not... true... " Florence said. "It's not true. I had nothing to do with this energy war. My father paid for your psychotic science experiment and after he found out what you were doing, he pulled the plug."

"And you expect us to believe Giovanni Belladonna acquired moral compass!" Dr. Giro exclaimed. "He spent his life deceiving humans in business, in politics. Belladonna family status is false!"

Discussions drowned the dying storm, but all she heard was repeated tapping. Surprised to hear anything with people speaking over each other at their highest decibels, she glanced at a jittery uniformed soldier next to her. They were not conversations. They were thoughts. Hundreds of spastic mental voices scraped the telepathic barrier.

"Quiet!" Florence demanded.

She balanced on wobbling legs, knowing timidity and tears wouldn't win the battle. Pink energy spread across her cheeks, encompassed her head and body, then deepened to scarlet red fire burning around her. Necks craned to get a better look. She glowed as much due to psionic energy as to perspiration.

Her chin lifted as she spoke, "My father's actions... aren't mine. His crimes... aren't mine, and I have generations of wealth unrelated to his crooked dealings, thank you very much." She knew her words were moot. Individual thought had become a jumbled disaster. Dr. Giro's influence enveloped the room.

She met her rekindled lover's terrified eyes. His cheeks and upper body sagged as he executed the smallest, vigorous head shake. She saw Wesley's lips say, "don't do it," and heard him begging her through their mental connection not to open the vault. Hunter switched roles to bodyguard and carried an odd smirk as he moved to protect the president. Allister's neck rolled around as he muttered incoherence.

"Let's talk about you, Dr. Giro. The sixth, is it? Or was it seventh? I can't keep track, there's so many of you."

"Quiet." He glared at her. "Or I'll do more than put you to sleep. Apprehend her."

"Hey, they take orders from me," Hunter said.

"Not anymore."

Realizing Dr. Giro's attack strategy, she'd used up her telepathy keeping Allister, Hunter, and Wesley's minds intrusion-free. Energy fled like a flock of birds. She buckled.

Two dripping wet soldiers wrestled back her arms and, in the struggle, she ripped her gown at the waistline. "Let me go!" she protested. "Your identity is fake, Dr. Giro. We found your secret."

Wesley came from behind Hunter, who put his arm out and said, "Suggest you stay put, Prez, or it's a wrap for you."

"Tell them who you really are!"

The soldier choked her, ensuring submission, while the second inserted a needle into her neck and pressed the plunger. Liquid invaded her bloodstream. Her vision blurred. Both legs folded under her and the injection seized her consciousness in an iron grip.

CHAPTER SIX

An Imperfect Sacrifice

Allister Adams

World Energy Summit, Deep Cove, Vancouver

Allister's shoulders contracted. Dizzy and weak in the limbs from seeing Florence overpowered, he brought his elbows to his lap and rubbed his clammy hands together.

Was now the time to leap up and pummel Dr. Giro to his death? Or would the doctor's influence over the soldiers incite a shootout at the slightest movement, incinerating bodies left, and right? Or was his anger misguided altogether when the real enemy was the U.S. government?

Freedom to act, or react, had become a curse. It bound him to the chair with fear of uncontrollable outcomes. The heroic moment (or what idea of heroic had been ingrained in his skull) was conceived from an energy war camouflaged in altruism. This conglomeration of allies and enemies had come to decide which future to stand for, when Dr. Giro had already decided for them.

Swept by a dense, sickening odor, Allister sat up straight, held his breath and knees for beloved life. Dr. Giro's Eastern European olive skin had changed to a decaying grey. Wispy white hair had grown past his shoulders but didn't fill in at a receding hairline.

"Hmmm. Your transformation begins so soon," the doctor muttered and coaxed a curly purple strand from Allister's scalp. "Now, I present you Uragon Princess, Zosma Caster."

Zosma graced the stage, floating in all her limitless beauty. She bowed to the speechless, entranced ensemble. Allister felt his mouth stretch and cheeks creep up. Her innate charm emboldened a smile's humble beginnings.

The guests didn't share his reverence. Shrieks from some beget screams from others, and the most intelligible reactions were limited to, "Oh my gosh," and "What is that thing?"

Allister tugged at his shirt collar as he studied Zosma's body for language. Her eye twitched. Her fingers balled into a fist. The muscles in her neck tightened. She'd achieved negligible assimilation to Earth's culture and customs, and judging by her response, was incapable of discerning inconsiderate awe from contempt.

"Do not be alarmed," Dr. Giro said, arms clasped behind him. "This delightful creature is saving planet by letting us use her energy. Show them what you do, Zosma."

Hovering, palms to the ceiling, Zosma raised her arms, and energy ignited her body in a radiant blue aura. Globes of firefly light split into twos, then divided again, and again, multiplying as if experiencing mitosis, until they resembled crushed sapphires. Her creations drifted amongst the guests and captured the room in childlike magic. A daring, curious few extended their hands.

"I have to admit I'm skeptical," the Moroccan king said. "A good majority of us received a thorough report proving this energy emits harmful radiation."

"Not in small doses and not when contained. This is where U-generators come in. My engineer, Mr. Ashur has found way to extract and store and distribute what you see."

Dr. Giro spoke with such verve, Allister had to shake the sincerity in his voice. He turned around to watch the augmented reality presentation projected onto a giant screen. The revenue model C20 had built guaranteed a 1000 percent return on investment through moderate taxation and annual premiums.

"Is inexpensive to use, because it is infinite. It cannot burn off, or burn out, or dry up. More important, and this is essential, it is not harmful to environment, and power cell storage does not diminish over time."

The Z-energy's magic reversed. Speckles fused into balls, and these balls merged into larger spheres. They spun, transformed to streaks, and her timid alien hands absorbed them. She was nervous. The longing for belonging gripped minds of the strongest and weakest alike. He couldn't recall where he'd heard the piece of wisdom.

A dignified applause followed the conclusion of her power display.

"How does it work?" the Nigerian king screeched. "I was promised technology that would preserve my country and sustain my people, not a light show, blue prints, and graphs!"

"It is simple," Dr. Giro answered. "Generators draw from source."

Zosma cried out. Her back arched, and she fell, banished like Lucifer from the heavens, and slammed to the merciless floor. Her crystalized crown tumbled. She contracted into fetal position as energy siphoned from her body,

"What'd you do to her!" Allister shouted.

"From our base ten thousand miles south, the invention we call U-generator has taken 5 percent of available energy. They will be conductors, powering homes, cities, cars, and soon, spacecraft."

Her eyes bounced between a fiery blue and misty black. "What will happen to me?" Zosma asked.

"A sacrifice must be made. You will join your people in Realm of Others, and billions live because of your selflessness."

Captain Brandt snatched Wesley and dragged him across the stage. Hunter clanked his fists. The captain's plasma cannon aimed at the detective's chest. "I wouldn't try me if I was you," he warned and pressed the weapon to Wesley's head.

The chord in Allister's nerves was struck. Two red paint pantones were mixed together; anger and fury, and slapped on his face. Charging at Dr. Giro, he spat through gritted teeth, "I knew you were a maniac!"

"And I knew you would come for retribution," Dr. Giro said, and stepped toward him. "You can choose. Kill me now and save Zosma. But President DeVries will die."

What a barbarous trap laid beneath the leaves of Allister's persistence and sticks of his intention. There in the middle of the stage he halted, ensnared. The auditorium should've been swamped in chaos and horrified screams. Instead, they were like silent spectators at an opening weekend film.

Dr. Giro waved his sausage-sized finger up and down. "Has it ever crossed your advanced mind that even if you kill me, you cannot save her." He nodded at the audience. "They will use what I have built to preserve themselves."

The Transporter gems emitted buzzing energy waves and time slowed to a standstill. He saw Zosma's body crumpled beside the cracked crown. In the other direction, Wesley had squeezed himself into the smallest occupiable space. Hunter didn't seem intent on helping. Florence had recovered from drug-induced slumber and propped herself on her elbow. Strangely, the syringe in the masked agent's hand was 90 percent full.

Allister made his final turn to Dr. Rabia Giro's inhuman stare. A dastardly grin stretched across gaunt features and the black mist moved too, defying the gem's effects. His own hesitation yanked the rug from under him and the world unpaused. While the scene sped up, Allister let his knees give way and sat on his heels. His head bowed, his fingers intertwined, and he rested his knuckles against his forehead.

There were too many decisions to be made to make one.

Dr. Giro retraced his steps to tower beside Zosma's debilitated frame. "Everyone wants to have power. But as you see, it is not about what you have, it is about what you do with it." His mist filled her body to the brim, and when Zosma got up, a thunderstorm raged in her eyes. "Kill them."

—

FLORENCE BELLADONNA

FLORENCE UNSHEATHED THE SWORD, flicked her wrist, and touched its edge to the soldier's neck beside her. "Don't you dare."

"Watch where you're pointin' that thing," he said and removed the mask.

Sighing, she lowered it. "Bazzo, thank goodness."

The other soldier yanked off his mask and shook out shoulder-length hair: Dorian.

"Get the officials as far away as you can," she instructed, tearing the dress's Cinderella skirt to reveal black tights. "I'll deal with her."

Zosma flew to the stairs' edge. Blue energy flocked to her converging hands. Florence's heart skipped a beat at another bellow of thunder, at shrill screams, at Bazzo yelling, "Run! No, don't look! Stop recording!" The last stragglers jolted out of Dr. Giro's influence and scurried to the exits.

Blush-colored light burst from her psiborg leg. Sword handle and blade upright, inches from her sternum, she took a deep breath and staggered her feet. The power swirled and expanded beyond the weapon's edge, building a psionic wall at the exact moment Zosma released the ergokinetic discharge. Florence braced herself, though no training prepared her for a collision likened to a meteoric mass in motion. Following a forewarning crackle from each, the Z-energy and the force field collided with a deafening *boom*.

Florence slid back. The psychic barrier cracked. She gulped. The psychic barrier held. *Zosma, I don't know you, but I know you're in there,* she projected.

Panting, palm perpendicular on the blade's flat side, she pushed the sword forward, intent on repairing the damage. Resewing torn psionic threads, it dawned on her that if the alien woman put an ounce more power behind the subsequent blast, her efforts were irrelevant.

Restored life was evident in the field's vibrancy and a Z-energy burst stronger than the first deadened her yell.

Megatons of deflected energy blew a hovering Zosma from her position. Some absorbed energy permeated her psionic field, disintegrating it. Whatever energy remained sent Florence smashing upwards through wooden stairs.

Florence winced and shook her head, lying in a bed of sticks created by her collision. No time to exhale, nor count how often she'd fought a cosmic-powered adversary, she gasped. Zosma landed on top of her, pinning her down. Florence's muscles ached for an intermission, yet her determined fingers groped for the sword as she dodged the alien's death delivering blows.

Seconds later, she struck gold. Psionic power fizzled at her palm's center, blowing Zosma back two feet at most. She snatched the dragon handle, rolled onto her knee, and swiped across Zosma's guts. Too slow. Zosma dodged with a full rotation and loomed, menacing fingers curled, cutting air circulation to Florence's lungs. Legs stiffening, she rose.

"This world's strongest psychic," Zosma said, "A being who knows too much and does nothing with it."

Florence may have been an appetizer on Dr. Giro's hit list, but the killing machine wasn't moving onto the main course until finishing every morsel. An impenetrable mind's effortless execution.

became cackling. The walls joined in and reverberated its sound. He quieted and gave his possessed henchman a light shoulder slap. "Make sure she watches him die first."

Florence dried up like a well and held out her hand. She called on the one thing she hadn't lost in twenty years. The sword of Psion, left behind in Zosma's violent flurry, obeyed the telepathic command, soaring hilt first into her trembling hand. She secured a tight grasp, moved around Wesley smooth and quick, and planted both feet. Adrenaline was a hell of a drug.

Hunter's metallic fists hit the ground like a sledgehammer. Waves of marble slabs rumbled and rocked the hallway. A column buckled. The ceiling caved.

"Florence!" Wesley exclaimed and pulled her to him by the waist. A section of the mural smashed where she'd been.

Gasping, their sweaty, dusty foreheads touched. She squeezed his wrist. He kissed her temple.

"I'll give you a window to run to the door," Florence whispered and disconnected from their embrace. "Promise me you'll take it."

"You're in no con—"

"Wesley, promise me."

Mid-nod, she yanked him down by the shirt. An uprooted column swung with lethal ambition, rammed against a row of its unbroken siblings, and disqualified the foundation. Lungs overwhelmed by powdered marble and eardrums by crashing sounds, they clambered from under the ceiling's hailstorm.

"Detective Steele, stop before you do something you'll regret," she said, squatting.

"The one thing I regret is pulling you outta the ocean."

"I tried." Right foot back, left foot forward, she drew her elbow up by her ear. Her sightline ran beneath the blade and she pointed the sword at Hunter's heart.

"I can hear the headlines now." He nodded to Wesley and used a theatrical voice, "President DeVries dies shutting down rogue organization, taking Russia, Korea, and China out of the clean energy race. Great narrative am I right? You'll be a bonafide American hero. And, psh, Cynque news won't report on you costing hard working Americans millions, if not billions of dollars. The public doesn't find out that kinda stuff anymore. No one'll know there isn't a solution to the goddamn problem. Until it's too late."

Moonlit metals gleamed in the dismal hallway, and two worthy combatants entered a game of strength versus strategy. The Sword of Psion's true edge led her advance, and the jagged steel's forward slash clanked across his torso. She pivoted in a full circle on her left foot, backhand sliced through his midsection, and passed back the right foot to switch positions. The blade flattened to him and she parried his retaliatory punch. Hunter cursed and stumbled, and slammed into a leaning column. Her nimble wrists propelled the sword into a swinging frenzy, which ended with her arm at her side. Blood restricted hands clenched the handle. The blade faced out, tip down.

"Let's see if steel can cut through Steele, shall we?"

"Your fake ass legacy dies with humanity, DeVries." Hunter snickered as he searched the shadows.

"He's gone. Give it up."

His aggression zeroed in on Florence. "You know the thing about Dr. Giro, he thought of everyone. You rich fucks only thought about yourselves."

She ducked his left hook, rotated 180 degrees and roundhouse kicked him with the psiborg leg. Hunter's head banged against the marble. Leaping to meet him at his resting place, she thrust the sword's point down. Hunter stopped it from puncturing his skull between prayer-positioned hands and threw her backward. She lost the sword. She lost her balance. She lost her edge.

Hunter swiveled a leg in a semicircle to a swift recovery onto both feet, retrieved the weapon, and hurled it forward. Florence darted sideways, catching the handle during a rapid open turn, then jumped column to column, poised to deliver a sharp, critical blow. He had other plans and threw a metal forearmed front guard over his eye. Her overhand, centered-slice wedged in his skin. He grabbed her by the stomach and flung her. The marble column that had been her aid became her enemy. Her back screamed on impact, and she landed face down in scattered debris.

"Hope he doesn't mind if I kill you in reverse order," he said, lurching to conclude his slaughter.

A plasma pistol's three blasts singed the air and ricocheted off Hunter's shoulder. A fourth and fifth heated the element protecting him. The sixth cost him his equilibrium, and he flew aside.

Blessed by the moon's light for his bravery, Wesley stood tall to take on their adversary. "Stay down, Steele. We'll get your head cleared."

Struggling to her hands and knees ended in Florence collapsing on her back. She stared upwards at the unveiled heavens begging her home. "You didn't take—" The sentence hid in her throat, afraid what truth its completion would manifest.

Wesley's window was gone. She felt submerged underwater. Drowned in a fateful moment and the world's hollow noises. His barely audible voice gauged if she was okay. Her arm fumbled for the sword. Manicured nail tips scratched at the dragon head handle, but they could not drag it to her. She extended her shoulder, eyes pressed shut, mouth stretched tight. *Crunch. Crack. Thump.*

Her lover's protesting screams, and, "Sorry it had to end this way, Prez," came before the human vertebrae snapped.

"We... Wes... Wesley," she choked out. Blood cold as a corpse, Florence witnessed Hunter drilling his mutilated body into the wreckage.

—◆—

ALLISTER ADAMS

THE THUNDERSTORM HAD PASSED, giving Bazzo and Zosma's heated combat the attention it deserved. Electricity and Z-energy blasted this way and that. Bazzo shouted Allister's name. Zosma grunted in pain or anger or disinterest. Chairs ripped up by the nails, flung across the room. Then came a tremendous scream.

Allister sat on his haunches and refused to acknowledge her behavior. He didn't want to see her murderous. Becoming the monster, they claimed, solidified her candidacy as an imperfect sacrifice.

"Stop it, Zosma," he said.

His blood moved too fast for him to process the energy's needling pain, and he heaved his leg from under him and flattened his foot. Z-energy enveloped his knuckles. A firm push to his knee and Allister stood spread legged, posture straightened, and squinted. Bazzo held his wrist, his face contorted and boiling red. A metal rod had speared his hand to the wall, too long and entrenched for him to free himself.

Allister took a step at a time and spoke soft, calming words, "Resist his influence, Zosma. You're not a killer."

She screamed, "You have no idea what I am!"

The radiating telekinetic field shattered, dented the walls and blew Allister into metal panels. Z-energy had scorched his chest worse than any plasma blast. Smoke rose from the affliction, and his unsteady hand dropped, too scared to make contact. "I-I know you're more than a weapon." A sharp inhale, and both forearms blocked her double kick. His pushback drove her into the air.

It was too much to ask that she remain there. Too much to assume that he'd gotten through to her. A Z-energy ball formed as she swung forward. He didn't feel the explosive force, though he flew, smashed a wall to scraps, and landed face down in the grass outside. Close call. Bringing his left arm to defend the strike had given him bonus rounds in the ring. Muddy coolness soothed the third-degree burn. He laid there thinking of words to slow her, confident no human sentiments would penetrate.

Zosma sped his direction, a purple blur. She jumped. Allister's arms tucked. He rolled away. *Boom*. Her feet hit the ground. Rocks and dirt spewed outward. He got up, swallowed hard and leaned on the house's siding.

A living energy source. A fallen world's princess. A compassionate, curious, and delicate specimen with a spirit luminous as the stars. What else could Zosma be? The mother of his children? Welcome on Earth? Yes. And more. He'd convinced himself no one should define her complicated and beautiful existence by a single attribute.

Fortresses of guilt and sorrow had dominated his mind and soul for months. The emotional constructs, which occupied so much mental space, drove weakness, and such weakness drove impulsion in place of intelligence. There he was, a victim, staring at her as she endeavored to knock his head clean off his body. The burn's stinging subsided, and restored skin sewed across his chest.

He grabbed her fist before it connected with his face. Hoarse, he muttered ancient Uragonian scripture, "Resilience lies in the sturdiest minds."

"And purpose is forged by unchained eyes." Zosma said, almost singing. "How did—"

Her pupils glowed the blue he loved, the intrepid blue of her heritage. Their fingers curled over each other. Touching her was like picking apples from his mother's garden on a summer day, stargazing with his father on the roof. Innocent, uncomplicated joy he longed for.

She went on, "I thought I was a solution. That is what he told me. I am sorry."

"Don't be sorry." He traced her jawline. "You've been exploited and hunted wherever you go. And here you are. Alive. You can do anything, you can be anything. You don't have to be a weapon."

"Then, I suppose neither do you."

Allister saw his reflection in her burning irises and pulled her body to his. Her sweet smell sent shivers down his arms. "Can you see yourself?"

Two of her three fingers caressed his cheek. She nodded.

Dr. Giro's heavy footsteps crunched splintered wood and crumbled rock. "The brave," he said in more guttural growls then human tongue, "are always first to die."

"Rabia is not what he seems, do not—"

Mist swallowed the light in her. She staggered.

Dr. Giro's face contained no fear. No invitation to battle. Hands clasped at his waistline, the doctor eluded flickering light, vacant, dark eyes locked on Allister. Like planetary bodies in a solar system, their orbit began. Allister was a great storm with his sights set on landfall. His fury hungered for vengeance and Dr. Giro fed it with the gasoline of his indifference.

Z-energy exploded up his left arm and bathed his body in its chaotic light. Tiny, frothy bubbles formed on his mouth's corners. "It's over, let her go," he said.

"Allister, I have toiled my entire existence, ensuring Earth reached necessary milestones for Z-energy integration. I will not be swayed by an insipid child pretending to be hero. No, she will not be let go. She. Will. Be. Used."

The first punch shattered the doctor's sternum. Allister retreated, huffing and puffing, forgetting he'd taken a swift, venomous step and swung with his two-hundred-pound body's entire weight. The kneeling doctor held up a plump, hairy hand covered in blood so red, it was damn near black.

Zosma shrieked.

Dr. Giro stood. His fingers still, his knees steady. No shock. No pain. "I will not stop," he said.

Facial bones cracked under Allister's numbed, blood-soaked fist. Dr. Giro doubled over, touched the dent in his wilted, fractured cheek.

"Allister, don't!" Zosma screamed and retired to sobbing.

He opened his hand and looked at it as the blood rushed to his palm, anxious to see what happened next. "Let her go," he repeated.

"Harnessing Z-energy is my destiny," Dr. Giro sneered.

Spit and mucus and vital fluid should've been stuck in Dr. Giro's throat. He should've needed to swallow, to pause before catching his breath. He didn't and continued, "I have waited."

Hand under the doctor's chin, Allister squeezed the Adam's apple and hoisted him off the ground. He waited for a whimper, an attempted gulp. Dr. Giro didn't beg for oxygen or absolution, though Zosma begged on the doctor's behalf.

They were connected, and they'd be connected as long as Dr. Giro lived. Z-energy coursed from Allister's elbow to his wrist to the nails digging into his enemy's fragile, wrinkled tissue. A fierce blue surge took an unsolicited voyage through the doctor's jerking body, frying bones to ash, scorching muscles and tendons to dust, melting skin until it evaporated above them. Death's torturous squeals became a jagged-tooth mouth spouting maniacal laughter.

A humanoid body shaped by dark mist smashed onto the stage. It squirmed on its back like an overturned insect. Far too massive to be squashed, it succeeded in standing, albeit hunched over. Five fingers melded to four, lengthening to long sharpened claws. A quartet of hungry eyes, red as an African sunset, blinked. A beak-like nose was molded in an elongated, reptilian facial structure and three misty horns billowed above its head like a crown. It straightened to an assertive posture and exaggerated spiked shoulders formed on the outskirts of a broadened muscular chest. The plump midsection narrowed into a skeletal waist as its body stretched to ten feet tall.

Allister's mind malfunctioned, denying the transformation happening before them. Any words reserved for shock, came as primitive sputters. Sickness swept his stomach. Mouth trapped open in astonishment, he tripped on his way to Zosma's side and toppled next to her.

Incoherent, curled up in a ball, she muttered "no" and a name he couldn't understand. He gave her obsessive care, persuading himself for the instant he stroked her arm; he'd done nothing wrong. But there was no one else to blame for Dr. Rabia Giro's execution. Allister had unleashed the sinister being dominating the room's center.

"I have waited three thousand years," the creature croaked, extending its arms to their full wingspan. Its carnivorous teeth gnashed in a deep, red mouth and a furious howl transformed it into black mist. The suffocating cloud tore light from their filaments, and blanketed the room in absolute darkness.

———

The smoky creature reshaped itself and bulldozed the stage, stray chairs, limp bodies, and scrap wood and metal from its path, intent on subduing the Uragonian princess. Allister squared his shoulders, primed to shield her.

"Allister, please," Zosma said. Reattaching her broken crown, she switched their positions, him shielded and her in front. Energy flooded to her. "Zaian power is cosmic. You are no match." She erected a shimmering telekinetic field.

"Zaian? Who is he?"

"*It* is Dylurshin Hexforth. The Great Betrayer. The Last Zaian. It has many names and even more faces."

The thing she referred to as Dylurshin pummeled her defensive measure. Its shrill banging sent blue globules splattering.

"I believe," she strained to say, "I can vanquish it, though I fear this innocent city will suffer as well."

"You're going to—no you can't!" He held her armored shoulders. "The pulse'll destroy Vancouver. Maybe you too."

Zosma touched his rising and falling chest. "I cannot stop this," she whispered.

Her ace of spades: an energy pulse. The card that won all hands, ended all games, emptied all pockets.

"I don't want to leave you." He stroked the nape of her neck "But, I don't think... I won't survive."

"Your people need you."

Bazzo.

"I swear to Taldykin, my Father Star, my actions were not of my own malice. Please make it known to him." She glided back, her forearm upright and said, "In unchallenged respect and devotion."

"Forever and always," he replied, holding his the same. Their eyes linked in commitment. Their limbs touched in promise.

"I'll hold Dylurshin for as long as I can."

Airborne, she rotated around herself, hands above her head, and as if composing Beethoven's ninth, she brought them to her sides, signaling the symphony. The Z-energy field fizzled from the top, whittling down. Down until it vanished at her toes and left her vulnerable to obstruction.

"If it is my energy you seek, Zaian, then I shall deliver it to you in all its boundless wrath."

"You will hurt me no more so than your ancestors did," Dylurshin said, as it collected its influence to challenge her.

The room lightened to a solemn grey and reluctantly relinquishing his concern for their conversation, Allister called Bazzo's name while he braved the misty presence occupying the small auditorium. A spine-chilling cry left the Aussie's throat. He followed subsequent cries of agony to the outskirts. A metal rod clattered beside him, launched from the wall somehow. Maybe electromagnetism.

"Mate," Bazzo sputtered, "Allister, I'm over here."

Bazzo was huddled in the room's quiet corner, cradling his own forearm. Allister had seen gruesome injuries on himself and on others, but none made his stomach turn quite like the festering, gaping hole in Bazzo's hand.

"Zosma says sorry," he said and dipped to offer his shoulder, "here."

Bazzo gave him the intact hand and asked, "She on our side now?"

"I got through to her. She's gonna try to... We need to go." Allister hauled himself to his feet with a firm grip on Bazzo's waist.

He limped to the grass lawn, Electric Wonder in tow. A nickname drafted in contempt took on a sweeter, more endearing taste when mixed with the dapper young man's valiance and selflessness.

Zosma screamed in displeasure and frustration. House fragments soared past them. Slicing, shooting, grunting, roaring, Allister fought the compulsion to rush back and aid her. He'd get in the way. He'd make things worse.

"How you holding up?" he asked Bazzo.

"Doubt I'd be moving if it weren't for you."

Dorian's triumphant silhouette greeted them from the cobblestone driveway.

He deserted their brief bromance, nearly dropping Bazzo to dash ahead and throw the hug he'd saved for Dorian around his neck. Signature dimples appeared in the corners of his mask-free smile, as he hugged Allister's torso in reciprocation.

"The Sonic Superhuman," Allister said, "it's good to see you."

Dorian nodded despite the playful chokehold and squeezed in response.

"Mind explaining the friggin' floating demon or whatever the shit?" Bazzo asked him, winded and hobbling to catch up.

"Zosma called it by the name Dylurshin Hexforth. I don't know what it is. I just know it's my fault it's free."

"Is she aiming to kill the thing?"

"Yeah, in not so many words," he answered and turned to address his mistake. The gazillion pieces comprising the mansion's roof, walls, siding, and foundation had been reconstructed, imprisoning the cosmic duel's sights and sounds. "The first pulse'll hit a two-mile radius, the second and third'll wipe out the Pacific Northwest region. We should, uh, keep it moving."

Dorian tapped him and pointed at the stomach-down body sprawled at their feet. Scalp visible at the crown. Wrinkled white blazer. A motionless Captain Brandt squirmed and cried out, "Huh, whoa. What fuckin' happened?"

"You tell me."

"My mind's... clear. My mind ain't been clear since... Allister, tell me you didn't." The captain snatched Allister's elbow. "You killed him? You killed Dr. Giro?"

"It was—it was an accident," Allister said, trying to pull away, trying to explain away the pangs in his conscience. "He had Zosma and I, I didn't know what else to do."

Captain Brandt relaxed his grip. "Oh, this's bad son."

"I don't have to explain myself to you."

"It don't matter anymore either way, you made the choice. Whatever Rabia was, is gone," Captain Brandt said, "This thing wanted somethin', and it's been moving us around on the chessboard to get it."

An impatient gaze penetrated the captain's thin follicles. Zosma's radiance leaked from corners, cracks, and crevices, implored to be seen and known of its impending eruption.

"I..." Brandt followed his concern. "I'm sorry I wasn't there for ya, Allister. You got a lot more livin' to do, don't do it angry." He jerked away, scrambled to his feet, and sprinted to the fractured house.

Allister took a step after the captain, forgiveness and rage battling in his bones. Dorian blocked his advance. He took another step. With an aggressive head-shake, Dorian splayed both hands on his chest.

"Where's Florence?" he asked. Wild, frantic eyes darted over the yard. Agent. Soldier. Agent. Soldier. Soldier. World leader. Agent. One picture of Florence Belladonna's charred corpse and his intestines knotted in anxiety. *Not again,* he thought. "Bazzo, where's Florence?"

"I-I left her to help Dorian."

A blue beam tore off the mansion's roof. Then, fast, furious, and fatal, it twisted and widened and ripped the house apart. Z-energy exploded outward in a fiery kaboom, threatening to overtake a marching Captain Brandt before his plan could take shape. His selfish disruptive field climbed his boots, coated his upper body like a suit of armor, and covered his hands as they flew out to the side. Translucent, rippling energy unfolded from the captain's hulking shape and expanded into a generous wall.

The pulse fizzed to nothing as it reached the edges. A restrained Z-energy vortex spiraled skyward for miles and miles, the disruptive barrier chasing it the whole way. Allister clenched his fists, nose thrust ahead of him like a bloodhound. The blast drowned Bazzo's shouting, but he picked up every other word, catching "Allister" and "glowing" on repeat. Unbeknownst to him, the Transporter gems had showered him in the brilliance of temporal energy.

———

Florence Belladonna

The roar's distinguishable low pitch beckoned from the conference room at the same time telepathic backlash stormed her skull. And while she'd been lying on rough, uneven marble, committed to having her final resting place be next to Wesley, Florence recalled the petrifying face in Allister's mind that had accompanied the same infernal sound.

In whole or in part unexpected, Hunter had been relinquished from the mist's possession and his rampage paused. Recognition of her immobile form shone in his face, became shock, then graduated to horror at Wesley's mangled remains.

He bolted. She bolted after him.

Gore's rotten stench would not leave her nostrils. Bathed in tears, rain and sweat, she ran like Cinderella after the clock struck twelve. Curly locks resurrected by moisture bouncing in the wind, serrated sword glinting in streetlight. Dreams dashed, gown ruined; there was no more magic and, worse, no more potential for magic. She thought about the years she and Wesley had wasted, thinking if they stayed apart they stayed alive. Falsehoods forged in fear.

During her mile-long sprint, the scenery shifted from towering cedars to houses clad in poverty. One leg, made of a metal alloy foreign to earth, had unlimited stamina. The other, of muscle, bones, and tendons, was susceptible to fatigue and injury. She slowed. With every third or fourth rapid breath, her feet dragged in an irregular cadence.

Questionable orange lights were strung under an overpass infested with shabby trash-filled cars and pitched tents. The street smelled of urine and desperation.

Four undercover C20 agents had skulked into the spotlight. Her seldom seen savagery provoked, she swiped behind her, cut off an agent's gun-wielding arm, snatched him by the collar, and tossed him at the oncoming attacker's feet without taking a single breath. A swift psiborg leg kick to the advancing agent's throat sent him toppling over himself in the air. He hit the street with a wet thud.

No sign of the metal-skinned culprit.

Wires whisked around her ankles, forcing them together. Air battered her face as she fell and slammed on the asphalt. A trigger clicked. She rolled onto her back and the plasma beam burned a crater where her head had been. Though he missed her, the agent gloated from above, prepared to fire again. She swept her legs right. His body flailed, and the gun flew. Florence cut the wire, returned to her feet, and stabbed him through the thigh. He cried out.

Clink. Clink. Clink.

She retracted the sword and turned to the graffitied wall under the bridge. Hunter leaned on a pickup truck, wearing an arrogant metallic smile. He finished clapping, interlocked his hands, and stretched them above his head.

"You and Giovanni are cut from the same cloth, honey," he said, chortling. "In fact, you're worse. Because you pretend to be good."

Her human leg faltered, and forced her to steady the antique blade's reddened tip against the street. "Stand up straight," her father had said, "and conduct yourself with poise and precision, or no one will take you seriously." She pressed down on the dragonhead hilt and told herself not to fall over, not to give in.

"You. Killed. Him," Florence said. For those spoken words the sword was no more than the long leg of a cane, needed to hold her up and keep her going. "He was your—"

"God, you're being dramatic. Just tell me you weren't going to say friend. Wesley was far from a friend, sweetie, and from what I hear, pretty far from a lover too." Hunter stopped within arm's reach. "He was a liar. I take that back. He was a politician. Too caught up in self-interest to see the bigger picture, our preservation."

And in that sentence Florence remembered she carried a weapon, not a crutch. She screamed, confident her sword's jagged edges ripped his colon and dislodged his spinal disks as it plunged through his abdominals. Confident it inflicted some damage.

Anything. Anything was better than his smile, and the sound of metal scraping metal, as he moved himself forward on the blade.

"I'm metal inside and out," he said.

His gigantic metal fingers hugged her waist too tight and her abdominal muscles fought oncoming suffocation. She pounded his knuckles with her fists. His grip tightened. She tugged her body upward and kicked wildly. Still, her hip bones, ribs and spine were squeezed closer together. She called upon her telepathic gifts, but was ultimately forsaken by them. They required more concentration and less grief.

Hunter wrenched the Belladonna sword out. "Pretty," he said and held the stain-free metal to the sky. "It'll look good on my accent wall."

CELINE NEPHTHYS

"BEN-TII, THERE'S NOTHING you could have done," King Nephthys said. He removed his chechia and smoothed the few silver strands on his head. "Let America have their energy war."

Celine hated riding in "metal cans," though her father insisted. Her head swayed, and shoulders rocked at each pothole and road bump. They'd gotten ten miles from danger, yet she felt the foreign creature's strength inflating.

America. Russia. China. Korea. They were oblivious. Pumping millions into Dr. Rabia Giro's Z-energy passion project, with no way to decipher the deeper motivation, his history on their planet, or his hand in the advancements of human science and technology. The Antarctic ice knew when the creature landed, and the revelation was too much to accept or turn a blind eye.

"Driver, stop," she said.

The vehicle lurched and stopped. She opened the door, and one bare foot settled on the pavement.

"It is not our battle, Celinicus Nephthys." The king tugged at her jumpsuit. "If you die here, there is no one to protect the planet."

"Then, I will not die." She placed her youthful fingers on his aged ones, turned, and rose her intense, wooden eyes to meet his. "Do not worry, Baba."

He let go. "May your mother's spirit be with you."

Wind pushed the door shut and the car peeled down the hill to the city.

Celine's arms curled in considerable effort to inspire the resurrection of a stone structure from beneath the asphalt. The ground pushed the man-made street aside, unveiling her makeshift chariot from a two-foot-wide fissure. She nestled her feet on its warm slate as it levitated higher and skated across a cloudless night sky. Hot breeze fanned her boiling temper, and she contemplated her and Rabia Giro's initial encounter. Remembering his deep ancient voice wrapped her in paralyzing fear. She'd been unable to admit to Allister, and herself, that the creature's presence struck a chord in Earth's consciousness.

A leaf flitted beside her ear.

"Yes, I feel it too," she said. "The creature called Dylurshin rises."

She caught it, twirled it in her fingers, and released it to its descent.

—•—

BAZZO SPARKS

BAZZO HAD WARNED at the top of his lungs the gems were glowing. Allister didn't listen or didn't hear him in time, or he didn't care.

In either case he'd vanished, Bazzo presumed into the inferno. Running to the sky for freedom, dust curled and swished above a conglomeration of collapsed concrete, marble, and stone. The World Energy Summit had come to an end.

Dorian helped him take apart the undercover uniform, rip its cotton strips and swathe his devastating hand injury. Fluttering eyes disobeyed his brain's commands to stay open. Blood loss soaked the camouflage colored scraps and for the first time, Bazzo examined his white, near transparent skin. Despite his neurological numbing trick, physical overexertion and its accompanying aches shot through his body. He crumbled. Dorian caught him under the arms to lower him and rubbed his back while he retched bile and acid from his guts.

Dry heaving, he asked, "Did Brandt—?" The question dried in his mouth, answered by what lay on the lawn.

Captain Brandt's shredded white jacket dancing in the wind. He'd been incinerated. The captain had spent his whole life making the wrong decisions and then woke up and decided to make the right one. Feeling his mortality, Bazzo wondered if it balanced out, if there was time for deliverance in those seconds linking righteousness and the afterlife. "Damn," he said, wanting to piece himself together and not knowing how to begin.

A pebble dislodged, bounced over a mountainous peak of debris and plopped on the grass. Numerous boulders followed its lead rolling to and crashing at the base. The birds knew of a danger he didn't, their wings flapping as they fled from treetops. There was a 66 percent chance the person he wanted to emerge would be the person who emerged, and Bazzo wasn't feeling particularly lucky. Dorian took several cautious steps back.

The dark pulsing mass burst free and ascended to its ten-foot glory, using red energy bolts to snatch, pull, and piece itself together.

Bazzo watched on hands and knees, jaw propped open and exclaimed, "What the fu—?"

Zosma's bruised body appeared to have been dashed against a concrete slab and remained sprawled over it. Allister's blood-stained body appeared to have suffered the blast's consequences and lay limp on uncovered rocks. Both beneath the giant living cloud, neither awake.

He aspired to stand, weary and trembling. His body expressed its disapproval with nauseating waves.

A lumbering Oshkosh MTVR truck smashed through the gate that guarded the property and squealed when it got to the unconscious bodies. Lowest to the ground, Bazzo peered between six deep tread tires. C20 agents exited the truck, shackled Zosma and Allister's bodies, and loaded them onto the covered cargo bed.

Mist particles slithered over, under, and through the getaway truck's mainframe, then were molded menacing and whole in front of it. The military vehicle vroomed in reverse out of the uneven driveway.

"Bridg... "

Acceptance was the qualifying event that dredged up her captivity. Accepting that Rabia Giro, who, in hindsight was a deranged scientist and not much more, had been replaced by this demonic creature made of pure mist. Accepting the demonic creature's sheer power to defeat Zosma *and* Allister. The reality was, if they hadn't stopped the thing, there wasn't much Bazzo could do. Bridget, himself, and the world were about to suffer irreversible devastation.

Not the bravest crayon in the box, eh, he thought and realized Dorian had crawled out of his peripheral.

"You are as weak and tiresome as your ancestors," the demonic creature said, shaking the forest with its galactic baritone. "And I hope easier to dispose of." The creature's clawed arm stretched upwards, twisting, lengthening and solidifying.

Aaaaanddd his arm just turned into a bloody sword. This is fucked. Bazzo mustered more energy and gambled two-to-one odds in a staring contest. "Ain't got a clue what you're on about," he said, holding his healthy fist tighter than he thought possible, "but you got my sis and my friend and... " Accessing nearby street lamps' electricity, a sparse collection of electric currents formed around him. He went to project the attack, found his arm paralyzed, and retired to grunting and swearing amidst booming villainous laughter.

The thick, sword-shaped limb refused to gleam in the moonlight as the creature took giant clawed steps toward him and touched the sharpened tip to his hammering heartbeat. "It would seem history does repeat itself."

CELINE NEPHTHYS

"YOU DO NOT BELONG HERE," Celine said and ejected from the chariot. The creature sneered, losing concentration, and the hunched, blonde man ducked and fell away. Her transportation-turned-projectile zoomed through the air and collided head on with Dylurshin's upper body.

Ascension of Earth's faithful crust to catch Celine as she plunged feet first, its leveled platform shape and the way it welcomed her as it lowered her to the grass, was proof and promise of their harmonious relationship.

The serpentine hiss signaled the entity's return to offense. She assumed its loud roar had stemmed from *annoyance* at the distraction, not pain, seeing as how inky mist crept ahead and splashed near her like an incoming tide.

"Celinicus Nephthys, the one that got away," Dylurshin said, "You reek of insubordination."

"I will not stand by and watch your dreams become what they truly are, nightmares." Celine's voice hovered between patience and agitation. Fingers closed into fists then opened to channel her geokinesis. "The Earth identifies you as the exiled from the stars. What business do you have on my planet?"

It snickered. "This is no more your planet than it is mine." Dylurshin's body lengthened, opted to stay an upside down pear-shaped blob, pounded the ground and blew outwards.

She lifted her foot and stomped. Displaced rocks, mud, and clay catapulted to six-foot heights. Solidified, they absorbed the assault before shattering back to a loose mixture. Renewed vigor raised her palms from hip level, to waist level. The soil's millions of tiny hands grabbed Dylurshin's body. Climbed and thickened as more attached. Her palms went from shoulder level, to eye level, guiding the dirt on its journey upward, and ended above her head.

Sand dripped from Celine's spine. Her hair, indistinguishable from the wind. Transmutation was inevitable when testing the upper limits of her gifts.

I can't falter, she thought.

Wooded soldiers summoned to aid her, slinked past, coiling around the cosmic force to extinguish the hostility within it. Vines, foliage, any natural thing in her power's reach swarmed to encase the creature in a compact cocoon.

Charged black and red energy rays formed fissures on the surface of the cocoon, expanding until they blasted it to harmless wreckage.

"Concerted effort Mentarian witch, you are strong indeed."

Exhaustion pulled her body to the lawn. "It's all I have," she mumbled. Her eyes pierced the ground as though looking at Dylurshin's clawed arm and sharp-edged blade would validate its ability to overpower her. Dirty nails caressed the supportive soil, and she drew in the elements to keep her dissolving anatomy intact.

Disadvantaged by mental strain, Dylurshin's influence poisoned the conversation betwixt her and the trees, channeling its own requests through the mother called Earth. Dispirited and disloyal roots corkscrewed around her in rapid succession.

Inadequacy shackled her creative spirit. Wild thoughts and personal fears convinced Celine she didn't have the imagination or strength to achieve her desired elemental manifestations. She knew what Dylurshin was, but she didn't how it came to be, she didn't know why it was there. The missing knowledge extinguished her fire. It felt implausible to overcome a threat without privilege to its weaknesses or its intentions. There was no soft underbelly, no Achilles' heel.

Moving fast, the ominous face advanced, ready to impose its influence on her geological power, as it had done a year before in her slumber. She would've rather died than suffer its exploitation, than have her gifts usurped for certain evil. Stroking the roots constricting her arms, Celine prayed for a final favor.

"My brothers and sisters, hear me," she said, "You have been influenced by this parasite. Listen no more to its sweet words of preservation. Do to Dylurshin with stone, what it has done to me with wood."

Earth obliged with a quaking invitation of bedrock from beneath topsoil, subsoil, and weathered rock fragments. The rumbling rectangular prism surfaced, and surrounded the entity, surging past its height and sealing at the top. Shrieks echoed as Dylurshin battered the prison's interior.

The roots retracted. She swallowed doom's bitter taste and engaged her audience. "Stone won't hold it for long."

A long-haired teenager reached for her hand to help her stand. "I'm fine," she said and picked herself up off her haunches.

The handsome young man known in the world's high society as Bazzo Sparks flexed his exposed abdominals and pulled his abused body into an "L" shape.

"Cel-Celine." He mustered a one-sided smile. "Glad ya came." She inhaled, turned to the street and replied, "We cross paths far too often for coincidence."

"No complaints here." He coughed, choked, gagged, and cleared his throat. "Dorian, Dr. B... gotta find Dr. B."

Her skin cracked like sunbaked clay. "You can barely stay awake. I can't hold myself together. And he is too afraid of his own power to fight." Thick veins crossed her forehead and spread down her body's left side. "This region will be lost to Dylurshin's influence. You need to warn the American—"

The crumbling tower cut in on her counsel. Dylurshin Hexforth had vanished and so did the last of her energy.

———

FLORENCE BELLADONNA

FLORENCE OPENED HER MOUTH, and inhaled the fondest memory of Wesley DeVries.

Twenty-two years old. Optimistic, but not naive. She tended to let her reputation precede her and strode into his office, prepared to accept an internship, even though there were no open positions. The instant they shook hands, what had been about making change in the world and challenging the political sphere's norms, became about his dimples and the way his eyes thinned when he smiled. Scarlet painted lips reshaped from a thin, entitled line to an intrigued smirk.

At the onset, her brain bulldozed any ounce of attraction. Earnest green irises brightened with intelligence instead of infatuation. She'd gone on to explain to him why his economic infrastructure for the New SoHo development project wasn't viable, still a bit naive to the inner workings of global politics and the dangerous creature she was destined to become.

Fifteen years later, life's unpredictable and unfair dealings had stripped her heart's fervor and left it frozen in a way it might never thaw, let alone reignite.

She'd been seduced by sweet vengeance and betrayed, riding tied up in a stolen pick-up truck's bed. Her wrists grappled with the itchy rope constriction. Primitive, yes. Loose, no. She rotated by fishtailing her legs, brought her heels to her butt, and pushed herself past the truck's rear wheel guards. Shoulders swinging left, right, left, right, she gained enough momentum, swung her torso up, and used her legs to scoot her back against the tailgate. She propped her shoulders on it as her head gave in to gravity and came to a rest on its bumpy metal cap.

Serene space spread above earned her mind's focus.

"Hang tight gorgeous!" Hunter called back. "We're here!"

Here. They weren't here. They were there. Somewhere in the vicinity, lay the flesh and bones of an assassinated U.S. president. New sounds and smells were there too—wailing sirens gunning up the hill and scorched grass.

Straight through the rear window molding, jacked up, armored police cars blocked the road. Canadian officials surrounded them, weapons aimed high, likely for Hunter's skull, incognizant of its metallic protection.

"Pull over now!" a high-pitched voice instructed over an intercom. "Pullover or we open fire. I won't ask again."

"Ha!" the detective spat.

The engine revved. Gunfire blazed. Hunter abandoned ship. The sleek Ford F-150 slammed into the vehicular barricade like a runaway train, causing instant engine explosions. Florence hadn't a free limb to anchor herself and ducked, curling her knees to her forehead as bad suspension sent the truck off of its left wheels. The vehicle's side crunched on impact with the road. Her backbone banged the rear wheel guard before she flipped overboard, hurled from safety and into the hard sidewalk. The metal continued sparking and scraping as the truck skidded to a stop up the street, smoking and damaged.

"I'm here on a special mission," Hunter said, showboating a massive firearm. "Got a U.S. fugitive in my camp, and I'm gonna drag her over the border, dead or alive."

Bewildered troops consulted the police captain.

Gun barrel steadied on the open window, she shouted, "Keep your sights on him, eh!"

"Sooo, which of you suckers is gonna lend me their whip?"

"Take him down!"

The cavalry obeyed. Round after round of tracer bullets lit up the neighborhood, ripped his leather jacket to shreds and ricocheted off his metallic form. Not the slightest bit tickled by their assault, Hunter charged his plasma weapon. "You know, I was going to let you all live. But you ruined my custom jacket."

Frantic shouting, plasma beams firing, blood spattering, and maniacal laughing consumed the private acres.

Will to fight. Will to live. Will to move. She searched her waning psyche for fiery passion to do the aforementioned and found a shrinking heart that snuffed out hope and possibility. Hunter was right. Her inclination to self-preservation or selfish devastation (they're very similar), drove her to give up, to lie there, to wait to be penetrated by stray gunfire or impaled by scrap metal rain.

Florence's bodyweight squished her hands. She wriggled onto her stomach and inch-wormed across the street. Pause.

The sword of Psion sword lay parallel to her, center stage to Hunter's wrath.

There came another blessing right after, the hairless tan face and tight-lipped glower belonging to Dorian Xander. He stood by the bulldozed gate, searching his palms for... There they were: waves born from sonic absorption ignited and basked his grim expression in a psychedelic purple glow. *Shoom. Shoom. Shoom.* Converted concussive energy blasts pumped through his palms.

Hunter shouldered one and deflected it. On the second, he lost his footing. The third and biggest consumed his figure and knocked him through the Canadian military's blockade.

"Dorian!" she called out. He stepped into the street and looked around at eye level. "Down here!"

Dashing her direction, he spotted the sword and scooped it up before he reached her side. A clumsy hand inspected her bruising and then he wedged the sharp edge through the winding rope's knot and after a little pressure, thousands of tiny fabric incisions unraveled.

Florence Belladonna, the infamous telepath, known for stealth, beauty, a quick tongue, and quicker blade, planted the sword's tip in the pavement and hoisted herself up. If this were her last fight, at least she fought for something and someone she'd believed in. Unevenly heeled footsteps, accompanied steel dragging on asphalt and a low, hoarse, feminine growl. "Give it a rest, Steele."

"Round two so soon?" Hunter asked and launched a vehicle her direction.

It screeched and whipped around. A second wind coursed toes to fingertips, and Florence slid underneath it, flipped to a standing position, and though limping, ran toward the detective.

A detached door twirled, feet from slicing her in half. She jumped, planted her enhanced foot on it, and leaped into the air. Psiborg leg surrounded by pulsing energy, her body swiveled, and the sword's sharpened edge clanged, scraped, then slashed Hunter's metal exterior. He flew back, tumbled over the street, and landed on his stomach. Both of her feet planted.

"Go ahead and kill me," he said, breaking into nervous laughter, "won't be your first and won't be your last."

Florence skulked toward him.

He stayed on the ground, gripped his wound, smiled like he'd won some game. "His first born. His little lady. Go on, make Lord Giovanni Belladonna proud."

Get a grip Florence, she thought, sword raised over his neck. *He's not worth it.*

"You saved my life once." She sheathed the blade, circling him and focused. "I'll spare yours."

Telepathic power penetrated his cavernous mental space, sifted for the deepest, darkest memories. Buried under toughness, misogyny, apathy were childhood scenes. Crying for hours hiding in the closet while his parents abused substances. Lashings whenever he was disobedient. Being offered up as an experiment. Left to die after the experiment failed.

Hunter's tortured screams fought a helicopter's thunderous arrival for attention, and the metallic mutation covering his upper torso, hands, arms, neck, and head reverted to human flesh, cell after cell, organ after organ. The detective, stripped of wit, charm, and guile, crouched into a fetal position.

Blustering wind took over her face. She turned its direction and muttered, "The bloody nerve."

Airforce One's new VH-94 helicopter enlivened the morose mid-night sky with glaring spotlights.

Dorian had returned from somewhere. Her first thought was the mansion grounds. Bazzo's comatose body rested on his thin shoulders. He lingered at the curb while searchlights inched toward illuminating his scrawny shape.

Dorian, don't run, she projected. *They'll find you.*

He lowered his head, knelt, and laid the body on his back on the sidewalk. Survival. Living on his own terms. Solitude. Desires sprinting through his mind faster than he, toward the damp forest. She stopped reading his thoughts.

The idea was to go to Bazzo's side and examine his condition, but she stood sculpted in contemplation, loneliness concrete in her veins. She could've fought a little harder, run a little faster, been a little smarter.

A pair of dress shoes and a pair of heels clicked in unison.

"They could've sent anyone up here. Why did they send you?" Florence asked.

"You're under arrest," a gravelly voice said. It belonged to Townsend Black, a cabinet member and DeVries's right hand man during his tenure as Senator of New York.

"You're the ones who should be arrested." She pointed to Hunter. "Trusting that unhinged psychopath to lead your takeover."

"President DeVries knew the risks when we planned the summit," Townsend argued, stone-faced, "It was meant to lure C20 out."

"Bullshit, Townsend!" Florence screamed. She stepped forward, used her inside voice and said, "Bull. Shit. Risks can be mitigated. Best of luck feeding that story to the American people."

"Easy, Florence," Clara Whyzelle, the press secretary, interjected. "We've known each other a long time. We can work through—"

"Dr. Belladonna," he sneered. His arms were already crossed. His hip already cocked. "Our pursuit of C20 and this operation is a private matter which doesn't need your input, just your cooperation. You're to come with us for questioning and we'll go from there." He turned his back on her and marched to their transportation.

"Is it just you?" Clara asked, getting closer.

Florence wiped dirt and tears off her chin and tilted her head at the sidewalk. "And him. I'm certain he needs a medic."

"Where is Allister?"

"We didn't come together. So, I don't know." Her posture sank, no longer obligated to feign poise. What she'd witnessed was incomprehensible.

"I'm sorry to lose Wesley, he was an amazing president. An amazing person. And I know he meant a lot to you. But, if Allister's been compromised, we need you to help us stop this thing."

CHAPTER SEVEN

COSMIC BLOODLINES

Allister Adams

C20 Lab, Antarctica

Sleep hadn't visited Allister in the seventy-two hours since he'd been captive. Crystalizing icicles burned the skin under his cheeks. It took convincing from his inner voice to admit the incessant teeth chattering belonged to him, and he hit the brakes on hours of continual thoughts. Both hazel eyes, stung from the cold, fluttered closed, and his bearded, angular chin sank. He'd had Zosma in his arms as their lips touched in sweet surrender.

Part of him killed Dr. Giro in homicidal hatred. Part of him killed Dr. Giro in a noble effort to free Zosma. But, "I wouldn't kill anyone," he'd said to Celine. It was a lie now, a lie he'd live with forever, even if he told it before he knew his limits. He wrangled with the two parts of himself, deciding which one was more at fault for the murder. It didn't matter the ratio, she wasn't freed. No, quite the opposite, Dylurshin, a mysterious being, was freed from the constraints of a human host. He should've known better.

Brandt sacrificed his life to disrupt the Z-energy pulse. Florence was killed by the blast or missing. Celine was too shaken to fight alongside him as prophesied.

Allister's body was suspended in an X-shape, covered neck to knuckles to ankles in a layered titanium alloy suit reinforced by steel. It bore an advanced civilization's sophisticated mark and

285

did nothing to keep him warm. Thick, link chains tugged his arms as far from his chest as possible, and nearly ripped the tendons that connected his shoulders. Legs positioned in a similar way, his quads flexed in fear of them being torn from their sockets.

He recognized the lab's interior design, dappled with ice, bereft of furniture. Indistinguishable from the one Dr. Giro had built at the Andromeda Project, it was as pure of disturbance, as it was spotless. The containment center sat in a corner and shined with the Z-energy's light.

Walls and archways carved inside towering crystals brought out the alien in the architecture. C20 was a castle under the Antarctic ice sheet. Dylurshin Hexforth's castle.

He took the time to navigate detail after detail, looking for what he'd missed. His mistakes may have cost them the world.

In 1973, the Arecibo observatory contracted the world's top ten scientists to make adjustments to its communication capabilities. Twenty years before Rabia Giro was born, yet, Rabia Giro was on that team. He'd commissioned the blueprints, and those updates were the sole reason Neight Caster's distress transmission was received by Nicolas Delemar seventeen years later. A plan had been set in motion.

There wasn't a question whether General Nicolas Delemar and Captain Jared Brandt had been on puppet strings. Their ambitions, magnified and manipulated, woes, amplified and accelerated, pit against each other in lethal rivalry and predictable betrayal. Lining up the facts, the two men had impacted Allister's life in detrimental ways; Nicolas having killed his father, Captain Brandt having killed his mother. He'd been an intentional target in Dylurshin's power-mongering game.

Allister suspected he served a purpose, otherwise Dylurshin wouldn't have taken the utmost care in making sure he lived through the energy pulse.

His spirit extinguished, profound disillusion engraved on his brow, regret's sharpened point corkscrewed his stomach.

Fed up with patience, Allister's head thrashed about. Strength, none. Regeneration, slow. Z-energy, nonexistent. Time. The silver lining on an otherwise hopeless cloud. Allister had time. His tense muscles relaxed. *I have time.*

The Transporter gems' temporal energy heat cured his goose-bumps. It raised his body temperature and escorted a vibrance to his cheeks. White light jolted from under the body prison, rushed around in a circle like a fish too big for its bowl until time slowed to a stop, and the present tumbled away at warp speed.

Allister saw the C20 base's deconstruction. Research groups left, then arrived in the Antarctic region. He witnessed colonial exploration, glacial ice shifting. One thousand years in the past, two thousand years in the past rushed by in a speedy, reversed time lapse, a fight, a crash landing. The play button pressed on 470 B.C.E., Antarctica's barren glaciers dwelled in transfixing silence.

High-pitched whistling pierced the air. An opaque, dome-shaped vessel had been double-crossed by its own speed as it struck the mesosphere's extreme cold and molecular friction. It blazed a hot orange, and four tapered metallic legs rattled behind it. The italic, circled "AE" followed by a sideways "8" insignia had all but burned away, and the space ship's violent impact ruined the surface. Giant icicles eroded to either side, building walls, as it slid atop ice toward a head-on collision with a towering glacier.

He identified those alien symbols. They hailed from the closest neighboring galaxy, Andromeda, where Uragon had existed.

Wind gusted against the exposed cockpit, demonstrating the colossal strength to slow, and then stopping the ship's path to obliteration. Its internal contents were an easy target for his awe, and he spotted a giant, refrigerator-shaped airtight prison. Clouded condensation on the device's cracked window tormented his curiosity.

Of the six aliens strewn about the main cabin, two were awake. The one closest to its edge was male. Tall, lizard green, slimy complexion, an oblong head, and pointed ears, a physiology Allister recognized, but wasn't as unique as the four gorgeous grey wings that protruded from his spine. The being groped the ground and folded his (only) two fingers around an emerald green staff.

"The chamber is broken," he said in a low pitch to his companion. Two glowing eyes, the color of the sky right before you leave the stratosphere, stared at the prison window's vertical fracture. "It will escape."

"I know," the second coherent alien replied, as she surveyed a scathing incision in her torso. Vocals high as his were low, stifled in agony, she said, "Mallen, has your power worn?"

"I pray to Gatelius, no."

Allister gulped. Fogginess lifted and revealed the capsule's terrifying contents. Mystical darkness pervaded a blackened exoskeleton: Dylurshin Hexforth. It blinked, peered around, and discovered the crack for itself.

"Wendell!" the one called Mallen shouted.

Steel, iron, and glass burst outward. Wendell created a funneled wind and scattered debris to the ship's other areas, while Mallen surrounded them in angelic light and whisked, no, *transported* them and the five other aliens onto open ice.

A third alien stirred and came to. "Look sharp, warriors," the purple-haired female said and spit on the ice. Her three-fingered hands touched a double-sided saber attached to her hip and she sprang to her feet. *Was she Uragonian?* Allister asked himself. The spiked, armored suit. The skin and hair shades of lilac and light plum, without a doubt.

Alien to alien, Allister assessed their physical attributes and otherworld attire. His palpitating heart waited for anything to click and connect the dots. A salmon-skinned man opened square, black eyes, his four-fingered fist clutched a golden dragon's head handle attached to a lustrous sword. Temporal light coursed through visible veins, which took hard, 90-degree turns in Mallen's arms and legs, as they intersected his golden armored tunic. Wendell was a woman dipped in sky blue complexion then covered in a durable chainmail. She had white, straight, torso-length hair. He guessed her kinetic wind manipulation had guaranteed the ship's less-than-catastrophic entrance as it braved the brutal atmosphere.

The unrecognizable others mobilized as fast as they could and gathered their strength to battle. A quick, jagged, and toothy grin followed a smoky eruption into the already dim Antarctic sky. The cosmic force known as Dylurshin Hexforth, plunged as a singular particle stream down the aircraft's ravaged cabin, and took its beastly form on ice.

Grateful he couldn't feel anything in the outskirts of time, Allister blinked and watched the scene take a turn for the worse.

"This is not the prison planet, which means we have been thrown off course," the beady-eyed beast directed. "An interesting turn of fate, would not you say?"

Bleeding blue liquid over her hand, Wendell stammered, "We take him. Even if we die, we must make sure he does not return to Andromeda."

"I do believe you mean, return to the Empire," Dylurshin corrected, digging an arm in the ice.

Icicles jutted toward her. She dodged, and a miniature cyclone blew them to shambles. The other warriors engaged and fell, one by one, as Dylurshin turned their powers and insecurities on them.

"A century in space. A century imprisoned, never again," the dark figure said. "What a beautiful place for exile."

"Everyone is bound by time, Dylurshin, even you," Mallen said. Exhaustion aside, his voice stayed deep, clear and commanding. He held his staff for support and did a double-take on it, as if realizing its weight on the outcome. "The chains of Infinity. If I can imbue the chains."

Energy swarmed around him, building for a purpose known solely to him. It surged through the two-pronged weapon and sent sizzling power to the ship's remains. Sturdy chains pulsed with an ivory glow, slithered along the ground, and slinked up Dylurshin's legs and torso, searing its tough exoskeleton. It howled. Yes, Allister realized, in pain.

Dylurshin transformed its wispy limbs to sharpened, hardened, bardiche blade-shaped extensions. Mallen blocked the first cross body slash, swiped the next gut-aimed slice away, blasted a sideways swinging chop attack, then twirled the staff to deflect the barrage of daggers that zoomed his way. One slow step lead to a stagger, and needing the weapon for balance, allowed a jagged limb to impale him through the torso. Mist dissolved inside Mallen, and he slumped to his knees.

The spell ended. De-powered chains jangled against the ice.

"My companions, no matter how many centuries go by, remember our mission," Mallen said, driving his staff into the frosty earth. "To keep the Great Betrayer from returning to claim Andromeda's galactic throne. Tell this story to your children and their children and their children. You will not win, Dylurshin. As long as the Eight exist, you will never win."

Dylurshin screeched.

From the heavens themselves, the Transonian's temporal energy rained down, smashing into the battle's six participants. His power illuminated and stole their bodies, extending to the sky.

Antarctica showed the courageous no empathy. The temperature dropped. Light flurries were upstaged too soon by rampant snowfall, and a cold, furious breath from mother nature signaled a blizzard's beginnings. Mallen lay there, whispering what sounded like coordinates, knowing death wouldn't come to relieve him, as Transonians were functionally immortal. The rectangular prison and its chains kept him company, a cruel reminder of failed justice.

"It happened here," Allister said. Time sped up. He watched more ice arrive until the alien, the capsule, and the chains evanesced, frozen inside a glacier. Moments later, the year 2052 embraced him.

———

FLORENCE BELLADONNA
CIA Headquarters, Langley, D.C.

HAVING FALLEN ASLEEP in her clothes, Florence stirred on top of scratchy would be cream sheets. She threw off the covers soaked a dark tan by her anxiety and nightmares.

"What time is it?" she asked, not expecting an answer.

"Nighttime," Bazzo said, lazing in the chair beside her. "Didn't think you'd be out longer than me."

"I didn't want to wake up. Are they waiting?"

He nodded. "C'mon, that thing's got Bridg locked up, and I think they know where." Bazzo's cheeks peeled to the ends of his face. He pushed himself up from the armchair cushion. "Christ, never got this banged up workin' for ya dad."

June 19, 2037 was her first day as assistant project manager on Wesley DeVries's scrappy team. She finished his sentences. She tied his ties. She briefed him for his meetings. She told him when he was flat out wrong. Florence worked for him for a year and a half, then left to power through medical school and her residencies. Their spark hadn't birthed into a flame.

She was a doctor by the time they kissed; they'd been friends eight years before they were lovers, and the kerosene of adoration and respect for each other exploded like a wildfire across a parched forest. During his presidential campaign, (which she ran), press outlets asked in interview upon interview if she was the first-lady-to-be. "I think I'd know by now," she'd usually say, giggling. Then, she'd squeeze her shoulders and smile bright, so they knew she was being sincere.

She and Wesley were in Spain when he won the election. A beachside villa in Majorca, filled with decompression, relaxation, and his proposal for her hand in marriage. In a tuxedo, Wesley DeVries had knelt on the patio, as the Atlantic waves yelled against the rocks, protesting their happiness.

Due to rising suspicion in Florence's superhuman abilities, January 15, 2049 was the last night they spent together before she had to be shuffled out of the public eye. In those few short months, the flight toward engagement, the life they'd dreamt, disappeared from the sky without a trace.

"Ey," Bazzo said for the third time. "You sure you're up for this?"

"Yes, I just... yes," she replied. Florence had escaped the infirmary bed and stood still as stone midway to the door his shoulder held open.

She'd performed a physical examination on Bazzo in the helicopter and remembered his hand injury coating her cut-up fingers in wet redness. Now, the hand was safe inside a lightweight plastic cast. The medical technology had breathable, various-sized holes, which resembled the makings of a spider web from elbow to wrist and became solid from palm to knuckles.

Bazzo's able hand guided her into a hug. "I know what you're thinkin' and you couldn't've predicted..." he folded his lips in. Maybe he knew she'd lose her composure if he said the remaining words aloud.

But she found them waiting at the edge of his mind for her unwelcome telepathic probe.

"Couldn't've predicted what?" Florence asked.

Bazzo answered by pulling her closer.

"It's okay," she whispered, her voice emptied of sorrow. "I need to hear it or I'll keep acting like it never happened."

"Wesley's death wasn't your fault. You deserved to be as happy as any of us."

A crossroads would've been better than the sudden emergence of this singular, dark path, luring her to live a life dedicated to self-approved justice. It scared her that, as time went on, she'd become more and more like Giovanni. Revenge was an acceptable motivation, just not the best one to operate under.

The suited woman who guarded their shared infirmary room turned to them. "I'll be escorting you to the meeting location," she said with simulated politeness. "Please follow me."

CIA branding was splashed over windows, wall charts, and agent and doctor uniforms. They walked, heads down, and exchanged no words. As they did so, she imprisoned her feelings in the topmost tower of her emotional castle.

It would be unfair to degrade the twin glass structures leading to the conference space by referring to them as doors. Frosted crescent moons, carved from their base up to their celestial height, gave it a semi-opaque appearance. Jewel-encrusted edges slid away from their central meeting point and the escort opened her hand to the disappointment of fluorescent cloth furniture and an acrylic table. "Mr. Black, Mrs. Whyzelle, as you requested."

They entered.

Townsend rolled his sleeves. "Perfect timing, have a seat."

"I'll stand. Are we clear-headed?" Florence asked.

"I suppose," Townsend answered. "But I'm certain you'd know better."

"Excuse you?"

"I think what he meant is, he understands the value you bring," the press secretary soothed. Words continued to fall out of her mouth, "We-we'd like to catch you up to speed on our developments."

Her forehead straightened as her power dulled, and the false brown complexion returned to her psiborg leg. Florence massaged the artificial limb, running her fingers over its ridges, divots, and psychonium crystals.

"You'll be happy to know Detective Steele is in the Vault." Townsend leaned back. "He doesn't remember what he did, and Cynque says he's not lying."

"He's not," Florence responded. "Dr. Giro influenced Steele's mind."

"I'm sure he'll plead innocent."

"I'm sure you'll let him off too. He's the only superhuman who'll work for your corrupt dollars."

"Not the only one."

"Get to the point, Townsend."

"The point is, you all work for us. You always have and unless you want our civilization to vanish underwater, or burn to nothing in the next ten years, you always will."

Her arms crossed, and she squeezed her torso tight in a self-hug of sorts. "Can we not talk about this anymore?"

Clara Whyzelle's cough ended the tense hush. "We should get started," she said.

"Bazzo, this is my former colleague," Florence said with questionable respect. "Townsend Black, director of National Intelligence. Townsend meet Bazzo, acting CEO of Belladonna Corp."

"I'd shake your hand but..." Bazzo wiggled his elbow as if to explain his impoliteness with his ailment. "You look like a dick." He sat down.

"Don't worry about it. Unfortunately, I know who you are." The director's scrawny legs stretched, then retracted. He acknowledged Florence's impatient glare with a nod and a shrug and motioned for Clara to turn on the paneled visual wall.

"It was an undertaking to get former President DeVries to admit him and his father had any involvement in the Andromeda Project and the Z protocols," he said, "And we thought he'd be able to fill us in on the 2040 landing's specifics, like, why it was such a fucking disaster."

Zosma had been taken to a holding facility in Washington and since Neight was thought dead (circa 2042), Russell Ashur had to test and activate the Energy Containment Center. It suppressed the Z-energy before a second Cumberland, Kentucky incident transpired on a larger scale. Two major milestones, Rabia's arrival and Neight's resurrection (in 2044) sparked the conflicting conversation around Z-energy adoption for commercial use. Of course, it's also where the remaining breadcrumbs ran out.

"Talk about a world security breach," she said, "You let an alien bring toxic energy... my God, I can't even say it, it's so ridiculous."

"I wasn't in office. I don't even think I was divorced yet." He rubbed his trimmed beard. "Can you blame them? They were fascinated by intergalactic technology and magic, these 'artifacts,' and the quote, unquote apocalypse." He scratched his head. "Some called Neight a god. Some called him the anti-Christ."

"As interesting as Neight Caster is, I'd rather discuss—"

"Let's get talking about the demon holed up somewhere with my sis'," Bazzo said.

"Yes, the 'demon' calls itself Dylurshin Hexforth."

She tipped her head, as if she'd misheard him. "Pardon?"

"Rabia's activities followed a linear path; the Z-energy was always at the end." Townsend tapped the table. "Dr. Giro was never alive. It's a name, an alias, used for consistency and, to be honest, so far behind the scenes it didn't make it into any major historical accounts. Whoever that body belonged to before, I suspect the creature swallowed their identity the moment it seized control. And same for the others it's inhabited over centuries. We don't know what Dylurshin is. We don't even know if it's living. But judging by what we've found, it may not be from Earth."

"If it's not from Earth, where... ?"

"We're still figuring it out. There's a lot of information to process and package."

The folder's name. The assistance to five of the greatest scientific minds. The mismatch in birth years, and wide-ranging appearances. The genetic inconsistencies in his familial lineage. They made sense. Lips pursed, Florence peered out the conference room glass. CynqueT-wielding workers shuffled up and down hallways, talking over each other. They organized and prioritized incoming intel.

"You got your hands on Nicolas Delemar's Cynque," she said. "And spent time combing through it. I hope you have warrants."

"Delemar's Cynque is government property you stole," he retorted.

"Water under the bridge," the press secretary added and laid a vintage leather knapsack on the table. "Remember this?"

Florence lifted the flap and unveiled the contents. "Nicolas Delemar found it working at NASA," she said, puzzled, "in a dig, near, um... Tyre. Correct? Tyre, Lebanon."

"Right, precisely."

"What the hell's this have to do—?"

"Bazzo. Enough." Battle-worn nails traced a language etched in a slab dated 400 B.C.E. "If my memory isn't completely shot, Tyre was still the capitol of the Phoenician empire during this time period. You think Dylurshin landed there?"

"No," Townsend answered, "it's where we think it first infiltrated."

"The language in this scripture is closest to Old Latin," Florence said, and hesitated, shaken by the psychometric connection to what NASA had coined the Infinity calendar. Prolonged exposure to the relic's rusted iron sent a tingling up the bones in her wrist. She screamed as it reached her spine. Psionic energy scribbled over the text in coral pink, and a blush glow cascaded up her metal calf and thigh. She dropped the artifact to embrace the leg. It didn't hit the floor.

"It's not a calendar. It's a warning." Her sentences were swathed in inconsistent hyperventilation. "Mentions a dark cloud, time as a weapon. I think in literal translation it says, bound by time. A battle lost." Florence's eyes widened. "The book from the Vancouver house."

The tablet clanged against the marble, devoid of her power.

Clara's shriveled hands placed *The Book of Ancestry* before her. "We found it during our post-summit investigation."

"You are a weasel, aren't you?" Florence shook her head at the lazy excuse for unauthorized trespassing and thumbed the bound manuscript. She mumbled her way through paragraphs and caressed symbols, portraits. Thousands of pages of the same archaic Latin dialect told her family's and other families' constant opposition to an entity hiding amongst humanity. Families: the *Ventus* family, which split and became the *Nephthys* and *Sparks* families. And her own *Mente* family, which became the *Belladonna* family. All handwritten, it had been passed down through generations of psychics, elementals, Uragonians and more. The antecedents from the Andromeda Galaxy, Sichico Mente, Wendell Ventus, Kajam Tion, Frederick Xander, Evonna Caster were given chapter-long biographies that detailed their planetary origins. They'd been worshipped on Earth as gods and goddesses until they procreated and wove themselves into society. Their deaths were never confirmed, only their eventual absences from recorded human history.

Good God, we're not superhumans, she thought. Florence ripped the sword of Psion from her hip and turned the embroidered sheath over from hand to hand. Her father's eighteenth birthday gift was weighted with a different meaning and significance. On one side, a carbon copy of the creature she'd encountered in Allister's mind. On the other, eight planetary bodies represented the civilizations governing Andromeda, five of which had landed on Earth. It explained her aversion to technology, keeping note-books and not tablets or the Cynque. The responsibility to pass on the genes and the stories was now hers, though she knew kids wouldn't be in her future. Wesley's grotesque demise brought the threat of vomit to her parched mouth.

"Dylurshin is an alien. A very, very old one who comes from the same galaxy as Neight and Zosma."

"We can't sit around and chat anymore Dr. B," Bazzo said, hitting the table again. "We gotta save Bridg and Allister and Zosma and us, the world."

"I can't reach him this far... and we're in no condition to take on C20 and a cosmic entity."

"What're you saying?" he asked.

"I'm—"

"What's this?" Clara interrupted, positioned close enough to look over her sunken shoulder.

Florence had stopped on a sketched and shaded diagram. The rectangular contraption's origin, its purpose and function, and its measurements: height, length, and width were doodled in cursive, layered over the image and hiding in the corners of the page. She read the title, *The Temporal Chamber of Dylurshin Hexforth*. She broke a cold sweat. Her lungs worked overtime to catch her breath, to keep her heart from leaping through her chest. *The Temporal Chamber of Dylurshin Hexforth* was a page swamped with answers she hadn't been looking for: a prison devised by the King of an everlasting people, engineered by the finest blacksmiths in Andromeda and empowered by the white energy of time. The ancient book's script claimed with such certainty it would work, that she, now uncertain of most things, stole its confidence and said to the room, "It's the silver bullet."

———

300

ZOSMA CASTER
The Subconscious

LIKE A TORN PAGE from a vintage *National Geographic* magazine, plains, mountains, foliage, and desert, each took up a quarter of Zosma's brain. The hidden world intended to keep her mind at peace, hoping it would keep her body at peace, and in turn, keep Z-energy at peace.

There was no way for Zosma to walk in this world, but the open rooftop of iron and stone had allowed her to rest in a dragon chaise and observe its simple, serene beauty. The Uragonian guard had blocked the intruder's suspicions and hostile attempts to infiltrate.

The triangular door protecting the sacred land from chaos was open. Mist and blue energy contaminated her utopia like an oil spill. Half her mind was bathed in Uragon's binary starlight, and the other half was covered in midnight's shadows, even scales soon to tip.

Legs weakened, Zosma groped for the tower's ledge. "You got in," she murmured to the wind blowing past her.

"You preserved it well, I must admit," Dylurshin said. It materialized in a puff of distorted particles. "How long do you think you can resist me?" Ruby energy flowed through cavernous veins underneath its thin, misty skin. Glowing in fiery triumph, it orbited her at a slow pace and waited for her answer.

"I can resist you forever," she said, monitoring the land they fought for. "I will resist you forever."

"I do not need forever," Dylurshin sneered. "Only long enough for implementation."

Her knees buckled. It clicked, and she remembered the tender moment that had unlocked the door. To stop her from killing anyone, Allister in particular, she'd opened herself to let memories, love, and sensibility out, and in doing so, let Dylurshin in.

"What say you now?" it asked. Light slid away, sealing what felt like permanent doom.

"I... I will not be a weapon," she struggled. Flashbacks, flashing short clips of the battle she'd lost in Vancouver. Z-energy didn't know how to kill Dylurshin.

"For centuries your people denied what Z-energy is, and for decades, King Neight Caster denied what you represent." Dylurshin's arms aimed skyward and turned into gushing faucets of dark energy. It floated higher. "It is a matter of time before I scour your mind for the location of what I seek. And when I activate the artifacts you will be nothing more than what you are: a power source."

Fog covered her miniature kingdom's former beauty, then climbed the castle's exterior. Her body gave up resisting and smacked the rooftop. Putrid particles smothered her charming patio, moved up her legs and down her arms, crawled in her mouth, and through the smallest openings in her eyes. Dylurshin and its influence had won.

Neight Caster
C20 Basement

Neight contemplated the options laid out for him, knowing that dampening technology taunted him from within. Patience was a virtue, but the choice to stay captive had more to do with his Z-energy depletion, than the virtue itself.

"Hmmm."

A razored claw slid down the titanium-infused barrier. It occurred to him, as he examined the incision's thickness, that he and Zosma's prolonged presence on Earth had created a new timeline yet to be revealed. He opened his hands to receive knowledge, inhaled stale air, and growled, "Dylurshin Hexforth has returned."

Influenced engineers and scientists, led by Russell, prepared each U-generator to move to its final resting place. Low grey fog snowballed from the doorway, hovering at knee level. The C20 minions' mindless pacing dispersed eerie shadows alluding to the formation of a physical body.

"There are methods for saving humans that do not involve tampering with immeasurable power."

"So you keep saying," Dylurshin said, as the mist became a recognizable physique. "While you have baited this primitive people with ancient power and empty promises, I have done my diligence to enhance humanity's intelligence and, thereby, potential."

Activity on C20's base had ceased, presumably by Dylurshin's force of will.

"I wish suffering on no living creature," Neight replied. "However, they cannot harness this energy."

"You say yourself this dying rock has ten years left. Z-energy will be their guiding light, their fire, and when they awaken to it, I will usher in a new age as their faithful guide." It trudged to the completed U-generator's base. "This masterpiece was built by a human mind, Russell Ashur. You are so afraid of this human advancements. Why?"

"I am afraid of what they will do under your said guidance, besides conquer worlds and build an empire spanning two galaxies. I have seen it in my dreams. I have written about it in my prophecies."

"You behave as if you do not already support an empire spanning two galaxies, King Neight," Dylurshin countered. "Or have you have so quickly forgiven the tyrant who drove us here?"

"Your words are as hollow as your soul, murderer."

"Hmph, the fear in you is refreshing." It traced Russell's immobilized figure. "We are all murderers. You have killed. I have killed. They have killed. Whose conscience here is free of judgment?"

"How did you know about the unlimited energy bands?" Neight asked quietly.

"I am greater than you. I came before you. That is why."

Glowing hands opened window to the past through cryptic language. Neight saw that Dylurshin had body-snatched its way through human history, using influence to exploit their impulses, fears, and limitations in the process. Its consistent mission was to seek the smartest and rise to power with them.

The Z-energy magic spell explained Rabia Giro before he was Rabia Giro, when it was Dylurshin, cast out from Andromeda and escorted by the galaxy's soldiers of fortune to unknown sector four. Legendary tales lost to generations more concerned with the future than the past. Centuries of secret war and Dylurshin's presence on Earth became myths. The crash landing a legend, and Andromeda's children, human, more or less.

"Survival of the fittest is a concept I have lived since before you were imagined. Darwin conveniently forgot to express gratitude for my hand in the evolutionary theory's development. I have given humanity the ideas and the tools. I have offered it my cosmic awareness."

Thin blue power drifted past Neight's shoulders. His head dipped. "I have seen your truth. You spent a lifetime studying Z-energy."

"For one goal," it sneered. "The end of Infinity."

Neight had what he needed: a motivation. The entity referred to the Aenecan race, Andromeda's supreme governing institution known for their immeasurable abilities and extended lifespans. He sank to the floor. His flickering energy battled black misty needles filling the capsule and attempting to drill through his skull.

Dylurshin tilted toward Neight. "Where are Uragon's Z bands of unlimited energy?"

There was no answer to the question. Z-energy tumbled through Neight's hand and moved across to the other. Blinking at what felt like light speed, he opened his mouth. "Scattered like the others, cloaked behind an elusive barrier, protected by a mystical guardian."

"A king's deceit is his greatest weapon. You see, I realized in my research, a planet's core is a significant barrier for such cloaking. Knowing Andromeda's wise emperor, he would prefer these artifacts to exist somewhere he could watch them." Dylurshin added force to its intention and kept talking, "I formulated a hypothesis. If the core was destroyed with Uragon, how is it you, Zosma, and Allister can use Z-energy?"

Once upon a time the Uragonian's sentient power came from within themselves. The Z-bands' creation brought their power together, creating the source known as Z-energy to protect the bands from discovery. When Andromeda's leaders chose to disband the artifacts of Evale, the Z-bands of unlimited energy became the exception.

Collectively, they decided the power of ergokinesis (the ability to control all energy forms), as granted by the bands, was too dangerous to have drifting in space, ripe for discovery. Uragon's impenetrable core, acting as the artifacts' guardian, housed the energy source, and the Z-bands. Like the Cavern of Transports had held the Transporter gems.

Neight's silence surpassed the allotted time for dithering over an acceptable, yet honest answer, and moved into a prolonged hunt for necessary deception.

"Quite impossible," Dylurshin said, "I agree."

He used the wall to get to one knee, chanting a spell, "A people of darkness, who dwell as mist. A threat unknown, in shadow's nest. Influence I do not give into thee. Formeth a barrier of Z-energy." Repetition assured success. Under his breath, he said the short rhyme again and again. It triggered. Sizzling and sparking, a comet's brilliance flashed inside the capsule. The ominous mist disintegrated. Neight stood tall. "The more I rest, the more I wait, the more I learn and the more I know," he said. "Today I speak no more."

"Very well, Neight Caster. Harnessing the Z-energy is the sole reason for my being. It will happen if you like it or not." Dylurshin conceded, slinked away, and siphoned into Russell's hunched back, bringing the base back to life with his mortal breath.

"Are we ready for deployment, Mr. Ashur?" Myra said. She removed her glasses and searched Russell for confirmation.

He checked Dr. Giro's work station. The swiveling stool, empty and immobile, collected dust. Russell shook his head slightly. "Dr. Giro said to wait for him to get back."

"It's been days. You saw the news. I doubt he lived."

"You may refer to me as Hexforth," the beast announced.

Russell swept a hand across his forehead and staggered back, as Myra ducked behind him. Its height and mass overpowered them, but they blinked and blinked again. Dylurshin penetrated their truth and delivered lies, so they saw him as they thought they knew him: Dr. Rabia Giro. Only possible in closed quarters and on a limited number of subjects, Neight knew the impressive illusion required much of the entity's attention.

"Ahem, Hexforth." Myra shivered off the effects of the encounter. "It looks like the energy is resisting the transfer request."

Dylurshin's snout lowered. "I have been a fool not to see this."

"Did you find what you were looking for?" Russell asked, glued to the screen.

"Indeed, Mr. Ashur, my theory was correct."

Fatigued, Neight slumped to the capsule floor and rested his weary head against the metallic interior. "What theory?"

"Now the king speaks." It turned and stalked to the U-generators stacked side by side, then addressed him, "The secret you have been keeping is, I do not need to locate them. They are here, inside Zosma. Whatever vessel houses the sentient power, be it a core or a living being, is the artifacts' guardian. I destroy the guardian, and the Z-bands of unlimited energy appear." It placed a single claw on the device. "Mr. Ashur, you know what to do."

"Prepare to deploy the first generator," Russell said to Myra. "Coordinates are set for Morocco."

"I could not have done this without you, Neight Caster, and to show my gratitude, you may live long enough to see my plan come to fruition."

Cackling shook the room, and in the mist's absence, 100 percent visibility returned to the basement.

Obtaining the Transporter gems, preserving Z-energy, fleeing Earth, missions complicated by the unknown working against Neight in literal shadows. Dylurshin had outlived innumerable civilizations, imbued with the patience and wisdom of a true immortal.

Allister Adams, his proposed savior, had been hindered by lack of direction and kept humanity's future hidden in foggy uncertainty. And it was then Neight knew he'd placed too much pressure on a mortal, bound by emotions, by youth, by his (80 percent) humanity. It was not his war to win, not alone.

What of the other lost children? he thought. *If the descendants didn't know where they came from...*

He took a deep breath. Understanding was the key to action, was the key to success. Stroking the downward facing horns on his magnesium-alloy battle helmet, he chanted, "A more meaningful gift than a battle won, is the strength to see through deception. I give to thee, clarity, from a life we've lost, in your time of need." Light in every color in the spectrum streaked from his palm toward the being who needed it most.

DYLURSHIN HEXFORTH
C20 Lair

PRIOR TO ARRIVAL on Earth, Dylurshin had been enslaved in its weakest form, uneducated on how to use the Zaian mist at maximum power. Three thousand years among humanity had given it time to explore and master inhabiting non-superpowered mortals. Dylurshin's choice worked to its advantage, as the binding contract guaranteed that mental, physical, and spiritual control endured until the victim's natural or unnatural expiration. It enjoyed a fresh challenge every fifty to seventy-five years. Practice makes perfect.

Using a host body was unavoidable on a planet where its presence and alien form would lead to widespread alarm. And doing so limited the number and depth to which it could influence anyone else. Fellow gifted beings had proved the most challenging when random factors such as distance (from it), the subject's own power, confidence, etc., caused complications or stopped it altogether.

Those limitations vanished once it'd been inadvertently unleashed from the human shell known as "Rabia Giro."

Dylurshin floated in the meeting place for the directors, evading the troublesome and discomforting overhead light. The screens flickered on. Jane Wenyin, Chung Tae-Won, and Aleksander Karjavine wore scowls, high, tight hairstyles, and clothing buttoned to the neck.

"Dr. Giro, are you there?" Jane asked.

Unable to mimic the Eastern European accent, Dylurshin spoke in its deep, raspy tones. "I am."

"United States president is dead," Aleksander started. "This could cause war."

"Betrayed and killed by his own. An age-old story I made sure to tell." Influencing the Roman senate into assassinating Julius Caesar came to Dylurshin's mind.

"You've jeopardized our initiative," Jane added. "They're calling the demonstration and our proposal a 'hostile, terrorist takeover' of the world's energy. We're losing supporters by the day. No one wants to cosign on living sacrifice. Alien, or otherwise."

"Your inexperience fuels your concerns, spare me."

Chung Tae-Won tripped over his words. His buggy eyes bulged further out of his round face.

"Your financial investments allowed me to create the U-generator system, and now you will reap the benefits in silence." Dylurshin's angled chin lifted and the light blinked. "It will be impossible for your un-evolved minds to comprehend the operation's next phase."

"What you say?" Aleksander asked.

"This is unbelievable, preposterous!" Chung shrieked.

"I save you from renegade anti-superhuman group to work on project," Aleksander said. "And this is how you repay opportunity?"

"False! I seized an opportunity I have been waiting for since Ancient Greece and Persia drew the Peace of Callias treaty. The opportunity to take humanity to a place it could *never* go in my absence. To usher your race into its evolutionary pinnacle, to teach you the art of self-preservation, in exchange for my unchallenged leadership."

The light died.

"The U-generators are en route to their respective destinations. Your counsel is no longer necessary." Its arm flicked across its body. Thrown daggers shattered the screens, quieting protests and insufferable whining.

War? They knew nothing about war, or sacrifice, or self-preservation. Humans had not been called to learn such skills, fighting amongst themselves versus fighting the more evolved, and learning from smarter beings. They were malleable, misguided. They could be manipulated and molded to create better specimens, generation after generation. His experiments proved it.

Dylurshin floated higher in the air, particles crawled on its skin. It was the last, the last Zaian. It knew war, sacrifice, and self-preservation. Spending millennia watching strategic, innovative, and powerful civilizations in the known universe rise and fall, Dylurshin knew what it took to succeed, to overthrow. The time had come to employ a highly effective tactic: influence.

———

CELINE NEPHTHYS
Rabat, Morocco

CELINE PRESSED HER TOES on red sandstone, scouring for life in Rabat's eerie, soundless streets. Through sizzling heat, a helicopter caravan and military cargo plane lowered themselves into the open dome. The U-generator had arrived.

Alone on the roof. Alone in her resistance. She wrestled her conscience, not knowing whether her actions protected Earth or damned it. The varied aftermaths of Z-energy integration spun inside her head on the drums of a slot machine, never matching up to one which made sense. Her brow scrunched, and nature's whispers painted an unforgettable image of mass annihilation behind her eyelids.

She knew Dylurshin would protect it. King Marshall Nephthys had said in a public statement that, "No military resources would be allocated to combat a fabricated terrorist threat. The time to advance is now. And those weak and fearful will be left to die."

Wind strong enough to bend trees and tip livestock, bayed like a wolf, joining in chorus with the rolling thunder's boom overhead. Earth had begun building its ammunition.

"I see." She nodded. "I see what must be done."

Celine smelled the acidic air and laid eyes on the supercell soiling the sky, as the coming storm barreled toward them. Her heart pulsed, heavy with the weight of anticipation. A brilliant serpentine lightning bolt bit the helicopter's broadside. Tumbling, wild and in flames, it crashed into a school. The explosion snapped her from assessment to action. Children's screams touched her ears and consciousness.

Rushing across the awakened city on a rising dirt and soil pillar, her short breaths and swift strides ensured each heel caught the earthen bridge paving her warpath to the trespassers. A leap into the air, followed by a triple somersault landed her on the centermost point in Morocco's capital.

Silhouette illuminated by forked flashes of the planet's anger, she shouted, "Hear me, Earth, as I ask you for unquestioned command over your elemental power." Her open hand raised. "Grant me the strength to bring this threat to the ground and bury it ever so deep beneath your crust."

Thunder's cry shook the atmosphere, accepting her leadership. Her words dove into neighborhoods, corridors, streets, transporting commands, and delivering them to the land, the sea, the heavens.

The aircraft sent by C20 approached, firing rapid plasma beams. Celine scampered the length of the roof, spinning, leaping and flipping, while summoning chunks of rocks from the building to protect her. The mindless enemy paused to recharge, reposition their guns, and reap the benefits of her vulnerability. She gasped and faced forward.

Short-range missiles birthed from the helicopter's belly rocketed forward. Praying the parallel building's proximity was ripe for her emergency landing, she bolted toward the farthest edge.

A slip in judgement led to a slip in footing. A traitorous gale ripped the breath from her lungs as she landed hard on her elbows. Sweat slid down her nose, darkening rose-colored stone drop by drop. Missiles shed their shiny exteriors in preparation to detonate.

Her eyes were stained black with her power's overwhelming exertion. "Show them," she said to sand sticking to her moist palms, "When united we are unstoppable."

Loaned speed by a typhoon's world ending gusts, desert dust recruited an infinite number of allies, standing tall against their common enemy as a sky-reaching sandstorm. Her concoction stampeded over her kneeling figure, compacting, snowballing.

The missiles' premature explosions backfired on the flying vehicles as the sand wall slammed into them. Engines burned. Metal ripped away. Military choppers plummeted through homes and businesses to their demise.

Whipping around, she spread her fingers. An earthquake rattled the ground beneath, split Rabat down the middle and molded a ravine to the lithosphere's depths. The cargo plane, or as she liked to refer to it the "airborne metal can," fell to its permanent grave, hit boiling magma, and melted with the energy-less U-generator in tow. Like perfectly executed surgery, she sealed the crust closed.

Quieting skies concluded their spells. Lightning quelled thunder. Exhausted winds did their duty to scatter cloud cover, and dust became its light, jovial self, dancing few and far between in the air.

Celine turned, uncovered and vulnerable, to tens of thousands of awestruck faces. Screaming children and wailing adults trapped under compromised historical buildings, education centers, and mosques, blocked any victorious feelings. No one would be able to fathom that for the dozens dead and hundreds injured, billions had been preserved.

ALLISTER ADAMS

COLD STRANGLED ALLISTER'S BONES. Seconds, minutes, hours, days bled together without access to the rhythmic cycles of the sun. Mounting rage triggered barbaric yelling and obscenities, and the metal suit clanged, as it swayed back and forth with his body's defiance. Deep gulp after deep gulp, his hyperventilation subsided.

He held the sacred breaths in his chest, hoping to reclaim his sanity, then let them go one at a time to warm his lips.

His shackled hands quivered. Temporal energy would not come to them, and he felt like a junkie suffering withdrawal, having overdosed on their power by seeing so far back in time.

Devilish smoke entered the lab, winded through chair legs, between test tubes and under microscopes. Creeping up the metal tabletops, the mist molded Dylurshin like pottery into a revolting insectoid creature flaunting scarlet energy-engorged horns. "Can you believe those beautiful Transporter gems are younger than me?" A small smirk crossed its symmetrical, inverted raindrop-shaped face. Its claws wiggled. "We can build generator upon generator, but nothing surpasses the sovereignty of the artifacts of Evale."

His mind suspended the plot to escape and listened to instinct. "So-so why me?" Allister asked, shivering, "Or Z-Zosma? Or h-humanity for that matter?"

"I am here to straighten your trajectory and to give you the purpose you so deeply yearn for."

"Gee, thanks, but uh, N-Neight's got that covered."

"Neight Caster is a charlatan. Claiming to be your champion, yet he plots exodus in every waking instant. He abandoned you to pursue his own devices, as was always the prophecy."

"You're lying!"

"Have I ever lied to you, Allister Adams?"

No. Dylurshin was as horrifying as it was honest.

Four vermillion slits narrowed at him. "You do not need the fallen king, you never did. Neight bestowed in you miraculous genetic advancements which will guide—"

"He did what?"

Dylurshin's top fangs fit snug into its bottoms like a well-preserved carnivorous fossil. Light fluttered. Electricity hummed. Paneled walls came to life and populated the foreground.

Mapped alien chromosome 24 and 25 encompassed the wall. The visual zoomed into chromosome 24, which originated in the Uragonian genome and made up a whopping 10 percent of his total DNA. The other, number 25, hadn't been identified and made up the excess 10 percent.

Chromosome 24 rotated and froze. Two separate gene sequences provided augmented mental capacity, longevity, and regeneration, and, as a bonus, Allister was granted access to the Z-energy through his left arm (an obscure, but relevant limitation).

He couldn't be an alien. He would have three-fingered claws or purple skin or purple—

Hair. If the genes in either chromosome coded for physical traits, he figured he'd know it. Then again, without daily supervision those few idle strands the iconic violet of Uragon's people, may have multiplied and claimed majority of his curly mane.

Being superhuman was unnerving, being an alien, even a fifth of one, was...

"Twenty percent," he said aloud on accident, "it-it's just 20 percent."

"The blueprint. The beacon to lead your people into the coming age of Andromeda." Dylurshin's wiry claw neared his concealed hands. "You, who can carry us from this doomed place. It is why I have insisted upon your allegiance." At full height, it circled him like a great white. "And when Z-energy enhances the technological infrastructure of humanity... ah, the keys to preservation."

His head turned from the creature's taunting speculations. Salivary glands pumped spit out with his words. "It's not worth it if-if it means sacrificing her."

"I am willing to wager my own immortality the individuals suffering on this rock would not agree."

A greedy and lost population held steadfast to whatever reality they'd created for themselves. Humans were dependent on the planet and their fellow man for everything, and somehow, at their weakest, most desperate point, there was no mutual appreciation, only expectation, squabbling, and consumption.

"What self-aware being chooses love over continuation?"

"Anyone with an ounce of a soul," Allister said in a strained whisper.

"My soul was taken." Dylurshin swam through the air and stopped behind him to bend, as if telling a friend another friend's secret. "I gather by your vigor, the gems showed you my story." It tapped the shackles holding him hostage. "I believe that stems from your mother's side of the family."

"Everyone is bound by time, even you," he sneered.

Any facts they'd found on the creature skimmed the surface. A scarier thought furrowed Allister's brow: if Dylurshin was older than Neight by more than the two and a half millennia it had spent on Earth, how long had it existed?

"There is little you can do to hurt me, if anything," it announced. Mist raked his clenched jaw, adhered to the imprisonment, and sank between the cracks. "And all the while I have been planting seeds of doubt, isolation, rejection. Letting the fresh spring fountain you call the human mind nourish those seeds. They take root, sprout and grow."

Smoky black tentacles slapped, stuck, climbed, and dodged Allister's frigid, belligerent breath and dove down his throat.

"Traitor!" Dylurshin bellowed and wrenched backward, losing density.

He choked, as regurgitated, tar-colored mist scathed his esophagus. With cyclonic force, the angered alien burrowed into the ceiling ventilation, and Allister watched it escape through filmy, wet eyes.

—✦—

BRIDGET SPARKS
C20 Prison

"You look a mess," Bridget said. Her nails were coated with ice and sharpened to frosty points. "I see you brought a friend. I thought I told you I wasn't keen on group play."

Russell lingered in the open doorway. Per usual, his khakis were bundled and stuffed into his knee-high snow boots. A fur-hooded parka did a bad job hiding an untucked plaid shirt.

"You said she was dead," the guard snarled and entered.

"Dead?" She laughed. From her roots, she dragged four fingers through hair and unsnagged the last tangle. A tantalizing Bondi beach tan had transformed into pale blue skin, as if warm blood no longer circulated. A jester's mischievous smirk lit her face. "I learned a new trick," she cooed. "Wanna see?"

"Don't move," the guard said. His gun rose, charging plasma.

Russell stepped forward. "Bridget, listen to him. I don't want you to get hurt."

"Even better." She got up and smoothed her shirt's hem. "I'll get to show the whole crew."

She hurtled herself at the guard whose weapon was unprepared for her attack. A double punch crisscrossed the guard's flustered face. Her hand thrust forward to push him away by the throat. Her hand touched warm, living tissue. He squealed. Molecular movement slowed beneath her fingertips.

The guard's uniform fabric stiffened as its fibers surrendered to the same ice further cooling his now frostbitten skin. His plump face twisted and solidified in frozen anguish. Death wasn't sufficient, and the immobile sculpture of the recoiling man toppled and smashed against the steel floor.

She gawked at the internal organs and body parts cluttering the floor. The temperature plummeted.

"I told you your powers weren't gone. Did some research." Russell pulled the parka around his shaking body. "You have a

319

rare fo-foreign gene, triggered by tra-trauma, allows you t-to t-take on certain elemental pro-pro-properties."

She rubbed her fingers, a motion known for jump-starting her electric powers, and murmured, "I think I'd prefer electrocution."

"Come with me," his voice cracked.

"I'm not falling for this."

There came a primal roar. They ducked as shingles showered down on them.

"What in bloody hell?" she shrieked.

"I need to get you to the hangar, this-this operation is way out of hand."

"No shit, I told ya that two months ago." Bridget leaned in. "Now, I'm gonna ask ya one question. Answer sideways and I freeze ya balls off. Got it?"

He nodded.

"Is Baz alive?"

He nodded again. "I think so. What I mean is, I'd know if he wasn't."

Her concerned expression met his timid gaze. He didn't break eye contact as he explained Vancouver's blowout, which had been mislabeled a superhuman gang war.

"The World Energy Summit was an international disaster. President DeVries got killed, Captain Brandt too."

Satisfactory performance.

Bridget was the first to stand. "Christ. I miss all the fun." Tapping her forefingers together, she toyed with the original suggestion. "Let's move then."

They traveled past four other prisons in the open hallway, when, without warning, he cried out and staggered into the oxidized metal and concrete foundation. "I can fight this," he told himself. "I can fight this. We have to hurry. Hexforth knows I'm resisting."

What's he on about? she thought. Tugged from opposite ends by skepticism and worry, the more he suffered, the nearer she crouched, careful not to lay a hand on his bare skin for fear of what it might do.

"Babe, be straight, who's Hexforth?"

He pointed at a crevice. "There's a tunnel to the surface, I think it's this way." He yanked his glasses off, breathed on the lenses, and wiped the condensation. Placing them over his pouty brow, he blinked up at her. Dark hair buzzed on both sides and longer on top fell into eyes full of understated charm. His chapped, yet kissable lips spoke words that refused to register. "Hexforth is... I'm not sure how else to frame it. Dr. Giro's not exactly a doctor or a human."

Scorching hot attraction led a reasonable temp to her cheeks. Her parted mouth and infrequent swallows matched her doe-eyed look.

"Bridget, did you hear me? Dr. Giro's not real."

Ding. The elevator opened. A pillar of ashen air rushed at Russell's betrayal, swarmed the basement, captured any available oxygen, and forced them to separate.

"Mr. Ashur," the thing said, "you are needed in the hangar for the U-generator deployment."

Unlike any voice she'd ever heard. Unlike any creature she'd ever seen. Deliberate, calm mist moved and pulled to resemble Dr. Giro's faint shape. Her mouth dropped. It didn't solidify to washed-out flesh. To call it a demon would be short-sighted, but what else could be said of the hellish red eyes eight feet above her? Dwarfed by its titanic shadow and a mouth she was convinced devoured souls, she wrenched her legs closer to her torso.

"Neight showed me the monster you really are." Russell squeezed one eye closed and from the side of his mouth he said, "undid your delusions."

"What I am?" it queried. "What of my descent, my inhumanity? I gave you confidence, drive. I gave you worth. A worth your own people did not see."

Russell crawled to Bridget, one knee after the other. "No. No. No! St-stay, stay away!" Face paled, he turned to her and lowered his voice, "It's not going to let me go. You have to kill me."

Irrational nerve trumped irrational fear. "Actually, I don't," she said with stinging sarcasm and glared at the overgrown parasite's matte black exoskeleton. "I'll kill that instead."

"You think you can kill me?"

"Baz used to say, do your best," she jeered.

The being lunged, choosing the grim reaper's scythes as its arm's transformative choice. Pristine, icy whiteness bombarded Bridget's tightened fists. Her strained throat muscles emanated a spirited war cry. Her poised body discharged brilliant blue energy waves, and frigid air condensed the moisture between them into a frozen, opaque wall.

"You were nothing before me, Russell Ashur," it boomed, "and you will be nothing after."

Bridget gravitated closer to what was her last chance at intimacy.

"I used to believe that," Russell said in lust's low whisper, "until you—"

"It'll break through sooner than later." She retreated, unable to follow through on the fatal and selfish kiss. "Why'd you come down here?"

"Because I'm sorry," he said, then sank and wrapped his knees in arms. "I didn't intend for you to end up here, or for us to end up like... "

He'd dozed off. As for any hypothermia victim, Russell needed to stay awake to stay alive. Winter clung to his bare face, neck and his ungloved knuckles, and though she couldn't see, she envisioned his bones' violent vibration under the quilted coat. She'd spent a month disgusted by the cringe-worthy syllables that formed his name, promising to torture and end him at their next encounter. Watching him yield to the inevitable, she would've thrown herself in his arms to thaw his body, his guilt, and their connection. Yet, as cold as the room itself, Bridget had nothing to keep him warm but sympathy and an apology.

———

FLORENCE BELLADONNA
Antarctic Airspace

"DO YOU NEED HELP?" Florence asked.

"Nah, I'm alright. Airspeed's a tad high though!" Bazzo yelled back.

"It's the wind. Did you account for the wind?" Frowning, she observed his unpracticed, one-handed landing. "You should've let Giovanni fly," she said, balanced on the airplane platform edge. Polar air rushed beneath the glass-bottomed plane as they lost altitude. With a tenacious grip on the handle over the exit hatch, she shook her head.

"C'mon Dr. B, ya don't trust me by now?" he said. "Gio wouldn't do well in unfamiliar territory, and let's face it, I saw no good reason to program an Antarctica flight sequence before this a.m."

Landing gear squealed. They bounced up and down on the smooth, slippery surface that concealed the truth of their origin and a dangerous enemy. Taxi lights guided their path, and if he didn't stop within a few hundred feet, it would be across the River Styx.

"Bazzo, the reverse thrusters... "

Didn't activate.

"Ah crap," he said, "I knew I shoulda gotten them fixed. Plan B, Gio."

Age-old spoilers on the wings lifted at the AI's request, slowing their voyage to a steep drop.

She sucked her teeth and stomped her foot, scowl glued to the cockpit.

The front wheel straddled safety on the glacier's edge, and, in a rush to get them off the aircraft, the exit hatch lowered to the ice. Florence took her first step down the ladder, her sword cradled in one hand.

"See, easy as pie." Bazzo exited the pilot seat. Careful not to upset the plane, he reached back to nab a handle of Bundaberg rum on the dashboard, and said, "This'll take the edge off."

The vehicle groaned at his choice. She fell off the steps backward as the fragile, unsupported ice gave under the plane's weight. Cloth layers, piled on as a defense from subzero air, did little to pad her ten-foot fall. She scrambled to her knees and yelled, "Bazzo!"

She tried not to jump to conclusions, horrified as she witnessed the nose of the jet, then wings, and last, its horizontal and vertical stabilizers plunge over the edge. Even after hearing its crunch against the glacier's side and fire's faint crackle, which preceded the plume of smoke rising from the wreckage, she would not accept her companion's casualty. Her mind would not search its emotional closet for distress. Her heart's rusted gears would not crank to speed its beating. Her ducts wouldn't sign for the package of delivered tears. She grabbed the Cynque from her pocket, and fumbled to turn on its flashlight. Six senses on alert, she combed for evidence of human life, and inched to the vertical cliff, afraid she wouldn't like what she found.

Coughing. Grunting. "Little help?" the voice of her Aussie colleague echoed, winning its competition with the continent's winds.

Air released between her lips.

One set of his gloved fingertips had made it onto the frozen ledge. A miraculous feat when the other was in a cast strapped to his body. Bazzo strained below her light and hoisted himself up until both elbows rested horizontal in the snow.

"It was broken anyhow," he offered. *Kaboom. Kabloom!* A bonfire lit the ice shelf. Dark smoke surged to the sky.

Prepared for tenderness in her tailbone, Florence took his wrist, dug her nails into his puffy jacket and heaved her associate up. They laid on their backs, breathless, like children having run around and made angels in fresh fallen snow.

Bazzo looked over at her. "Sorry?"

"Don't be. I'm billing you for it."

"Fair enough," he said, stretching. Bazzo unzipped his parka. Inside, between his ribs and the cast, he'd nestled the thin glass bottle. "Cheers." He uncapped it and took a long swig. "Half in the bag and I can still feel the cold and my hand. I swear to bloody God." He thrust the bottle at her.

Cringing as a waft of vanilla and spices hit her nostrils, she rolled her eyes and refused his offer. "I'm not in the mood." She pushed the gold booze to him.

He got up and used his good arm to haul her to her feet.

Florence put on airtight goggles engineered for the South Pole's extreme conditions and gave a curt nod to the vacant ice sheet. What she sensed made up for what she didn't see. "The base is here, somewhere. Can you double check the coordinates?"

"Hold your horses," he mumbled. "No Cynque signal this far south." His fingers snapped, and a lone bolt landed on the ice and sparked a frenzy that fried C20's electromagnetic cloaking mechanism. "Gotcha."

A domed force field shimmered into reality. The ever-elusive C20 base loomed in windowless perfection, resembling a vertical metal castle inside an unshaken snow globe.

On second thought, she nudged him for the alcohol, endured the first sip, then tipped it back. Two months overdue. A bit musky, a bit salty, a bit sweet, abrupt and violent on the tongue. Still good medicine for what sliver of her soul she held onto. Done grappling with the aftertaste, she sighed in celebration of Bazzo's survival.

Rum kept the spirit of vengeance (for her) and liberation (for him) in their bloodstream.

He returned the liquor to its hideaway and zipped his military parka closed. Bazzo Sparks, though new to her life, was an odd extension of her family. She'd become uncharacteristically fond of this young, devoted superhuman trudging to save his sister. Possibly, trudging to his death. Florence admired the kinship he and Bridget shared.

Shame she was a criminal.

Florence draped her cable knit scarf over the thermal mask to envelop her chin and mouth. The katabatic winds objected to their intrusion and for every step forward, they slipped backward almost as much. Head on, they confronted the would be spotless white desert, greyed and blackened by sunlight's six-month absence.

"The dome!" she shouted.

Bazzo extended his hand toward the ground, drawing stolen electricity through his palm. He shouted back, "All over it!" The dome dimmed, brightened, dimmed again, and then dissolved to nothing. Soldiers spilled from the doorway, weapons raised and ready, and fanned out to defend the base.

"Plan?" Bazzo asked.

"Don't get shot!"

Unwilling to wait for hostility, she grabbed the sword's handle with all the strength she had and charged ahead.

ZOSMA CASTER
The Subconscious

GLISTENING RED, GREEN, blue, indigo, and yellow light penetrated Zosma's inner psyche and collected itself into liquid globules. Melded to one creamy color and elongated at the top, it shifted from whitish transparency to opaque silvers. The head and face of a womaformed, accompanied by a bone-straight brunette mane.

Next came a black tattered cape, and muscular trained arms outfitted in matching gloves to the elbow. The double-breasted jacket covered a V-shaped torso, and a narrow waist gave way to long legs accessorized in thigh-high boots. Leesa Delemar had returned.

Undisturbed fog in the barren space drifted away from the new arrival, and suctioned into a representation of Dylurshin within her mind. Its wispy shoulders rose and spread, guarding the way to the hidden portrait of Uragon's countryside. Guarding the way to Zosma.

"What is this insolent phantom?" Dylurshin asked, as he attempted disassembly. "How did you infiltrate this domain, counteract my power?"

Light washed over Leesa like a waterfall, though enlivened her complexion none. Death's irreversible color saturated her skin.

"You know me, Hexforth," she said, eyes blazing. Her telekinetic grasp imprisoned every atom in the creature's body. "You've known me for eons. Where. Is. Zosma?"

"You are a figment. A figment of her imagination."

She took a step. The blue Z-energy wall stifled behind Dylurshin's oppressive presence glimmered with obedience. The energy filtered through her outstretched fingertips and its numbing force shot from her palms. Z-energy penetrated the entity's core, and obliterated its physical form. Leesa ran full speed across the triangular threshold to the perilous war-torn terrain, cape flapping in the turbulence of a troubled mind. She somersaulted to dodge sharpened rocks jutting up out of the ground, and doubled back, a stone's throw from falling.

"Zosma!" Leesa yelled, "If you can hear me, say my name!"

An infinite drop separated her from the fortress consumed by molecular mist. Dylurshin's grin enveloped a sky in reddish grey dominance. "Is this Neight's pathetic attempt to save his daughter? With an astral projection?"

Sinister black lightning struck the frail edge. Leesa screamed, arms flailing, eyes frozen in diligence, as she fell into the endless canyon.

"Leesa," Zosma whispered. Names of people she'd cared for, people who'd helped her, people who needed her to wake up, were dealt on mental cards. And with all those cards on the table, it became clear she'd won the hand. Whatever the game, her prize was free thought. For all she stood to lose for existing, there was no future in which Dylurshin could win. "Neight... Florence," she continued. "Allister."

Speaking each name grew her sense. Zosma's fist clenched on the ground. Surrounded by the luminosity of a newborn star, her limp, overrun figure fought the outside influence.

"I will banish you, if it is all I do," she said to Dylurshin.

The reversal began. She purged herself of the mist, forced it to retreat down her body and across the roof.

A wave, similar to the destructive ones she'd elicited so many times before (the kind that annihilated people, cities, planets), rippled through the picturesque reincarnation. And for the first time, the Z-energy restored beauty.

"You are more than evil," Zosma said, hand raised above her, "but you are less than me."

"No! I have come too far!" The final syllable echoed in surround sound as Dylurshin dove, open mouthed, to devour her.

A concentrated beam shot down its throat and exploded outward, eroding what parasitic power remained. Binary star's magnificence vaporized wisps of leftover mist.

"I'm here," Leesa said, and stopped her fall. "I'm always here."

"But where did you go? I thought you were lost in the chasm? And before, you were restrained inside the wall? I could not feel you." Zosma peered at their feet. The locked tower now open, theories broiled in her mind. Leesa wasn't a human spirit lost in limbo. She was the physical representation of the energy inside her. An energy that had never left and was always there, so long as she had the consciousness and confidence to call upon it.

"You understand now. We are meant to navigate this universe together."

"Yes," Zosma replied. "I will make sure Dylurshin does not find what it seeks."

CHAPTER EIGHT

THE LAST ZAIAN

NEIGHT CASTER

"ZOSMA REPRESENTS THE FUTURE of our great universe," a voice, smooth as a string instrument, breathed into Neight's ear. "If her birth was not to be, it would not be. And so, if my death is not to be, it will not—" His dead soulmate's final declaration expired as he came to.

Subdued staff, including Myra, fussed over a master screen encompassing the center of the basement. It showed fifteen flashing white circles on a world map.

"They're in place," she said, "Agents are moving in to secure each perimeter, so we don't have a repeat of Morocco." Her hand fumbled for the back of a chair and landed on Russell's scarf. "Shouldn't Mr. Ashur be back by now?"

"He is preoccupied dying a traitor's death," Dylurshin answered.

Ten additional U-generators had been activated during Neight's brief slumber, meaning 75 percent of the Z-energy circulated the globe. Zosma was strapped to a table using titanium bands and locked inside a translucent box. The containment center's remote operating mechanism held the leftover 25 percent captive, hindering her defenses.

His eldest daughter screamed, awakened by the excruciation of energy force sucking through her pores. When the final four generators activated, the entirety of Zosma's power would irrigate to the machines, leaving her torn to pieces.

Dragging himself to stand Neight said, "It cannot be," and repeated, "It cannot be. Stop this, you do not know what you are doing!"

A single row of sharks' teeth arranged in a permanent smile snapped together inside powerful jaws. "I have shown enough mercy today. Engage the centrifuge!" Dylurshin thundered.

Three agents walked over to activate the prison centrifuge, and achieved several unsuccessful pokes to the big green button.

"What is happening?" Dylurshin asked.

"Influence, over the living, the weak, the broken, the scared. Confidence, in the living, the strong, the resilient, the fearless. A difference between two ancient things who placed their faith in alien beings. Humanity has shown it has choices, and they speak in liberated voices. I draw power and prayer from our sacred Z-energy source, help bring an end to Dylurshin Hexforth."

He spoke the incantation three times. Long muscular arms rotated counterclockwise to an imaginary drum beat. The incision he made in the capsule flashed blue, split the titanium down the center, lengthening and widening into a full-blown hole.

"I misjudged your capacity for compassion. An admirable quality in a ruthless tyrant," Neight said.

"You do not know tyranny until you know the truth about Andromeda's Sanctuary. Its laws, its morals, its practices. A creation baptized in conquest's red fire, doused in dishonesty's sour taste."

Neight needed to buy time. Though the currency of their conversation had diminished in value over the last few months, it meant he'd have to spend more. He shook his head, stepping to freedom. "It will be a pleasant surprise for you to see Zosma's true power."

"She is nothing," Dylurshin scoffed. "An obstacle I will overcome like innumerable others."

"It's a demon!" a bewildered scientist exclaimed, jabbing a finger at Neight's crouched body.

Though hunched to a quarter of his eight-foot height, elongated fangs, a square jaw, and velociraptor-shaped talons were a stark contrast to a female Uragonian's gentler features. The grimace he wore alongside spiked shoulder pads and forearm guards didn't help.

Myra doubled back, her glasses fell, and she fell on them. Through swift nasal inhalations, she stammered, "What... what... are..." without finishing the question, she scurried to the emergency exit and escaped with fellow fleeing scientists.

Stalling to ensure the basement's emptiness, Neight said, "You have misjudged your new 'people.' Imagine they saw you for what you are?"

Disoriented, wild particles jumped away from Dylurshin's form in heightened emotion, betraying the calmed delivery. "They will worship me when I fulfill my promise to preserve them, to make them the apex of mortal existence. Nothing will stop this civilization's ascension to Andromeda. Not you, not her, and not the little hybrid boy you have put your faith in."

Their lingering banter tiptoed toward conflict.

"You lost our previous battle, yet you challenge me now, knowing I am limitless," Dylurshin taunted.

"Last time, I let my arrogance dictate my actions. This time, I let your arrogance dictate my actions." His hands twisted one above the other and touched. Z-energy jogged fingertip to fingertip, and as his palms spread apart, Neight said, "Your influence over that contraption is no more!"

Energy blades sliced Dylurshin's arms, severing its connection to the containment center controls. The amputated mist defied gravity. It observed the missing limbs while they drifted upward, straining to elongate and reconstruct them.

Neight let his daughter's exhaustion-laced cries lead him to her. She trembled, unable to keep her body intact, as if a black hole had been opened in her abdomen.

His Z-energy charged fists pounded the entrapping box with all intended brutality, yet, it did not bend, moan or crack, constructed to repel the energy's force inside and out. Four decades it had been since they'd both been of sound mind and body, aware of their surroundings and their Uragonian heritage. "Remember what I told you," he said. His unwrinkled forehead touched the box's ceiling, wishing to press against hers in sincerity as he'd done in her youth. "Daughter, my dearest princess, hang onto your, self with everything you can."

"How did it consume me?" Zosma asked, swallowing multiple times before finishing the sentence, "I am controlling, distributing, accessing it all, at once."

The three verbs brought recognition to her brow—she and the energy were one and the same. Neight and his queen didn't know the mistake they'd made when they transferred the power thriving in the core of Uragon.

"I am to blame," he muttered, disconnected from her unfocused gaze.

"You did this to me?"

Neight caressed the semi-opaque material like it were her smoldering cheek. "Creatures will strive to dictate who you are and what you are meant for, but when *you* know who *you* are and what you are meant for, it is all that will matter in the end." He showed his armored forearm and said, "The Caster bloodline survives the wrath of an infinite system."

She nodded, and despite their separation, her flashing arm quavered on the upward journey to meet his. "In kinship and in loyalty," Zosma choked out, then tightened her lip, "Go. Nothing is accomplished by our... sentiments."

336

He obeyed. And recoiled, drawing his cape. Black daggers coated in sinful red energy, hurtled at him from Dylurshin's chest.

"They rise, they fall," he said, spreading his arm. Blue energy waves blasted them to oblivion. The ram-horned, magnesium alloy helmet tapped his heel. He rotated, scooped up the protection and fastened it to his head.

Fanged teeth barred, Neight charged forward. "Face me, Zaian filth!" The faceplate extended, hiding his eyes. He picked Dylurshin up and threw it. Writhing mist would've made contact with the wall, instead it parted like the Red Sea. He'd put his full force behind the follow-up right hook, sending his knuckles through metal and ice.

"What do you know about the Zaians?" Dylurshin asked, rebuilding itself amongst cold steel.

Neight tore his fist out. "I know they are about to be extinct." Swarming darkness caught him by the chest plate, swiveled him around, and tossed him so hard the basement's crystal wall shattered. On his knees, both forearms created an "X," and a sparkling barrier blocked a dark energy-powered bombardment. Outdone, one arm fell and the second wavered, pleading for him to surrender. "That is enough!" he bellowed. A Z-energy orb diffused the attack. Repelled by the energy expansion, the body made of liquid mist belonging to Dylurshin demolished heavy-duty machinery and shorted the main CPU.

Mist chopped about like untamed waters and converged at Dylurshin's open palms. "Indeed," it said, and cocked back.

Drawing both hands together, Neight prepared for a similar attack. The helmet's horns and crest glowed, adding fuel to his fire. In silent execution their blasts collided, respective energies booming and crackling as they tugged in war.

His retaliation weakened. His Z-energy reserves further depleted. The hostile attack overtook him, knocking the steaming helmet away as he flew next to the broken capsule. No rush to get up, Neight laid there checking for injuries outside of a bruised ego. A head to head battle was not the best move. "Allister."

"Great minds, Neight Caster, great minds. Mr. Adams, it is time for us to use those artifacts you have," Dylurshin said, and caught the fallen king's eyes as it finished its sentence, "Your savior is here. How does it feel that he cannot save you?"

ALLISTER ADAMS

TORTURED SCREAMS hammered Allister's ears, but his head, forbidden to look their way, stayed straight and narrow. Posture deflated, Allister heard himself talking in a layered demonic voice, saw himself straggling on two feet, while his consciousness had been submerged in mental limbo and drowned in an abyss inside his own awareness. He neared Neight's defeated figure.

"I believe my comprehension of the Transporter gems can make them more useful." Dylurshin turned to him. "Begin."

Mist soared in his neural pathways. His legs planted shoulder width apart. His arms stretched to full wingspan, fists twitching with anger that didn't belong to him. Dylurshin steered the ship and wasn't willing to turn around. Though screaming "no" in his head, a temporal energy sphere somersaulted around him and its tendrils lashed Neight, who'd risen and firmly grasped his shoulder.

The alien's glossy, shoulder length hair, his skin grey or lilac depending on the how the light hit, and strange, yet handsome widened nose and inflexible jaw, flickered, whitening from the effects of molecules breaking down for transportation.

Neight had mentored him through the hellish Andromeda Project experience, offering guidance, wisdom and at times his own reality altering powers, to guarantee Allister's success. Continuous personal sacrifices required the alien refugee's resolute faith that he, Allister Adams, a Uragonian descendent, was the right choice. The right choice for the Z-energy, the right choice to wield the Transporter gems, and the right choice to advance humanity.

"You must wake up," Neight whispered. "Time is of the essence."

Allister searched the disappearing face for distress and found the same peculiar devotion to him. Neight's obsidian eyes, wrapped in a golden iris, reflected the permanence of space. No planets, no stars, just the swallowing blackness of antimatter and negative mass between galaxies.

Propelled through the subconscious void, he swam like an Olympic medalist. *I—I'm sorry Neight, I'm so sorry,* he thought, prohibited from speaking his own words. Their reinforced connection and his regenerative powers hacked at Dylurshin's dominion, dead-set on crafting an antidote for the influence that bordered control.

"What you seek, the gems will find. If you can come to free your mind. If I have learned one lesson in five centuries, forgiveness does not require love, but love does require forgiveness. Goodbye, Allister."

Shrouded in temporal energy, overpowered by gravitational force, Neight was sucked into a singularity. Sentenced to nothingness.

Allister's spirit touched the edge of awareness, reconnecting to his body, jolting him awake. Crunched in a standing ball, he lurched, blinking as the tumultuous environment went from fuzzy to clear. His eyes followed his ears, and where he looked, he saw Zosma. Her hands, torso, and one leg were energy, everything else, waning flesh, soon to suffer the same fate. Fury surged in his gut—verve through his bloodstream.

"Alert—" The CPU's screen glitched, flashing red text and fuzzy maps "—Nineteen remaining generators are in place. Initiating energy transfer."

Sans minions, Dylurshin became engrossed in the details and Allister limped to the shining box containing Zosma.

"Zosma, are you listening?" he whispered, hands groping the prison for a way in.

"Yes," Zosma said. Like the sun's corona during a lunar eclipse, blue light burned around the yellow in her eyes. "Whatever happens, Dylurshin cannot find the Z-bands of unlimited energy."

"Ninety-percent energy access transferred," the CPU's monotone voice announced.

Allister restrained sniffles. "It won't. I promise, it won't. They're not here. They're out there in the universe somewhere. You'll be fine as long as we shut down these generators."

Zosma shook her head against his assumptions. "They are here. I brought the artifacts with me. If Dylurshin finds them, it means a desolate future for the human race and, Allister, that creature threatens more than you or I could fight to save."

Her agonizing yell correlated to a chunk of energy whirling around the hole in her.

"Ninety-five-percent access energy transferred."

He waited for her to quiet, to talk through his asinine idea, "There's a device here. Somewhere in Antarctica, I think. It can hold Dylurshin, it's-it's held Dylurshin. But what if... I-I can't save you."

She dry-heaved her initial answer, and willing her to breathe, he gripped the box's hard edges until he lost the feeling in his palms.

"Then don't," Zosma choked out and sank back.

Emotional restraint notwithstanding, tears and snot soaked his chin, knuckles and the rectangular prism preventing her escape. His single wish to reassure her resilience with a gentle stroke through her hair would not be granted.

Energy siphoned into the growing whirlpool. Sirens warned them the chemical reactions had reached their peak. Fiery propulsion blew him backward.

He recovered in shirt scraps, ignoring the micro cuts, the abrasions, the bruises. Zosma, fighting the energy's chaotic eruptions, assumed a humanoid shape and levitated—skull half intact.

Hot tears trickled down his cheeks. Allister pushed off from the cracked floor and returned to the worthiest stance he could muster under the circumstances. He had to be the rock. He had to be the anchor. The reason for her to keep fighting. Shrinking the distance between them, he said, "Zosma, I would do anything to give you the happiness you deserve. No matter how complicated this got, I wanted us to be together."

She planted a cool, pure energy kiss on his quivering lips.

"If our mutual adoration is written in destiny, it will be."

The heat of a dying star emanated from her body. Her tender lips dissolved, joining her radiant silhouette.

"You will submit to me!" Dylurshin howled. Its particles froze midway through separation, as it rushed up to attack.

"That which we fear most, we do not keep far from sight," she said earnestly. Her flailing hair fizzled into energy and, by telekinesis, she dispersed their enemy's body to the distorted space's opposing corners. "Hurry, Allister, find it. Let my death not be in vain."

BAZZO SPARKS

THEIR LONG, SLOW STRIDES had become bursts, and rubber snow-boots kissed a surface of frosted glass promising to keep their bodies upright by adhesion and carry them into battle with lightweight. Electric fury had whizzed from Bazzo's eye sockets, shoulders, arms, and hands. Florence's psionic energy had added sharpness to her sword's slice. They fought their way inside, dodging firepower while swiping, electrocuting, disabling and dismembering C20's defenses. His victims lay injured. Hers lay dead.

"These agents are oblivious," he said, stepping over bodies to the entrance. "Show 'em some mercy."

They all had names, he supposed, and families, loved ones.

"Keep that in mind when they're shooting at you," she replied.

"I do." Ignoring his hand's phantom pangs, the light headedness and tipsiness creeping in, he took another shot and slung the bottle.

"You should've left the rod in there."

"Electromagnetism ey Dr. B, took it right out." He shuddered at how the flesh had squished, and bones had crunched during the metal rods' passage in and out of his hand. "Thought I was a goner for sure."

Giovanni Belladonna's Cynque accessed the central glass elevator like Townsend Black had promised. Ground tremors plagued their mile-long journey to the prison floor, so Bazzo and Florence squeezed the handrails in uncertainty, nervous pupils fixed on the ceiling.

"Message received from Mum. Would you like me to open?" his Cynque asked.

He smiled. "Yes." A picture of Bridget as a scraggly teen shimmered above the watch. "They miss her. Will be good to get her back to Oz."

"You know she was on death row for murder before she joined the Andromeda Project?" Florence asked.

The image retracted. "So?" His face scrunched. "She killed a scumbag in self-defense. I know the story, they tricked her into signin' them papers."

"Ms. Sparks has bi-polar disorder and a long—"

"Don't Ms. Sparks me," he said over her. "My sister is brilliant—"

"With a history of violence that borders sociopathic," she finished.

"Yeah?" Bazzo raised his voice. "Ya know I worked for a person like that. He made off just fine."

"He was rich," she snapped. Florence opened her mouth, tilted her head. "I don't know if they'll let her go home with you."

Imagination left his eyes vacant, and he went monotone. "I reckon you can pull some strings. If you want to."

They reached the underground prison area in silence. C20 agents blasted an ice construct spanning the hallway. Heated plasma sent cracks throughout the wall, inspiring its reversal to liquid. Bazzo peered at the cavernous melted hole near the top, behind which, Bridget fretted over an unconscious body.

Ding. The doors opened.

"Bridg," he said in disbelief, walking. "Bridg, I'm here!"

The agents turned from the ice wall. Florence yanked him by the hood and dragged him to a hollowed opening. Titanium reinforcement, jagged ice, and the foundation's concrete exploded at them.

"Have you, lost it?" she shouted. "You're going to get us both killed!"

"Is that what you're worried about?" Bazzo asked, face red as a brick. He, the irresponsible older brother assumed his baby sister would care for herself, not get into trouble. In a whirlwind of priorities and efforts to hide his farmhand upbringing, he disconnected from the psychotic young girl he'd taught everything from how to walk to how to drive. Glower deepening, he said, "Screw this. I've been patient enough."

"Wait, what are you doing?"

The soldiers halted their attack, shuffled their feet as they switched positions. He listened to the weapons recharging; a rare and convenient pause, during which he exited their hiding spot and tried to fire. Anger helped fight his mind's fatigue and gave electricity the courage to spark. But the hissing currents scurried off as fast as they had arrived.

I'm outta juice, he thought.

Reactive plasma cores whirled to life, and excited atoms for a fatal blast were quieted by his verbal white flag.

"I surrender," he said again, "long as she goes free."

The lead agent took him by his parka's fabric and punched him in the stomach, then kneed him in the face, smashing his nose. Bazzo rolled along the ground, wheezing, and stopped face up. Bewildered, he dabbed the bloody stream with his coat sleeve. A crippling grip closed around his neck. The agent lifted him up and hit him in the stomach again. He whimpered.

"We don't take prisoners," the C20 agent said. Fur topped, construction boots crunched against debris and ice shingles, towing Bazzo deeper into the underground cavern by his golden locks. "Come on out, Ms. Sparks."

The agent tossed him on his stomach. He let the frozen metal paneling treat his nose's swelling. Shivering. Nausea. The rum was no good to him, churning in his anxious belly. Intoxicated blood had been pumped to his brain and liver. It did not bring warmth.

His chin rose to heeled footsteps. Bridget climbed through the ice creation, heat-deprived flesh coated in miniature crystals, and he realized it wasn't an ice creation, it was her ice creation. *You gonna hang out back there?* he thought at Florence.

"Late as usual, Baz," she said, low and casual. "What took ya so long?"

"Ah, c'mon, Bridg. This's record timing." He waited for Florence's answer, or another blow to the body. Neither happened.

The agent snatched his head back and saddled the weapon against his temple. "I'll take those as your dying words."

"No!" Bridget yelled.

The plasma blast didn't echo in the corridor, Bazzo's (would be) sizzling brains didn't splatter the immaculate ice walls. Instead, her emotional outburst had hardened all 60 percent of the water in the agent's blood, organs, muscles, and brain, rendering him immobile. Drifting condensation spread, inviting icicles to form pointed homes on his chin, fingers and gun barrel. Bazzo fell away from the sculpture, which was polished off with a preserved misshapen scowl. Searing orange energy reduced the statue to shards.

"Less talk!" Florence yelled, diving under open fire. She sprung off her hands to her feet, rotated the sword and executed a whirling backspin, slashing an agent across the chest. His weapon clattered on the ice and she roundhouse kicked him into slumber.

The whiff of a smoking gun sailed above his upper lip's stubble, and a click whipped his neck to attention. Staring down the barrel, he gulped as the gloved finger moved the trigger.

"Ack!" the agent squealed. Florence's legs wrapped around his neck in a vice grip. Yelling, she twisted her body, flipping him over her. *Thud.* The agent hit the ground. She turned and hurled her sword edge-first like an all-star pitcher, impaling the agent zeroed in on Bridget.

"Hmph, mercy." She strode to the squirming body and wrenched her weapon from his lungs by its hilt.

Bazzo watched her, gawking. Merciless. Like Giovanni.

The entire base shook. Blocks of ceiling buckled, dislodged and fell. Bridget's icicle nails clenched his collar and ripped him from danger. Concrete smashed where he'd been laying as his coat yielded to her semi-instant freezing ability. With her help he tore it off, watching it become solid ice and join the mess on the floor as fractured shingles.

"Christ," Bazzo said, nose too tender to wipe, voice too nasal to take seriously. "I was worried about ya, but I must say baby sis, ya look tiptop." He smiled, tottering to a blood drenched agent. Bazzo undressed him, stole his parka, and shook as he zipped it to trap what body heat he had left.

"I don't think Russell's gonna make it," Bridget said.

They found the engineer, taking up as little surface area as possible, any effort to keep warm. Florence knelt down.

"Weak pulse," she said.

There wasn't time for hesitation, yet Bazzo did, wondering whether he could play a supporting role in rescuing Allister. Half in the bag. Nostrils bleeding. Hand pulsing with agony. And not an electric current in sight. He'd be comic relief for sure, but no help. And as powerful as Florence and Bridget were, they had limitations, and getting in the middle of a brawl with two (or three) cosmic beings was absolute suicide.

"I vote we get him topside first, and sort it there."

"We risked our lives to come down here and stop Dylurshin."

"So, what, you want to leave him to die?"

"I need to get to Allister or this was a waste."

On her knees, Bridget traced the air about Russell's motionless face. "I got an idea," she said, marveling at the ice clinging to her skin. "I'm gonna bring down the house. Make 'em all come running to you. Take him."

"Come off the grass," Bazzo scoffed. "Didn't ya learn ya lesson the last time. You're comin' with us." He scooped Russell into one arm and fell over from the unforeseen weight. "Ya gotta be kiddin' me." An additional attempt ended them both on the floor. He moaned. "Sorry, I'm more banged up than I thought." He laid there, staring up in Bridget's wet, twinkling eyes, looking for the electric blue color from their childhood. Frozen irises stared back.

Bazzo got up, determined, and called to Florence for help.

"We don't have time for this," she whispered.

"Less talk. Just lift."

Their shoulders sharing support, they succeeded in dragging Russell's deadweight a few feet, then were thwarted by wreckage. They lifted him again, cleared the obstacle, and collapsed after a handful of imbalanced missteps.

"He can stay with me," his sister said to their backs, "he'd want it this way."

So did Florence. Bazzo turned to look at Bridget.

"Finally embracing who I am, the good, the bad, and the beautiful, and it'll be the last thing I do." She swallowed. "I was a bloody mess. Tell Mum I'm sorry, and Dad too. I got lost there for a bit." She swallowed again and took a breath. "But I've had a lotta time down here to think. I have to do this."

"Ya don't have to do anything Bridg, except come with us."

Flowing tears froze on her wintry cheeks. "Go home Baz, it's time."

"It's a done deal, let's go," Florence said and tugged him toward the elevator.

Ice prowled up the towering infrastructure, aiming to turn the base into a crumbling memory. Bridget commanded the sub zero cold of a continen, causing breaks in the sound crystalline walls. Cracking, splitting, they caved in a rumbling avalanche. Bazzo punished himself by watching, for watching, and flinched, each time a monstrous icicle crashed inches from her. Even as the glass elevator swept them to a sturdier level, he knew that in moments, she'd be lost amidst glacial salvation.

Unable to bear it, he hid from her sacrifice. Seeing it made it true. Made it final and real and heartbreaking. And for those seconds he preferred the quiet darkness in his head, at least then he could imagine Bridget dying in peace, beautiful and un-maimed.

Taking a last remorseful look, let's just say for closure, Bazzo saw the spot where she'd been kneeling, empty.

Allister Adams

C20's base. The Andromeda Project's laboratory. They had commonalities. Homes to the Containment Center and research breakthroughs in genetics and technology. Pristine. Organized.

Sacred to the "man" who'd introduced himself to Allister as a scientist devoted to preserving and advancing humanity.

Allister had accepted Zosma and her fateful expiration, sprinted to the hall, and, operating on a hunch, began his vertical climb to the place where Dylurshin strung him up like slaughtered meat.

Difficult to navigate tunnels and platforms put him back in familiar locations again and again. He came through a tunnel's mouth, heels first, stopped, and turned around to the manufacturing facility below. A transparent elevator shaft. A narrow bridge to another identical platform and tunnel entrance. "I thought the lab was here," he said.

His mind sifted for previous images of the base, comparing those encounters to find similarities or differences in what lay before him. *The Steps.* Steps leading up. He hadn't seen those before.

Agents exited the other tunnel, blocking access to the steps. *Dammit,* he thought, then followed up with, *Shit,* as he scrambled back. They opened fire at the sight of him. His right foot planted. He flipped sideways and spun backwards so the scorching plasma hit the walls instead of him. Landing on both feet, he ducked the projectile chunks of ice and steel blasting outward.

The base moaned like an old house. Firepower ceased. Hush settled. The agents' heads traveled up and left, down and right, hunting for the origin of the noise. The ground's sudden quaking triggered their disoriented shouting. Using the opportunity to reroute, he dashed onto the bridge. He'd planned to make it across, charging through the enemy mob like a rhino. His shoulder angled low and teeth pressed together, mistakes he quickly realized. He didn't grasp why the ground shook with such resolve. Why it had decided right then to bring this behemoth known as C20 to its deserved demise.

Allister couldn't stop and he couldn't go back. Not while fissures shot up the shining walls on either side. Not while fully formed rifts divided those walls into fragments. Or while the platform dislodged, taking the bridge with it. All he could do was gasp, force himself to fall, and slide, heart racing, onto his stomach.

Whoom, it fell. *Klunk*, it smashed into the bridge lying beneath. Pause. *Creak.* Said bridge objected to the burden. Ear to the ground, his grip tightened. *Whoom. Klunk.* Pause. *Creak. Whoom. Klunk. Boom.* The base shuddered and the platform's final impact puffed arctic dust up over him, clouding his surroundings. He pried his aching fingers from a handprint embedded by fear, inhaling, to assess his medical condition. The crash rang in his ears and slamming into metal had battered his ribs. He defied his lingering grogginess, exhaled, and rose onto his raw, splintered hands and cold, bruised knees. Not bad, considering. *Am I back where I started?*

Wreckage continued to fall around him, and he looked up to see the bridge had plummeted three stories, taking out the underlying cross bridges and their platforms as well. The glass elevator car had cranked past him during the ordeal.

Florence? he projected, swearing he saw her and her sword.

No answer. And no roars, no sizzling Z-energy, no combat. No Zosma. The last 5 percent must've siphoned off.

There were a cluster of damaged robotic assistants he hadn't noticed before, donating their weight to the giant steel seesaw they shared. One hand and one knee at a time, he crawled toward solid ground. At a slight angle, the dutiful bridge pretended to wait for him, sitting still while he inched. But as unsecured machinery skated across iced over metal, it squeaked and tipped into diagonal decline. Gravity. Gravity became his nemesis, pulling the weighted objects closer. Rolling downward, he cursed and tucked his knees. The shallow slant now near vertical, an airborne Allister, machines, the bridge, and his chances for success plunged.

C20's robotic assistants exploded on contact with solid ground. The bridge crunched in on itself against the same merciless foundation. And he, having strayed from their trajectory, plowed through a frozen ceiling.

Though he added injured back to the ailments list, his pained squint acquiesced to lit up eyes. An incomplete mural looked down at him.

If complete, eight planets would've been spaced in even measurement around the circle like numerals on a clock. Painted at the position of twelve midnight was one third of a large golden planet with an italic "AE" in its center. He identified it as the planet Aeneca, home to the Aenecans. To the left, was a smaller violet planet with an italic "U" in its center, which represented Uragon. Beneath that, was a crimson planet with an italic "P" in its center. He knew it as Psion, a planet comprised of psionic beings. A golden ring looped from the perimeter of the largest circle, around and through the other smaller circles and, like a waxing quarter moon, the missing side eased into darkness.

Allister assumed the mural's remaining visuals rested on the broken pieces beside and under him, but he got the gist.

The eight governing planets of Andromeda's Sanctuary... painted on a ceiling, like a fresco in the late fifteenth century. The temple, the place of worship, didn't belong to the entity. Dylurshin wouldn't keep architecture that glorified those civilizations; it despised them and all they stood for.

Some sort of explosive aftershock echoed from the base's belly. He rolled onto his stomach and covered his head. More mural caved. Titanium alloy pieces crashed around him, one of which clanked against the large contraption he'd fallen next to.

Quiet followed.

The dusty, dormant control panel was intact post impact. Intrigued by the computer's resilience, his instincts coaxed him into hasty exploration. First, he saw an "AE" and the sideways "8" insignia.

"Oh my fucking god," he said, backing up for a wider POV on what he deduced was an alien ship's cockpit. An observation deck. A captain's chair. Weapon controls. Communication modules. The cargo ship that Dylurshin had arrived in three thousand years ago, Allister was inside it. It was inside the base.

He returned to the responsive screen, its lit-up surface occupied by Uragon's symbol-based language. Black circle. Two heptagons inside it, on the left and right, had a green to white gradient. The symbol meant "time." Black circle. White circle inside it. No gradient. "Binds." Black circle. No other shape. No gradient. "All." The sentence led his examination to corners and to crannies and to empty supply compartments in search of the hidden chamber designed to hold Dylurshin. Squatting and thumbing his ear, he hypothesized where it would be if not in the inconspicuous places. The Transporter gems glinted, teasing him. He pounded his fist in his hand.

"Welcome," Dylurshin said.

Again, it embodied the darkness, blending in shadows, poised for an ambush. It had amassed substance, looming twenty feet tall. He knew if Dylurshin had emerged to confront him then the heaviness keeping him scrunched down, the sick traveling up his esophagus, and the stirring in the pit of his stomach were valid. Zosma was gone.

"There is nothing left. Her purpose is finalized. Surrender to me, Allister Adams."

Allister swallowed the news. Growling, he flew through the air with accelerated motion, grabbed Dylurshin by the horns, and dragged it across the ground. A dark energy barricade blocked his battering fists, while a duplicate, but smaller creature split off from Dylurshin's silhouette.

"I have sacrificed too much," it bellowed, gesturing for the clone to attack. The left hook clobbered Allister's cheek. "Fought too hard." Dylurshin's dark energy blasted him in the shoulder. "And planned too well to lose." The clone kicked his leg in and slashed him across the chest.

The cold air couldn't help but add its own sting to the cuts, reminding him it was, in fact, freezing. Up to that second, his body had done a fine job pretending their battle took place in regulate d temperatures. And, he'd spent the previous five minutes convinced his trembling had everything to do with anger and nothing to do with human frailty. Delirium tapped him on the back. He scoffed at it, jaw parallel to his knees, hands resting on his thighs.

His lip's trickling blood ran its course. A dizzy spell spun the room like a top, and he went to whisper, "Get it together," and spit onto the metal instead. The words couldn't find his brain, or his brain couldn't find the words.

Dylurshin snarled, as did its clone, a primal, foreign thing. Pulsing ruby energy ran through rifts in their mist contortions like rivers through canyons. Both circled him, neither in a rush to end his life or their time together inside the intergalactic vessel.

Who's turn was it to attack? Whoever wore the goading grimace. Allister stood opposite the alien in defense, put his left hand up, maintained dodgy aim by steadying with the right, and waited for Z-energy's charge to reach his elbow. *Zoom. Zoom.* Two circular blue beams penetrated Dylurshin and its clone's exteriors. Distorted in suffering, the mist shapes made all the noise they could, until their exoskeletons hardened and the residual energy short-circuited, and evaporated. They were not stopped. They were not slowed down. Panting, Allister faltered as Dylurshin's retaliatory overhand swing slammed into his curved spine and pinned him on the floor.

"The Z-energy is more power than humanity could ever dream. More than I had ever dreamed."

"This isn't a future for us, it's a future for you," Allister fought to say, "Humanity doesn't need you, Dylurshin, we can advance on our own."

"In the grandest of theories, you could." Dylurshin's dense limb pressed hard to crush his will and his way. It cackled and said, "However, your preservation is not guaranteed without a strong arm to guide you."

Hot gaseous breath burned his nostrils. Allister huffed and puffed, grunting and pushing to relieve the enormous weight. The mist thickened and slinked up his legs and around his chest. *Poof.* Gone. The Transporter gems had reacted on their own and in luminous disintegration, he fizzled away. The black cloud of mist folded in like a collapsing star and regenerated clump by clump.

"Two and a half million light years away, there is an emperor, disguised as a king, who's kept an entire galaxy in blind submission," Dylurshin said. Its tentacles swirled, sniffing the cockpit for him. "He could not kill me, so he sent me here because I know his secrets. I am destined to bring him to justice."

Allister's mental encyclopedia listed no knowledge on the Zaian race Dylurshin belonged to, as his knowledge came from Uragon. His brain studied the floating blob down to its complicated depths.

The last Zaian, an exiled creature that had sewed itself into human societies. Acted as innocent as an extra thread. Banished for crimes it was driven to commit. No, Dylurshin was not evil in the maniacal sense, if you were the type to understand how a creature's past can dictate their decisions and motivations.

"You do not have the wherewithal to activate the capsule, Allister. Summoning that much temporal energy will annihilate your feeble hybrid body," Dylurshin hovered, hissing, "Transonians are immortal. You are not."

Mallen. The alien buried somewhere in Antarctica had innate transportation abilities. He was a Transonian, "a keeper of time and space." The planet Transom's collective temporal energy had given life to the Transporter gems. Allister wondered if the trouble he had with the gems was that, as a Uragonian descendent, he didn't share their power.

Thinking back, enchanting the Chains of Infinity had taken more strength than transporting six beings to different continents in a world Mallen didn't know. Allister could barely transport himself without going unconscious. He'd never used the Transporter gems as an offensive weapon. Open a portal here and there, move around the world (sometimes on purpose, sometimes by accident), and see the past. If his time was to be spent mastering their use, he was way behind schedule.

In that humbling moment, accepting his limitations and the need to keep learning, his mind unlocked. The gems could teach him. What was a twenty-year-old earthling's gifted knowledge versus four-thousand-year-old artifacts' experience?

Dylurshin did not advance. Dylurshin did not retreat. It paced in obsessive compulsion back and forth along the ship's observation deck. An intriguing position... or not. *That which we fear most, we do not keep far from sight.* Chest aching at the resonance of Zosma's wisdom, Allister exhaled and said, "It's in the center."

The mist's rotting odor drifted to his hideaway. The fumes meant Dylurshin was too close. Too close for further contemplation. Too close for further hesitation. Too close for—

It materialized in his peripheral, swollen with malicious intent. A single condensed breath threatened to compromise his advantage. And in the throes of danger, one of his mother's most profound sentences replayed. "Neight taught me our futures are tangled up in plans we may not want to be part of, but they're part of us," she'd said in the cave beneath C20. "Every decision you make matters."

Cowardice had no advantages. Fear had no benefits. The temporal energy surged in his veins and he looked at the flashing Transporter gems.

"The Great Betrayer," Allister said, limping out of hiding, "you're in pain. You're alone."

"You dare question my being!" Dylurshin's axe-shaped appendage chopped at him.

His left arm shot up to take the brunt of the swing. Crackling on impact, Z-energy erupted and thwarted the blade's penetration.

It lifted the axe and chopped down harder, drilling him into the ground.

"I saw the Temporal Chamber when our minds were linked!" he yelled.

Enveloped in bright white light, his chin raised. As Dylurshin had foretold, he expended more effort than he thought possible. Temporal energy flowed in streaks and weaved through the observation deck. The Transonian gift rebuilt the ancient capsule of star's crust ten billion times stronger than steel. Tranquil air became a blustering distraction, throwing debris about.

Dylurshin growled, "I will not be undone by mortals," and thrust its sharpened limb forward.

Razored edges would've glinted along the thick spears' blade, if it weren't spawned by a cosmic demon's imagination and non-reflective dark mist. The ruthless weapon greeted Allister's epidermal layer with a harsh point. With its agonized squish and his agonized scream, the tip pierced his spine through his abdomen, and protruded from his back. Twisting, sinking deeper, shredding his organs.

His skin drained to a pasty brown. Amidst guttural choking, his mind went blank. The room quiet. Allister stood in the sparkling pool of space. Privileged to a birds' eye view: Antarctica, then Earth, then the solar system, then—at least two hundred and fifty million stars woven on the divine cosmic ether, painted on the canvas known as the Milky Way galaxy. In those brief seconds, so entrenched in time, he understood its nature. Circular. Spherical. Infinite. The beginning was the end was the beginning was the end. He learned not to look forward into the future or backward into the past. Look around, pinpoint a location, and go there.

Allister landed back inside himself. His hands dug into the misty weapon tearing him open and resisted.

The chamber's door opened, re-enchanted by a time energy tempest. Soaked in the entity's doom, the Chains of Infinity moved with sinuous grace, rattling over metal floor, and coiled around the swelling cloud known as Dylurshin Hexforth.

"I destroyed that abomination," the cosmic being screeched—expanded and contracted, flexing against their constriction.

Mist it had sent to influence humanity, returned from failure. Twenty feet became ten. Ten feet became five. Weapons became claws, then fingers. Three horns flattened to a smooth round head. The chains absorbed the mist into their shining links and cranked in reverse, dragging the alien away. Dylurshin crashed to the ground, a calcified exoskeleton. "No. No. No!" it gurgled in protest, striking the cockpit, though its strength was naught.

"Everyone is bound by... time, Dylurshin," Allister said, huddled on his knees, blood running from the wound. "... Even you."

"You do not understand," Dylurshin protested, scratching at the metal for assistance. "Vor Vegacent is the tyrant, not me. The Aenecans will return here and destroy you." The door shut, activating the temporal power that had filled the chamber thousands of years ago. Dylurshin returned to dormancy. Infinite patience and planning, undone by arrogance. The ancient prison vanished in a burst of light.

———

ZOSMA CASTER
The Subconscious

A BLUE BLAZE BURNED across the subconscious world, destroying happiness and contentment as it crept to her protective fortress.

"How much longer will I live?" Zosma asked.

Believing it her dying day, she paid homage to her physical body, every curve and nuance carved in pure energy. When the energy engulfed her and the tower, it would be over. "Humanity would be saved."

"You've been misinformed about the way our relationship works," Leesa said, perched on the ledge. "I blame fear. Your fear of what you are."

A haven overrun, usurped by greed. The land portrayed a similar sight to Uragon's final hours, a sight she'd seen minutes before blasting into space on her way to Earth. Minutes before entering a quarter century slumber.

"What am I? What are you?"

"I have existed since Uragon's conception," she began, rising. Her body basked in the approaching flames, she turned to Zosma and said, "Living in the hearts and souls of its people for a hundred thousand years. I wasn't aware then I was pure magic energy."

Starlight touched Leesa's skin, to bring it color, to bring it life, but it declined their charity. "Some five thousand years ago, an intergalactic being breached Andromeda. It sought to shroud our galaxy in its darkness, and there came a need for the collective power of Uragon."

The Z-energy became infinite. It would never burn out, exhaust... diminish. The Z-bands had been welded in the same imperishable star's core as her armor and imbued with the supreme energy. Artifacts formed to join seven others in a war that took a galaxy to the brink of death and damnation.

"Z-energy possession is a natural occurrence in the Uragonian gene sequence, but you, you, have been gifted with so much more." Leesa held Zosma's degenerating hands. "Together, we are the source."

Zosma crouched to the stone patio in anguish. "What about the artifacts?"

"I was the guardian. Your psyche, the mystical barrier." Her hands created a circle, and Uragon's Z-bands of unlimited energy were redrawn line by line and colored into reality. They shone a fierce gold, flashing like a pulsar with radiation. "The time has come for you to bond with them and take control."

She watched turbulent energy race at them. "I cannot take these. They symbolize destruction!"

"They do." Leesa fastened the artifacts onto her forearms. "It will be up to you to change your perspective, and then everyone else's." She swept an arm out, drawing the inferno in on its arrival. A single torch played above her fingers. "You're ready to take back your power." She jammed the torch into Zosma's chest, and, in expansive rippling waves, disappeared.

The tower caved on itself. Zosma floated down, willing her feet and legs into existence as her face returned to its violet beauty. Golden shin guards, the girdle, her mother's heirloom necklace, a white high-collared cape, and the Uragonian crown, physical components rebuilt to perfection. Smoke and embers drifted in the aftermath. Moisture-robbed terrain smashed under her two toes. She breathed, smiling in gratitude, knowing the hard work of repairing the utopia was ahead.

Allister's gruff yelps sucked her consciousness to reality and threw it at her crumpled body. She opened her eyes to the C20 engineering room. Z-energy no longer consumed her. Ice had lost its grip on walls and crumbled ceilings, drizzling into growing puddles. And for some reason, bone-chilling quiet surrounded her like a blanket too thin. Had his cries been a hallucination or—he screamed again.

She listened for his heaving and his heartbeat with no better sense of his location. Her wild intuition impelled her. Stepping over stray generator parts, squeezing between crushed machinery, ducking under hanging wires, and rushing past the cracked energy-cancelling barrier, she pressed her ear to the wall and yelled, "Allister! Are you in there?"

"Zo-Zosma?" he exclaimed, fighting for air.

Though his voice was consumed in a fit of coughs, she'd heard what she needed to hear. Her finger's downward swipe severed the metal separating them, and as she shoved her palms out, it peeled to reveal him. She glided the short flight.

Hovering horizontal, centimeters above his gouged insides, her finger brushed his swollen eye and traveled along his cheekbone. "It is trust that makes you strong." She nuzzled her crowned forehead close to his exposed, thumping heart. "And it is love that makes you invincible."

Sickening squelching sounds gave her a reason to rejoice. It meant mended lungs and intestines, reconnected blood vessels and nerves, fused bones, and reattached ligaments. Signs of revival. From lower sternum to his neck, an invisible needle retraced the skin with an invisible thread, closing the gaping chest wound.

Lifting his head, he took her hand and said, "I don't get it... how?"

"The bands. I did not have a choice."

Allister eyed the golden bands and laid his head to rest on the floor. "We'll deal with it. You're alive, that's all I care about."

Days prior Zosma had been a devoted member of the organization C20. Weeks prior she'd been willing to sacrifice her life for a purpose that was not hers. Falsehoods forged in fear.

"The universe has spoken its truth," she said to him, "it is written, and so it will be."

Zosma willed a blue telekinetic field into formation, suspending them in the air. It rose through the hole in the ceiling, pushing aside fallen fixtures, breaking intact platforms piled on top of each other, and blasted out of the avalanche-sealed crater.

Two figures trekked toward nowhere atop the frozen land mass, clothes blowing in wind. They swiveled at the emphatic boom caused by her exit. The psychic, Florence, shouted and pointed up at them, then tugged at the other human. It was Bazzo Sparks.

Antarctica showed the courageous no mercy, but Zosma did.

———

ALLISTER ADAMS
CIA Headquarters, Washington, D.C.

"BLOOD PRESSURE GOOD, neurological functions good, cognitive response good," the doctor said. Face wrinkles appeared above his mask, indicating a smile. "Quite the recovery, Agent Adams."

"That's not my name," Allister mumbled.

Besides, he'd been admitted in perfect condition. His previous treatment history lived in a screen attached to the bed, and in a holographic projection from the Cynque. So, his hospitalization four months ago, came into question.

"It's how I've been told to address you. Nothing personal." The stout doctor reread the assessment through a monocle embedded in stylish headgear. "If I may make a suggestion." Chip by chip, the mask retracted to reveal a buttery face, rewarded by years of life-saving sagacity. "Your accelerated, regenerative abilities, as astounding as they are to a young, crime-fighting superhero—"

"I'm not a superhero."

"Right. Nevertheless, you're aging faster than normal. I'm not sure what this says about your lifespan, but be mindful of your body's reactions to trauma. If you go too far, you may not heal, or if you do, you may not wake up."

Well, fuck, he thought. Power had a price tag.

"Thank you, Doctor..." He read the name. "Rojas."

Dr. Rojas glanced up past his forehead for the sixth time.

"I know! My hair is fucking purple, man, sheesh."

"It's not the color that concerns us, it's the genetic trigger."

"Don't suppose I could convince you to uh, share the results?"

The doctor typed onto the tablet and no details on the visible screen next to him changed. "Cynque, close file," he said to the room.

"At once, Dr. Rojas," the computer replied, blanking the displays.

Allister huffed. "Of course not, the secrets have secrets in this place."

"You're all set. Dr. Belladonna wants to take a final look at you before we move forward. Take care," he said.

Florence survived. Apprehension swelled in his throat, when he'd expected relief and a pinch of joy.

"Move forward?" he asked.

"Cynque, examination mode, please." The doctor's mask extended from the same headgear and snapped over his mouth, as if it would prevent his leaking the answer. "She'll be in soon."

They were hidden on the CIA research and training facility's fortieth floor. Langley had been re-zoned and upgraded to a full-blown military city. And it had taken a credible official (obviously Florence), pulling numerous thin strings to get them to admit an alien, and two unstable superhumans into the building for treatment. Then again, there were not many other places they could go, especially unsupervised.

Bazzo and Zosma alternated from eavesdropping to chatting outside the door like children. Dr. Rojas scanned his Cynque against the examination room entrance. It slid sideways and Bazzo strolled in.

"Bang up job, mate," he said. Following their firm handshake, he rearranged the sling on his shoulder.

"How's the hand?"

"Ah, minor damage. I need surgery. New bones, nerves and such."

Allister's eyes fell to the hospital blanket.

"What're ya gonna do? With my pockets this stuff's replaceable. Not everything is ya know," he added, shrugging and nudging his head at Zosma, "I put in a good word for ya. Just do me a favor and don't let anyone inside her—" He whistled while tapping his temple.

"Bazzo, I'm sorry about Bridget. She was a good girl."

"Who're you tellin'? Bridg was special. Bright, hilarious... kind back in those days. When we got our powers, she wanted to tell the world, learn how to use 'em. But we had a few incidents on the farm and... she spiraled from there. She grew up so fast. I don't know how I lost track of her." Entrapped in his childhood, Bazzo rocked on his heels, inhaled, and tapped the bed's railing. "Wasn't scared of much besides herself. She was a brave one, loads braver than me. Bloody shame nobody gave her a chance to show it."

Leaning forward, he touched Bazzo's slouched shoulder and nodded in agreement. "She came through when it counted most."

"If you ever need anything Double A, you gimme a ring," he finished, sniffling. "I prefer blue sapphires to diamonds though."

Bazzo curved his mouth in a resilient smile to offset a film of tears welling up. He retired to the exit.

Zosma, who dillydallied by the door as Bazzo strolled out, sidled to the bedside and squeezed Allister's two extra fingers. "A unique skeleton, indeed," she cooed. "I do not gather you need five of these."

He sat up higher, coming to eye level and cupped the back of her neck. "If we didn't need them, we wouldn't have them. What about this wild flower hair color? Can't be natural."

"As natural as the genes that code for them," she teased. She spun matching clumps, one of his and one of hers, in their shared focal point.

Heads angled to the side, two pairs of lips came closer and closer, breaths mingling before a long-awaited kiss lit yearning bodies on fire. Her thick fingers ran down his spine, pulling, until there was no space between them.

"Ahem." Florence's austere expression extinguished the passionate encounter. "Zosma, can I see you in private? When you're done." She plopped a duffel bag by the door and said to him, "FYI, you're being permanently relocated."

Cold-blooded. Not a beat missed. Not a tender tone detected.

Complicated questions and logistics lingered above Zosma and Allister's grazing noses and below their connected foreheads. Their dirty laundry was multiple loads of confusion, different colors washed, rinsed, and hung to dry together. She drifted to the window.

"You covered them up," he remarked, noticing she'd wrapped glossy sand-brown fabric taut around her forearms.

"My aim is not deceit. It is to avoid anyone posing questions I am unable to answer."

"Hey, I get it, I still can't explain." He ran a hand through his mini-afro and said, sighing, "We'll talk later. I could use some downtime too."

"I care for you, Allister Adams," Zosma said, engaging her telekinesis to open the door. "It is the only thing I keep faith in these days."

Left to ponder the last few months' gains and losses: no greater gain than Zosma; no greater loss than his mother, there came a Cynque news alert: "Vice President Evan Muenchow is scheduled to be sworn in tomorrow, replacing the late President DeVries. He's chosen a controversial candidate for vice president, proclaimed independent Dr. Florence Belladonna. A dual citizen with a long-standing political tenure who has already faced multiple assassination attempts. She would be the first female of African-American descent to hold such a high-ranking position in the presidential cabinet."

"You've got to be kidding me. Cynque, summarize article."

It read aloud in a fabricated female newscaster's nasal voice. "This comes mere days after twenty untested energy-conducting machines were delivered to major cities: Berlin, Cairo, Hong Kong, Vancouver, and Morocco, to name a few. Their true purpose largely unknown." Cynque news went on to bash C20, other questionable organizations like the Andromeda Project, and initiatives like the Z protocols, suggesting the world's twenty wealthiest people and their governments start offering explanations. The U-generators had since become two-story eyesores among the few prospering metropolitans in the world. "And to make matters worse," it concluded, "we're told they can't operate without a source. I speak for billions when I ask, what are they hiding from us?"

What are they hiding from us? A trinket's glimmer in the unzipped bag teased his focus. He shuffled to it.

Heart pangs followed, as he picked up the medal for outstanding military service given to him by Captain Jared Brandt. At six years old, the shiny thing and its heroic meaning had so fascinated him. He couldn't bear to part with it, and Brandt couldn't bear to make him. The man he'd called "Uncle Brandt" was different back then. He was family. The doting godfather's kindness immortalized in plated gold.

Allister polished the smudges with the hospital smock's silk fabric, remembering the unintentional transportation inside the disruptive field. The Z-energy pulse had reached its height and brief words redeemed Captain Brandt.

"They're gonna sacrifice Zosma, an' you'll be the only one who can stop 'em. If ya love her," Brandt had said, as he slipped into the arms of lady death, "don't make the same mistakes I did. Instead of killin', find a way to live for somethin' bigger than our own selfish needs."

FLORENCE BELLADONNA

FLORENCE SLIPPED INTO A NIGHTMARE, tormented by the black velvet box she'd found in Wesley's desk. Sensitivity had no place in the position she'd accepted, but two fingers pulled it closer, and she sighed, fighting off a tsunami of memories and sadness.

"Vice President Belladonna?"

Her executive assistant's grating voice went in one ear and out the other.

She waved a hand over Florence's eyes. "Vice President Belladonna, are you okay?"

No. "Yes."

Not the focus, so, out of focus, the executive assistant rested in her peripheral, hidden behind nostalgia. Florence caressed the miniature treasure chest. Inside glinted a promise—to have and to hold, to love and to cherish, as long as they both shall live. She picked up the 10k diamond, enormous and obvious, the opposite of their relationship. At the time, she had a soft spot for gaudy things. Life forced simplification on her. She twirled it around, imagining their wedding dance, then struggled to slide it on, reliving when Wesley had done it for her. This time she wouldn't be breaking both their hearts, by giving it back to him a month later. She squeezed her hands and lowered her forehead to them, swallowing loss lodged in her throat.

"I can give you a minute," the young woman offered.

Twisting off the ring put her on the path to self-control. Florence nestled it into its home and slammed the box shut. Emotions trapped inside velvet, in the company of diamonds. Keeping her lips close together, she asked, "What do you need, Mrs. Gibson?"

"You've been requested to oversee Detective Steele's interrogation." Her assistant leaned down to whisper, "Also, three files were retrieved this morning. President Muenchow wants you to have a look and schedule a meeting first thing next week."

"Have you looked at them yet?" she asked.

The freckle-faced, red head's light green eyes expanded. "Not yet, it's password protected. I had them sent to your Cynque." She tiptoed to the conference room door while Florence became entrenched in her now reattached Cynque device, and the unlocked files.

The word "classified" had been graffitied in the bottom right corners. Four digital images snapped by the International Space Station, depicted a remote area in the Pacific Ocean. "Taken in early 2052," she mumbled, getting closer to the holographic projection. Unusual energy readings showed disruptive wave emissions increasing two-fold month by month and based on a loose predictive model they'd peak at year's end. Scientists believed them the principle cause for seismic activity, rise in super hurricanes, and abstract climate patterns.

"Is now an appropriate time?" Zosma asked.

Florence locked the Cynque, dissolving the image. "Come in."

Zosma obeyed, but didn't come too far in, pacing the room at its fringes and observing the humans bustling outside.

"I must accept blame and take responsibility for actions I performed, even under the entity's persuasion," Zosma said. Her purple hand traced the glass. "I apologize for my hand in taking the love of your life from you."

"Did you know what you were doing?" Florence asked, standing, hardened, unsure if she were speaking as vice president, a devastated significant other, or a fellow super-powered creature.

"I suppose I was aware." Zosma frowned and looked away. "Vulnerable, influenced, yet aware. Disguised as Rabia Giro, I could not ascertain the threat Dylurshin posed against myself and your people, until his actions validated what, deep down, I knew to be true."

"You mean, when you found out he wanted to kill you. Got it."

"Coinciding coincidences, Florence Belladonna. Imagine the tall tales of fright told in your youth, and the diabolical creatures in them carved in your night terrors." Blue light surged beneath her palm. "Imagine, having just one of those demons resurrected from human flesh before your eyes, knowing it wants a single thing in the entire universe, and that thing is you." Three stretched fingers balled into a fist, snuffing it out. "I fought it for my sense of self, yes, I deserved it. And once reclaimed, I fought to save you from Z-energy's destruction."

"Celine Nephthys destroyed the first deployed generator. You owe her a big thank you."

"I would wager we all do."

Five percent had kept her alive. The looming question was, how did she get the rest?

Zosma ambled the perimeter, stopping parallel to her, facing the opposing direction. "You have asked me here, why am I the one speaking?"

A funny coincidence, the same power struggle she and Leesa Delemar had experienced, existed with Zosma as well.

Hands stuffed in navy trouser pockets didn't hide that her Cynque was back, which meant Florence Belladonna was back. "I had to handle the repercussions of—" She hesitated at the obligatory use of his name. "President DeVries' assassination, the policies he'd presented to Congress, the laws he was writing. I'm reviewing what's in the pipeline, finishing what I can and crafting my own."

She didn't have a choice, except it wasn't about collecting a fat paycheck, it was about upholding morality. She'd gotten the confession she wanted, time to get to the point.

"The world isn't ready for Zosma Caster," she blurted out. "I need you to become Leesa Delemar again."

"Have you given thought to the psychological effects on Allister?"

Demanding face-to-face conversation, Florence stepped toward the alien princess, tilted her neck up, then admitted, "It doesn't matter. I told the world leaders you left."

"I would think after what your planet has been through, you would learn deceit gets you nowhere," Zosma said, following her lead and moving closer. A hair taller, glaring down, she countered, "I will hide. Not behind a disguise."

Her stiff hand gestured over Zosma's body and landed on the Z-bands. "How do you expect to live like this? With those?"

"I saved this world from its greatest threat."

Exhaling, Florence placed her hands on Zosma's shoulder armor. "You're its greatest threat."

She meant to say "we." From the public's perspective, take physiological traits off the table and the signifying difference between her and the alien princess was the damage they inflicted. As a collective, the recognizable aliens and the unknown descendants were the other, their categorization, irrelevant nomenclature.

"Bottom line, an alien's an alien. Whether it's you or Neight or Dylurshin, and goodness knows what else is out there. It's all the bloody same." She let her hands drop and walked to the table. The velvet box returned softness to her tone. "The goal is for us to be allies. I made a promise to Dolores. I have an obligation to look after Allister, you, and now the 175 million Americans left, plus the entire free world."

"So, are we your prisoners or your soldiers?"

Florence glanced over her shoulder and replied, "Depends on how well you cooperate."

Mrs. Gibson shrieked. Her eyes darted at the ground, the nearest escape, and the purple alien woman. "I'm sorry I interrupted. Dr. Myra Eberle is here to see you."

"I'll be there shortly, Mrs. Gibson, please get her some alkaline water or espresso, thank you."

"Yes, of course."

"And Mrs. Gibson. Next time, request entry."

"Yes, Vice President Belladonna." The executive assistant ducked away.

"I am already Leesa Delemar, aren't I?"

A rather cruel reality check on Florence's part. Telepathic manipulation had guaranteed anyone Zosma encountered saw Leesa Delemar, not an armored princess.

"There's no reason people should be afraid," she said, staring at the closed door. Her assistant's short-term memory erased, she turned to Zosma—

In mid-transformation, three fingers became five, and her eye color changed to the Z-energy's blue. Violet hair darkened to autumn brown. Lilac skin turned olive, and golden armor melted into the Andromeda Project uniform that Leesa died in. The energy faded.

"With great power, comes great sacrifice," Zosma said in Leesa Delemar's rough voice.

Florence saluted her. "Welcome back, Lieutenant."

ALLISTER ADAMS

TWO PLOTS OF LAND. Dolores Adams on the left. Patrick Adams on the right. Allister may not have known what Neight told his parents about the responsibility running through his cellular structure, but success depended on his choices; his choices depended on his ability to seek understanding.

Florence had said he needed closure. Lackluster creativity bore engraved headstones, empty caskets, and a private ceremony. Traditional. Sincere. Fiscally responsible. As a registered superhuman under the CIA, Allister and "Leesa" had been relocated to a property in Northern Virginia. Far enough from the military city to keep him sane, and close enough to keep watch on what happened there. Agent Allister Adams on permanent standby in a world of fractured democracies, civilian unrest, and superhuman terrorism.

Allister crouched to touch the dirt. Intertwining fates had already brought the children of Andromeda together, though, true motives and morals were to be revealed. He expected the coming adversity to show where alliances were strongest, weakest, and non-existent. Friends sometimes became enemies, enemies sometimes became lovers, a neutral party, like Dr. Rabia Giro became an unstoppable behemoth. A temporary win wasn't worth celebrating.

He returned to the modest single-story house. Maintained acres concealed them from the outside world and the nearest neighbor was two to three miles away. Just like home.

Leesa sat on the kitchen island reading the daily Cynque news.

He closed the door behind him. "You know you don't have to wear that stupid costume in the house."

"You miss Lieutenant Delemar?" she asked, lowering her arm.

"I don't need a reminder of what I've lost," he whispered, nuzzling her neck with soft kisses. "I'd rather cherish what I've gained."

"An intriguing philosophy. I enjoy bearing witness to your mental evolution." Trouble twitched in her eyes, as she morphed into her alien form. Zosma rested a fused finger on his cheekbone's highest point. "If Neight has been sent to Andromeda's Sanctuary, he will be punished."

No sooner than the final touches completed on her three-toed feet, both his hands encircled her waist. "Your father's survived worse, right? He'll make it back... right?"

She curled to his reassuring embrace. "I have never witnessed anyone, save for Dylurshin, survive the wrath of the Aenecan king. Either way, Vor and his armies will come. Because it is me they wanted all along."

EPILOGUE

DYLURSHIN HEXFORTH

Castle Infinity. Eroter City, Planet Aeneca, 400 B.C.E.

HUNDREDS OF ROOMS, heavenly high ceilings, and hallways of grandeur painted with tales of the universe—the fundamental elements of Castle Infinity. To be inside Castle Infinity, could only be an honor or a curse. An honor to serve there, to stay there, to be born into the royalty they possessed. A curse to be a criminal there, in transition to exile in one of their prisons.

From a sky-scraping tower of prisons to an open room lined with Aeneca's best soldiers, Dylurshin Hexforth was dragged through the castle's beauty. The Zaian slave felt honor, knowing his vengeful deed could bring down all that surrounded him. But victory was heavier than Dylurshin thought. A bodice of magical particle compression chains wrapped round its thin neck, wiry arms, and torso, spiraled into a metal skirt covering its bent legs.

The win was delivered, though immediate satisfaction and freedom were left out of the package. Dylurshin rested, weighed down by its thoughts—paralyzed by its concerns. Would they kill it? Aenecans were as infinite as they were unpredictable and treacherous. Marching. Chanting. Weapons clanging against armor.

"Where is the demon!" someone yelled. That someone was Vor, Prince of Aeneca, ruler of Andromeda. Young but powerful, naive but arrogant. The massive hall's entrance shimmered away. The prince was unarmed, clad in golden armor, his straw yellow hair tied in a warrior's ponytail. Blue veins traced his flexed arms, and a lighter shade of blue skin stretched over a domineering athletic frame. Nearly twenty-five feet tall, Vor stopped behind the creature beneath him, and his army stopped behind him.

Dylurshin stared at the ground, until both scarlet colored eyes moved upwards alongside a triumphant grin.

The expression sent Vor into an impulsive rage, and he gripped the chains. "You are an abomination. I will give you the foulest punishment you can dream. You will not see Zellatris Rose or the Z-energy as long as there is light in my body." Vor tossed Dylurshin to the floor.

"A terrible attack on the ego of your people, to know the Uragonian Queen prefers a Zaian slave over an Aenecan royal," Dylurshin jested.

Vor stepped around and marched down the parted row of soldiers. "Zellatris was manipulated by your influence into doing unthinkable deeds."

"She was manipulated by you and your father into marrying Taldykin. To merge the families and establish your hold over Andromeda. I only opened her eyes to the truth and helped her discover her potential." The creature paused, adjusting to increased discomfort. "You knew what she was. You just wanted the energy tamed, so it wouldn't harm you."

To defeat an Aenecan was challenge enough. To kill one, a feat once believed impossible, had been perfected and performed. According to reports and surveillance, the act occurred during an Aenecan's most vulnerable time, rejuvenation. Black smoke invaded the castle. And under a strange influence, no one reacted, no one moved, and the Queen of Uragon, Zellatris used her immeasurable energy to destroy the Aenecan king particle by particle, atom by atom, until he was no more than the stardust he'd been born from. "Are there any more of you left?" Vor asked. Bulging arms clasped behind his back, he tipped on his heels, and stood a front the throne occupied by his father less than two star cycles ago.

"I am the last." A traitor. A murderer. A scientist. An explorer. A list of credentials worth raised eyebrows, and enough mischief worth severe punishments.

"Have you ever wondered why that is?" The soon-to-be-king twirled to face Dylurshin. "It is because you are vermin. Meant to be stomped out to avoid infestation. My father should have killed all of you, but his pity overruled his duty as king. I will not suffer the same mistake. I cannot kill you," Vor admitted, "I can, however, make sure you never get to finish what you started."

"Aenecans are poison!" Dylurshin screamed in protest, trying to dematerialize beneath the magic chains. "I know your secret. The one you hide behind your demigod virtues and robust politics. You have this entire establishment believing an Aenecan can do no wrong."

"An Aenecan can do no wrong," the prince repeated in a conniving tone. "That is why you will be exiled to the prison planet in the outer sectors of Andromeda's sanctuary. It should bring you nostalgia and peace to exist at the edge of the Milky Way. It is where your people came from to begin with."

"Our people, it is where our people came from."

Vor scoffed.

Xonden, the prison planet, a barren desert of a world with a cruel queen—it followed an obscure path around a tiny yellow star. Only one other planet in the system held life, a planet called Earth.

"Dylurshin Hexforth, you are guilty of treason, exploitation, and falsities, against a royal of Aeneca. Not to mention facilitating malicious acts against Andromeda's Sanctuary, and the supreme governing member of its institution. You will be escorted to Xonden, and live out your days in permanent exile," Vor decreed. "You leave on the next cycle."

The Aenecan army disbanded, melting like wax statues into the floor, leaving Vor and Dylurshin alone.

"These chains can't hold me for eternity. Even in your pomposity I know you know this."

"I have enlisted the help of the other civilizations to create a Temporal Chamber especially for you. It will be ready by star fall."

"A worthless exercise, prince. If it is not Zellatris, it will be another," Dylurshin said. "Know this, if you know nothing else— your best endeavors will be spent manipulating the Uragonian people into thinking they are your allies, when you seek only their elimination. I vow to you, Vor Vegacent, you will see me again and when you do, I will have Z-energy in my charge and destroy you with it, as Zellatris did your father. The Aenecan Empire, falsely believed to be Andromeda's Sanctuary, will fall."